THE TRY~

v

CW00558025

THE SWAN IN SUMMER

BARBARA LENNOX

ISBN 979-8-8412-0863-1 (paperback)
ISBN 979-8--35123469-4 (hardback)

1st edition September 2022
10..9..8..7..6..5..4..3..2..1

DEDICATION

To my late parents, who gave me that greatest of gifts,
a love of reading.

BONUS MATERIAL

Link to a two-page synopsis of *The Wolf in Winter*

Link to a scalable map of The World of *The Swan in Summer*

Link to a Spotify playlist for *The Swan in Summer*

Link to trailers for *The Swan in Summer* and *The Wolf in Winter*

CHARACTERS AND SETTINGS

CHARACTERS

(Principal characters in bold)
* characters who appeared in *The Wolf in Winter*

In Dalriada:

***Feargus** – King of Dalriada
Brangianne – his sister
Yseult – his daughter
Ciaran – Abbot of St Martin's Monastery
Eoghan – Steward of Dalriada
***Ferdiad** – Fili of Dalriada
Adarn/Azarion – Blacksmith at St Torran's Sanctuary
Oonagh – villager in Carnadail
Ethlin – Feargus' late wife
*Loarn and Oenghus – Feargus' foster brothers
Bearach – Castellan of Dun Sobairche
*The Morholt – late Champion of Dalriada
*Ninian – apprentice healer at St Martin's
Brother Caipre – former infirmarian at St Martin's
Aedh – late husband to Brangianne and former Lord of Carnadail
Daire – Oonagh's late son
Aiofe – villager in Carnadail
Niamh – villager in Carnadail

In The Lands between the Walls:

In Lothian:

*Corwynal – half-Caledonian son of the King of Lothian
*Trystan – King of Lothian's son, Corwynal's half-brother
*Rifallyn – King of Lothian
*Blaize – half-brother to Rifallyn, Corwynal's uncle, also half-Caledonian
*Ealhith – Corwynal's Angle slave
*Aelfric – Angle from Bernicia, son of Herewulf of Gyrwum
Caradawc – Ealhith's son
*Madawg – Leader of Lothian's war-band
*Janthe – Corwynal's mare
*Rhydian – Trystan's stallion

In Galloway:

*Marc – King of Galloway
*Gwenllian – Marc's sister, Trystan's mother
Garwyn, Bishop of Caer Lual and Galloway

In Gododdin:

*Lot – King of Gododdin, Overlord of Lothian and Manau, Duke of the Britons

In Manau:

*Arthyr – Consort of Gwenhwyvar, and War-leader of the Britons
*Gwenhwyvar – Queen of Western Manau
*Bedwyr – Arthyr's companion
*Caw – King of Eastern Manau

In Strathclyde:

*Dumangual – King of Strathclyde

In Selgovia:

*Essylt – Queen of Selgovia
*Kaerherdin – Her half-brother

In Caledonia:

*Arddu – God of the forests and empty places

Others:

*Maredydd – trader from Rheged
Manawyddan – God of the Sea

SETTINGS

In Dalriada:

Dunadd – principal stronghold of Dalriada (Dunadd hillfort in Argyll)

Dun Sobairche – former royal residence of Dalriada, in Old Dalriada (Dunseverick in County Antrim)

St Martins' Monastery – Monastery near Dunadd (Kilmartin, in Argyll)

St Torran's Sanctuary – Monastery on Loch Abha (Torran in Argyll)

Loch Abha – Loch Awe in Argyll

Cruachan – Ben Cruachan in Argyll

The Narrows – Outflow of Loch Etive (at Connel in Argyll)

Crionan – western port for Dunadd (Crinan in Argyll)

Loch Gair – eastern port for Dunadd (Loch Gair on Loch Fyne)

Carnadail – settlement in Ceann Tire (Carradail on Kintyre peninsula in Argyll)

Ceann Tire – Kintyre peninsula

Arainn – Island of Arran

Tairbeart – settlement and port in Ceann Tire (Tarbert in Argyll)

Dun Averty – stronghold and port in Ceann Tire (near Cambeltown in Argyll)

The Isle – Islay

Dun Bhoraraig – principal stronghold of Oenghus (Dun Bhoraraig on Islay)

Dun Ollie – principal stronghold of Loarn (near Oban)

Dun Treoin – private residence of Abbot Ciaran (hillfort of Duntroon, near Dunadd)

In the Lands between the Walls:

The Mote – Principal stronghold of Galloway (The Mote of Mark, near Rockcliffe)

The Rhinns – Southwest coast of Galloway (area around Stranraer)

Carraig Ealasaid – island claimed by Galloway (Ailsa Craig)

Alcluid – principal stronghold Strathclyde (Dumbarton Rock on the Clyde)

Iuddeu – principal stronghold of Western Manau (Stirling)

Dun Eidyn – principal stronghold Eastern Manau (Edinburgh)

Dunpeldyr – principal stronghold of Lothian (Traprain Law hillfort)

Trimontium – town on the border of Lothian (Melrose)

Meldon – principal stronghold of Selgovia (Black Meldon hillfort in the Scottish Borders)

Beacon Loch – site of a battle in *The Wolf in Winter*, also known as Llyn Llumonwy or Loch Laoimin (Loch Lomond)

Other locations:

Rheged – Briton Kingdom (Cumbria)

Caer Lual – stronghold in Rheged (Carlisle)

Glannaventa – Port in Rheged (Ravenglass)

Gwynedd – area with a number of Briton Kingdoms (North Wales)

Kernyw – Briton Kingdom (Cornwall)

Dumnonia – Briton Kingdom (Devon)

Armorica – Briton Kingdom (Brittany)

The Narrow Sea – The English Channel

Atholl – Caledonian Kingdom (roughly Perthshire)

Circind – Caledonian Kingdom (roughly Angus)

Island of Eagles – former location of the Caledonian warrior and druid training camp (Glen Brittle on Skye)

Bernicia – Angle Kingdom (Northumberland)

Dun Guayrdi – Angle pirate stronghold also known as Bebbanburgh (Bamburgh)

Gyrwum – Angle Eorldom in Bernicia (Jarrow)

Erui – Ireland

Ulaid – area occupied by various Scots tribes (Ulster)

Ailech – lands of the Ui Niall (Northwest Ulster))

Laigin – Scots' Kingdom in Erui (Leinster)

TRIBES AND NATIONS

The Britons:

The Kingdoms of Gododdin, Lothian and Manau (Votadinae tribe)
The Kingdom of Galloway (Novantae tribe)
The Kingdom of Strathclyde (Dumnonae tribe)
The Kingdom of Selgovia (Selgovae tribe)
The Kingdom of Rheged (Carvetii tribe and others)

The Scots:

The Kingdom of Dalriada (The Dal Riata tribe, originally from the
    north of Ireland, Ulaid (Ulster) but who've expanded north into
    Western Argyll)
Dal n'Araide (tribe occupying lands to the south of the Old Dalriada)
Ui Niall (tribe occupying lands to the west of Old Dalriada)

The Caledonians (a generic term for all 'Pictish' tribes):

The Kingdom of Atholl (Caledonian tribe)
The Kingdom of Circind (Venicon tribe)
The Kingdom of the Creonn tribe
The Kingdom of the Carnonac tribe

The Anglo-Saxons (Germanic tribes from the continent):

The Angles – Originally from Denmark, now occupying Northumbria
    and spreading into lowland Scotland
The Saex – Originally from Saxony, occupying lands to the south of
    Northumbria
The Jutes (not mentioned) – Originally from Denmark

MAPS

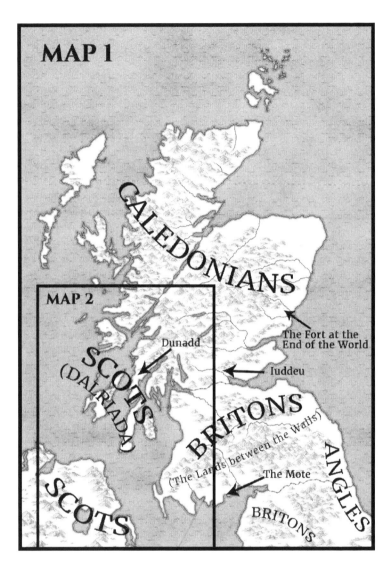

THE FOUR PEOPLES OF *THE SWAN IN SUMMER*

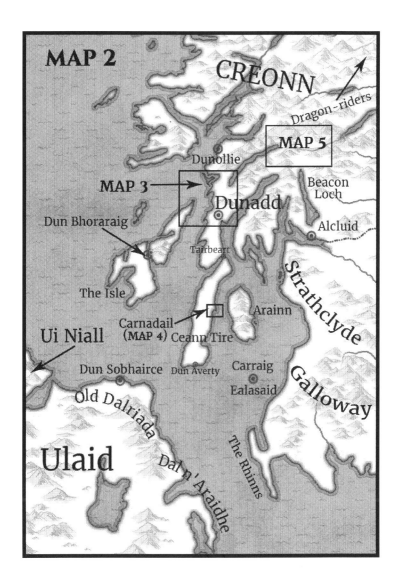

DALRIADA AND SURROUNDING LANDS

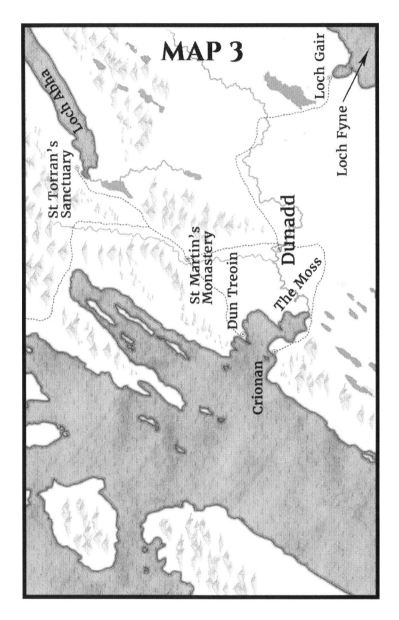

THE AREA AROUND DUNADD

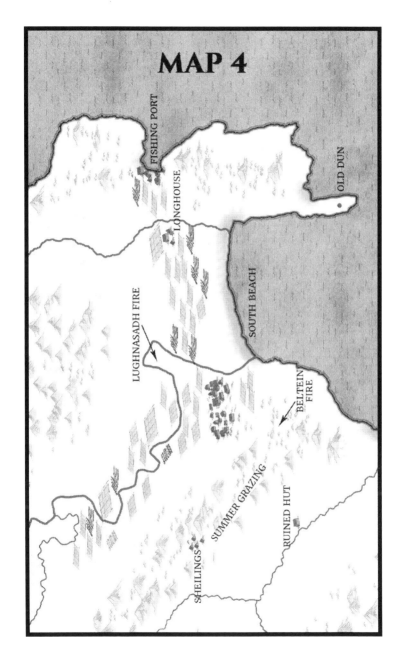

MAP 4

FISHING PORT

LONGHOUSE

OLD DUN

SOUTH BEACH

LUGHNASADH FIRE

BELTEIN FIRE

SUMMER GRAZING

RUINED HUT

SHEILINGS

THE SETTLEMENT OF CARNADAIL

THE TRYSTAN TRILOGY

ENDING AND BEGINNING

Dunpeldyr in Lothian,

Spring 491 AD

Tomorrow, a man I have loved and hated will burn his father, and everything will change. But not for me. I will remain the woman I have chosen to become, neither wife nor lover, mother nor sister. They call me The Healer here in Dunpeldyr and care little of where I came from or why. Yet once I was The Dark Swan of Dalriada, sister and daughter of kings. But here, beneath the stone-built walls of the fortress, I am just a woman watching a man pace through the night under the loom of an old moon, from torchlight to moonlight, carrying darkness within him.

He will be thinking of the past, of love and death, of a father and an uncle, a son and a brother, of what might have been and what could never be. And so I too will think of the past, of him, and the times before him, times that turned me into what and who I have become.

I will recall a summer of freedom, and a night long before that, a night that shaped me, and I will remember the day before, when a future full of promise lay before me. I will think back to the girl I was then and try to imagine the woman I might have become if that night hadn't happened. I wonder whether, if the two of us should meet, girl and woman, we would have anything in common except for a name. She was called Brangianne, as I am, and it is her story I will recall. And so I will think back to a sparkling Beltein morning over twenty years ago . . .

THE SWAN IN SUMMER
PART I

CARNADAIL IN DALRIADA,

BELTEIN, 468 AD

AND DUNADD IN DALRIADA,

SPRING, 486 AD

PROLOGUE

Carnadail, Beltein 468 AD,

twenty-three years earlier

THE NIGHT OF CHANGES

Beltein is the Night of Changes, the night that marks the turning of Spring into Summer. It's a night of fire and feasting, of loving and laughing, a night when couples slip away into the deep green shadows and aren't seen again until dew gathers, cold and clear, on the first morning of summer. They say a child conceived at Beltein will be touched by the gods for the whole of its life; a boy will grow to be a great warrior, a girl so lovely she'll break all hearts.

But Brangianne's child would be neither for he'd been too impatient to wait for Beltein. She and Aedh had only been wed since Imbolc, yet already a child had claimed its place in her womb and her heart, but she didn't regret not waiting. Her child didn't need to be a warrior or a beauty, just a whole and healthy heir for the Lord of Carnadail who, even now, was waving to her as they rowed him ashore from his ship.

I'll tell him tonight, she thought, a little shiver of anticipation running through her as she watched the coracle ground on the beach. Aedh jumped into the shallows, splashed ashore and ran towards her, caught her in his arms and, laughing, swung her off her feet. He smelled of tarred ropes and bilge-water, salt and wind, and the deep waters of the Sound.

'Any trouble on the journey?' she asked lightly, once he'd set her down, determined not to let him know how much she worried when he travelled the dangerous shipping lanes between Ceann Tire and the old Dalriad lands that lay to the south in Ulaid.

'Galloway raiders, you mean?' He threw an arm around her waist, and they walked up the beach towards the steading and the Longhouse he'd built for her down on the machair. 'Not a sign of one. They'll all be in harbour for the Beltein truce and, anyway, word has it they're raiding the Dal n'Araide coast this season, which is good for Carnadail, if not for the Dal n'Araide.'

'Was Feargus at Dun Sobhairce?'

He shook his head. 'Your brother had already left for Dunadd so he could be with Ethlin for Beltein. The gods will give them a Beltein child or he'll demand to know why not!'

'Don't joke about it! They've been wed for over five years now and no sign of a child. A king *needs* an heir.'

'As does the Lord of Carnadail.' He smiled a slow, glinting smile that made her heart turn over. 'So, what about it, wife? Shall we make a warrior tonight?'

She smiled back at him but held her secret close. *Later*, she thought, *when we're alone*. Beltein was for lovers, so let them be lovers for a little longer, since after the Night of Changes change would come all too quickly.

'We'll make whatever the gods decide,' she said. 'Though with you a farmer and me no beauty, we're unlikely to produce either a warrior or a heart-breaker.'

'No beauty?' he exclaimed in mock astonishment. 'But don't they call you the Dark Swan of Dalriada?'

'Bards' nonsense!' In truth, however, she was secretly pleased by the description, for didn't swans mate for life? 'It just means my neck's too long.'

'It's not too long for me.' He bent to nuzzle the neck in question. 'You're *my* Dark Swan,' he whispered, his grip tightening around her waist as he guided her willing steps through the gateway to the steading yard and towards their house. 'My very own Dark Swan ...' he murmured, kicking the door open. It had been a long time, weeks ...

A cough came from behind them, and Aedh let her go. Two of the men from the ship had followed them and were grinning from the entrance to the steading. One had a wooden chest on his shoulder, the other a large sack.

'Curse it, can't a man make love to his own wife without ...? Oh, never mind! Take that stuff to the forge. Wait, I'll come too.' He turned back to Brangianne. 'Later, then ...?'

He smiled down at her, the deep warm smile of the man she'd loved for half her short life and intended to love for all the rest of it. Her heart swelled in her chest, beating hard against her breastbone, until she was sick with longing.

'Later,' she promised, and watched him walk off, whistling, into the bright Beltein morning.

'Not here!' Brangianne laughed and snatched back her hand when Aedh tried to pull her away from the bonfires. It was the middle of the night by then and flames were leaping from the hilltop above the settlement. Cattle were bellowing as they were driven between the fires and everyone was shouting and laughing, drinking and dancing. Already couples were disappearing into the shadows of woods and fields, which was all very well for the common people, but the daughter and sister of kings expected certain privacies. 'Let's go home.' She caught Aedh's hand as he'd caught hers and, blinded by firelight and

deafened by the roar of the beasts and the drumming of their
own hearts. They ran down the hill, across the stream and over
the machair to the walled steading.

The place was dark, for the fires had been doused in readiness
for the morning when they'd be re-lit from the need-fire. There
was no moon that night, only a shudder of starlight on the water.
A wind was coming off the sea, carrying the smells of salt and
kelp and something she didn't recognise. But it didn't matter,
because they'd reached their house by then, a fine house, her
pride, and their undoing.

Brangianne woke to Aedh calling her name. She'd intended
telling him something but couldn't remember what it was, for
the Night of Changes had come and gone, changing everything
in its wake.

'Brangianne?' It was a breath of sound, barely heard above the
distant crackle of fire and the harsh hesitant breathing of a man
trying not to breathe.

'I'm cold, Brangianne, I'm cold.'

A pulsing yellow flicker came from beyond the doorway.

'Aedh?' Her voice was hoarse and her throat hurt as if she'd
been screaming. Why would she have been screaming?

'Hold me . . .'

She was lying by the door, a crumpled heap of torn cloth and
aching flesh that stank of something she refused to give a name
to. Every part of her hurt. There were tears and blood and . . . and
other fluids.

'Brangianne . . . ?'

He was sitting opposite her, his back against the wall, the
flickering light from the doorway burnishing his bruised face. It
had taken three of them to hold him, for he'd fought while one of

them had . . . had . . . They'd made Aedh watch. Then the leader of
the Galloway raiders had come into the Longhouse, dragged the
man off her and tossed her some gold in payment before cursing
the rest of them out. They'd let Aedh go after that, so why didn't
he come to her now? Why didn't he gather her up and let her
weep against his shoulder and tell her everything would be all
right? Why did he look so—?

'Aedh?' He slumped sidewards with a mew of agony. 'Aedh?!'
There was blood. A lot of it. And the foul smell of ruptured guts.
They'd slit his belly open. He'd tried to hold the wound closed,
but now it gaped in its awful vileness. And nothing would be all
right ever again.

'I'm cold,' he whispered as, outside, fires raged.

It took Aedh three days to die, and in those three days
Brangianne came to understand that a woman might survive a
rape but a man couldn't survive a wound in the belly. She didn't
know how to deal with such an injury, and nor did the birth-
woman or the old druid priest. They just shook their heads and
left her to do the little she could. Aedh said he was cold, so she
kept him warm, though he sweated with the pain. He was thirsty,
so she tried to make him drink, but he could swallow nothing.
The wound swelled and stank, and Aedh shuddered and moaned,
lost to reason. Outside, the people of Carnadail repaired what
could be repaired, speaking in low voices as they did so. They'd
escaped lightly, for on the night of the raid they'd all been at the
Beltein fires where she and Aedh should have been. If only she
hadn't insisted they return to the Longhouse! Now Aedh was
dying for her wilfulness.

Brangianne didn't sleep for the whole of those three days and
nights, but remained beside him, holding a hand that was cold

and clammy and finally – though she didn't realise it at the time – quite dead. She wept no tears, though she longed for them. The sky wept for her instead, a dull, penetrating drizzle that held all the chill of winter. She too was cold by then, cold and calm and somehow distant. They burned Aedh in the old way, down by the shore at low tide, so the sea could take away his ashes, but nothing could take away what had happened. Nothing but revenge. One day, she swore to herself, she'd have the raider who'd raped her and killed Aedh in her power. She'd force him to his knees, cut through his belly with a blunt and jagged knife, then watch, unsleeping, for all the days it would take him to die.

Perhaps the gods listened to her, for the tide that took Aedh's ashes out to sea washed a body onto the beach, that of the man who'd raped her and whose torso bore the same dreadful wound he'd inflicted on Aedh. But it wasn't enough. Did the man who'd led those raiders to Carnadail during the Beltein truce think she could be placated with a scrap of gold and a single dead man? She'd go to Feargus, she decided, and demand he punish Galloway on her behalf. Later, however, she thought better of it. What good would a war do? Why make other women weep in ruined homesteads over dead and dying men? So Brangianne kept her silence and brooded on her hatred of Galloway and all who lived there, all the time turning over and over in her fingers the whore's payment the leader of the raiders had flung her – an armlet on which was set, in enamel, the raven of Galloway. *One day I'll have my revenge on you too*, she promised the raiders' leader. But that was for the future, because it wasn't long before there were other matters to concern her.

'A boy,' the birth-woman declared when the pain and screaming was done. 'You have a boy . . .'

Brangianne had assumed she'd lost her child, for how could any life have survived that Night of Changes? So she hadn't told Aedh and had let him die not knowing he'd fathered a son. But as the days passed, and weeks turned into months as the year waxed and waned once more, she came to understand that the gods had taken one life from her but hadn't begrudged her another.

Until they robbed her of that too.

'. . . a changeling child,' the woman told her, for Brangianne's son was smaller than he should have been, a sickly boy who refused to feed.

He died at sundown a few weeks later on the night of the Imbolc feast, a night of stars in a frozen careless sky. His little life ebbed on the last tide of winter and his soul slipped free to wander the otherworld with his father. At least he wouldn't be alone. She sat all night with the cooling little body in her arms, and at dawn she walked out to the old ones' dun on the very edge of the promontory. A single rowan tree grew against the remains of the wall, gnarled and leafless but still alive. She burned him there, then buried what was left in the half-frozen earth among the roots of the witch tree, swearing as she did so that never again would she watch a man die and not be able to help him, or suffer a child to weaken without the skills to bring him back into the world.

As for the gods, she was finished with them. They'd made a game of her life, had given her everything, then, for no reason, taken it away. They were cruel and capricious, and, as if to prove it, a few days later Feargus arrived. He too had been betrayed by the gods, and his face was drawn with grief, for his beloved wife Ethlin had finally given birth to the longed-for heir to Dalriada – and died of the birthing.

'A Beltein child, born at Imbolc,' he said bitterly. 'What a son he would have made!'

'You can marry again, Feargus, have other children.'

He shook his head. 'I don't need another child. Ethlin died, but our daughter lives. That's why I'm here – to take you back to Dunadd to care for her. Who better than her aunt?'

Brangianne's arms ached to hold a child, and though she thought no-one could fill the gap left by her son, it wasn't long before this one did, a fierce, red-headed creature who was Royal Princess of Dalriada and tyrant of her father and aunt's grieving hearts. A pretty thing even then, a child confident of her own beauty, a girl who'd grow up to break hearts. *She who must be gazed upon.* That was the meaning of the name they chose.

They called her Yseult.

I

Dunadd, Spring 486 AD,

seventeen years later

A VERY ANGRY SWAN

*S*he was in the camp north of the Loch of the Beacon, with the mud and the rain, the flies and the smell. Especially the smell. It filled her nostrils and robbed her of breath, making her gasp as light and shallow as a landed fish. The mud clung to her shoes and soaked the hem of her skirt, weighing her down. Flies buzzed around her face when she waved them away from the open wounds of the men she was trying to help. But there weren't enough bandages, had never been enough poppy, and those left in the camp, where the exhausted remnants of Feargus' army had finally come to rest, were the ones with the worst wounds of all. Day by day, they sickened and died, just as a man and child had sickened and died in Carnadail, seventeen years before.

The wounded men lay on the raw wet earth, a long line of them stretching into the distance, all of them crying out for help, for water, for their mothers. Brangianne was weary beyond all imagining, her eyes gritty with despair as she moved from one man to the next, and when she came to the end of the line she *was so tired she laid herself down, for she too was hurt. For a long time no-one came, but when someone finally bent over her, it was no-one she recognised, a dark-haired coldly handsome man of her own age with eyes the colour of storm-clouds. He smiled at her, a wolf's smile in a proud disdainful face, before turning into a wolf indeed, a silver-streaked wolf with slate-coloured eyes, and she was a swan, a dark-feathered swan beating the air with her wings. The wolf leapt away and loped north, heading for the winter-mantled mountains. She wanted to follow him, to fly into the clear northern air and leave the camp and the mud and the flies behind. But her feet were bound with ribbons, and they were all holding her back – the men crying for their mothers, and Feargus and Yseult too – all of them holding her down when all she wanted to do was fly . . .*

'Brangianne!' The door, flung open, slammed against the wall and jerked her out of the dream. 'The Morholt's arrived!'

Yseult tugged at Brangianne's blankets, one of which was tangled around her feet, and snatched them away when she tried to pull them back. 'His ship's at Crionan. He'll be on his way to Dunadd by now. Come on! If we don't catch him at the gate we won't hear any news until the evening. Get up, or I'll go without you.'

Brangianne groaned, shut her eyes and tried to hold on to the dream. She wanted to follow the wolf, to escape the camp and the men and her own helplessness. She wanted to wake and find the war hadn't happened. But it had. Her brother had been tricked by a man called Corwynal of Lothian and defeated by the treacherous Galloway Britons. And she'd been defeated too, for, despite her reputation as a healer and a surgeon, she'd failed to heal more than a handful of men. Now, almost a year later, dreams of the camp in the forest still troubled her nights. But this dream had been different from the others, the man a stranger, and she wasn't sure what it meant.

'—and I won't tell you what he tells me,' Yseult threatened. So Brangianne, who wanted to hear the news from Ulaid as much as her niece, gave in and allowed Yseult mastery over her blankets. She swung her feet to the cold floor and looked for the skirt she'd been wearing in the infirmary at St Martin's the previous day. It wasn't clean – there were spots of dried blood near the hem – but it would do, so she pulled it on, threw on an overtunic and reached for her comb.

'There's no time for that!' Yseult grabbed her by the arm and pulled her towards the door, allowing Brangianne no more than a cursory glance in her tarnished silver mirror. But even a glance was enough to reveal what she feared; the woman in the reflection was a dark-haired untidy woman of middle years who looked more like a peasant than the sister of a King. Yseult, in contrast, was every inch the Royal Lady, for that attractive baby had turned into a pretty child, and now, at seventeen, was set fair to rival her mother's pale-skinned, fine-boned beauty.

Time she was married, Brangianne thought. *Before there's any more trouble.* She herself had been married at fifteen, but though Yseult, as Royal Princess of Dalriada, had been promised often enough to this one or that according to Feargus' political whim, nothing had been settled as yet.

It wasn't long after dawn, and the men who slept in the hall and adjoining huts were just stirring. The main doors were still shut, and the place stank of smoke and dogs and unwashed bodies, so she held her breath and followed Yseult through the side door and down the steps to the kitchen, where the scent of freshly cooked bannocks was more wholesome. But Yseult didn't allow her to swallow a mouthful of ale or snatch a bannock. Instead, she pulled her through the door that led to the terrace and thence to the track that wound between the roundhouses and workshops that crowded Dunadd's upper level, eventually reaching the great gate that pierced an outcrop. There Yseult insisted they climb up to the western rampart where she hung out over the edge to look along the causeway that approached Dunadd from the harbour at Crionan, a couple of miles west of the fort.

'What a beautiful day!' Yseult threw her arms wide as if to embrace the whole world.

It was indeed. The sun, set in a cloud-dappled forget-me-not sky, sparkled on the bends of the River Add as it wound its way through the glittering wetland of The Moss that lay between Dunadd and Crionan. Beyond the Moss, the woods that crowned the low hills to the south were a patchwork of greens, thick with bluebells and ransoms. It was barely a week after Beltein, and, despite a lingering chill in the breeze, the day promised to be warm. But Brangianne couldn't share Yseult's joy in the morning. The dream still gripped her, and she found herself brooding over the events of the previous summer.

Why did men go to war? Why had Feargus, normally the most rational of men, allowed his foster brothers and their treacherous Caledonian allies to persuade him into that disastrous war against the Britons? He'd aged in the last year; his face was gaunt, his brow furrowed, his red beard streaked with white, his temper even more ungovernable than usual. War had brought defeat, and defeat had been followed by a tribute demand from Galloway in return for releasing Oenghus and his men. Then, as if that hadn't been bad enough, the harvest had been poor and the winter unusually severe. Nevertheless, they'd survived, and, with the tribute delivered at Beltein by The Morholt, Dalriada's Champion and Yseult's uncle, Feargus had begun to emerge from his black mood. Now, with spring greening the fields, hope burgeoned once more. With luck, The

Morholt, who after delivering the tribute was to have travelled on to Ulaid, would have brought an answer from their allies in the Old Country to whom Feargus had written asking for aid.

'There they are!' Yseult leant dangerously far out over the rampart and pointed along the track that skirted The Moss. A small party was approaching, cloaks flying behind them, sun glinting from spear-tips and jewellery, but Brangianne could make out neither the distinctive figure of The Morholt himself, nor his companion, the silver-haired Ferdiad, Dalriada's Fili – royal messenger, bard and, when necessary, spy.

'It's not The Morholt! It's Bearach!' Yseult exclaimed when the party reached the lower gate. 'What's he doing here?' It was a good question, for Bearach, the elderly Chamberlain of Dun Sobhairce, their stronghold in Old Dalriada, rarely left Ulaid. Yseult sprinted down the stairs, ignoring Brangianne's protests, and dived into the group of Dun Sobhairce men to accost Bearach.

'Where's my uncle? Is he still at Crionan?'

Bearach's face fell at the sight of her, something that rarely happened when men looked at Yseult.

'No, my Lady.'

'Is Ferdiad here?' Brangianne asked, having caught up with her niece, for sometimes Ferdiad travelled alone to Crionan in The Morholt's ship.

'No . . . no. Lord Ferdiad . . . couldn't come.'

'Is he ill?'

Bearach glanced at his escort, most of whom were staring admiringly at Yseult, and waved them out of earshot. 'No, Ferdiad's not ill precisely.'

'The Morholt then?' Yseult asked. 'But he's never sick!'

'No, he's not sick.' Bearach still wore that stricken expression. Then, after a quick glance around, he lowered his voice. 'He's dead, my Lady! Your uncle's dead!'

A challenge. A Briton. A Briton from Galloway.

Brangianne's hands curled into claws as she listened to Bearach's story. Beside her, Yseult's bright colour seeped away so dramatically Brangianne was afraid she might faint. After a moment, however, she recovered, whirled around, and went running back up through the fort.

'Come back, Yseult! Don't you dare disturb your father!' But it was too late. Brangianne sprinted after her but was too late to prevent Yseult from pushing past the guards at the back of the hall and bursting into Feargus' chamber.

'The Morholt's dead! A man from Galloway killed him, and I want you to—'

'Nonsense!' Feargus' brows snapped together. The outer doors leading to the Royal Terrace were open to let in the light, and her brother was sitting at his table, Dalriada's portly Steward, Eoghan, standing next to him pointing out some detail in one of the many fragments of parchment piled in front of him. Now, seeing Yseult, Eoghan straightened and bowed deeply, but Feargus continued to scowl at his daughter before turning his devastating green gaze on his sister, a question in his eyes. *Can you not keep your niece under control?* Then – as he took in her stained skirt and frayed cloak – *Can you not dress like the sister of a King for once?* She began to make some excuse, but Yseult interrupted.

'It's true! Bearach's just arrived, and he told me—'

'It's true, Feargus,' Brangianne cut in.

'Enough! Both of you! If Bearach's brought news, I'll hear it from him, not some garbled version from a pair of hysterical women! Ah, Bearach . . .' The door from the hall opened once more and Feargus rose to welcome the man who dealt with the business of their lands in Ulaid, in the Old Country, as everyone had begun to call it since Feargus, twenty years before, had moved the seat of Dalriadan power to Dunadd. 'I apologise for my womenfolk. They were . . . overcome by your news.'

Bearach flushed at the hint of censure in Feargus' words, for any news should have gone first to the King. 'Sadly, Sire, Lady Yseult is correct. The Morholt is indeed dead.' He handed Feargus a sealed scroll of parchment. 'Lord Ferdiad has sent you further details.'

Feargus broke the seal and began to read, impatiently at first, then more slowly. He sank back into his chair, the colour draining from his face, and his fingers were trembling by the time he reached the end.

'What's happened?' Brangianne asked, her mouth dry with apprehension. Had their allies in Ulaid turned their backs on them? 'What does it say?' But Feargus just laid the parchment on the table and stared at it as it rolled itself closed once more.

Eoghan poured Feargus a cup of wine and pressed it into his hand, and he drank it down much as a man will drink strong ale before going into battle. A little colour returned to his face and he looked up. The effort it took him to control his expression was evident to everyone in the room but, when he spoke, his voice was steady enough.

'My thanks for bringing this news so quickly, Bearach. I hope you won't object to returning to Dun Sobhairce as soon as your ship can be re-provisioned? I'll come myself in a few days. Tell Ferdiad to expect me – and that he'd better be sober.' Bearach nodded and left the room, and Feargus turned to Eoghan. 'Call the Council.'

Eoghan bowed and left the room also, leaving Feargus to stare down at Ferdiad's letter as if it was a serpent.

'Father? What's happened?'

He tossed the roll of parchment to Yseult. 'Here. Read it for yourself.'

She unrolled the letter and held it so Brangianne could read it over her shoulder, but it was difficult to make out, barely legible and water-stained in places. It was so unlike Ferdiad's usual impeccable Latin and honeyed phrases she found it difficult to believe it was from him at all, for it was little more than a brutal statement of the facts. He'd gone to Galloway and made a bargain in an attempt to win the tribute back. The Morholt had offered to fight a Galloway challenger and, despite it being common knowledge that there was no-one in Galloway to match him, the challenge had been accepted. This challenger, his name blurred so Brangianne couldn't make it out, had met The Morholt at the Galloway island of Carraig Ealasaid. It had been a fair fight and an even one, Ferdiad wrote, but in the end this man had killed The Morholt, though he'd taken such a serious wound himself he was unlikely to live. Ferdiad accepted complete responsibility for what had happened and invited Feargus to punish him in any way he thought fit. It was only at the end that he wrote of the bargain he'd made. In order to get the Galloway king to accept the challenge, Ferdiad had agreed that if The Morholt was defeated, the tribute would be doubled.

Yseult let the letter fall to the floor and looked at her father, her own face as pale as his.

'What . . . what will you do?'

'I don't know, Yseult,' he said, his voice exhausted. 'I really don't know.'

And that frightened Brangianne more than anything, for Feargus was never at a loss for a plan or a scheme. They didn't call him Feargus the Fox for no reason.

'I want to help,' Yseult said. 'Tell me how, and I'll do it.'

He looked up at her, his face softening into something approaching sorrow. 'Oh, you'll have to help, Yseult,' he said before turning to Brangianne. 'Both of you will have to help.'

'I'm going to kill that man from Galloway!'

Yseult paced back and forth on the Royal Terrace that lay below the hall, her hands curled into fists, her eyes a green blaze, her hair, the same russet as Feargus', tossing like the flames of a Beltein fire. Her skirts flicked about her ankles and brushed against the herbs Brangianne had planted between the stony outcrops, filling the air with the heady scents of thyme and woodruff. 'I mean it!' She stopped in front of Brangianne who was sitting on a bench set against the western wall, her cloak clutched tightly about her despite the warmth of the day.

'Don't be ridiculous!'

'If only I was a man!' Yseult raised her fists to the sky and shook them in frustration, then glowered down at the king-making stone with its foot-shaped depression, a stone on which no woman had ever stood. 'If I was a man I'd be part of father's Council and have a say in things.' She glared up at the hall where those of Feargus' advisors who lived close to Dunadd had been summoned to discuss the crisis. 'If I was a man, I could challenge that Galloway murderer. I could go there and kill him!'

'Well, you're not a man,' Brangianne said tartly. 'So let there be an end to all this talk of killing!'

Yseult shook her head. 'The Morholt was my mother's brother, and I'm his only kin. It's my duty, Brangianne. For the honour of our Family and my own honour I need revenge on that man from Galloway!'

Revenge!

Brangianne shivered as the past trailed icy fingers across her skin. Once she'd wanted revenge herself for a man cut down in his prime and a child dying before it had lived. She'd sworn she'd kill the man responsible for those deaths, the leader of the raiders. Yet she'd done nothing about it. Worse, she'd pushed that oath to the back of her mind, and could no longer recall the man's face, not even the colour of his eyes, though their expression haunted her dreams.

Seventeen years before, she'd left Carnadail and never returned. Now she was afraid to do so, knowing she'd have to face the judgement of the ghosts who'd demand the vengeance she'd promised them, a vengeance she didn't know how to get. *One day*, she'd always thought, a day she'd pushed further and further into the future.

What mattered to her now was the other oath she'd sworn that Imbolc morning when she'd buried her child, the oath that had given life meaning since those dreadful days of seventeen years before. Never again, she'd sworn, would she stand helplessly by when a man was hurt or a child was dying, and now, after years of study and practice, she was the best surgeon and healer in the whole of Dalriada, skilful enough for Feargus to have called on her to help with the wounded after the war. Too late, in the event, for most of them, but that wouldn't happen again. Next time there was war she'd travel with the army, whether Feargus liked it or not. If there was a next time. But perhaps there would be. Was that why her brother had taken the news of The Morholt's death so badly? Did it mean another war?

'. . . maybe you're right,' Yseult broke into her thoughts. 'Maybe it would be better if I didn't kill him.' She sank onto the stone bench beside Brangianne, but her eyes were still glittering, and her lips were pressed together. 'Killing him would be too easy. I want him to *suffer*. I want to *make* him suffer. And I know how I'd do it. I might not be a man, but that doesn't mean I don't know how to hurt someone, how to drive them to their death.'

Her voice lost its fierceness, and her eyes welled up with tears that fell, sparkling, down her cheeks.

'We don't know Ninian's dead, love.' Brangianne hoped he wasn't, for she was fond of Ninian, the son of one of Feargus' clients. He'd been fostered with Abbot Ciaran in the Monastery of St Martin's that lay a few miles north of Dunadd and had become the best of her apprentice healers. He and Yseult had grown up like brother and sister, but their youthful affection hadn't survived the flowering of Yseult's beauty. The previous winter Ninian had lost first his heart, then his head. He'd made some stupid offer and, having been rejected – for what else could Yseult have done? – he'd announced he was going to become a priest, and a celibate one at that. He'd left Dunadd for Rosnat, the seminary in Galloway, and they hadn't heard from him since. Feargus had told them he had reason to believe he was dead. How, he couldn't – or wouldn't – say but, whatever had happened, Yseult felt responsible. The child of Beltein, having turned into the beauty she'd always promised to be, had become a breaker of hearts.

'So you're planning to break the heart of this man from Galloway, are you?'

'I could do it!' Yseult insisted. 'Men are always falling in love with me. I broke Ninian's heart without even trying, so how much easier would it be if I really meant it? I'm going to make the man who killed my uncle fall in love with me and then ... then I'll make him suffer.'

'Good plan,' Brangianne agreed dryly. 'Except he's in Galloway and you're in Dalriada. Except he's very likely dead. Except you don't know who he is.'

'Ferdiad knows.'

'Ferdiad! I don't want to hear that man's name ever again!' Dalriada's Fili was far from Brangianne's favourite person at the best of times, and these were the worst. 'When your father gets hold of him, he'll very likely wring his scheming neck! Which is no less than he deserves. It's Ferdiad you should be wanting to kill.'

'Why? He loved my uncle.'

'Then why not leave all that revenge to him?' Brangianne wondered if Yseult understood the nature of Ferdiad's love for The Morholt. Probably not, for no-one understood Ferdiad, that careless breaker of hearts of both men and women. The one person he'd seemed to genuinely care for was The Morholt, so Brangianne didn't envy the man who'd killed him, for Ferdiad's revenge would be ... comprehensive. 'You'd do better worrying about what your father wants you to do to help. What he wants us both to do.'

They didn't have long to worry for, just then, a servant came to inform them that, the Council being over, the King had summoned them both.

The King. Brangianne shivered uneasily. Not her brother. Not Yseult's father. Not a man who didn't know what to do. They'd been summoned by the King of Dalriada, the leader of their tribe and the head of their Family, a man required to made unpalatable choices, a man prepared, it turned out, to sacrifice everything and everyone to buy his way out of trouble. And that included not only his daughter, but his sister.

Blaize threw his satchel into a corner and subsided gratefully into the chair that had been set out for him in the little Oratory of St Martin's.

'Arthyr sent me,' he told the man sitting opposite him, a tall man, older than Blaize and considerably more serene.

It had been a long trip: the journey along the northern wall from Iuddeu, haggling for passage at Alcluid, the voyage down the Cluta and up Bute Sound in a death-trap of a wallowing trader, an awkward landfall at Loch Gair and the ride over the hills to St Martin's on a spavined nag they called a horse in these parts. And all because Arthyr, as War-leader of the Britons, wanted to know how things stood in Dalriada. Which was why Blaize had come to Dalriada, not to see Feargus, its King, but Ciaran, Abbot of St Martins, a man Blaize had known for a great many years and who shared his views about the present and his fears for the future.

Despite his fears, however, Ciaran smiled warmly at Blaize, a smile that stripped away any secrets he might have been thinking of concealing.

'I thought you were advisor to Lot, who I hear is to be the Britons' next High King?'

Blaize sighed. He was still advisor to Lot, King of Gododdin, but Lot's idea of that role was for Blaize to replace Corwynal as his eyes and ears in Iuddeu, since Lot had never wanted Arthyr as War-leader and still saw him as a rival for the High Kingship. Corwynal, curse him, had gone chasing after Trystan to Galloway and had yet to return, leaving Blaize advisor not only to Lot but to Arthyr, an even more demanding man than the King of Gododdin.

'So, how *do* things stand since the war? Has the tribute been paid?'

In the cool tranquillity of St Martin's Oratory, Blaize felt every one of the miles he'd travelled. His bones ached, there was stubble on his cheeks, dirt beneath his fingernails, and a stench of horse and human sweat about his person. Ciaran, in contrast, was as immaculate as ever, his long silver hair combed smooth, his bleached habit spotless, the rings on his fingers gleaming in the wan spring sunshine that fell through the open door leading to the orchard. He looked very much a man in control, but perhaps that impression was an illusion, for when the Abbot stood up, with a grace that belied his years, to pick up a letter that lay on a chest near the wall, his hands were trembling, and not, Blaize thought, with old age.

'If you'd come to me half a moon ago, I'd have said that, in the circumstances, they were as well as could be expected. The tribute had been sent and thus a possible war with Galloway averted. But there have been . . . developments. This is just one of them. Here – read it for yourself.'

Blaize glanced at the inscription; the letter was addressed to Feargus, and the seal had been broken. He unrolled the crackling parchment and read through it, quickly at first, then more slowly. A pain began to pulse somewhere behind his breastbone as he tried to grapple with the magnitude of what had happened.

'Galloway doesn't have a Champion,' he said stupidly before his brain caught up with his tongue and he remembered the young man who'd left Iuddeu in a fit of pique, a young man who'd wanted to make a name for himself and been denied the chance, a young man who'd gone to Galloway to join Marc.

It's Trystan! Blaize was certain of it. And, if the letter was to be believed, he'd been so seriously hurt he might even be dead by now. If he was, how would Corwynal react, or Marc for that matter? Badly, Blaize thought, in both cases. And all for the sake of a shipload of tribute.

'How did Feargus take it?'

'Much as you might expect. Disbelief followed by fury.' Ciaran sat down once more, leant his elbows on the arms of his chair, and steepled his fingers. 'He blames Ferdiad, not unreasonably.'

'Not The Morholt?'

'Oh, this challenge won't have been The Morholt's idea. He missed the battle by the Loch of the Beacon, since Feargus had sent him and Ferdiad to Ulaid to sort out a dispute, and he swore revenge. In his position as Dalriada's Champion, he could do no less. But he wouldn't have thought of this. No, this bears Ferdiad's mark.'

Blaize had met Dalriada's Fili on a handful of occasions. The man was charming and devious, and as fork tongued as a snake, but he hadn't struck him as a fool.

'Why would he risk Dalriada's Champion being defeated, no matter how unlikely, given the possible consequences?'

'Your guess is as good as mine, Blaize. I spoke with Ferdiad before he left with the tribute from Dunadd. He was going to Dun Sobhairce to meet The Morholt and collect the rest of the tribute before taking it to Galloway. I had no sense that he intended anything other than delivering it as planned. Something must have happened to make him do this. But his reasons don't matter. What's done is done, and we have to deal with the consequences.'

The two men looked at one another. They'd known each other for a long time, and though the lands they served were enemies they'd become friends. Each understood how tenuous civilisation was, how easily it could be destroyed. So they'd begun to work together to preserve it where they could, and to reach out to others who thought in the same way. *The Brotherhood*, they called themselves.

'The consequences may be worse than you fear,' Blaize said. 'This unnamed Champion of Galloway; I believe it's Trystan.'

Ciaran had heard of Trystan, of course, and also knew of Corwynal, for both had played a major role in Dalriada's defeat, but Ciaran wasn't a man to hold a grudge.

'The poor boy! And hurt almost to the death . . .'

'If he's dead, Corwynal will kill Ferdiad,' Blaize said flatly. 'Fair fight or not. As for Marc, Trystan's his sister-son and heir. So, unless it wasn't Trystan or, if it was, he's survived, this means war.'

He glanced through the letter once more, noting the ragged hand, the blotched script, as if the writer had been drunk or weeping, or both, and some important details were missing. Which meant Blaize would have to go to Galloway to see Marc and find Corwynal and, if he was alive, Trystan. Yet another journey. The thought of all those miles made his bones ache.

'I fear you're right,' Ciaran said. 'So you'd better return to the lands of the Britons, but not necessarily to Galloway. Feargus is going to Dun Sobhairce and he'll get the details out of Ferdiad, no matter how drunk our wayward Fili might be, and once I hear from Feargus I'll send word to you at Iuddeu. That's where you need to go. Arthyr should know of these developments, whether or not your nephews are involved, because this does indeed mean war.'

War! Such a little word for such a destroyer of worlds. All it would take was one spark and, like the dry furze after a summer's drought, all the lands of the north could catch alight in a conflagration that could all too easily roar out of control. War, between lands, between tribes, between clans, between brothers.

'Between Galloway and Dalriada,' Blaize concluded sourly, thinking of all the efforts he, through Lot, had made to bind together the alliance of Britons and avert this very thing – all the Brotherhood's plans ruined because of a quixotic inexplicable decision by a snake of a Fili. 'This year?'

Ciaran shook his head. 'Probably not. Marc will have to give us time to find more tribute, at least until after this year's harvest, and I think Feargus can be relied upon to draw out the proceedings until the autumn storms begin and the seaways close. But next year? If Feargus can't raise another shipment of tribute or chooses not to, then, yes, I fear it may indeed come to war. Although war between Dalriada and Galloway may be the least of Feargus' problems. There have been other developments, Blaize, not least being that there are warships on the stocks in the sea-lochs of the Creonn.'

Blaize frowned. 'Not an unusual event, surely, given that the Creonn have been at war with the Carnonacs for years?'

A war that had kept the Creonn, the Caledonian tribe whose lands lay to the north of Dalriada, relatively quiet as far as raiding Dalriada was concerned. Or it had done.

'Indeed. But my sources tell me the Creonn have come to terms with the Carnonacs. And you know as well as I why that is and what it will mean.'

Blaize did indeed. It meant the scavengers were circling. It meant the Creonn had heard of Dalriada's defeat and decided the time was ripe for them to wreak revenge on a weakened Dalriada in retaliation for a defeat inflicted on them a generation before. The Creonn had long memories.

'Feargus should never have got involved in last year's war.'

'True, but Loarn forced his hand. It was Loarn's lands that were being raided by the Creonn and he wanted something done about it. So when the Caledonians suggested they could rein in the Creonn in return for Dalriada's help against the Britons, Loarn believed them and convinced Feargus to support him.'

Blaize snorted. 'No-one has ever been able to control the Creonn. They can barely control themselves. Each Clan is as likely to fight another Clan as their enemies. They're an undisciplined rabble.'

'Now, perhaps, but once, twenty years ago, they acted together, when they hired the Dragon-riders to command their war against Dalriada. But you know the story.'

Blaize nodded. Feargus, a young man newly come to the Kingship, had destroyed the Dragon-riders and thus defeated the Creonn, a victory that had consolidated his rule of Dalriada, and nothing had been heard of the Riders since. They'd dwindled into myth and now were little more than monsters to threaten children with. Without them, the Creonn were a spent force, at least on land. So why was Ciaran bringing them up now? What did he know? More, certainly, than Blaize who'd regarded them as nothing more than history, a horse-riding warlike people whose origins were forgotten, a people who'd marked their faces in the Caledonian manner, but with designs that made no sense, a people who'd worn heavy armour and whose horses – great beasts bred from the last of the Legions' stallions – had been as armoured as their riders. A people Ciaran wouldn't be talking about if they belonged only to the past.

'Are you saying they're back?' Blaize's voice, in his own ears, sounded shrill. 'Then where have they been all these years?'

Ciaran shrugged. 'Somewhere in the north, I expect. Little word comes out of the Caledonian lands of the western seaboard, as we both know. As to whether they're back, I don't know, but I fear . . .' He smiled grimly, a smile that didn't reach his eyes. 'Let's hope I'm wrong, because if I'm not, we'll end up facing something more serious than a few raids. Feargus should never have listened to Loarn last year, but he needed to appease his foster-brother, who's grown ambitious . . .'

So there were scavengers even in the heart of the Royal Kindred.

'What's Feargus doing about all this?'

'Everything he can to stay in power and in control. He may even succeed. But he can't pay the tribute all over again without help. What you and I – and your War-leader – need to worry about is where he's going to find that help. But this could be an opportunity, Blaize. The last thing Arthyr will want in the west are lands controlled by Loarn, or the Creonn. Sadly, both are real possibilities if Feargus doesn't get the aid he needs. He's turned to his old allies in Ulaid, and that's where he's going, taking his daughter Yseult, who I rather fear will be sold to the highest bidder to pay for ships and men and tribute. And, what's more—'

He broke off and lifted his head, listening. Beyond the closed door to Ciaran's Oratory, the one leading to the rest of the Monastery, Blaize heard raised voices.

'—he's already sold his sister.' Ciaran finished what he'd been saying with a wry smile and got to his feet. 'I must ask you to leave me now, Blaize, since you're hardly in a condition to meet my royal visitor.'

'Feargus?'

'No. Brangianne, Princess of Dalriada, Lady of Carnadail. They call her The Dark Swan of Dalriada and, from the sounds of it, she's a very angry swan indeed.'

He laid a hand on Blaize's shoulder, urged him to his feet and steered him gently but firmly towards the orchard even as someone banged urgently at the door leading to the monastery complex.

'Get some rest, Blaize, before you head back to Iuddeu,' Ciaran advised him. 'But first, perhaps – indeed there's no perhaps about it – you should take a bath.'

'I want to become a nun!'

Brangianne burst into Ciaran's Oratory, brushing aside the objections of the novice who'd followed her from the main gate insisting that the Lord Abbot couldn't be disturbed.

'It's all right,' Ciaran said to the novice. 'My visitor has left, and I was expecting the Lady Brangianne.' He closed the door in the novice's face, went over to his chair, sat down with his elbows on the armrests, steepled his fingers and regarded her evenly. 'This, I assume, is about Eoghan?'

'You know?! You mean Feargus discussed it at the Council? In front of everyone? How dare he!'

Brangianne had intended to be humble, to put her case calmly and rationally but, at the memory of what her brother had asked her to do, all thoughts of humility were swept aside in a flood of righteous anger. 'I'm going to kill him! And I'm going to kill that man from Galloway too, whoever he is! In fact, I'm going to kill everyone from Galloway,' she went on, warming to her theme. 'And everyone responsible for that stupid, *stupid* war with the Britons, especially Loarn and Oenghus. I blame them for this. As for Ferdiad, when I get my hands on him, I'll stake him out and . . and . . .' Too late, she realised she was hardly advancing her cause and that Ciaran's lips were twitching with barely restrained amusement.

'It appears it's not only Yseult who shares your brother's temper,' he observed. 'Do stop pacing about, Brangianne. Sit down and let us have this discussion quietly and calmly.'

Quietly and calmly? Her heart was pounding and her mouth was dry. Her whole body was trembling and had been ever since Feargus had informed her what it was he wanted her to do, and with whom. Although, when he'd first told her, her immediate reaction had been to laugh.

'You're joking, surely! You can't seriously expect me to marry Eoghan!'

'I am indeed serious. You know how hard it was for me to pay the tribute to Galloway, especially after the bad harvest we had,' Feargus reminded her 'Now, because of Ferdiad, I have to find it all over again.'

'*You* didn't agree to whatever Ferdiad arranged!'

'No, but since he's Dalriada's Fili and speaks in my name, I'm bound by it. If I don't pay the agreed tribute, I'll look weak, and I can't afford to appear weak right now. Nor, however, can I afford the tribute from my own lands and clients. But Eoghan can.'

'Eoghan's rich because he's your Steward. Everyone knows – including you – that he's been skimming the annual tribute for years.'

But Feargus just shrugged. 'All Stewards do that. You may not care for Eoghan, but you have to admit he's efficient and, right now, I need him and his wealth if our Family's to survive. And his price is marriage into the Royal Kindred.'

So it was no laughing matter after all, and Brangianne had been shaking with fury and panic ever since, but a possible way out of the situation had occurred to her.

'I have to become a nun, Ciaran,' she said. 'I won't – I can't – marry Eoghan. He's the grandson of a wheelwright. How dare he aspire to the sister of a King! It's not to be borne!'

Yet it wasn't entirely pride that made the whole thing so objectionable, even though the man was little better than a peasant. It was Eoghan himself, Eoghan with the cold damp fingers, sour breath and wet eyes the colour of stones. And it was the thought of what marriage with him would mean, for Feargus didn't intend this to be a marriage in name only.

You're not too old to bear children, he'd pointed out, and Brangianne, horrified, had understood that Eoghan didn't simply want to marry into the Royal Kindred, but for his children to be Royal too, and thus have a claim on the throne, something he could never have himself. The children he expected her to bear. And that meant ... that meant ...

Her skin had crawled at the thought.

No, it wasn't to be borne. She'd given up all thoughts of marriage and children many years before. It wasn't that she'd had no offers, or that there hadn't been men she'd been fond of and might, once, have wanted to share her life with. But she hadn't loved any of them. She hadn't even desired them. Ever since that night in Carnadail she'd felt no desire, no joy. Nothing. She blamed the leader of those Galloway raiders for this more than anything – that he'd robbed her of joy, that he'd turned her into a half-woman, a failure she had no intention of exposing to anyone, especially Eoghan.

'What of Yseult?' Ciaran asked. 'She isn't banging on my door, demanding to become a nun. Yet she too is to be married. How did she take it?'

I said I'd do anything to help. And I meant it. Yseult had been pale but determined, even when she learned Feargus intended taking her to Ulaid to find her a husband, someone with men and ships and gold. 'Better than me. But she's always known she'd have to marry a man of Feargus' choosing. She's been betrothed often enough.'

'So why didn't you expect the same fate? You must be aware of the number of men who've asked for your hand in the last seventeen years.'

'I didn't want to marry any of them, and Feargus respected my wishes. I thought he always would. I thought I was *safe!*'

'From what? Eoghan in particular, or men in general? Perhaps it's life itself you're afraid of.'

'What do you mean?'

Ciaran got to his feet and held out a hand. 'Come. It's a fine day. Let's walk down to the river.'

The Monastery of St Martins lay a few miles from Dunadd in a narrowing of the valley that ran north towards the long inland Loch Abha. The Monastery's extensive precinct had been built on a gravel terrace between the river meadow and the wooded hillside beyond. It was a place of great sanctity, for the valley, with its rings and avenues of stones, had been sacred long before the coming of the Christian priests, and as Ciaran led Brangianne through the orchard that lay between the monastery buildings and the outer wall of the enclosure to a small gate set in the wall, the peace of the place settled on her shoulders. Slowly but surely, the pounding of her heart began to ease.

Beyond the gate were the monastery out-fields and grazing lands, and a path led across the water-meadows to the river, over a little bridge, and into the woods on the further bank that, at that time of the year, were thick with violets, wind-flowers and wood sorrel. A bench stood beneath a willow that overhung the river, and there Ciaran sat down and patted the seat beside him.

'So, we were talking about life. Then tell me – what life would you like to lead?'

It was a good question. Was it the life she would have had if the Galloway raiders hadn't come to Carnadail that Beltein night all those years before? Occasionally, she wondered what that future might have been like. A hard life, probably, for making a living from the land was never certain. Yet there would have been children and, with them, all the joys and griefs of motherhood. She would have been a different woman, and perhaps, if she met that woman now, she wouldn't recognise her. The oath she'd sworn in Carnadail had changed her into what she'd become.

'I'm a healer,' she said. 'That's my life. That's what I want.'

But that life was to be stolen from her by The Morholt's death, for although Feargus indulged her in what he saw as a harmless pastime, she doubted if Eoghan would permit his wife to mix with the sorts of people Brangianne was in the habit of treating. But that might persuade Ciaran to grant her wish.

'I spend most of my time at the Monastery already,' she pointed out. 'Especially since Brother Caipre died. You need another infirmarian, so why not me? I always intended to make my life here one day . . .' *When I'm old*, she'd thought. *When I'm tired of life in Dunadd. When I'm ready to live a life behind walls.* She shivered at the thought. Giving up her freedom had never been part of her plans, but it might be the only way. 'Why not now?'

'Because, my dear Brangianne, there's a great deal more to entering the church and taking your vows than a desire to avoid a distasteful marriage or the availability of a position you think might suit you. The church isn't a refuge but a destination and, as with all destinations, a journey is involved, one you've not truly begun. The journey towards Christ is like life, and life, my child, is something you haven't begun either.'

'That's not true! And I'm not a child. I'm thirty-four years of age!'

'Goodness! So old! Time you began then,' he said, quite unmoved by her declaration. 'Or rather, time you began once more.'

'But, Ciaran—'

'No, listen to me.' He laid a hand on her knee for emphasis. 'You're a good healer, perhaps a great one, and we're grateful for your work here at the Monastery. You came to me seventeen years ago and asked me to teach you the healing arts. I've taught you everything I know, and you've gone further. But have you ever wondered why I agreed to teach you? Did you think it was because I wanted to pass on my own knowledge? Or because I foresaw that one day you'd come to me with a genuine desire to take your vows?'

He held up a hand as she opened her mouth to protest.

'No, Brangianne, it was because I saw a woman who was hurt in her spirit and for whom the knowledge I had – the vocation you ultimately chose – was part of the healing she needed. But only part, Brangianne, for you're not yet whole. You've still not forgiven yourself for what happened all those years ago, even though you know, in your heart, that if you went back seventeen years with the knowledge you have now, you still couldn't save them.'

She shook her head. She'd lived when they'd died. How could that ever be forgiven?

Ciaran patted her hand. 'But I can see you need my help, so I will help you. I'll speak to Feargus and persuade him to grant you a summer of freedom. Anything can happen in a summer. In return, I'll expect you to spend that summer thinking about your life and striving to make it whole once more. But I warn you that it won't be easy and that there will be conditions attached.'

'Why would Feargus listen to you when he won't listen to me?'

Ciaran smiled. 'I can be persuasive when I choose, and Feargus, as you know, likes to keep his options open. He's seen how powerful the church in Ulaid has become, and he wants that power for himself and his Family. It might not help him now, but he could be persuaded to take the long view and might not be displeased to have you take your vows. He'd expect you to become Abbess of St Martin's eventually, of course.'

'Abbess?' she asked, surprised, but not immediately dismissing the idea. To run the monastery might be interesting. She could expand the infirmary and make St Martin's a centre for healing and—

'You won't ever be Abbess, however, because you don't have what it takes,' Ciaran went on, crushingly. 'Your faith is based more on a desire to punish the Old Gods than a genuine belief. Then there's the question of the revenge you haven't quite given up on. Revenge, as you know, is a sin. It's forgiveness you need, not revenge.'

He regarded her sternly and, as she sensed her escape route closing, panic surged once more. Eventually, however, a smile tugged at the old Abbot's lips. 'But Feargus need not know my views on your suitability, or otherwise, for the church. I'll allow him to assume whatever he wishes if he'll grant you freedom for a summer.'

Freedom! If only it was that easy. 'What about Eoghan? He's not likely to take a long view.'

'Oh, I think he might. Feargus need only mention how little confidence he has in finding a suitable match for Yseult in Ulaid.'

'You mean Eoghan really wanted Yseult?! That I was his second choice?!'

But, despite her protest, she wasn't really surprised. She'd seen the way Eoghan fawned over Yseult, the way he followed her with his wet eyes, licking his fat red lips when he believed no-one was watching. The thought of those soft damp hands on Yseult's pale skin made her feel as nauseous as the thought of them on her own. *Men are always falling in love with me*, Yseult had declared. They lusted after her too. 'Feargus would never give him Yseult!'

'No, but he could allow him to think he might. And who knows? Perhaps when your brother returns from Ulaid he'll no longer need Eoghan.'

Anything can happen in a summer. Brangianne took a deep breath. Maybe things would turn out all right after all. The sun was shining and the scents of violet and woodruff filled the air. Across the water meadow, the Monastery's golden-thatched dwellings gleamed in the sunshine. Although she didn't relish being trapped behind its walls, the Monastery would be a peaceful place to spend her summer, but when she told Ciaran so, he shook his head.

'I'm afraid you won't be staying at St Martin's, Brangianne. I said there would be conditions, didn't I? I told you you had to learn to forgive. But not the leader of the raiders who killed Aedh. It's yourself you have to forgive, and there's only one place you can do that. Not in Dunadd, and not behind the walls of St Martin's. You need to go to the place where it all began. You have to go back to Carnadail.'

A SUMMER OF FREEDOM

Beltein was the Night of Changes, but Beltein had come and gone and nothing was any different. Oonagh was still in Carnadail, though there was little to keep her there. Not anymore. No family, not since the previous year, not in Carnadail. But maybe she'd stayed because she'd been waiting for something to happen. And now it looked as if something was about to.

'What's that on the sail?' one of the women asked as the ship edged its way into Carnadail's rocky northern bay through a smirr of rain. 'A duck?'

'A goose?' another hazarded.

'It's a swan, you ignorant peasant.' Oonagh rolled her eyes. She was the only one of them not to have been born in Carnadail and, as such, was regarded as an expert on all things foreign. 'That's the King of Dalriada's sign, so it must be the King's ship.'

'Why would the King come here?' someone wanted to know, and one of the other women began to sob noisily. 'He must know!' she wailed.

'Oh, shut up and don't be so foolish!' Oonagh despaired sometimes. 'The King hasn't come. The ship's just stopped to take on water.'

It was unlikely, however. Carnadail had two bays, the beach to the south and the fishing port where the women were standing. But the beach was shallow and the approach to the port was tricky in any sort of a wind, so most ships in need of water headed for Tairbeart to the north, or Dun Averty to the south. In Carnadail, they wouldn't expect to see a ship until the traders arrived in the autumn, yet this one had come barely two weeks after Beltein. Now, having negotiated the rocks near the headland, the sail was lowered, the oars run out, and the ship was rowed into the rocky protective arms of the port. The anchor stone was dropped over the side and the ship drifted to a halt.

Maybe the King really had come. If so, Oonagh had a word or two to say to him. Feargus the Fox they called him, but Oonagh thought of him as Feargus the Warmonger, for his war with the Britons had taken Daire, her only surviving child, as well as most of the able-bodied men of Carnadail. Then winter had come, which couldn't be laid at the King's door, but the hunger could, for the tribute demanded by the Steward in the King's name had been the same amount as usual, despite the poor harvest and the lack of men to gather it in.

Oonagh would be glad of the opportunity to ask this King what he intended to do about all that, and her heart beat a little faster when she noticed a tall man leaning on the strake near the bow of the ship. The rain had eased by then and the man threw back the hood of his green cloak to reveal a head of foxy-red hair and a glint of gold about his neck. Beside him stood a girl, her long copper-coloured hair lifting and tangling in the wind.

Is that the Flame of Dalriada? Oonagh wondered, for the stories that came south with the trading ships spoke of Feargus the Fox's daughter, Princess Yseult, who'd grown with the years into beauty. Oonagh, who had pretensions to beauty herself, would have given anything to see her more closely, but when a coracle splashed down from the ship neither father nor daughter made any move to get in. Instead, it was laden with chests and sacks.

'Those aren't water barrels,' someone said.

'We should hide,' one of the others insisted.

'What are we going to do?' The woman who'd been sobbing started up again.

Oonagh clicked her tongue. *What a flock of sheep!* 'I'll tell you what we're going to do. We're going to get on with our work and not stand here gawping. Aoife and Niamh, you stay with me. We'll greet whoever's come. The rest of you go back to the fields. And for Briga's sake can someone shut that child up!'

A baby was wailing, a sound that grated on Oonagh's nerves, but its mother hushed it into silence, and the rest of the women left, their children trailing at their heels, leaving Oonagh with two of the more sensible of Carnadail's residents. Which wasn't saying a great deal.

'It'll be a new Steward,' Niamh said, eying the boxes and sacks.

'We don't need a new Steward,' Aoife insisted.

Yes, we do! Oonagh thought of the squabbles that had blown up recently, the fences left unrepaired because no-one could agree whose responsibility it was, the cattle left to graze the already over-grazed fields because no-one could decide when they ought to take them to the summer pasture, and the increasingly pungent middens that should have been turned over but hadn't been because no-one wanted to do it.

'Why would they send us a new Steward when they don't know we don't have one?' she asked.

'Who is it then?'

It was a good question, but Oonagh didn't know the answer, so she watched in silence as, on the ship, someone went across to the King and his daughter – if that was who they were – embraced the girl, exchanged a few words with the man, climbed into the waiting coracle and was rowed towards the shore by one of the crew.

'It's a woman!' Aoife said unnecessarily for they could all see it was a woman, her long dark hair blowing about in the wind.

'It's her!' Niamh exclaimed as the coracle neared the shore. 'It's the Lady of Carnadail! She's come home!'

'Dead? What do you mean, dead?' Brangianne demanded of the three women who'd met her on the beach of the fishing port and explained why the Steward of Carnadail wasn't there to greet her. 'How did he die?'

'A fall,' the youngest one said.

'Fever,' declared the oldest at the same time.

The third was a tall striking woman of her own age, deep-breasted and narrow-waisted with an odd foreign look in her wide cheekbones and dark red hair. She appeared to be their spokeswoman. 'He had a fall, my Lady, from his horse – he's a devil, that animal – then developed a fever. He died at Imbolc.' She shrugged as if the death of a Steward was a minor inconvenience, but it was far from minor to Brangianne since she'd been relying on the man to find her somewhere to live and generally deal with everything, leaving her free to . . . to do what?

She still wasn't sure why she'd agreed to come to Carnadail, or what Ciaran expected of her now she was here, but she'd been given no choice. Secretly, she'd hoped Feargus would refuse to let her go, but whatever Ciaran had told her brother had succeeded for he'd graciously granted her time 'to put her affairs in order' before marrying Eoghan, an event that wouldn't take place, he informed her, until he and Yseult returned from Old Dalriada, a trip that would last three months or so. To her surprise, Eoghan hadn't objected to her summer of freedom, and had wished her a pleasant trip and told her the Steward of Carnadail, who was some sort of kinsman, would take care of everything for her. Clearly, however, he wouldn't. Not now he was dead.

'Did you send word to Dunadd?'

The two women who'd spoken first wouldn't meet her eyes, and it was the red-head who answered. 'Of course, my Lady, but the man we sent hasn't returned, so maybe . . .' She shrugged. Maybe he'd never arrived. Or maybe he hadn't been sent in the first place.

Brangianne opened her mouth to say that another message would have to be sent, but thought better of it. Eoghan, with an eye to his own interests, might take it into his head to come in person, given that the dead Steward had been his kinsman, and Eoghan was the last person she wanted to see. The people of Carnadail had managed without a Steward for three months, so could surely manage for a little longer. Aedh, as Lord of Carnadail had always acted as his own Steward, so why shouldn't the Lady of Carnadail?

'Well, it can't be helped, and I'm here now, at least for the summer, so I'll be your Steward until I can find you a new one.'

The three women exchanged doubtful glances, but Brangianne ignored them. She was the daughter of a King, and sister to another. She was Brangianne the Healer, Dark Swan of Dalriada and Lady of Carnadail. If she could manage to be all of these things, why not a Steward also? How hard could it be? She'd move into the dead Steward's House and rely on his servants to do all the work. He had servants, didn't he?

'Ran off when their master was . . . died,' the older woman told her. 'Stole what wasn't nailed down, including the best of the fishing boats, but they didn't touch the Longhouse. It's still standing.'

'The Steward was living in the Longhouse? *My* Longhouse?' Brangianne stared at them aghast, having expected her old home near the southern beach to have fallen into ruin after she'd left seventeen years before. 'I can't stay there!' She whirled around. Perhaps the coracle was still on the shore, the ship still in the bay... But both had gone. She could just make out the ship through the murk, hull-down in the Sound; she was alone in Carnadail. 'I can't stay there,' she whispered, turning to face the women once more and shivering as the rain, increasing from a drizzle to a downpour, began to soak through her cloak.

'It's your home, my Lady,' the younger one said in some confusion.

But it wasn't a home anymore, and she couldn't bring herself to go there. *Not yet. Not today. Not until I'm ready...*

Only the red-headed woman seemed to understand why Brangianne might not want to return to the place in which her husband had been killed and her son had died. 'You can stay with me.' She fixed Brangianne with a look that had all the fierce defiance of a hawk. 'My name's Oonagh. But I'm no-one's servant.'

Brangianne met that look with one of her own, the cool gaze of the daughter and sister of Kings.

'I didn't imagine you were,' she replied, and the woman's expression shifted to an amused mockery that stripped away Brangianne's masks of status until the two of them were nothing more than women bound by something Brangianne didn't yet understand.

Oonagh's house lay on the far side of the river on a little terrace that overlooked the stepping-stones and the western end of Carnadail's long south facing beach. The other houses of the settlement clustered close by, hazed by the smoke that seeped from the thatched roofs and doors of the roundhouses. The settlement was enclosed by a wooden palisade that hadn't been there in Aedh's time, a defence to keep out raiders.

'You live alone?' Brangianne asked, noticing that all but one of the bed-places was empty and that the house was spotlessly clean and far too tidy.

'I do now. Since the war. Since the winter.'

The war had taken her only son, a winter fever her husband. The son's girl had given birth to a child, but the winter had taken that too, and not long afterwards the girl had been found floating in the pool below the falls. Oonagh told her all this in a flat, emotionless voice, as if it had happened to someone else.

'You've no other family?' Brangianne asked her. In Dalriada, family was everything.

'I did once. Maybe I still do, but no-one I'd care to make a claim on.' Oonagh busied herself about the fire, ladling pottage into a wooden bowl and setting it down with a clatter. The subject, Brangianne understood, was closed, so as she ate the pottage – it was really rather good – she looked curiously about the little roundhouse, but all she saw were gaps – an empty peg where a man's cloak had hung, a chest that had held a son's best tunic, and, on the loom, an unfinished length of cloth that might have swaddled a new-born child. Oonagh followed her gaze and seemed to see the same gaps.

'I'm not planning on staying in Carnadail,' she said, but it wasn't until the following day that Brangianne understood why that was.

Seventeen years before, a man and a child had died. Now others had died, and Oonagh wasn't the only woman to have lost her family. Worse than that, the land itself was dying. Brangianne hadn't noticed the previous day, but now, on a bright blustery morning, she saw all too clearly how thin the fields were, how choked with weeds. Fences were broken, old thatch was rotting on barns, goats were roaming the infields, bellowing thin-flanked cattle were crowded into overgrazed fields, and the reeking midden was overflowing. Even the palisade she'd seen the previous night had collapsed in places, though that hardly mattered since there was no-one to defend it. Few men were left in Carnadail: a handful of fishermen, a miller crippled with the bone disease, and the teenage son of the blacksmith who didn't know how to make anything except nails.

Most of this would be the fault of the dead Steward, for this malaise must have begun long before the war and the winter. Like Eoghan, the man had probably been skimming the tribute for years, and his kinsman must have known about it. When she got back to Dunadd, she'd have it out with Eoghan, she decided, but that was a pleasure for the future.

Later that day, she gathered the people of Carnadail together and told them it had been without her knowledge that Carnadail had been stripped of its men and produce. But things would be better now. She was Lady of Carnadail and they owed her their allegiance, their labour and their produce, but she knew allegiance had to be earned, so she'd work alongside them in the fields and with the flocks. She'd brought little with her from Dunadd, but that little would be shared with them all.

It was a fine speech but was met with hostile stares, and she didn't entirely blame them. She'd tried to put what had happened in Carnadail seventeen years before to the back of her mind and had succeeded too well, for in doing so she'd forgotten her responsibilities to the place and the people. Now she had to put that right. Her summer of freedom looked as if it was going to be a summer of work, but she was used to that. Carnadail was sick, but it wasn't dead yet, and Brangianne, above all things, was a healer.

She'd been so certain that day. Seven days later, the only certainty left to her was the conviction that she couldn't stay in Carnadail a moment longer.

So you'll run away as you did seventeen years ago? Ciaran's voice came from the fresh salt wind hissing in the heather. She'd come up to the moor, saying she wanted to inspect the flocks, but in truth it was to escape the stench – and expectations – of the village. Once she'd reached the shielings and the flocks, however, she'd carried on walking across the open moorland until she could see no-one with a claim on her.

I didn't say it would be easy, my child.

Ciaran had been right; nothing about Carnadail had turned out to be easy. *A summer of freedom.* It was laughable now because, rather than finding freedom in Carnadail, all she'd found was failure. *I'll be your Steward. I'll put things right.* But she knew little of fences and flocks, less about the Law, and nothing about how to apply it. So many of the decisions she'd made turned out to be wrong that she'd stopped making decisions at all. No-one was happy, but none of the villagers tried to help her, not even Oonagh whose silent criticism was only slightly better than the sullen suspicion of the other women.

'Why didn't you leave?' Brangianne had asked her once she'd seen how bad things were in Carnadail.

'Some of us didn't have the luxury of leaving,' she'd replied. *But you did. You do now.* Oonagh's words had gone unspoken but were true, nevertheless. She could run away as she'd done once before, and that was exactly what she was going to do.

It's not like you to give up so easily. Ciaran's imaginary voice was annoyingly persistent. *I thought you were a healer.*

'I can't heal this, Father. I've tried everything.'

Have you tried praying? And with that he was gone, and she was alone. Even her God and his son were very distant here in Carnadail. The church was a ruin, the old priest having died the previous year and, with his going, the Old Gods had emerged from rock and tree, spring and stream, and their worship, never far below the surface in Dalriada, had taken hold once more.

'But I know you're still there, Chrystos,' she said out loud, as if by doing so she might banish the little spirits back to their dwelling places. 'I know you're listening. So, please, give me a sign to tell me what to do.'

She held her breath, waiting for something to happen, but no bird passed overhead. No cloud shadow swept over her, and the note of the stiff spring breeze remained constant, whining through the heather and carrying with it the scent of bog myrtle and the deep waters of the Sound. She wished now she hadn't spoken, for who could tell who might be listening, or who might answer?

The wind was stronger up on the moor and was gusting into a gale that tugged at her skirt and shawl and tangled her hair. The horizon to the south had darkened and spoke of rain to come, and she was a long way from shelter. A deer track ran south along a ridge in the moorland, crested a rocky outcrop, and zigzagged steeply down to the settlement. That would be the quickest way back so, fighting the wind, she struggled along the track to the outcrop, and was about to pick her way down the far side when she stopped, transfixed by what she saw.

Beneath her lay Carnadail as she'd never seen it before, as a bird might see it, tiny and remote. She could make out the houses by the river, the smoke of their cooking fires streaming inland, the stepping-stones and ford that led to the water-meadows, the patchwork of fields, some of them dotted with cattle and goats, and there, behind its sheltering belt of trees, the place she'd been avoiding, the Longhouse. And that was her other failure, for she'd been unable to approach the old dwelling-place, far less go in. *Not yet. Not now. Not until I'm ready*, she'd thought the day she'd arrived. Seven days later, she still wasn't ready, and had begun to think she never would be.

She stared down at the long thatched building, the cluster of barns and outhouses, the stream that curved beyond the trees and through the dunes. All these things she remembered with the deep ache of forgotten familiarity, but not everything was as it had been seventeen years before. There were holes in the roof of one barn, weeds in the infields and no stock in the outfields. Only one creature moved near the Longhouse, the dead Steward's horse, a black stallion, a wild beast no-one but Oonagh could get near. *Horses are in my blood*, she'd said, as if it was something to be ashamed of. The Devil, they called him. A killer, if the story of the Steward's death was correct. But was it? As the days passed, Brangianne had begun to wonder if it might not have been the horse that killed him but the women. If so, she couldn't entirely blame them, but maybe it meant she too, as the new Steward, was in danger.

That particular thought hadn't occurred to her until that moment, but it reinforced her decision. She'd return to the settlement before the rain started and get one of the fishermen to take her up the coast. She'd walk back to Dunadd if she had to.

The storm was approaching fast. The sea had taken on the colour of the sky, the slate-blue of storm-clouds. To the east the island of Arainn still bulked clearly against the more distant land, but to the southeast Carraig Ealasaid, that outpost of hated Galloway, had vanished in the low scudding cloud. The sea was flecked with white, and the waves curled towards the Ceann Tire coast to smash themselves to spray on the promontory and boom on Carnadail's long south-facing beach. Even from high on the outcrop above Carnadail she could hear the rhythmic thump of great masses of water beating the iron-hard sands. She was glad she wasn't on a ship in that sea and pitied anyone who was.

Then she caught sight of a scrap of white at the mouth of the bay, moving swifter than the waves, and knew, beyond doubt, that this was the sign she'd demanded. A boat racing the storm.

'Bail! Or, by Woden's balls, we're all drowned men! Come on, you weak-stomached Lothian bastard! Bail!'

The wind had blown up out of nowhere somewhere around dawn after an unpleasant night during which Corwynal, Aelfric and Trystan, in their little skiff, had reached the channel between the mainland of Dalriada and the island of Arainn that loomed darkly through the low haze. Carraig Ealasaid, which they'd left the previous day, was lost in the murk, and they could barely see the Dalriad shore through the gloom. Aelfric had taken one look at the sky to the south and begun muttering under his breath. He'd been relying on daylight to find their way north through the channel, but little could be seen except for the caps of great waves that roared up behind them, one after the other. All they could do was keep the boat heading north and try to stop it broaching, though, in truth, Corwynal's only contribution to the proceedings was the contents of his stomach as an offering to Manawydan, an offering as welcome as his recriminations to Arddu.

You promised me Trystan's life! In Lothian. You promised!

But the God's reply was without anger, pity, or a shred of interest. *He lived. He lives even now. As to the future however . . . ?* Corwynal could sense the God slipping away.

I offered my own life for his! I still do!

The life of a man who refuses to live? What use is that? You will have to do better. You will have to give up something you don't value but can't live without.

It was a riddle typical of the God, but Corwynal didn't have the patience to puzzle it out.

Anything!

The God laughed because he'd heard that before, the raucous mocking laugher of a gull as it swept low over the boat. Gulls took the spirits of men through the gateways of the world, didn't they? The thought sent Corwynal scrabbling below the half-deck to see how Trystan was, afraid his offer to Arddu had come too late. But

Trystan was still fighting for life, though he was no longer conscious.

My son's dying. He accepted it then. *My son. Dying.* A truth all the worse for being unspoken. *Trystan, you're my son.* He'd come so close to saying it on the Rock but had held back for reasons that no longer made sense. And now it might be too late. All through the night he'd lain next to Trystan, trying to protect him from the worst of the buffeting, holding him close to his heart and willing him to live. *Anything!* He meant it. If Trystan could fight so hard for life, how could he do less?

'Come on, man! Bail!'

He did his best, filling and emptying an old leather bucket until his shoulders ached, but it made little impression on the amount of water sloshing about their feet, water that made the boat sluggish and increasingly reluctant to rise to each successive wave. They'd already thrown everything they didn't need overboard. All that remained were their weapons and the little white dog who'd been as sick as Corwynal and who now pressed herself against Trystan, shivering and whining as they ran before the wind. By the middle of the morning, they no longer knew where they were. All they could see to the west was a forbidding land that fell steeply to the water, dense with trees and fringed with booming boulder beaches or long tongues of rock. They were close enough that Corwynal could smell pines and heather, and seaweed rotting on the tideline.

'Woden's balls! Do you hear that?' Aelfric hauled on the steering oar, making the boat slew to one side and angle down the face of a breaker. It wallowed in the trough before the sail caught the wind once more and the boat surged forward. But in the quiet of the trough Corwynal had heard it too – the roar of breakers – and from the crest of the wave he could see, ahead of them, a long finger of land fringed with black teeth and white with breaking water. Aelfric was steering away from the rocks, but they reached out, pulling the boat towards them.

'The tide's taking us in! We can't weather the point!' Aelfric wrenched the steering oar around until they were heading to the west of the rocks, rather than the east. Corwynal scrubbed the spray out of his eyes and peered around as they slipped past the outliers of the reef. All he could see was a steep shore to the west, a low finger of rocky land to the east, and ahead, where the gale was driving them, a long grey beach on which the breakers were beating like a drum. At the western end of the beach, however, there seemed to be a break in the surf, as if the water was deeper there, a pool or a river, perhaps. It was a faint chance, and Aelfric took it, angling the boat towards that break, but as they reached calmer water a squall came screaming across the bay. The boat tilted sickeningly and Corwynal heard canvas ripping as the sail split, and a crack as the mast shattered. It crashed down on the little deck, and the upper part caught him on the side of the head, knocking him to one side. He made a grab for the gunwale, but it slithered out of his grasp, and he tumbled into the sea. The shock of it drove the breath from his body, then the water closed over his head, and everything went black.

'Breathe! In the name of God, breathe!'

Brangianne pounded on the man's chest and put her mouth to his to force air into his cold body. He smelled of the sea and tasted of vomit, and the dense stubble on his face was rough against hers. His chest rose and fell, but he showed no sign of being able to breathe on his own.

'Breathe! I can't do it for you for ever!' She was angry now – she didn't need yet another failure – and pounded harder on his chest. 'Breathe!' Finally, as if he sensed her fury, his chest rose of its own accord, and he choked as he struggled for breath. She helped him roll over and he crawled to his hands and knees, vomiting the sea from his stomach and coughing it out of his lungs. And so, against all the odds, one man at least had survived the shipwreck when she'd been certain all would perish.

He was dressed in leather leggings, a short dark tunic and a shirt that had torn when she'd pulled him out of the sea, exposing the pale skin of his chest. There, almost black against his skin, was the pricked design of a wolf. A Caledonian then. In Dalriada? Yet she was sure she'd seen this man before, or someone like him. That cold face was familiar, as was the long dark hair shot through with silver and, when he finally opened his eyes, they were the slate-blue of the storm clouds streaming north in the gale that battered the coast. She seemed to know them too.

'Who are you?' she asked. 'What's your name?'

He squinted up at her, blinking away the blood trickling down his face from a shallow wound in his forehead. He looked dazed, was probably concussed, and his gaze went past her as if she wasn't there. He was searching the sea and the beach but finding nothing.

'Dris?' he muttered. 'Elfrich?' He lurched to his feet, staggered, and would have fallen if she hadn't caught him. 'Dris!' he shouted. 'Elfrich!'

They must be his companions; she'd seen others on the little boat as it hurtled toward the shore. Was he the sole survivor? Then something moved in the hissing shallows, a creature that struggled to its feet and shook itself, a little white dog that ran along the beach, barking furiously.

At the eastern end of the beach, beyond the stream, wreckage was scattered over the rocks and a big man was struggling ashore with someone in his arms.

'They're safe,' she told the drowned man. 'Your friends are safe.' It occurred to her that, being Caledonian, he might not understand her. 'Safe.' She smiled reassuringly and pointed at the headland.

He followed her finger, gave a cry of relief, pulled himself out of her grasp and, like the dog, sprinted along the beach.

But for herself, a wave of horror stripped that reassuring smile from her face because she knew what was about to happen.

'No! Not there! Please, not *there!*'

She ran after the Caledonian, but her wet skirts slowed her down, and by the time she was breasting the dunes it was too late. The big man had reached the steading, the other man still in his arms, opened the door of the Longhouse and carried him inside.

The house was cold and dark and had the mouldy smell of abandonment, but provided shelter from the storm. Trystan was alive, but still unconscious. Aelfric had laid him down in the corner of the main room of the dwelling-place and crouched by the ashes of an old fire, striking sparks from a flint to set light to a small pile of straw and twigs. Eventually, he coaxed a little flame into life, and sat back on his heels to feed the fire with more straw.

'Thought you'd drowned.' He peered at Corwynal in the flickering light.

'I think I had. A woman saved me.'

'Woman? What woman?'

Corwynal turned around. He'd assumed the woman who'd rescued him would have followed them into the house, but no-one was there. Had he dreamed her? His head ached abominably, and he felt nauseous and dizzy. There was a lump the size of an egg in his hairline and a long shallow cut that was still bleeding.

'Where are we?'

'Well south of Dunadd, that's all I can say. And the boat's wrecked. I tied what's left of it to the rocks and hid our weapons above the tideline. I'll get them when it's safe.'

'We'll get them in the morning.' Corwynal stripped off his sodden shirt and tunic and draped them over a stool next to the fire to dry them. 'We'll rest here tonight and make our way north in the morning.'

Aelfric looked at him doubtfully but said nothing and turned to feed the fire with another handful of straw. But it must have been damp for the fire sent up a great billow of rancid smoke that irritated Corwynal's sea-raw lungs and forced him back outside once more where he leant dizzily against the wall of the house, coughing like a stag. Eventually the spasm eased, and he straightened to find he wasn't alone in the abandoned yard of the steading. The woman he'd thought he'd dreamed was standing there, clutching her shawl around her shoulders and staring at him.

He stared back, his vision swimming. There was something familiar about her, but he was sure he'd never seen her before. She was close to his own age; strands of silver glinted through the dark brown of her hair, and her eyes were grey, or maybe green. They were the sort of eyes whose colour shifts with the weather, darkening and lightening as clouds pass over the sun. She wasn't beautiful, not as men find women beautiful; her nose was too pronounced, her mouth too wide, her face too long. Yet there was grace in the way she carried her head that made him think of a swan, and an authority at odds with her appearance, for she was dressed as any peasant woman in a muddy skirt that had seen better days and a stained and fraying over-tunic.

'You're a Caledonian,' she stated, her eyes flickering to the designs on his chest and arms. It wasn't a good start, he thought. Since the war, Caledonians were unlikely to be welcome in Dalriada. He made a vaguely reassuring gesture, but she didn't appear to be convinced. Her face was pale, her hands clenched by her side, her body wracked with shudders.

'You understand me, don't you?'

He nodded.

'Where are you from?' Her eyes narrowed. 'Not Galloway, I hope.'

From Lothian— He caught himself in time. The name Corwynal of Lothian might be known in Dalriada, the man who'd tricked their King then tried to kill him.

'From Iuddeu,' he said. 'We're traders. Iuddeu is in Manau.'

She lifted her face to the wind, jerking her chin at the storm-lashed horizon. 'You came from the South.'

It began to rain, fat drops of water striking his naked back and making him shiver. *She hates Galloway.* It wasn't surprising, given the war the previous year. And now their Champion had been killed by a man from Galloway, though she was unlikely to know about that yet. He'd have to be careful, but his head ached too much for thought and he was shivering with the cold. Any lies he told would have to be as near to the truth as possible.

'We were in Galloway,' he admitted. 'But we were attacked and my . . . one of us was badly hurt. A priest treated his wound, but it's gone foul. I thought to take him to the Monastery near Dunadd since I'd heard about the skill of the Scots healers there.'

'Gaels,' she snapped. 'You call us Scots – it means pirates. We're not pirates, though you Britons are, especially Britons from Galloway. We call ourselves Gaels.'

He nodded, annoyed with himself for the slip. He should have remembered that, especially when he didn't like being called a Pict.

'Who attacked you?' she asked.

He shrugged. 'I don't know. Rivals? Traders from Iuddeu aren't always welcome in Galloway.'

'No Briton, or Caledonian, no matter where he's from, is welcome in Dalriada.'

'We're shipwrecked,' he said. *And, as such, have guest rights.* He didn't say it, and instead made a half-hearted attempt at a smile. 'All we want to do is rest up for a day or two then make our way north.'

'We're many miles distant from Dunadd. Two or three days by land.'

He looked past the strangely empty dwelling place. On the shoulder of the rising land to the west stood a small palisaded settlement, smoke rising from a cluster of roundhouses. Beyond the settlement, trees closed in, cloaking the hills and spilling down to the rocky coast. The weight of those miles settled on his shoulders as he contemplated the difficulties of moving a dying man through that forest.

'Is there a boat we can buy? Or horses?' He touched the silver on his wrist, sufficient, he reckoned, to buy a small boat or a couple of horses and a cart. 'Where can I find the headman of your village? Maybe he—'

'There is no headman. This is the land of the Lady of Carnadail.'

'Then if I could speak to her—'

'You are speaking to her,' she said flatly. 'So, no, you can't buy a boat or a horse. All we have are fishing coracles, and they're all needed. As for horses, the only one we could spare is that one.' She jerked her head at a remarkably fine-looking black stallion grazing one of the weed-choked fields. 'But he's wild. You'll just have to walk.'

She turned away, and he stared after her, shaken by her hostility. To have come so far, with so much difficulty, to have thought they were safe, that Trystan might live ... Arddu had cheated him, as he always did.

'The hospitality of Feargus Mór of Dalriada is famed even

among the Britons, but it's clear his generosity isn't shared by his subjects,' he said bitterly.

The woman caught her breath on a gasp of outrage, and she whirled around, lifting her hand to strike him but, with a visible effort, stopped herself.

'We're not wealthy people.' Her eyes were like flint. 'Even less so since the Britons of Galloway stripped us of everything we had in their demand for tribute, so I can't give you what you want. But you may stay here for the night. I'll send someone with dry clothes and food, and tomorrow you can leave for Dunadd.'

'Wait,' he said as she walked away. 'Is there a healer in this place?'

She turned back to look at him, or perhaps not at him. At the house. She shivered, but not, he thought, with the cold.

'No.' She turned once more, stumbling in her eagerness to escape, as the door of the Longhouse opened and Aelfric came out.

'We need wood for the fire,' he announced, then caught sight of the woman. His jaw dropped, and his face split into a grin. 'It's her! The woman who sewed up my arm! The healer!'

So Arddu hadn't cheated him after all.

Brangianne closed her eyes, squeezed them shut and wished she could sink into the earth. The big man pulled up his sleeve to show her a well-healing scar, but she'd already recognised him. He was one of the sailors from the Rheged trading ship that had run aground in Loch Gair earlier that year. He'd recognised her too, and knew she was a healer.

I can't be. Not here. Not in there!

'Please.' It was the dark-haired Caledonian. 'Please. My . . . my companion's hurt. He needs help. Please, come and look at him.'

She felt a touch on her arm, and her eyes flew open to meet his and saw such a raw mixture of hope and desperation that she took a step back. 'Don't touch me!'

He glanced at the big man and jerked his head at him, muttering a few words as he did so.

'You needn't fear us,' he said once the big man had gone, heading for the beach. He spread his hands. 'See, we bear no weapons. I've sent Aelfric for driftwood for the fire. Now, please –'

'You don't understand!'

It wasn't him she was afraid of, or the big sailor. It was the house and whatever waited for her there, another dying man, another failure. Ghosts. Everything she'd avoided since coming to Carnadail. Everything Ciaran had insisted she face up to. The past reached out and took her by the throat.

'Please,' he repeated, holding out a hand but not touching her this time. 'There's nothing to harm you. Come. You're cold. We're all cold, but there's a fire inside. Come . . .' Still he held out a hand, his voice soft and reassuring, the sort of tone a man might use to a restive horse. 'Come. . .'

She shook her head. 'My husband was cut down by Galloway raiders in that house. It took him three days to die, and I had to watch. Our son died there too. I can't go in there.'

She thought that would be the end of it, but this wasn't a man who gave up so easily.

'Will you allow another man's son to die there too?'

It was the worst thing he could have said, and she flinched and took a step backwards.

'He's my son.' The Caledonian's voice was breaking. 'I'd do anything to save him. Anything, if you'll just try. I'll beg if you want me to.' He readied himself to kneel, this man she was convinced had never knelt to anyone in his life. But she shook her head; he'd already defeated her, for if there had been a chance of saving Aedh or her son, wouldn't she too have promised anything? Wouldn't she have begged? She dropped her face into her hands, but it wasn't to weep. Not yet. She took a breath, then another, steadying herself for the inevitable, because everything had been leading her here. Ciaran. Her failures in Carnadail. Her demand for a sign. She wished now she hadn't asked for a sign because some God – she wasn't sure which – had heard her and sent her a drowned man with a dying son.

'I didn't ask for this,' she said bitterly, and dropped her hands to look at the man. Once more she felt a sense of familiarity. Where had she seen him before? And when? He was looking back at her, frowning, as if he couldn't place her either. His gaze was a little unfocussed and the wound at his temple was still bleeding.

'That head wound needs stitching,' she told him, trying to delay going into the Longhouse.

'It's nothing. Please . . .' He held out his hand once more. 'There's nothing to be afraid of.'

She wasn't so sure about that, but took his hand anyway, feeling calluses and sand and the stickiness of blood, and let him draw her towards the door of the Longhouse, to the place she could avoid no longer. She was a healer, wasn't she? And she had work to do.

Corwynal wasn't as confident as he'd sounded. The woman was afraid, and he thought she might have reason. Were there ghosts in that house? Vengeful ghosts perhaps? He opened the door and a puff of acrid smoke, for all the world like a fleeing spirit, billowed out. The woman gasped, but he tightened his grip on her hand and drew her over the threshold. The fire was burning brightly by then, and he could see more of the place in which they'd taken shelter: bare walls and dusty furniture, a table and a chest, old dry straw and bracken on the floor, a torn hanging on one wall, a ragged leather curtain screening off a room at the far end. The building stank of smoke and mould, steaming sea-drenched cloth and emptiness. Perhaps that was what the woman was seeing, the gap in the world where a family should be. Perhaps she heard the echo of their voices.

Trystan lay on the far side of the fire, moaning faintly. The little white dog was curled beside him but lifted her head when they came in and whimpered like an ailing child. The woman froze at the sound, but the dog got up and trotted forward, wagging her tail hopefully, and the woman gave a shaky laugh of relief, let his hand go and knelt beside Trystan. Corwynal crouched on his other side, watching her face, and saw it soften as all women's faces softened when they looked at Trystan. And, with that softening, he knew she'd help.

'He doesn't look like you,' she observed, placing a hand on Trystan's forehead.

'He favours his mother.'

'She must have been beautiful, your wife.'

'She *was* beautiful, but she was never my wife. She belonged to someone else.'

The woman blinked at that, but just nodded. 'How old is he?'

'Eighteen.'

She flinched and looked down at Trystan once more, her expression unreadable, but when she looked up her eyes had narrowed, and she was looking at him with a peculiar intensity, assessing, judging, but not, thanks to the gods, suspicious.

'Very well. I'll try to help him, but this you must understand; I may fail. The wound has begun to go foul – I can smell the corruption. If it's gone too deep, there will be little I can do. I may make matters worse, and he may die under the knife when otherwise he might have lived for a few more days. This you must accept. I've treated wounds like this before, at the camp at the head of the Loch of the Beacon after you Britons defeated my people. Few of them survived, so his chances are small. You must accept this too.'

Corwynal nodded, his mouth dry with terror. *Anything* he'd promised both Arddu and this woman.

'But he's young and looks strong,' she went on. 'He's survived thus far. It may not be too late though it's late enough, so I won't wait until daylight.' She glanced around the room and once more appeared to see images he could not, but blinked them away. 'He shouldn't be moved, so I'll have to treat him here.'

'I'll be grateful for anything you can do.'

'Oh, you'll have to be more than grateful,' she retorted. 'If he lives, he'll take some time to recover, weeks certainly, more probably months. He'll have to stay here in Carnadail in my care.'

'I'm not leaving him.'

'I wasn't suggesting you did. But if you're to stay here too, you and your companion, you'll have to work for your keep. This land has been stripped of its menfolk for my . . . my King's war. Few returned. Then there was winter fever, which took many from Carnadail, so we're short of labour. We need farmhands, men to tend the fields and livestock and help with the harvest. Promise me your labour for the summer, and I'll do what I can to heal your son.'

A whole summer? Corwynal swallowed hard, wondering how they could maintain their deception for that long. But he had little choice.

'We'll do whatever you ask.' He held out his hand. She looked at it blankly, and he realised she expected him to bow to her, but still he held out his hand. 'My name's Talorc,' he said. 'Aelfric you know already. My son's called Drust.'

She reached out and clasped his hand in hers. 'I'm Brangianne, Lady of Carnadail, but in Dunadd they know me as

Brangianne the Healer and reckon me the best surgeon and physician in Dalriada. I hope, for the sake of your son, that they're right.'

THE STEWARD OF CARNADAIL

'We should kill them all.' Oonagh thumped a cauldron of porridge down on the hearth in the Longhouse, and the wholesome aroma of seethed oats banished the stink of dust and mould, at least for the moment.

'After breakfast, I assume,' the Lady said. 'Given that you've made enough for five and not two.'

Oonagh thinned her lips, dropped her eyes to the porridge and stirred it fiercely to stop it from catching.

The boy was still asleep, a little white dog curled up next to him, and the dark-haired one was lying over by the wall like the dead. From outside came the regular thunk of logs being chopped for the fire. The big one, it turned out, was handy with an axe.

'They're Britons,' Oonagh insisted. 'They could be warriors. They could have killed our countrymen, husbands and sons of women in Carnadail.' *They could have killed my son.* Her gaze flicked to the sleeping boy and away again. 'They're not to be trusted.'

'Are you?' The Lady came to join her by the fire, a bowl in her hands in which she was grinding some pungent herb.

'What does that mean?'

'I think you know what it means . . .'

Oonagh glanced at the other woman. *She's changed.* In the clear morning light, flooding in through the open door of the Longhouse, Oonagh saw the marks of a sleepless night in the other woman's face. Oddly, however, she seemed more at ease than the woman who'd arrived in Carnadail barely a week before, so full of her own importance. *I'll be your Steward . . .* Typical aristocrat! Oonagh had thought. All talk and no action. She didn't have faintest idea of what being a Steward meant. Oonagh could have helped her but hadn't. *Just go*, she'd thought. *Just leave us alone.* So, the previous day, when the Lady had stormed out of the settlement and hadn't returned to Oonagh's house by the evening, she'd thought she'd done just that. But the cursed woman had turned up in the morning to announce that she'd spent the night at the Longhouse – the place she'd been avoiding – and, by the way, there were three shipwrecked traders who needed looking after.

Traders indeed! The big one, so handy with that axe, was built like a warrior, and though the older dark-haired one, with the look of Caledonia about him, wasn't as broad in the shoulders, he still gave the impression of a man to be reckoned with. As for the boy, Oonagh hadn't looked at him and didn't want to.

'I don't know what you're talking about.' But the Lady just smiled.

'Things are never quite as they seem, are they?' she said, glancing about the Longhouse. It was built in the new style, an elongated oval with a smaller sleeping chamber, adjoining the main room, with its own outer door. It was much bigger than the other houses and Oonagh wouldn't have minded living there herself once she'd given it a good clean.

'I thought this place would be full of ghosts, that all I'd find was death. But I found life instead.' The Lady nodded at the man sleeping against the wall. 'He'd drowned, but I breathed life back into him, and I think I've saved the boy too, God willing.' She took a deep breath. 'So I've suggested they stay in Carnadail for the summer.'

'What?!' Oonagh stared at her. 'Are you *mad?*'

'They're shipwrecked. They have guest-rights. The boy's badly hurt, and he'll need my care if he's to recover. So I made a bargain. I'll tend him, and the others will work for me. We need men who can weed the fields, repair things and . . . protect me.'

So, she knew. The Lady might be incompetent, but she wasn't a fool.

'They're Britons,' Oonagh insisted.

'Actually, the big one, Aelfric, is an Angle, and the other, Talorc, is half-Caledonian. The boy's a Briton, but I don't think he'll be a danger to anyone for some time, if he ever was. Talorc told me they're traders, and I choose to believe him. I can believe anything I like, Oonagh. I might, for instance, choose to believe that your Steward did indeed die from a fall or a fever or both.'

She leant towards Oonagh and though she was smiling, there was steel in her eyes. 'Or I might decide to believe otherwise. You may not know this, but your former Steward was kin to Eoghan, Steward of Dalriada, the man I'm supposed to marry when I return to Dunadd. I don't know much about the law, as you all keep pointing out, but I do know this; if I tell Eoghan of my suspicions, and he decides to believe them, you'll lose your land-rights, what's left of your cattle, all your possessions, and possibly your lives.'

'*If* you tell him.' In spite of the woman's uselessness, Oonagh thought rather more of her than the others did.

We should kill her too, one of them had said. It had been Oonagh who'd talked them out of it. *She won't stay. She hates it here. Be patient.* Now, look where patience had got them.

'Are you going to tell him?'

'Not if you tell me the truth. How did the man die?'

'Stomach trouble,' Oonagh said flatly. 'A spear through the belly. Up on the moor in the old ring of stones, at Imbolc. They left him to die as an offering to the gods.' The Lady gasped and her hands flew to her mouth. 'He had it coming,' Oonagh insisted. 'But I had nothing to do with it. I spoke against it. All I did was take a knife and slit his throat. No-one, not even that bastard, should have to die like that.' She met the Lady's appalled gaze with a lifting of her chin. '*Are* you going to tell this man you're supposed to marry?'

'No, and I'm not going to marry him,' the Lady said after some thought. 'I came to Carnadail to escape. I ran away once and was thinking of running away again. But not any longer. I'm here for a reason.' Her gaze drifted to the sleeping boy, who was beginning to stir now, then to the man by the wall. 'But you're right; they're Britons so I have to be careful. As Feargus' sister, I have value to Dalriada's enemies, so I don't want them to realise that. All they need know is that I'm the Lady of Carnadail and a healer. I want you to tell the women these men are traders from Manau, and now my servants. My identity is to be as big a secret as what happened to Carnadail's Steward. Do you understand me, Oonagh?'

She understood all right. 'I suppose the big one might be useful,' she conceded. 'But as for that Caledonian . . .' She spat in the fire.

'I'll find him something to do. So, do we have a bargain?'

Oonagh seemed to have little choice so nodded curtly. 'They'll stay here?'

'Yes, best keep them away from everyone. I'll be staying too, to look after the boy.'

'You can't stay here on your own!'

'I was hoping you might stay with me, in the women's room.' The Lady nodded at the small chamber beyond the leather hanging.

Oonagh jumped to her feet. 'I'm not staying here with *them*.'
But she didn't mean *them*. She meant *him*. The boy.

'Come and look at him, Oonagh.' The Lady caught at Oonagh's
skirts as she made for the door and jerked her to her knees so
that she fell heavily right beside the boy she'd been avoiding.

He was fair-haired and handsome, not at all like her son, but
much the same age, sixteen, maybe seventeen. Half-boy, half-
man, and hurt, clinging to the edge of life. Her son would have
clung too, would have called out her name as he slipped over the
edge . . .

'Do you really want him dead?' the Lady asked. 'Can you
imagine what his mother would feel if he died?'

'He's not *my* son,' Oonagh said flatly, but didn't get up. The
boy was stirring, his head moving back and forth on the pillow. A
lock of hair had fallen across his forehead and, before she knew
what she was doing, she'd reached out to brush it away. 'He's
not,' she whispered, her throat suddenly raw with unshed tears.
But inside her, that yawning cavern, that boy-shaped gap in the
world, had begun to close, for here was another boy to care for,
another boy to love.

Talorc . . . Talorc . . . The name dragged him back from a
nightmare of sea and waves, a boat bucking in the surf, water
closing over his head. He heard breakers pounding on rocks, but
in his nightmare they were drums beating in time to the clash of
weapons, drums that echoed from the black mountains of the
Island of Eagles, a world in which his name had been Talorc. It
was a name few men would know south of Atholl, and even fewer
women. Yet it was a woman who spoke his name, her voice
threaded with the lilt of Dalriada.

He threw back the blanket and rolled to his knees, reaching

for a weapon that was no longer there. He was in a long low building whose door was open, letting daylight flood in. Beside him, staring at him in alarm, her hand outstretched as if she'd just touched him on the shoulder, was a dark-haired woman. He remembered now – the storm and the beach, the Longhouse in the rain, the woman refusing to go in, denying she was a healer. But she *was* a healer. He'd watched her work by lamplight, probing the ruin of flesh in Trystan's side and drawing out a fragment of metal. She'd nodded in satisfaction before cleaning and salving the wound, and sewing it neatly with fine linen thread. She'd done everything she could, she told him, and Trystan's chances had improved.

'He's awake,' she said now, following his anxious gaze beyond the hearth-fire. 'He's still groggy from the poppy, but he should know you.'

Trystan was pale, his skin waxy, his hair lank. His side was neatly bandaged, and no longer smelled of corruption, but rather of some aromatic herb. His eyes were clear, and when he saw Corwynal they warmed with affection.

'You're alive!' he murmured.

'We're all alive, Drust, you, me, Aelfric. Even the dog.' The little white dog was pressed against Trystan's shoulder, her tail thumping the floor. 'We're in Dalriada, Drust,' he said, repeating the name so Trystan would remember what they'd agreed. He could say no more in case the woman understood Briton, but when she spoke it was in the Gael tongue.

'Tell him he's safe here, Talorc,' she said.

'Talorc?' Drust repeated, confused, but after a moment he nodded in understanding and looked up at the woman.

'I know I'm safe here.' He spoke in her own tongue and smiled at her.

Few women could resist Trystan's smile and she wasn't one of them. Her face lit up. 'So you speak our language, do you? Well,

young Drust, my name's Brangianne and I'm a healer, and this—'
She gestured to a red-haired woman who was crouching in the
shadows eyeing Corwynal suspiciously. 'This is Oonagh. She'll
help me look after you. I've cleaned and stitched the wound in
your side, so try not to move, because if you do you'll ruin all my
work. And look; I kept you the thing that stopped your wound
from healing.' She pressed a sliver of metal into his hand. 'With
this gone you should get better, but you must be patient and do
as I tell you.'

'I'll try,' he said meekly. 'Though I'm not very good at being
patient or doing as I'm told.' He glanced at Corwynal, a glint of
affectionate mischief in his eyes. 'As my brother will tell you.'

The woman's head came up at that, the smile wiped from her
face. 'Brother?' Her grey eyes bored into Corwynal's. Horrified,
he remembered what he'd said the day before. *He's my son.* Had
the blow to his head knocked all sense from him and made him
tell this complete stranger the one secret he'd kept to himself for
seventeen years?

Trystan looked confused at her tone and glanced anxiously at
Corwynal. 'Didn't you mention we were brothers?'

'Brothers?' the woman Oonagh scoffed. 'I've not seen two men
look less like brothers!'

'Please . . .' Corwynal reached for Brangianne's arm, but she
scrambled to her feet, pushed past him and strode out of the
house.

The wind had eased during the night, but the swell still roared
in from the south to crash along the beach. Torn streamers of
cloud scudded across the sun, their shadows dulling to pewter
the glitter of silver light on the sea. The woman stood close to the
high tide mark, her arms clutched across her chest, and, though
she must have heard his approach, she remained standing with
her back to him, looking out at the waves.

'You told me he was your son. You lied to me.' She whirled to face him, her eyes flinty with dislike. 'Did you think I would treat a son when I might not treat a brother?'

'Of course not! And I didn't lie. He *is* my son,' he said. 'I raised him, but he's always believed himself to be my brother. I shouldn't have told you that truth, but I . . . I couldn't stop myself.'

The dislike didn't go, but her anger muted to something more like puzzlement.

'You have the same father?' she asked eventually. 'His mother was your father's wife?'

He flinched at that. No matter how you looked at it, it didn't put him in a good light. 'You find that contemptible, I suppose. She was beautiful, and we were both young . . . Word by word, he was making her despise him. He could see it in the curl of her lips. 'I know that's no excuse but, please, let me explain—'

'I'm not interested in your sordid little story. As far as I'm concerned, Drust's nothing more than a young man who needs my care, and you and the Angle are going to work for us here in Carnadail. So let there be this understanding between us. There was a war last summer, which we lost on account of a treacherous Briton called Corwynal of Lothian.'

He felt himself go cold.

'Women lost husbands and sons in that war,' she went on. 'And Galloway's tribute demand crippled us, so be thankful you aren't from Galloway. But no Briton is welcome in Carnadail. You may be shipwrecked and you may have guest-rights, but none of that stops you being our enemies, and only your labour will reconcile you to me and my people. Do you understand me?'

He nodded, relieved their bargain still stood. 'Perfectly. You want us to have no past. Very well. It will be as you wish. I'll make sure Drust and Aelfric understand it too.'

The woman nodded and turned to walk back to the house, but he caught her wrist.

'And you?' he asked. 'Are you to have no past also? Is that part of the bargain?'

She tried to pull her arm away, but he held her tightly and forced her to look him in the eye.

'You're correct,' she said with chilling formality, her grey eyes cold. 'Nothing about me need concern you other than that I'm the Lady of Carnadail, and you, for the summer, are my servant. You'll address me as 'my Lady' and won't speak to me at all unless absolutely necessary. Is that understood also?'

So she had her own secrets, but he wasn't interested in them. All that mattered was the right to keep his own.

'Understood, my Lady.' He smiled and made a slight, faintly mocking bow before loosening the grip on her wrist. He was still smiling when she snatched it away and stormed off, stumbling in her haste to get away from him.

My Lady! he thought with derision. It wasn't how he thought of her. *Brangianne* was her name, a common enough name among the Gaels, common too among the Britons, being Branwen in that tongue, meaning the white raven. *The white raven?* It stirred some memory, as had her words the previous night: *A bad wound*, she'd said calmly after peeling away Trystan's pus-soaked dressings. *But I've seen worse*. Where had he heard those words before, and why did she look so familiar?

Perhaps her secrets mattered after all.

'I'm going to like it here,' Aelfric announced after the red-head, Oonagh, had shown them about the settlement of Carnadail.

'Why?' The Caledonian gave him a sour look as he pulled his borrowed cloak around his shoulders; it had begun to rain once more. 'The place is a mess, and we've agreed to work here.'

'*You* agreed.'

'All right, *I* agreed, but I had no choice. Trystan won't be able to travel for a month at least, and it'll take you that long to fix the boat.'

If it can be fixed, Aelfric thought doubtfully. *If I can get the wood and the tools – and the time*. Corwynal was right. Carnadail was a mess – weed-choked fields, over-grazed water-meadows, a run-down forge. The fishing fleet was nothing more than a handful of one-man coracles on a boulder and shingle beach protected by a crude breakwater. Things were little better inland. The settlement was a scattering of roundhouses and a stinking midden, enclosed by a broken palisade. Everything was in a poor state of repair, some of the houses unoccupied, and as for the inhabitants … But here things improved, in Aelfric's opinion, for most of them were women. Some were old, some young, some comely, some merely passable. The red-head was the most attractive of the women, though she was a bit old for him, and didn't like him or the Caledonian. She'd made that very clear and hadn't been pleased when the Lady asked her to show them around the settlement. She'd barely spoken to them and had sent them to wait in the rain while she whispered with a small group of women, some of whom, the younger ones, were eyeing Aelfric with interest. He tried out his best smile, and a couple of them giggled until Oonagh spoke sharply to them.

'Don't be a fool!' Corwynal muttered. 'Half their menfolk died in the war last summer. It might have been us who killed them.'

'Empty beds have to be filled.' Aelfric raised his arms above his head and stretched luxuriously. 'I could have a different one every night for a month.'

Corwynal laughed shortly. 'You won't have the energy! Have you seen how much work there is to do? Have you smelled the midden? I'll wager moving that will be our first task.' He frowned at a goat that strolled past, trailing a chewed tether behind it. 'How did it get this way? Isn't there a Steward here?'

But when Oonagh finished whispering and Corwynal asked her this question, she gave him a curt answer.

'He's dead,' Corwynal translated, looking troubled 'The Lady's their Steward now.'

The blacksmith was dead too, the forge now run by a boy younger than Trystan, and half the tools were missing. What was left was broken or blunt, but Aelfric managed to find a hammer and some nails.

'Tell her these are to repair the fences,' he told Corwynal when Oonagh glowered at him. 'But they'll do for the boat too.'

He'd go slowly with that, he decided, giving Oonagh one of his best smiles. Her dark eyes flashed, and she spat her disgust and disdain, but Aelfric wasn't put off. He liked his women to have a bit of fire. Oh, yes! He was definitely going to enjoy himself in Carnadail!

Corwynal's hands, despite his sword-grip callouses, were blistered by the middle of the afternoon. Oonagh has set them to repairing a fence that was part of a small enclosure next to one of the roundhouses in the settlement. Corwynal, lacking Aelfric's carpentry skills, had been given the task of splitting elm logs into fencing stakes, and neither he nor his hands were used to the work.

Oonagh watched disapprovingly from the door of the roundhouse, her arms crossed. From time to time, some of the other women came to join her, most to stare and whisper, but some to argue. Other fences needed repairing, he gathered, and tempers grew heated, but Oonagh drove them off, grumbling. A competent Steward would have calmed everyone down, but the Lady of Carnadail didn't seem to be a very good Steward. He began to wonder if she was as good a healer as she'd claimed, though she'd seemed capable enough the previous night, and Trystan had been better in the morning. But he'd recovered before, only to relapse once more. Doubt iced his veins and his promise to the God echoed around his head. *Something you don't value but can't live without.* What did that mean? It might mean nothing at all. It might mean there was no price to pay, because there was no life to pay for.

He threw down his tools and, ignoring Oonagh's angry protests, strode back to the Longhouse where he discovered, as he'd feared, that Trystan's condition had deteriorated. He was delirious, his skin flushed with fever, and kept turning away from a cup Brangianne was pressing to his lips.

'What have you done to him?' He dashed the cup from her hand, making the little white dog cower away in fright.

Brangianne jumped to her feet, red spots of anger mottling her face. 'I've done nothing but try to heal him! You brought him here! You risked his life on the sea! If he dies, it will be your fault, not mine! If you want to blame someone, blame the man who struck him down! Blame the man who failed to protect him. You claim to be his father. So why didn't you protect him?!'

A cold mass of fear settled beneath his heart.

'I've tried,' he whispered. 'I've tried all his life.' He turned and went outside to lean against the wall of the house, then slid to the ground as his knees weakened. His throat was thick with unshed tears, but he refused to weep. There would be time for that when it was over, so he went back into the house and crouched beside Trystan, across from Brangianne. The accusations hung in the air between them. *What have you done to him? Why didn't you protect him?* The atmosphere was like ice. *Ice*, he thought bitterly, as he watched Trystan burn up, *would have been useful.*

Brangianne poured some liquid into the cup he'd spilled and tried to get Trystan to drink. Corwynal took it from her, held him more firmly and, between them, they forced him to swallow some of the acrid-smelling infusion.

'It's willow-bark,' she said in a more even tone. 'It will help reduce his temperature, but the fever must run its course. All we can do is wait for it to break.'

For the whole of that night they watched Trystan ramble unintelligibly in his fever, but by midnight his voice had faded to a mumble as he moved restlessly back and forth, trying to find a cool place to lay his head. All that night Corwynal forced Trystan to drink, and though the fever didn't abate it grew no worse. Trystan was weak from a month of pain and fever on The Rock, then the sea-voyage, and now Brangianne's treatment of his wound. How much could a body bear and still live? Corwynal didn't know and was afraid to ask, but as the night went on his hopes ebbed as irrevocably as does the tide.

The others stayed away. Oonagh came in briefly with some food that neither Brangianne nor Corwynal could touch, but after one look at Trystan she left, her face tight and controlled. Perhaps she'd watched other men dying of fever and had lost her taste for it. Not long after dawn, Aelfric came to share their vigil, settling himself in a corner, though it wasn't Trystan he watched but Corwynal. Brangianne sat in silence, searching for signs of a change in Trystan's condition. But it was Corwynal who noticed.

'He's sweating!' He moved the lamp closer until they could both see the sheen on his skin. Brangianne nodded and even the dog looked up from her place next to Trystan and barked.

'Build up the fire,' Brangianne said, and Aelfric did so without need of translation. Corwynal looked across at her, desperate for certainty, but she frowned back at him. The treacherous hope that had briefly stirred subsided once more, and he sat back, watching Trystan sweat out the fever until it was over and he lay still.

'Is he . . . ? Has he . . . ?' He couldn't see Trystan's chest move, and his own chest was tight and painful, barely containing the greater pain in his heart. The dog, still crouched next to Trystan, looked up and whined. Brangianne touched her fingers to Trystan's throat and glanced at Corwynal, her face unreadable. His heart faltered to a stop. Had he . . . ? Was he . . . ? But she took his hand in hers and guided his fingers to the place where he could feel a pulse, faint and slow but steady.

'He's asleep,' she said.

'I thought—' *I thought he'd died.*

'He's asleep,' she repeated, sharper now, and he felt so sick with relief he had to stumble outside and retch until his stomach was empty. Then he walked away from the house into a cold and windy morning shot through with rain, beneath a sky streaked pink with the last ribbons of dawn. A stream ran down to the beach past the steading, and when he reached it he fell to his knees, buried his face in his hands and let tears of relief trickle through his fingers. Eventually he bent to wash his face, cup water in his palms and drink until he'd swallowed away his terror.

You promised me something you don't value but can't live without. Arddu's voice was in the rush and hiss of the breakers on the shore, the purl of the stream and the cry of gulls wheeling along the tideline. *Anything*, Corwynal had promised as the boat had foundered. He felt a hand on his shoulder and knew, without turning, who it would be and what Arddu had meant.

'Don't touch me.' He stood quickly to throw off her hand, warning her, feeling the beat of the God in his blood and the touch of doom in her fingers.

'Drust isn't going to die,' she said and, not hearing his warning, touched his shoulder once more. He was afraid as he'd never been before, for this wasn't a danger he could meet with sword or shield. Against this he was as unskilled and unarmoured as a new-born child.

He turned quickly and caught her in his arms. She went rigid, and he could feel the panicked beating of her heart against his. With every thud he felt love tear into him like the beak of a raven, ripping open his chest and dragging out his heart – the heart that had been untouched for so long he'd forgotten its very existence, as he'd forgotten the dream of the white raven and the black. So this was what the dream had meant, this the God's price, this the pain he had to accept, of loving this enemy, this far from beautiful woman, this other half of his soul – a woman who tore herself out of his slackening grip and struck him hard across the face.

'How dare you!'

'I'm sorry. I thought... I'm sorry.' Let her think him overcome by the fear of Trystan's death.

'I *told* you he was going to live!' She was shaking as much as he was. 'It's over now.'

He watched her stumble away from him. 'No, it's not,' he whispered. 'It's only just begun.'

Drust woke the next day, weak but lucid, to Brangianne's relief. Although his weakness remained, the fever didn't return, and, as the moon waned and waxed once more, and the summer solstice approached, he began to improve. Brangianne, quietly satisfied, since she hadn't been as confident of his eventual recovery as she'd claimed, continued to change the dressings on his wound and dose him with infusions to strengthen his blood. Oonagh quickly fell under his spell and found delicacies to tempt his fragile appetite, delicacies the rest of them never saw. Oonagh was even won over by the little white dog, persuaded by her impression of a starving animal who was too polite to beg and, as a consequence, she did rather well and began to fill out.

Talorc, once he was confident Drust was out of danger, stopped haunting the Longhouse, and she was glad of it. She'd been shaken by what had happened on the day Drust's fever had broken, though she tried to tell herself it had been nothing. Talorc had thought his son was dead. Small wonder he'd broken down and turned to the nearest person for comfort. That was all she'd been to him, all she could allow herself to be. No-one had held her like that for . . . had it really been eighteen years? So it was strange, and disturbing, that she'd wanted to hold and be held, to weep in his arms, to find comfort herself. Yet was that so surprising? Her husband and son had died in the Longhouse, and she still had those griefs to deal with. She couldn't allow herself to care about a stranger and an enemy, so she was relieved when he moved out of the Longhouse altogether and took to sleeping in the barn, telling everyone it was because he didn't want to share a room with 'that cursed little dog.'

But she thought otherwise. It wasn't the dog he was avoiding. It was her, and she was glad of it, for when they had, of necessity, to speak to one another, his misgivings about her instructions were all too obvious.

'Wouldn't it be better if—'

It was as if his criticisms fought their way past his control, though usually he could stop himself from saying any more.

'What?' she'd demand.

'Nothing.'

'What were you going to say? I insist you tell me.'

Sometimes he would, and generally he turned out to be right. Sometimes he'd hold his tongue, and whatever she'd told him to do would prove unnecessary or ill-advised. The one task he approved of was her demand that he 'do something about that devil of a horse'.

Brangianne supposed the Steward had ill-treated the black stallion because he'd been unable to ride him. 'He must have been a battle-mount,' Talorc told her, with something like adoration in his eyes. The Britons loved their horses, she'd heard. 'He wouldn't have put up with a fool.'

'I don't need a battle-mount, so make him useful.'

She'd thought, perhaps naively, that the beast could be trained to pull a cart, but suspected Talorc was doing nothing of the sort. A confrontation over that was looming, but when the confrontation came, it was about something else entirely.

'You said what?' Brangianne demanded of Corwynal. 'What right do you have to make decisions on my behalf?'

No right, of course, but the necessity had been clear enough. Two of the village women had come to the Longhouse, seeking Brangianne for a decision she'd promised them, but she'd seen them coming and had headed off for the woods, saying to no-one in particular that she had to pick some yarrow. So Corwynal had spoken to them instead. Or rather he'd listened, something Brangianne had failed to do. It was a complicated situation involving a dispute over a boundary that went back generations, but he was used to dealing with that sort of thing, and he hammered out a compromise that was grudgingly accepted by both parties.

'A decision needed to be made, so I made it. They're both satisfied.'

'That isn't the point! It's a question of the law. We have laws here, even if you barbarian Briton's don't!'

'We do have laws, as do the Caledonians, and, like yours, they're mostly a matter of common sense. But a bad decision's better than none at all. Did you want them hanging about the village, glowering at each other, while they waited for you to make up your mind?'

Let me help you. It was increasingly difficult not to say it. Instead, he criticised her with his silences and hesitations when she told him to do things he knew to be misguided. Nevertheless, despite his determination not to get involved, he couldn't always stop himself. On this occasion, however, he'd gone too far, but maybe it was time to speak his mind.

'You need a Steward.'

'No, I don't! The last man was a liar and a thief, like all Stewards. I may not always get it right, but at least I'm honest and I try.'

'There's a great deal more to being a Steward than honesty and effort,' he said feelingly.

She bit her lip at that and her hands curled into claws at her side. He thought she might strike him, but, after a visible struggle, she took a breath and looked him in the eye, something she'd avoided doing until now. Her eyes were as grey as summer rain clouds that held the promise of sun behind them. They were cool upland tarns in which a man might drown, and he was drowning now, but he kept on struggling to stay afloat.

He tried to tell himself he had no reason even to like her. She was short-tempered and infuriatingly wrong-headed. And yet he'd seen her be kind and caring, and sympathetic. He tried to tell himself she was no more than passable to look at, but he could feel his eyes soften when he looked at her and knew that, to him, she would always be beautiful. Worst of all, he found himself wanting to talk to her, to share his life, his past, his hopes, to tell her things he'd told no-one else. Was that love? If so, it was dangerous, and he had to stay away from her and keep his feelings to himself. He was willing to pay Arddu's price, but no-one, especially Brangianne, was going to know how hard he'd fallen, so now he met her eyes and forced his expression into his usual cold reserve.

'Very well!' she said through her teeth. 'Since you know so much about it, since you think common sense is better than ten generations of law, you can deal with all the other cases. Be my Steward and see how *you* like it!'

'As my Lady commands.' He gave her an ironic little bow, and she gave a squawk of rage and stormed off, leaving him to consider how much of a fool he'd just been.

But, fool or not, from that moment on, he was Carnadail's Steward, the person who decided what had to be done, by whom and when, what was owed in renders and tribute, what penalties were due for what crimes, and who should pay them. He decreed which fields should be ploughed, which hedges repaired, when the shearing should begin. He insisted the midden be moved and new latrine pits dug beyond the palisade. Everyone complained about that but, once it was done, the village didn't stink so much. It was all a great deal of work, but there were compensations. Brangianne, free of the complaints and requests she hadn't been able to deal with, turned into a different woman.

Her frown disappeared, and her temper improved. Occasionally, he heard her singing as she went about the place, though not very tunefully. At first she tried to find fault with his decisions, but their arguments soon cooled to discussions, and her demands muted to suggestions. The weather improved; it grew warmer as spring slowly ebbed away, as did the storms. It still rained, but lightly and mostly at night, and the barley and beans grew tall and strong. He could take no credit for either the better weather or the growth of the crops, but Brangianne seemed to appreciate him, to acknowledge – if only to herself – that he was good at this, that he might have secrets and was probably a liar but wasn't a thief. He hoped she might come to believe that, enemy or not, he was worthy of respect. He wanted her respect almost as much as he wanted to shoulder her burdens.

He was being a fool, of course, as Trystan and Aelfric were quick to point out. He'd claimed to be a trader but was giving the lie to that claim by demonstrating that he must once have been a

Steward. But he didn't care. It was work he was good at and though the people might not trust him and there was little he could do, in a single summer, to repair everything that was wrong, they came to appreciate him too because he listened to them and gave them decisions they could understand. He began to feel at home in Carnadail and to care rather more than was wise for the place and its people.

And for its Lady.

'A ship!!'

When the cry went up, they were at the port in a fish-drying shed belonging to one of Carnadail's fishermen. Brangianne was cleaning a festering cut on the man's arm while he grumbled to Corwynal about the cost of salt. Corwynal listened sympathetically, but remained obdurate about the price, and when the man complained to Brangianne, she told him he'd have to accept the Steward's decision. Aelfric, meanwhile, was haggling with one of the other fishermen for seasoned oak, but the man was being unhelpful, pretending not to understand Aelfric's mangled Gael, and Aelfric turned to Corwynal in frustration. Corwynal shrugged and told him to make do with what he had already and the Angle stomped off in disgust.

'The oak's for repairing your boat, isn't it?' Brangianne finished binding the fisherman's arm and looked up at Corwynal, a smile tilting the edge of her mouth. 'You think I didn't know?'

He shrugged. 'We have to leave eventually.' The summer solstice, The Night of Turning, was already a week behind them, and it wouldn't be long before the June evenings began to draw in. Summer was passing, Trystan was getting better, and soon their term of bondage would be over. Not that he thought of it as bondage anymore.

'You're making so little progress one would almost think you didn't want to leave.'

She'd spoken in jest, but he felt the blood creep into his face. Was it so obvious? 'I've become fond of Carnadail, and—'

It was then that the cry went up.

'Cor—!' The Angle stopped himself just in time. 'Talorc!' he shouted, and Corwynal ran outside, reaching for a weapon he didn't carry.

A ship he'd seen earlier, sailing north up the Sound, had changed course and was heading for the little port, its sail bellied before the brisk easterly wind, its symbol showing clearly in the late afternoon light, a symbol he recognised. It was the sign of the Black Ship, and the ship itself was The Morholt's ship.

Behind him, Brangianne stifled a cry of dismay and, when he turned to her, her face was ashen.

'Go back to the Longhouse, both of you! Find Drust and hide yourselves somewhere. Anywhere. Go on. Run!'

But Corwynal continued to watch the rapidly approaching ship until he saw what he'd begun to fear.

'I'll go,' he said. 'But I don't think there's any point in hiding...'

Nevertheless, he sprinted back to the Longhouse, Aelfric falling in behind him. As they reached the crest of the path Corwynal risked a glance over his shoulder. The ship had dropped its sail and the crew threw the anchor stone over the side, bringing the ship to a halt a spear's throw from the port's stony beach. A coracle was lowered, and a man, a harp-bag slung over his shoulder, leapt lightly into it, picked up the paddle and made for the shore.

Ferdiad, the one man who could ruin everything, the one man from whom it wasn't possible to hide, had arrived in Carnadail. And everything was about to fall apart.

THE FILI OF DALRIADA

'What are *you* doing here?!'

Ferdiad and Brangianne had never been friends. He was intelligent and charming, but she thought him manipulative and devious, and wouldn't have welcomed him under normal circumstances, far less these. But he just raised an eyebrow at her rudeness.

'A fine greeting from the sister of the King to the King's own Fili, come to claim your hospitality!' He peered critically at her. 'Well, Brangianne, you look— How shall I put it? Healthy, I suppose, might be the kindest thing to say.'

She glared at him, conscious of her sun-darkened skin, the mud on her skirts and her tangled hair. Yet Ferdiad didn't look his best either; his normally brilliant eyes were dull and rimmed with red, and his face was gaunt with grief and guilt. Nevertheless, she couldn't find it in herself to pity him.

'You're not welcome, and there will be no hospitality!' She should have left it there but was too angry to hold her tongue. 'You're not welcome because you're the cause of all our troubles – Feargus', Yseult's, and mine. Do you know what your bargain with Galloway has cost me?'

'Ah, you mean Eoghan.' He made a moue of distaste. 'Well,

I'm sorry for that, but you can't blame me for not foreseeing all the consequences of my well-meaning attempt to save Dalriada from having to pay the tribute.'

Not foreseeing?! Well-meaning?! Brangianne was so outraged she didn't know where to begin. Sorry, was he? She'd make him sorry! Her hands curled into fists and she half-raised an arm to strike him, but, with an effort, she controlled herself. There would be time for fury when she was safe.

Why was Ferdiad here? To take her back to Dunadd? To Eoghan? Or to Ulaid, to Feargus who might have some new scheme in mind, someone else for her to marry, someone who might be worse than Eoghan?

'Has Feargus found a husband for Yseult?' she asked, half-hoping he had. Someone rich enough to make her own marriage unnecessary. But Ferdiad shook his head.

'Not yet. He's had plenty of offers, as you might imagine, but can't seem to sell her off as easily as he sold you.'

'I'm not marrying Eoghan,' she insisted. 'And I'm not leaving Carnadail.'

He allowed his gaze to drift over the settlement at the harbour, taking in the cluster of rough huts by the shore and wrinkling his nose at the smell of drying fish.

'You like it here? How astonishing! The place is barely civilised. But don't worry; I haven't come to make you leave. I'm here to find someone.'

Who? There wasn't anyone in Carnadail he could possibly be looking for, other than the Britons. Yet why would he look for enemies of Dalriada in Carnadail, and what would he do if he found them? Kill them? Not on his own, of course, since he was no warrior, but he had a shipload of men . . . Or he could simply inform Feargus or Eoghan about their presence, both of whom would certainly decide to interfere.

'Whoever you're looking for, they're not here, so you might as well leave. Feargus gave me a summer of freedom, and I intend to make the most of it. I *do* like it here, civilised or not, and if I want to pretend to be nothing more than the Lady of Carnadail, I don't see it's any of your business.'

'Pretending?' His eyes sharpened. 'Pretending to whom? Not your own people, who must know who you are. So, to whom are you pretending?'

She bit her lip, annoyed with herself for letting her tongue run away with her.

'Well!' he exclaimed, his eyes gleaming. 'Let me guess. Are there, by any chance, strangers here?'

'Of course not!' But she'd never been a good liar, and Ferdiad just smiled and raised an eyebrow. 'Oh, all right,' she said, giving in to the inevitable. Hadn't Talorc said it wasn't worth hiding? 'But they're not really strangers. I knew one of them from St Martin's, an Angle, a trader from Manau. One of the others is a Caledonian - half-Caledonian – and the third's just a boy. They're not a danger, Ferdiad, and . . . and I need them.'

He'd gone very still, and his green eyes were glittering with something she struggled to give a name to. Hunger? Satisfaction? Was it one of the Britons he was looking for? Aelfric? Drust? No, it would be Talorc, though she couldn't have said how she knew it. Nor could she give Ferdiad an answer to his question because she didn't know the answer. Why *was* she still pretending? Why hadn't she told the Britons she was sister to the King of Dalriada? She was no longer afraid they'd take her hostage. Indeed, the very idea was laughable.

So why not tell him? *Him.* Warmth crept into her face at that particular thought. Yes, it was Talorc from whom she kept her identity secret, Talorc whom she'd come to respect, and whose respect and liking she wanted in return – for herself, not who she was related to. He wouldn't think much of a woman who'd lied about who she was. And now Ferdiad threatened her innocent little pretence, Ferdiad who, like Ciaran, saw a great deal too much.

'You . . . need them?' There was an odd catch in his voice. 'For what?'

So she was forced to tell him about the bargain she'd made, about how Drust needed her, how Aelfric was a good worker, how Talorc had become her Steward.'

'Your Steward?' He gave a shout of laughter. 'My dear woman—!'

'I need them,' she cut in. 'I don't want you to frighten them off.'

To her relief, he gave her one of his charming smiles. 'Very well, Brangianne, I won't frighten them off, but I do insist on meeting them.'

'Why?'

'Curiosity. Am I not allowed that? Don't worry, I won't give you away. You can go on pretending to be nothing more than the Lady of Carnadail, but you understand what that means?' He lifted an eyebrow. 'It means I out-rank you, so you'll have to address me as 'My Lord'.' His smile broadened to a grin that glinted with a mixture of malice and mischief. 'I may even insist you curtsy.'

'We could just kill him,' Aelfric suggested. It was the obvious solution. The man had come ashore alone and unarmed. How difficult could it be? But the Caledonian wasn't convinced.

'And what would that achieve? Apart from revealing us as something we're pretending not to be?'

'Listen, Corwynal—' Trystan began.

'Don't call me that!'

Aelfric sighed. He hadn't approved of this whole changing names business. Not that he was against half-truths or lies – he'd told enough in his time – but secrets had a way of being found out. He, himself, had come within a hair's breadth of giving them away when the ship had arrived and he'd almost called out Corwynal's real name. Although Talorc was his real name too, apparently, and Drust was a Caledonian version of Trystan. Nevertheless, they were still lies, and it would put them in a difficult position with the Lady of Carnadail when that Dalriad Fili told her who they really were. Because why wouldn't he, given that he blamed both Corwynal and Trystan, not unreasonably, for killing Dalriada's Champion?

'You might have forgotten your real name,' Trystan said. 'But Ferdiad won't. He wants revenge. That's why he's here.'

Trystan was standing in the doorway of the Longhouse, leaning against the doorpost for support, having refused to confront Ferdiad lying down like an invalid. Corwynal had taken a defensive position on the other side of the door, within easy reach of the weapons Aelfric had hidden in the thatch of the adjoining barn. Trystan's dog was trotting from one to another, clearly under the impression this was all a game. But it wasn't.

'If that's what he wants, he wouldn't have come alone,' Corwynal pointed out.

'He has a ship,' Aelfric reminded them. A fine ship, one he wouldn't mind taking the helm of himself. If the fresh easterly breeze continued veering to the south, it would blow them neatly to Strathclyde 'So we kill him, overpower the crew, and get away from here.'

'Overpower an entire ship? Don't be an idiot! Anyway, Ferdiad can't possibly know we're here, so he must have come for some other reason. And Brangianne won't give us away.'

Aelfric exchanged a look with Trystan. 'Is there any reason why she shouldn't?' the boy asked carefully.

Good question. She'd told them to hide, which meant she'd try to protect them. But would she do so once she knew who they

were? The Lady might be fond of Drust, and maybe himself – he
made her laugh when he mangled the Scots tongue – but what
did she think about Corwynal? Aelfric wasn't so sure, but one
thing he was certain of; the Caledonian cared for The Lady of
Carnadail and she was the only one who didn't know it. What a
fucking idiot! If he'd wanted a woman, why hadn't he picked one
of the village girls, all willing enough in Aelfric's by now
extensive experience? All except that Oonagh of course. Why had
the Caledonian fallen for the one woman he couldn't have?

Ealhith, Aelfric thought morosely, would never forgive him.

'I'm Lord Ferdiad, Fili to King Fergus of Dalriada,' Ferdiad
announced grandly, 'here at his request to visit the Lady of
Carnadail, who tells me you're traders from . . . where was it
again?'

When Ferdiad appeared in the steading yard, Brangianne at
his shoulder, Corwynal had expected the worst. Her expression,
however, was hard to read, and she seemed ill at ease and
defensive, as if Ferdiad knew something about her she didn't
want them to find out.

The attitude of the Fili was even more of a puzzle. Why
pretend not to know them? Hadn't he recognised them? Trystan
had let his beard grow, and Corwynal was thinner, but surely
those weren't the reasons. If anything, it was the Fili himself
who'd changed; he looked like a very different man from the one
who'd come to Galloway to offer The Morholt's challenge. This
man was grey and haggard, and he looked as if he'd been
drinking for weeks and had only recently stopped. Had it
affected his memory? Was he, perhaps, still drunk? Yet, apart
from a faint trembling in his hands, there was no sign of it. His
voice was crisp enough, and his eyes, screwed up against the

light as if his head ached, were as sharp as Corwynal remembered. He knew them all right but, for reasons of his own, had decided not to betray them. Not yet. Not until it suited him.

'We're traders from Iuddeu,' Corwynal said, going along with the pretence. 'We trade in furs and silver.'

'Really? With what nation?'

'Any nation that will trade with us: Lothian, Gododdin, Galloway, Strathclyde. Occasionally Caledonia.'

'Atholl?'

'Not Atholl,' Corwynal said, wondering where this game of Ferdiad's was leading.

'How strange,' Ferdiad mused. 'I once heard of a man called Talorc, but he was from Atholl.'

Corwynal's disquiet deepened. Why would a Dalriad know anything of Talorc of Atholl when he hadn't called himself that for over twenty years?

'It's a common enough name in Caledonia,' he said with a shrug. 'But I'm from Iuddeu.'

Ferdiad smiled and turned his green gaze on Trystan.

'And you? A Briton who bears a Caledonian name and a royal one at that?'

'I make no apology for my name, or anything else!' Trystan would have said more, but Corwynal threw him a warning look, and Ferdiad's smile broadened to a grin as he flung out his arms to encompass the three of them.

'So – a Briton, a Caledonian, an Angle, and—' He looked down at Trystan's dog, nosing with interest at his shoes, '—a little white dog! An unlikely combination, don't you think, Lady Brangianne?'

She opened her mouth to speak, but nothing came out, and she threw Corwynal a look in which appeal was mixed with confusion, as if she was as mystified by the game Ferdiad was playing as the rest of them.

'And it's just such a combination of men I've been looking for,'

Ferdiad went on, eyes glinting at Brangianne's failure to reply. 'Because I'm hoping they can help me find out what happened to the man my King has . . .an interest in. One who bore this.'

He pulled a chain from beneath his tunic, on the end of which hung something that caught the light as it spun, its garnets as red as blood, its pearls as white as tears, something they all recognised.

Corwynal's heart rocked in his chest. He'd been so taken up with trying to anticipate how Ferdiad would expose their part in The Morholt's death he'd forgotten everything else that had happened the previous year. But he managed to keep his silence, and Aelfric confined himself to a grunt of surprise. It was Trystan who gave them away.

'Ninian?' he asked in astonishment. 'You're looking for *Ninian?*'

'You knew Ninian?' Brangianne exclaimed. 'Why didn't you tell me?'

She wasn't sure what she'd expected, but it certainly wasn't this. Indeed, she was struggling to think at all. It was barely an hour since she'd been binding that fisherman's arm and accusing Talorc, half in jest, of not wanting to leave Carnadail. *I've become fond of Carnadail, and—*What had he been going to say?

'I didn't know you knew him.' Talorc spoke for them all but sounded as if he was afraid to give too much away. Why was that? And why had Feargus sent Ferdiad to find out about Ninian when he believed he was dead? Why had Ferdiad come to Carnadail? Was it because these three men knew something about Ninian's death?

'We met him in Trimontium,' Drust said. 'It's a trading town on the border between Lothian and Gododdin.'

'Excellent!' Ferdiad said. 'That's where I lost his trail. He went off, by all accounts, with a small party of men that included some Britons, a Caledonian and an Angle, which is why I'm so fascinated to find just such a combination of men in Carnadail. I can see there's a story behind this, and I do love a good story!' He strolled over to the bench that stood in a patch of sunlight next to the door of the Longhouse, sat down, stretched out his legs, crossed them at the ankles, and leant back against the wall with the look of a man ready to be entertained.

If so, he was the only one of them enjoying himself. Brangianne felt as if she was rooted to the ground, while Aelfric stood in the doorway of the barn, his hands curled into fists. Drust subsided painfully onto the stool on the other side of the Longhouse door, a white look about his lips, his dog pawing at his knee in concern. Talorc stood next to him, his hand on Drust's shoulder, his body tensed and his face turned away from her as if she was the enemy here, rather than Ferdiad.

The wind, veering into the south, brought with it the smell of weed on the high-tide line. Little white clouds scurried across the sun, sending bursts of light and shadow across the steading yard as everyone waited for someone else to say something.

'It's not much of a story,' Talorc said eventually 'We met him there by chance. He'd been in Rosnat, I believe, but when we met him he was travelling about as a healer. He came to Meldon in Selgovia with us. While we were there, some Caledonians arrived and persuaded him to leave with them.' He paused, glanced at Brangianne, and looked away. 'They crucified him.'

Crucified?! Brangianne's gorge rose at the thought. *Ninian, that gentlest of souls, crucified?!* She looked at the cross Ferdiad had held out, the cross with the dying man set about with garnets and pearls and stained with some dark substance that dulled the gold. Was that Ninian's blood?

'Why?' Talorc shook his head as if he didn't know, or didn't want to say, but she couldn't miss the flash of anger in his eyes.

He saw it! He didn't just hear about it. He saw *it.*

'They're a cruel people,' Ferdiad said. 'These particular Caledonians—' he went on, turning to Talorc, '—where were they from, again?'

'Atholl,' Talorc said grimly. 'And that's where Ninian's gone.'

Drust looked up in surprise, Aelfric muttered a curse and Ferdiad leant forward, his eyes sharpening. Brangianne was equally surprised, but not because he'd gone to Atholl. Because he'd been in a position to go anywhere.

'He's alive?'

'He was when I saw him last,' Talorc said. 'We followed the Caledonians after they'd taken him and he was still alive when we found him, so we took him back to a healer in Meldon. That was just after Beltein, and by Samhain he'd recovered and came to Iuddeu. But he only stayed a few days. It was a bad time of year to be travelling, but he couldn't be dissuaded. He told me he was heading west to Dalriada and spoke of forgiving his enemies. I didn't think anything of it at the time, but he must have meant the Caledonians who'd crucified him.'

'Forgive his enemies?' Ferdiad exclaimed. 'What a strange idea! I know I wouldn't. Would you, Lady Brangianne?'

She thought of the man who'd led the Galloway raiders, of Corwynal of Lothian who'd tricked Feargus, and the Galloway Champion who'd killed The Morholt. No, she wouldn't forgive any of them. '*I* wouldn't, but it's just what Ninian would do! He's no warrior, but he has more courage than anyone I know.'

Ferdiad got to his feet. 'Courage, perhaps. Stupidity, certainly. Because now I'll have to chase after him to Atholl of all places.'

'They don't like strangers in Atholl,' Talorc said.

'Then I'll need a guide.'

The two men looked at one another. Neither had a weapon,

but it was as if two blades had sparked together. Brangianne could feel violence in the air, but that wasn't what made her protest. It was panic. Summer wasn't over. There would be the harvest to get in. She couldn't manage without him – them.

'None of you are free to guide anyone anywhere,' she said, turning to Talorc. 'You gave me your word you'd work for me for a summer, until Drust was healed. Which he's not. You don't want to leave, do you?'

He'd said he'd become fond of Carnadail, and— It shouldn't matter what he'd been about to say, but for some reason it did.

He shook his head, but she wasn't sure if it was in response to her question or to the situation Ferdiad had put him in. 'My wishes are of no importance. But yours are. Ninian was your friend – and mine. If you want him found, you should send me with Ferdiad.'

She didn't know how to reply. He was right, but she didn't want him to go. She'd come to depend on him. Her summer of freedom wouldn't be the same without him – or the others.

Drust was frowning at Talorc, a warning in his eyes, a protest on his lips. Aelfric had pushed himself away from the barn door, ready, she thought, for action. But Ferdiad's expression, as he glanced from her to Talorc and back again, was that of a player of Fidchell who'd just seen a new opening in the game.

'Actually,' he said, cutting across Drust and Aelfric's as yet unvoiced objections. 'I think I'd do better on my own. I wouldn't, in any case, dream of depriving Lady Brangianne of her valued Steward.'

He smiled a slow smile of satisfaction, got to his feet and stretched, then extended a hand to her. She took it automatically, expecting him to bend and touch the back of her hand with his lips. But he didn't, and she realised he was waiting for her to curtsy to him.

'Lord Ferdiad,' she muttered between gritted teeth as she

dipped her knee to him, wanting to scratch that handsome smiling face, but knowing this was a small price to pay to keep her secrets.

'Thank you for your hospitality, such as it was.' He gave her a half-wink. 'But I mustn't impose on you any longer. I don't want to keep my ship waiting.'

The sun was low in the sky by then, and the long summer evening was darkening. A half-moon sailed between the clouds, chasing the sun into the west. Ferdiad turned to the three Britons, his eyes glittering. 'We'll meet again, I'm sure. Sooner or later.' It was both a promise and a threat. He held out his hand to Talorc. 'I'm sorry we're not to journey to Atholl together. It might have been . . . interesting.' He winked at Aelfric and then turned to Drust. 'Well, boy, I'm sure you'll make a full recovery in the Lady Brangianne's care, but you must be bored, so maybe this will help.'

He picked up the harp in its embroidered bag and held it out to Trystan who stared at him, then at the harp with something like longing in his eyes.

'I've no heart for music these days,' Ferdiad explained. 'But that shouldn't mean my poor harp is doomed to silence. Take it and bring it back to life.'

Smiling at them all, the little pieces in his game, Ferdiad left the Longhouse, leaving confusion and suspicion behind him, as no doubt he'd intended all along.

'What in the Five Hells are you playing at? You're not really looking for Ninian.'

Corwynal had followed Ferdiad to the fishing bay and caught up with him before he reached his coracle.

'Actually, I am.' Ferdiad's look of injured innocence was

almost comical. 'Feargus decided it was to be my punishment. He was somewhat... annoyed about my arrangement with Galloway.' The Fili shuddered as if remembering something considerably more violent than mere annoyance.

'Feargus believes he's dead, that we killed him, even though I denied it.'

'Feargus has a great capacity for believing whatever he chooses to believe, and for changing his mind whenever it suits him. So, yes, I *am* looking for Ninian, who has led me a merry dance so far. I came here as a last resort. He was the Lady of Carnadail's apprentice, so I thought she might have an idea of where, if he was alive, he could have gone. I didn't expect to find you three. I went to the Rock, you know, and the priests told me you'd left in a fishing skiff in a storm. I assumed you'd all drowned, so imagine my delight when it was clear the Lady was hiding something – or someone.'

So she hadn't given them away, not deliberately.

'Why pretend not to know us? Why didn't you just tell her and get it over with?'

'What a short-lived pleasure that would have been! I've all sorts of reasons for being here. I've told you one of them. You'll have to guess the rest.'

'You promised revenge, on Trystan, on me.'

'Of course I did!' Ferdiad said mildly. 'Did you think revealing who you were would be part of it? Well, it might be, but not now, not here, not yet, perhaps not ever. That would be too easy, wouldn't it? Like spearing fish in a barrel, and where's the sport in that?'

'Revenge isn't a *sport!*'

'It is to me. I've planned it you know.' His voice chilled to a glossy iciness that made Corwynal's blood run cold. 'Already it begins to take its shape. But it won't be quick and it won't be simple because I'm not simple. I'm not predictable – even to myself – so don't bother trying to understand me. You'll just have to wait and see what happens. I'll be interested to see what happens myself.' He smiled and stretched, as satisfied and languorous as a cat in the last rays of the sun. *No, not a cat*, Corwynal thought. *A well-fed serpent, sunning itself in summer, sated but still dangerous.* His thoughts must have been evident from his expression, for Ferdiad's face lit up with what, for the first time, seemed like genuine amusement. 'I'm not called Ferdiad the Snake for nothing.'

Beyond the headland, the sail billowed and caught the wind, and the ship heeled as it picked up speed, heading north, driven by the fresh breeze that had veered around into the south. Brangianne, watching from the crest of the track, had seen Talorc speaking to Ferdiad on the shore. She'd thought the two men might come to blows, so strong had been the antipathy between them at the Longhouse, but they'd only spoken briefly before Ferdiad thrust the coracle into the shallows, jumped in, and paddled out to the waiting ship. She waited for Talorc to come back up the hill because she had questions, but wasn't sure where to begin, what to ask, or if she really wanted to know the answers.

'So he's gone,' she said unnecessarily.

'Yes.' An awkward silence fell between them, full of unspoken things.

'Were you really Ninian's friend?' she asked once the silence had become unbearable.

'Yes.'

'Can you prove it?'

'Look.' He lifted one side of his tunic. There, beneath the pattern of a bird, which might be a goose or, equally, a swan, was an old scar, a little above his hip bone. A neatly stitched scar, purple against the pale skin of his body.

She touched the scar and felt the even puncture marks of the stitching. Around his back was a similar scar. It looked like Ninian's work. An arrow wound, she thought. Talorc was lucky Ninian had been there to deal with it, for men died of such wounds. When had that happened, and why? But she didn't ask. She didn't want to hear what might turn out to be a lie. Anyway, it wasn't proof Ninian had been his friend.

'Ninian would have healed an enemy.'

Was he an enemy? Was he *her* enemy? It seemed impossible for things to go back to the way they'd been just a few hours before when he'd told her he'd become fond of Carnadail and something or someone else. No, what he'd been about to say didn't matter. It could be the cursed horse for all she knew, or cared, the one he was training. For what, she didn't know but it wasn't, no matter what he claimed, to pull carts. That was a lie, one, perhaps, of many.

'I should have made you go with Ferdiad,' she said. 'Whether he wanted you or not.'

'Why didn't you?'

Her fingers still held the feel of his skin, shivering under her touch, and she pushed her hand into her skirt as if she might brush it away, then forced herself to look into those stormy troubling eyes and found her breath catching in her throat.

'Because you're useful to me.' Yes, useful. That was the word to use. That was all she could allow him to be.

'Useful,' he repeated. She could feel the distance grow between them, a chill wind rushing into the space, and she could breathe once more. 'Then, if you'll excuse me, my Lady, I'll go and make myself useful.'

He strode off towards the Longhouse, and she didn't see him again that evening. In fact she rarely saw him in the days that followed since, once more, he took to avoiding her. Any spare time he had he spent training The Devil, together with Trystan, now well enough to limp to the outfields. Annoyingly and unnervingly, she found she missed him, or at least the discussions they'd had, the suggestions that became plans: a field to be cleared, another variety of barley to be tried, long-term plans that belonged to more than a summer. So perhaps it was the plans rather than the man she missed, for they were part of her pretence that she was never going back to Dunadd.

But one day she'd have to, and when she returned, it would be to take her place at St Martin's, for the thought of marrying Eoghan had become increasingly intolerable. Ciaran would surely accept her now, for she'd come to Carnadail as he'd demanded, and, with the finding of life rather than death, she'd begun to forget that Beltein night of fear and blood and failure.

Until it all happened once more.

RAIDERS FROM GALLOWAY

The days turned warmer as the summer slipped irrevocably towards Lughnasadh. Days of sun sent the temperature soaring and great masses of cloud building up over the land. In the long summer evenings, thunder rolled about the hills, and the days would end with a storm as violent as it was short-lived. Sometimes the heat drew moisture in off the sea, and tendrils of thickening mist would waft in with the tide until Carnadail was wreathed in a salty seaweed-smelling fog that softened the edges of everything. It brought a welcome coolness to the evening, but also clouds of biting insects that were difficult to ignore.

In the fields, the barley grew tall and heavy with grain. The harvest would be poor, but The Lady of Carnadail had promised that no tribute would go to Dunadd that year. She, personally, would deal with the King's Steward, she said with a sharp edge to her voice. Corwynal would very much like to have dealt with him himself for he suspected the Steward of Dalriada was as much of a thief as the Steward of Carnadail had been. But he didn't say so to Brangianne. Indeed, he said little to her after Ferdiad's visit, for they were avoiding one another once more. *She suspects*, he thought. But of what he couldn't have said, and he thanked his

Gods he hadn't spoken the words that had been on his tongue in the fish-drying shed. He'd lost his heart, as Arddu had demanded, but saw no reason to suffer the humiliation of having it thrown back in his face.

Days passed, then weeks. Once Lughnasadh was behind them and the crops were in, summer would be over and they'd have to leave. Even now there was nothing to keep them, apart from Corwynal's promise to stay for the harvest. The boat was sea-worthy once more, and Trystan had recovered much of his strength, though he still tired easily. His wound had closed up, leaving scar tissue that tightened his side, but Brangianne assured him it would stretch with time. Nevertheless, Corwynal could sense Trystan's frustration building, and was glad of Ferdiad's unexpected gift of his harp. *It's probably cursed*, Aelfric muttered, but Corwynal could see no harm in it. It kept Trystan from boredom, and in the evenings he'd sing for them all, songs of the Britons he translated into the Gael tongue, and others Corwynal didn't recognise. They were good evenings. He could sit in the shadows away from the fire and watch Brangianne's face as she listened to Trystan singing. Sometimes Aelfric was there too, occasionally contributing one of the long dirges of his people, but usually he slept elsewhere. He'd worked his way through all the willing women of Carnadail – of which there were many – and was going around for the second time. He hadn't made any progress with Oonagh, however. She still glowered at him and called him an oaf to his face, but Aelfric just laughed.

It was a few days before Lughnasadh when everything changed, one of those days of sweltering heat that drew haar off the sea by late afternoon. Corwynal had intended taking The Devil, with whom he'd reached a wary understanding, up to the moors to check on the herds, but had stopped at the port to talk to some of the returning fishermen and hadn't yet left for the hills when the alarm was raised.

'Raiders!' A woman ran down from the village, grabbed a couple of children, and ran back up the hill to the safety of the palisaded settlement. The fishermen and women at the port dropped their nets and creels, scooped up the rest of the children, and sprinted after her. But Corwynal didn't join them.

Raiders? Now? Before the harvest's in? It made no sense. There was little to steal and the herds and flocks were all up on the moor. So he didn't head for the settlement. Brangianne had gone there that morning with Oonagh, so she'd be safe. But the Longhouse, so close to the beach, was vulnerable, and Trystan was there. Corwynal took two running strides, mounted The Devil, kicked him into a standing gallop, and lashed him with the reins. The horse leapt forward with a scream of outrage and lengthened his stride, his haunches bunching as they crested the rise between the port and the Longhouse.

Three coracles lay like stranded seals on the beach. Corwynal could see a vessel standing to out in the bay before it vanished behind a bank of haar. Four men were crossing the beach, four more cresting the first of the dunes. Others must already have reached the Longhouse since he could hear Trystan's dog barking, the crash of weapons and the yelling of men. *Aelfric's there!* he thought with a surge of relief, until he saw the Angle sprinting across the fields, leaping the low hedges as he made for the steading. Corwynal bent low over The Devil's neck, urging him to greater speed. Closer now, he heard the clash of metal on metal. Trystan must have managed to get his sword from the thatch above the barn door and, from the sound of it, was fighting the raiders. But, hurt as he was, how long could he hold them off? Fear clawed at Corwynal's throat as he hurtled towards the Longhouse, then his heart began to pound in his chest for, running down from the settlement, her cloak flapping in the wind like the wings of some great bird, was Brangianne.

'Get back!' he yelled, and Aelfric echoed his cry. 'Keep away, woman!' But she kept on running. He didn't know what to do. Should he head her off or keep going to the Longhouse? Brangianne or Trystan? *Don't make me choose!* But there was no real choice; he had to protect both of them, and that meant reaching his weapons. He lashed the reins once more, and The Devil squealed with fury and thundered towards the steading, clods of earth flying from his hooves. The gate was shut, but the wall was only breast height. *Come on, boy!* The horse gathered his haunches and leapt, soared over the wall and into the yard, trampling one of the raiders and scattering the others.

Trystan was in the doorway of the Longhouse, a sword in one hand, and was struggling to block the blows of one of the raiders. His stance was awkward, and he was grunting with pain as he parried each thrust. Corwynal jerked on the reins and yelled at The Devil, who reared, squealing and striking out with his hooves at the man attacking Trystan, turning the back of his head into a red ruin of bone and blood.

'Behind you!' Aelfric roared as he skidded around the side of the Longhouse and scooped up his axe from the pile of straw Trystan had brought down when he'd dragged out their weapons. Corwynal's swords lay there too, but he couldn't dismount to retrieve them since one of the men Corwynal had driven away when he'd landed in the yard had returned, a long knife in his hand, thrusting low to hamstring The Devil. Corwynal kicked out and jerked the horse back in a spinning rear. The man stumbled towards the Longhouse and fell forward as an axe thudded into his spine.

Three down! The music in Corwynal's blood began to sing. 'Trys, get in the house!' he yelled, but as he did so two things happened. The rest of the raiders burst through the gate from the beach, and Brangianne flew into the yard from the other gate. She pulled up short, her eyes widening at the sight of the three bodies bleeding into the mud, and Corwynal kicked The Devil towards her, forcing her back against the barn.

'Sword, woman!' He jerked his head at the weapons that lay at her feet. 'Quickly!' She stared at them as if she'd never seen a sword before. 'Now, Brangianne!' His use of her name broke her trance; she picked one up and he bent to sweep it out of her hand. The thrill of it went running along his arm as he drove The Devil into the mass of men were milling around the door to the Longhouse. The horse shouldered one aside as Corwynal hammered his blade down at another. On his other side, Aelfric was yelling his Angle war-cry and wielding his axe to deadly effect, but Corwynal had eyes only for Trystan, still in the door of the Longhouse, being driven back by yet another of the raiders. His face was bloodless, his lungs gasping with the unaccustomed effort and, before Corwynal could reach him, he failed to parry one powerful blow. The raider's sword slid along his blade, crashed into and over the guard, and sliced wickedly up his forearm. Trystan dropped his sword and staggered back into the Longhouse, his left hand gripping the wound, blood pulsing between his fingers. Corwynal slid from The Devil's saddle as the raider grunted in satisfaction and thrust his sword at Trystan once more. But Trystan rolled clumsily away and the raider's blade bit into the dirt floor of the Longhouse and, before he could wrench it free, Corwynal's own blade came down to half-sever the man's head from his body.

A cry of distress made Corwynal look up. Brangianne was in the doorway, staring at him in horror, her face drained of colour, except where it had been splashed by the raider's blood. He grabbed her arm and pulled her into the Longhouse. 'Stay inside! Both of you!' She fell to her knees beside Trystan; they were safe now. They were both safe, and he was free.

'Go on!' Trystan yelled at him as Corwynal returned to the yard and reached for his second sword. The grip smacked satisfyingly into his left palm and the music flooded through him, horns braying in his breath, drums beating inside his head, the metallic scent and taste of blood flooding his throat. He yelled something and threw himself forward, his two swords as bright as flames in his hands. The world slowed into the patterns of the dance, and he bared his teeth in a wolf-smile as the blaze of battle sang through his veins.

One raider died before he realised it. Aelfric calmly despatched another, the sun flashing from his raised axe. How many were left? Three? Not enough. As long as the music lasted, as long as the chords crashed through him and the drums beat in time to his heart, Corwynal wanted to kill and go on killing. He hadn't felt this joy since the battle by the Loch of the Beacon. Beside him, Aelfric crooned a war dirge as, side by side, they drove the raiders from the steading, forcing them back through the gateway where they turned and ran. They didn't get far. Aelfric cut one down with a casual sweep of his axe and Corwynal raced after another and brought him to the ground in a fanfare of horns. He turned, searching for the remaining raider.

The scream came from behind him. The music stopped, and the world returned, brutal and jagged. He ran back to the steading yard but felt as if he was ploughing through mud. One of the raiders, instead of fleeing for the beach, had doubled back through the yard, and Brangianne had tried to bar the entrance to the Longhouse with her outstretched arms. The man had pinned her against the wall, and she was screaming and struggling to get free. His heart in his throat, Corwynal hurled himself towards her and slammed his sword through the man's body, angling the blow for the heart. He pulled the raider off her, and she collapsed towards him, a red stain blossoming across her chest.

I thrust too deep! I've killed her! He eased her to the ground and dropped to his knees beside her. 'Brangianne, my heart . . .'

Her eyes were wide with panic, her breathing fast and shallow. Trystan crouched beside him, one arm roughly bandaged, the other clutched to his old wound.

'He was coming for me, but she threw herself in front of him!'

Corwynal ripped apart the bloodied bodice of her dress, and she screamed again, trying to fight him off, but he'd already let her go. Her skin was smooth and white, and quite unblemished. The handle of a small knife jutted from the chest of the raider. Brangianne had killed the man, not him. The weight of the man's dying body had pinned her to the wall, and his blood had poured all over her, but she was unharmed. Relief flooded through him, and he couldn't stop himself from gathering her into his arms and holding her hard against him. She stiffened at first then flung her arms around his neck and sobbed against his shoulder.

'You're safe, my love,' he murmured into her hair. 'We're all safe. It's over now.'

But it wasn't.

'Aelfric!' Trystan yelled. 'One of them's getting away!'

Corwynal unwound Brangianne's arms and ran for the gate. One of the raiders, thrown against the wall when Corwynal and The Devil had plunged into the yard, had recovered and crawled away from the steading. Now he was stumbling across the dunes, heading for the beach. Aelfric sprinted after him, but the man had too good a start, so the Angle stopped at the crest of a dune, took careful aim and threw his axe. But the raider jinked like a hare and Aelfric's axe missed him by a hand's width, and the man carried on, making for the coracles.

Corwynal tore after him though he knew he'd be too late to stop him from getting away and back to the ship. But someone could. Waiting by the drawn-up coracles was a figure wielding a length of driftwood, someone who swung it with killing force, bringing the raider to the ground, and went on striking the man over and over until he was nothing more than a heap of oozing meat, someone who waited calmly for Corwynal and Aelfric to reach the coracles before laying down her bloodied length of wood.

'That was for my son!' Oonagh snarled, tears glittering in her eyes. 'That was for my husband. That was for all of them. And that was for you Britons, you so-called traders. That was for you *liars!*'

'We have to get away, Trystan insisted.

Corwynal and Trystan were sitting on the crest of a dune later that day. Dusk had fallen by then, a luminous dusk that merged with the thinning mist, washing the hills to a golden blur and burnishing Trystan's face to bronze. Down on the beach, close to the river, a bonfire of driftwood had been lit to celebrate the victory against the raiders, and in the firelight Trystan's face was animated. His eyes were bright, perhaps too bright, and there was a sheen on his skin Corwynal didn't like the look of.

'Are you listening to me?' But Corwynal was reliving the day, the music and the fear, the exaltation and the terror. He was remembering words that couldn't be unspoken. *Brangianne, my heart. My love.* He hadn't exchanged a word with her since.

'They were from *Galloway*, Corwynal!' Trystan reminded him, cutting into his thoughts. 'They spoke Briton. "Find the boy." That's what they said. Someone in Galloway wants me dead.'

Corwynal nodded. None of the raiders had worn Galloway's raven symbol, but Trystan had recognised two of them and Corwynal a third, all hangers-on in Marc's court. It was a pity Oonagh had killed the last one, because it would have been useful to know who'd sent them.

'We should have expected this,' Trystan went on. 'There are enough people in Galloway who'd be pleased if I never came back.'

Corwynal nodded. He could think of a few, and Trystan was right. They should have expected an attack of this kind. Ferdiad had managed to track them to Carnadail, so someone from Galloway could have done so too.

'You think they're still out there?' Trystan lifted his chin at the darkening sea, still hazed with fog. They hadn't seen the ship again, but they'd delivered a message; Corwynal and Aelfric had gathered up the bodies, dragged them to the beach then piled them into the coracles and sent them out on the tide.

'I doubt it. They've lost twelve men already; they won't risk more. No-one who saw us got back alive, so they won't know we're here. They'll just assume Carnadail is better guarded than they'd anticipated. I expect they'll cut their losses and return to Galloway.'

'But, sooner or later, they'll be back. And that means we have to leave.'

'Who'll defend Carnadail if we go? What do you think would have happened today if we hadn't been here?'

Carnadail would have been ravaged, and its people knew it, which was why Corwynal had allowed them their celebration. Smoke drifted into the dunes, bringing with it the scent of roasting meat from the pit that had been dug in the sand. Everyone from Carnadail was on the beach, apart from Brangianne and Oonagh.

'What happened today was *because* we were here,' Trystan pointed out. 'The best way to defend Carnadail is for us to leave.'

'You're not well enough. That wound in your arm ... your side ...'

'My arm will heal. The wound in my side's torn again, but I'll survive that too. What I won't survive is another attack like today. I fought badly,' Trystan said bitterly. 'I didn't kill a single one of them.'

So that was what was bothering him, the fear that he'd never again be able to fight as he used to. 'You have to heal, Trys, and that will take time.'

'Agreed, but I don't need to stay in Carnadail for time to pass.'

'I gave my oath to stay for the summer, for the harvest.'

'Then break it. If you care for her at all, you must.'

'Her?'

'Gods, Corwynal! Do you think no-one's noticed? Everyone knows it but Brangianne herself – except you rather gave yourself away today, didn't you? Don't get me wrong. I *like* her, and I'm happy you've found someone to care about. But here? Now? Even you must know how foolish it is. What can possibly come of it?'

It was a question Corwynal had refused to ask himself.

'You'll make it worse for yourself if you stay, and worse for us all if you were planning on telling her the truth.' Trystan gripped Corwynal's arm and shook him. 'You aren't, are you?'

'I'm tired of living this lie.'

Trystan gave him a long searching look, let him go and turned his head away. When he spoke his voice was expressionless.

'If you're tired of it, it's best we leave. If you won't break your oath, ask her to free you from it. After what happened, she may be glad to do so – because she can't believe we're traders now.'

Trystan was right. Oonagh was right too. They were liars.

'I saved you some meat.' Aelfric slithered down the western side of the dune, the little white dog following him hopefully. He was holding two ribs of meat in one hand and a cup of ale in the other. The sight of the meat, dripping fat and pink juices, made Corwynal's stomach curdle. 'But if you're not hungry . . .' Aelfric waited only a moment before biting into one of the ribs.

'I am, even if my brother's lost his appetite.' Trystan snatched the remaining rib and shared it with the dog.

'You've told him then?' Aelfric cocked an eye at Corwynal. 'That we're leaving at Lughnasadh?'

'Lughnasadh?!' The Night of Gifts was just a couple of days away.

'It's a good day to leave. That ship will have gone back to Galloway, and everyone else will be drunk and in harbour. We'll be safe from everything except the weather.'

Corwynal looked from Aelfric to Trystan and back again, saw the resolution in their faces and knew they were right. The day he'd been dreading had arrived.

She was a blade slicing through skin, punching its way through tissue, scraping past bone. She thrust deeper, twisting as she hit muscle, pushing deep into the chambers of a heart. There was blood then; it seeped and flowed, pulsed and spurted, pooled and darkened, and she was drenched in it. In her dream she slashed and stabbed and sliced and hacked until the heart, exposed now, lay soft and still, glistening in its cage of bone, and she was no longer a blade. She was her own hands now, hands that lifted out the heart and held it, warm and wet and heavy in her palms, and it was her own heart she'd cut out, for her dress was sodden with blood and she was standing in a crimson pool that had poured from the gaping wound in her chest. She laid herself carefully down, at the end of a long line of men, still holding the heart, and waited for someone to come. But no-one did, and the heart cooled in her hands until, at last, there he was, a dark-haired man with eyes the colour of a storm, a man who bent over her and took the heart from her. 'Brangianne,' he said. 'My heart.' And suddenly he was a wolf, and the heart was in his jaws as he loped off towards the mountains. She beat her wings and stretched out her long neck and flew after him, but he vanished into the fog, and she was a white-winged bird, alone on a beach, crying, crying . . .

Brangianne woke to the sound of gulls and the pale fingers of dawn probing their way through the cracks in the door and shutters of the women's room at the end of the Longhouse. Her heart was banging against her breastbone, but her nightshift was unstained, her chest intact. It had just been a dream. Then it came back to her – the alarm from the settlement, a ship glimpsed through fog, men running across the beach, weapons in their hands, and herself tearing down to the Longhouse, her cloak flying behind her, like a dark avenging swan.

Not again! she'd thought. *This time I'll stop it!* Had she been mad? She could have been killed, almost was. Her gorge rose at the memory of the raider slamming her against the wall, the stench of his breath in her face, the feel of his hands . . . Just like that last time. Except this time had been different. This time she'd had a knife.

Now, however, all she could think of was the passage of that blade. Even as she'd thrust the knife into the man's chest, she'd been working out how to heal the wound she was making, of staunching the blood with moss, sewing the torn muscle together, stitching each layer of tissue and skin back into position, and wrapping the damaged flesh in clean bandages. But then she'd reached the heart, felt the blade catch and twist, and the heart had pulsed along the shaft of her knife until it pulsed no more. There was no healing for that particular wound, no healing for what she'd done that day, any more than there had been healing for what had been done to Aedh all those years ago. Ciaran was right. Some wounds can't be healed, just as some crimes can't be forgiven. She, a healer, had killed a man, and there could be no sanctuary for her at St Martins after that. She'd have to marry Eoghan.

It was still early, and there was no sound but the gulls along the shoreline and Oonagh's gentle breathing. Oonagh had wept herself to sleep the previous night, and Brangianne had envied her those tears, for her own tears wouldn't come, and her eyes were dry and gritty. She got up, threw a shawl about her shoulders and, not bothering with her sandals, walked to the beach. The tide had come and gone in the night, leaving the sand smooth, patterned only by the star-fish footprints of the waders that scurried ahead of her along the tideline. The fog that had concealed the ship was gone too, and the morning was clear and sharp, the sand cold beneath her feet, and when she reached the water, she hitched up her skirts and walked into the sea to let it wash away the memory of blood dripping down her dress.

I'll make them go, she decided. *Then I'll be safe.*

From what? Waves surged around her ankles. *From what?*

She headed back towards the Longhouse. There had been a bonfire the previous night. She'd heard the sounds of celebration coming from the beach and, later, Drust's voice raised in song. She hadn't thought there was anything to celebrate. Now all that was left of the bonfire was a pile of white ash – and Talorc lying asleep close to the circle of the fire.

Her first instinct was to walk away, but she found herself staring at the man who was even more of a stranger now than he'd been before. His hair had fallen across his forehead and there was a little frown between his brows, but his face was softer in sleep than she'd ever seen it awake. Of the snarling wolf he'd been in the steading, and in her dream, the only trace remaining was the half-seen design on his chest. He lay on his back, one arm outstretched, his hand relaxed. That hand had grasped the hilt of a hidden sword and hacked men to pieces. That same hand had held her against him as she'd wept against his shoulder.

She gasped at that particular memory, a soft intake of breath but enough to wake him. He opened his eyes and, seeing her, they were clouded and confused, a tumble of rainclouds in a summer sky, but they sharpened to slate as he rose in one lithe movement to face her. Her heart banged in her throat, but she forced herself to meet his eyes.

'You lied to me,' she said.

Everything of softness vanished from his face.

'Not about anything important.'

'Who are you to say what is, or isn't, important? You said you were traders, but you're not. You're warriors.'

He shrugged. 'I've been a warrior in my life, amongst other things. So has Aelfric. And I think you always knew it but chose not to ask me.'

She flinched and looked away, for it was no less than the truth. But it didn't excuse him, and she lifted her chin and forced herself to look back at him.

'You fought at the Loch of the Beacon, didn't you? You killed my people.'

He hesitated but didn't look away. 'Yes.'

'How many?' It was a stupid question. She'd seen what he could do. She'd watched, horrified, as he'd killed all those raiders so . . . so gracefully.

'I don't know. I . . . lost count.'

'You could have killed men from Carnadail. You could have killed Oonagh's son.'

He looked grave. 'Do you imagine I haven't thought of that? Yes, it's possible. But I give you my word that we took no part in the rout.'

'Your *word!* How can I trust your word, you . . you *liar!*'

He smiled faintly, a cold self-mocking smile. 'You can't.' He turned on his heel and walked off along the beach, and she stared after him, realising where her question had taken her. She'd wanted an answer – but not *that* answer.

'You gave me your word you'd stay for the summer,' she said, running after him.

'Yesterday changed all that. We can't stay here. It's not safe.'

He'd kept on walking, trying to outpace her, but now he stopped so abruptly she almost ran into him. 'It's not safe for *you*. That ship came from Galloway.'

'Galloway?' The sand shifted beneath her feet as the world swam dizzily between past and present. 'But . . . but *why?*

'Someone's looking for us, for Drust, and as long as we're here it puts everyone in Carnadail in danger.' He walked on, forcing her to run to keep up with him.

'Drust?' It was the last thing she expected. 'What can he have done to earn such enemies? He's just a boy.'

'That doesn't mean he doesn't have enemies. Drust arouses passions in people, love in one, hatred in another.' He smiled thinly. 'He probably made love to the wrong woman, so it might be a jealous husband or a resentful rival. It doesn't matter. What matters is that we have to leave. So free us from our oaths. You don't want us here, not now you know what we are.'

Don't I? 'Is Talorc even your real name?'

'Talorc's the name my mother gave me, so yes. I said I was a trader, and that's only a little less than the truth. Ferdiad was right. There's no Steward who's not also a trader, because that's what I am, or was, the Steward of lands in . . . in Manau. That makes me someone who wants early springs, dry summers and a good harvest. I know you think all Stewards are liars and thieves, and maybe most of them are, but nothing of what I've been in Carnadail has been a lie.'

'No Steward kills men so . . . so easily.'

'No, but I was a warrior once and haven't forgotten those skills.'

'Skills you taught that devil of a horse. He's a *killer!*'

'Skills I reminded him about. I told you he was a war-horse. That's what he's trained to do. He's not a cart-horse. He's a killer who saved your life.'

As he had, and he'd saved everyone in Carnadail too. She

owed him for that at least. But he was right. She, and Carnadail, would be safer if they left.

They'd reached the end of the beach by then, the stream below the Longhouse where the skiff Aelfric had repaired was drawn up above the high tide mark. Such a little thing, barely big enough for two, far less three. With that thought, she saw how to give him what he'd asked for yet keep what she wanted too.

'Drust has to stay. The wound in his arm is a serious one, and he may take wound-fever from it. And I need you to stay too; I can't manage the harvest without you. But Aelfric may go back to the Briton lands. The waters north of Arainn are treacherous and no place for an over-loaded boat, but one man would be safe, and faster too. He can come back for you in a bigger ship. By that time, Drust will be out of danger, and the harvest will be over.'

The summer would be over too, her summer of freedom. She held out her hand. 'Do we have a bargain?'

He stopped walking and frowned at her, not much liking this arrangement, and for a heart-stopping moment she thought he'd refuse. But he took her hand in his, hard and calloused, a warrior's hand, and, stained with ink, a Steward's hand.

'Yes, we have a bargain.' He let her hand fall, and, as the cold of the morning crept into her palm, he nodded and carried on walking along the beach, away from the boat, away from her.

She walked slowly back to the Longhouse, the sand, warmed by the rising sun, as soft as dust between her toes. A heron rose from beside the stream, scooped the air with its wings, and flapped heavily along the shoreline. Had she made the right choice? She was thinking about hearts again, hearts beating against her own. She was thinking of words spoken that couldn't be taken back, and of words unspoken and unasked, for fear of where the speaking or asking might take them. She was aware of a threshold but wasn't sure if it lay behind her or ahead.

I've become fond of Carnadail, and— She knew now what

he'd been going to say. —*and the Lady of Carnadail.* Although that wasn't how he thought of her. *Brangianne, my heart, my love. . . .* She went over and over his words, as she'd gone over that thrust of her knife, that killing, trying to make them mean nothing, but with as little success. Ciaran had promised her a summer of freedom in which anything might happen.

It seemed as if something had.

6

THE MAN WITH BEASTS ON HIS SKIN

'Oonagh! Oonagh! Oonagh!' The shouts of encouragement became a chant that drowned out the drums and whistles, and the stamping feet of the women who were spinning around the circle of the dance. The Lughnasadh fire, built on the water-meadow in the bend of the river, crackled and roared into a sky that had first turned to gold but was now an inky black shot through with sparks. The air was full of smoke and the scent of crushed grass and meat sizzling in a pit on the riverbank.

'Come on, Oonagh!' She shook her head. She was not – absolutely not – going to dance with that big oaf of an Angle.

'Go on,' Brangianne gave Oonagh a little push towards the dance. 'It's your last chance. He's leaving tomorrow.'

Oonagh would be glad to see the back of the man, with his smiles and his fractured tongue and his . . . size. By tomorrow morning he'd be nothing more than a scrap of sail out in the Sound, heading north until he was beyond Arainn. He was making for Strathclyde where he'd hire a ship and come back to Carnadail for the others. But she didn't believe it. Why should he come back? He was a liar and a cheat and a . . . a lecher. No, that wasn't the word. She didn't think there was a word for a man like him, a man who smiled and took his pleasures before passing on to his next victim – but victim wasn't the right word either, given that all the women had declared themselves willing to repeat the humiliating experience. Had they no pride? Sluts, the lot of them!

'Oonagh! Oonagh! Oonagh!' Her treacherous feet were tapping out a rhythm, and her body was swaying to the music. She was a good dancer, better than the others; half of them didn't know the steps. No wonder the Angle was making such a mess of it. Someone who knew what they were doing ought to show him.

The chanting broke into cheers and catcalls as she marched forward and took her place in the circle. 'Right, oaf, watch carefully and do what I tell you without arguing.'

It had been over a year since she'd danced. Last Beltein, it had been, before . . . well, just before. She hadn't realised how much she'd missed it. Now she threw herself into the pattern of the dance, weaving and twisting, jumping and turning. The Angle matched her step for step, lighter on his feet than she'd expected for a big man and a foreigner. Hands clapped, feet stamped, and the fire roared higher and higher as Oonagh danced and danced until she could dance no more and was forced to stumble out of the circle, laughing and breathless, to sink onto the grass. She was blinded by firelight and the sweat trickling into her eyes, and though she was aware of someone coming to sit beside her and a cup of ale being pressed into her hand, she didn't know who it was.

'I didn't kill your son, you know,' the Angle said, taking a deep swallow of his own ale.

Oonagh had been raising the cup to her lips. Now she lowered it once more.

'You don't know how he died.'

'I do. One of your friends told me.'

Some friend!

'A spear in the back, wasn't it?'

'He wasn't running away!' No-one had said so, but she knew they'd all thought it.

'Everyone was running away. There's no shame in that, only sense. Have you ever been in a rout? It's an ugly thing. But I wasn't involved in the rout, and the axe and sword are my weapons, not the spear. So it wasn't me who killed your son.'

She'd never know who had. It had taken her this long to accept it. A few nights before, after she'd killed the raider on the beach, she'd wept about it. That man had done her no harm, had been running away like her son, but she'd clubbed him to death, and it had felt good, then ... not good. Death and war were no longer so simple. Enemies and friends were no longer so different.

'I know.' She lifted the cup and took a deep swallow, then another. Her throat was dry from the dancing, her feet aching, but it had been good to dance. Something coiled tightly inside her had loosened. 'So you're leaving. Run out of women to bed?'

He grinned, a flash of teeth in the darkness. 'Only one left. And the Lady of Carnadail, of course.'

'She wouldn't have you!' She looked across to where the Lady was sitting with Drust, who'd been forbidden to dance on account of the wound in his side that he'd torn open again. He was surrounded by a knot of giggling girls and they were playing some guessing game that involved a great deal of laughter.

'No, probably not,' the Angle said cheerfully. 'And if she did, I reckon someone would kill me for it.'

He jerked his head at the far side of the Lughnasadh fire where the Caledonian was standing at the margin of the light, like some dark shade of Samhain. He appeared to be listening to the conversation between one of the older women and a fisherman, but his eyes were on the Lady.

'What a fool that man is!' the Angle muttered, and though Oonagh didn't want to agree with him she had to agree with that.

He's not the only fool around here, she thought, looking at the Lady. She was talking too loudly, laughing too brightly, drinking too much, too conscious, Oonagh reckoned, of the man in the shadows.

'It would be better if he went with you tomorrow.'

'You think I haven't tried to convince him? This plan; it's too complicated. Too much to go wrong. That's his problem, see, won't allow anything to be simple, and some things deserve to be simple, like pleasure. But what does he know of pleasure? Eating and drinking now, you'd think they'd be simple enough for anyone. Fighting, ploughing a field, helming a boat, all simple pleasures, riding a good horse – never thought I'd say that, mind! – and loving,' he added casually. 'That should be simple too, like dancing. You're a good dancer, Oonagh.'

She grunted, half-amused, half-irritated by the cheek of the man. 'I'm old enough to be your mother.'

'I doubt it. I'm twenty five. You?'

'Thirty one.' It wasn't so old actually, and twenty five wasn't so young. Not that she was thinking of . . . well, anything like that, not even when he put his hand on her ankle. But she didn't pull her foot away. His hand was warm and undemanding, his offer lightly made. Her rejection, she thought, would be as lightly received.

'I saved the best to last,' he said with that infuriating smile of his.

'Best of what?' She had a very good idea of what – or who – he meant.

'Best of myself,' he replied, surprising her. 'It's Lughnasadh. Don't you people call it the Night of Gifts?'

'So, what's the best of you? Some meaningless promise?'

'I don't make promises. Not anymore. I've broken too many . . .'

Like all the men she'd ever known. But at least he was honest about it. And that surprised her too.

The warmth of his hand had spread up to her knee, her thigh, further. She could feel the heat come off him in waves, her own blood taking fire at the half-forgotten smell of fresh male sweat. Warmth flowed through her body. It was from the dancing, she told herself. She hadn't danced in over a year, hadn't wept, hadn't laughed. There were other things she hadn't done, and it occurred to her now that the woman she'd become – wife of a dead husband, mother of a dead son – was only part of who she was, and that she'd forgotten the rest. She picked up the cup and drained it to the dregs, slapped his hand away from her ankle, stood up and walked away, and didn't turn back until she reached the edge of the firelight. He was still sitting there, gawping at her.

Hah! she thought. *You didn't expect that, did you?* It was a small victory, one simple pleasure among many. It was the Night of Gifts, but gifts would be accepted – and maybe given – on her own terms.

'Well?' she asked, lifting her chin. 'What are you waiting for, you big oaf? Weren't you going to show me how good the best of you really is . . . ?'

'He's leaving on the tide.'

Oonagh's voice sounded blurred, but voices heard on wakening often did, and this one had woken Brangianne from a dream of firelight, starlight and storm. Lightning flashed behind her closed eyelids, and thunder rumbled right inside her head.

'And good riddance!' Oonagh said fiercely, and the rumbling grew louder. She was milling grain, Brangianne realised; the thunder was the sound of stone grinding rhythmically in the quern. But that didn't explain the flashes of light behind her eyes. Cautiously, still keeping her eyes shut, she extended her awareness into the rest of her body then wished she hadn't. Her throat was dry, her belly sour. Her hair stank of old smoke, and there was a foul taste on her tongue. She was ill, she decided and, being a great believer in the restorative effects of sleep, turned over and pulled her blanket over her head.

'I never liked the man,' Oonagh continued, her voice muffled but still audible. 'They're all down at the beach, waiting to see him off. Fools that they are! And mark my words, my Lady, no matter what that man promised, there's not a chance he'll be back.' For a while there was no sound in the Longhouse but the grinding of rock against grain until even that fell silent. The next thing Brangianne heard was a muttered curse, the sound of Oonagh jumping to her feet, striding to the outer door, jerking it open and letting it bang behind her. There had definitely been something peculiar about Oonagh's voice, but Brangianne couldn't think what it was. Thinking was unaccountably difficult, and it was some time before she understood exactly what had been said.

He's leaving on the tide. There's not a chance he'll be back.

'No!' She sat up abruptly. The world reeled before steadying itself. A plea pealed through her head as if her skull was a cracked bell.

Don't leave me! Please don't leave me!

She scrambled to her feet, groped for her shoes and tied the laces with fumbling fingers. Then, forgetting her shawl and the ribbon for her hair, forgetting she was the Lady of Carnadail and had a certain dignity to maintain, she ran down the hill after Oonagh.

Please don't leave me!

She only stopped running when she understood that Oonagh had been speaking of Aelfric, not Talorc, that it was Aelfric who was to set sail on the tide. Talorc wasn't leaving after all, so there was still time . . .

Time for what?

A large crowd had gathered at the fishing harbour, several of the women weeping openly, but Brangianne had eyes for just one person, the man who didn't look up when she stumbled down the shingle beach. He was standing with Drust, both of them talking to Aelfric, giving him instructions or advice. But the Angle wasn't listening. He was scanning the crowd as if searching for someone and frowning, but when he caught sight of Brangianne pushing her way to the front his face cleared.

'My Lady!' By rights he should have taken her hand and bowed, but he grabbed her around the waist, lifted her up and kissed her soundly on both cheeks. 'You'll take care of these two for me?' he asked as he set her down, jerking his head at Talorc and Drust. 'Until I'm back?'

Brangianne sensed Talorc's eyes on her but found it impossible to look at him. Instead, she turned to Drust who grinned at her. 'We won't be too much trouble, will we?' he asked, appealing to Talorc.

'No,' he said curtly. 'And it won't be for long.'

'I hope not,' she said, meaning she hoped Aelfric would have a safe passage and a swift return. It wasn't until the words left her lips that she realised they could be taken quite differently. She hazarded a glance at Talorc; his expression was closed and distant and he was looking not at her but at the horizon.

'You'd better go,' he told Aelfric, nodding at the sky in which clouds were building. 'There'll be a thunderstorm come the evening.'

'On land maybe, not at sea.' Aelfric made no further move to leave, even though the tide was beginning to ebb. Eventually, he shrugged, took hold of the prow and dragged the boat into the shallows. 'Tell Oonagh—'

'Tell her yourself!' The voice, fierce and tearful at the same time, came from behind Brangianne as Oonagh pushed her way through the crowd. Then, without stopping to hitch up her skirts, she strode into the water after Aelfric, reached up to grasp him by the shoulders and proceeded to kiss him soundly, an assault Aelfric returned with enthusiasm.

'You come back, you hear me?!' she hissed once she'd stopped to draw breath. 'You come back and take these cursed Britons away, because if you don't, I'll hunt you down and—'

Aelfric stopped her tirade by kissing her once more, and, embarrassed, Brangianne looked away then regretted it, since she inadvertently caught Talorc's eye.

Brangianne, my heart . . . She'd barely spoken to him since the morning after the raiders had come. Last night, at the Lughnasadh feast, he hadn't come near her, and she'd been relieved, afraid of being alone with him, of having to talk about those words.

She was glad when the kiss ended, and Oonagh let Aelfric go and whirled around to glare at the loudly appreciative crowd. 'What are you all staring at? Haven't you got work to do? Isn't there a harvest to get in?' But that just raised a laugh, and she blushed, strode out of the sea and, with her head held high, shoved her way through the people and marched back along the path.

'I *will* be back,' Aelfric murmured, half to himself, as he watched her go. He pushed the boat out into the breaking waves, grasped the gunwale and leapt in, then rowed out to deeper water. Once past the rocks, he raised the sail to catch the westerly breeze and set course for the northern tip of Arainn. Brangianne remained on the beach, watching the boat head east. Behind her, the crowd thinned as first one and then another crunched their way up the steeply shelving shingle bank, and when she forced herself to turn around Talorc had gone.

'The bull's got away again, My Lord.'

Corwynal straightened up to ease the knots out of his shoulders. It was later that day and he and the women of Carnadail were gathering up the last of the hay. It had already been scythed and laid out to dry; now it was being forked over and loaded into a cart. It was backbreaking work, especially under a brazen sun on this, the first day of autumn. Brangianne was working with the rest of the villagers, her arms and face red with the sun, her hair grey with dust. Corwynal's own hair was gritty with filth, the dirt on his face seamed with sweat, his shirt sticking to his back. The last thing he needed was yet another chase after the cursed bull.

'I thought someone was watching him?' None of the women would meet his eye; no doubt whoever had been watching the bull, up on the moor where the herds were grazing for the summer, had abandoned the task to come and see Aelfric off. In their absence, the bull had wandered off and had probably got itself mired in some bog or other. 'All right,' he sighed. 'I'll fetch the ropes. Gather as many people as you can and meet me at the shielings.'

He returned to the Longhouse, saddled The Devil, looped the ropes around the saddle horn, and took the trail to the moor, fighting The Devil all the way. The horse didn't like the weather, and nor did Corwynal. It was too close, too humid, too still, and a mist of biting insects plumed from the heather. Thunderclouds were building on the high ground to the north, and a smell of iron was in the air. There would be a storm before long, and, judging by those clouds, it would be worse than usual. He was glad they'd got most of the hay in, but he'd need to find the bull quickly. He didn't want to be on the moor when the storm broke.

Aelfric would be north of Arainn by then, he thought, stopping at a bend in the track when he was high enough to see the whole expanse of the Sound, but couldn't see his sail. The wind had veered around to the north, not the best direction for making for Strathclyde, but he was sure Aelfric would rise to the challenge. Once ashore, he'd make for Meldon, collect Kaerherdin and some of his men, then hire a ship and return to Carnadail. Trystan hadn't liked the plan. 'More delay,' he'd complained.

'Safer, though.' Corwynal was still concerned about whoever was searching for them. 'When we go back to the Lands between the Walls, we might need the protection of Kaer's men.'

'We?' Trystan had narrowed his eyes at him. 'I was beginning to think you intended staying in Carnadail.'

'Of course not.'

He had no reason to stay, none he'd been given. Nothing kept him but a promise to remain for the harvest, and that would be finished in a couple of weeks if the weather held, a month at the outside. Then the summer would be over. But there was still time . . .

Time for what? Trystan was right; it was an unnecessary delay. He should have insisted on the two of them going with Aelfric today, even though Trystan had come down with another bout of wound-fever. Why was he staying for a woman who'd barely spoken to him since the day the raiders had come? Last night, at the feast, she'd laughed and joked with Aelfric and Trystan but hadn't spoken to him once. What had he been hoping for?

Irritated with himself, he kicked the reluctant Devil on along the track, cursing the bull, the weather and Arddu in equal measure. The God had been noticeably absent since the storm that had brought them to Carnadail, but now Corwynal was aware of him in his blood and heard his laughter, a low rumble of amusement that came from the north, from the heart of a line of slate grey clouds that crouched along the horizon like a pack of ravening wolves.

It didn't take long to find the bull. He was mired in a bog, as Corwynal had predicted, and by the time they'd got the beast out he was muddy to the thighs, stinking of bog water, and in more of a temper than The Devil, since the storm was no more than a couple of miles away.

'Best get into the Shielings before the storm breaks,' he advised the women and older children who'd been helping him free the bull. 'It's not safe out in the open. I'm heading back down the hill.'

'What about the Lady?' one of the women asked. 'She came up not long ago, asked where you were, then went that way.'

The woman pointed towards the south, to the crest of the moor where there was no shelter at all. A number of responses came to mind, but he voiced none of them. Instead, he leapt into the saddle, jerked the reins, making The Devil rear in protest, whirled him around and headed south along the track just as the storm broke.

She should have seen it coming; a storm on open moorland didn't arrive unannounced. She'd been aware of clouds gathering behind her, but they'd been the high white towers of summer and, ahead of her, the sun was still shining over the sea. Heather was blooming in drifts all around her, and the moor was heady with the scents of bog myrtle, juniper and moss. It wasn't until she reached the crest of the high ground that the clouds swallowed the sun. Only then, as the wind tugged at her skirts and clawed her hair into tangles, did she wonder if she ought to go back. She wished she'd brought her shawl with her, that she hadn't come at all.

She should have expected Talorc to be on the moor. She'd seen the two women from the shielings speak to him, had watched him throw down his pitchfork in disgust and stride off to the Longhouse. It would be the bull again.

She should have known, should have *thought.* Thinking, however, was impossible that day, and she wished she hadn't drunk so much ale the previous night. If only someone had asked her to dance ... But no-one had; the Lady of Carnadail was supposed to be above all that. She'd considered ordering Talorc to dance with her – he was her servant, wasn't he? – but when she'd seen Oonagh dancing with Aelfric she was glad she hadn't. All that clasping of hands, the meeting and parting, the touching of shoulders and hips, the dizzying circling and circling ... Instead, she'd laughed too much about nothing and pretended to be happy. Only now did she understand why she needed to pretend.

Don't leave me! Not because he was useful. Not because when he left Drust would leave too, and she'd come to love Drust like a son. But for himself.

'The Lord went that way,' one of the women from the shielings told her, pointing towards a boggy bealach between two low hills.

'He's not a Lord.' When had they started calling him that? *Lord of Carnadail.* The thought made something long-forgotten flutter unnervingly in her stomach so, instead of heading for the bog, she'd taken the deer-track that led south to the crest of the moor, the place where she'd asked for a sign and been sent a ship. *A summer of freedom, in which anything could happen,* Ciaran had told her, but she hadn't expected *this* to happen. She couldn't allow it to have happened. She'd have to make that very clear; she was a King's daughter, after all. Not that she intended telling him so. She didn't want to make a liar of herself. So what was she going to tell him? That she valued him? That she was grateful to him? That if circumstances were other then they might ... No, best to say nothing. Circumstances were as they were. Nothing had changed.

Dear God, what am I going to do?

She was answered by a rumble from behind her. It sounded as if a boulder had fallen from a cliff-face and was rolling across a field of scree. But there were neither cliffs nor scree on the moor, and the few boulders she'd seen were firmly embedded in the peat. Once more there was a rumble, but it was nearer now. She turned and her stomach lurched. A storm was racing towards her, cloud descending, trailing veils of rain, the dark heart of it shot through with vivid streaks of lightning. One jagged coruscating flash of light stabbed down from the cloud, and a heartbeat later – no more – there was a growl of thunder that shook the ground beneath her, a hiss of rain that quickly turned into an icy torrent of drumming water, and a roar of wind that left her in no doubt about the answer to her question. *What am I going to do?*

She was going to die.

'Cursed woman!' Corwynal muttered, urging The Devil on as he bent low over the horse's neck, searching for footprints. But the track had turned into a stream flowing between tussocks of heather that were whipping back and forth in the rising wind, and there were no tracks to be seen.

All the time he was cursing Brangianne, he was cursing himself too. What was he doing chasing after someone who didn't want him, and into a thunderstorm at that? He didn't even know if she was still on the moor. The woman at the shieling could have been mistaken; surely Brangianne wouldn't be so stupid as to walk out on the moor with a storm coming. Yet still he urged the horse on, kicking him into a canter when the gradient eased. She was out there. He was sure of it.

'Brangianne!' He could barely hear his own voice over the roar of the storm, the thunder of The Devil's hooves and the drumming of rain. It was colder now, the wind stronger than it had been, driving the rain horizontally. He thought about getting his cloak from the saddlebag, then abandoned the idea. He was already soaked to the skin.

The storm was overhead now, all around him, the air tasting of metal and smelling of sulphur. Lightning struck to the right and left and – terrifyingly – straight ahead. A great fork of lightning cracked the clouds open and struck a faint rise in the land barely half a mile away. The Devil screamed and reared, his hooves pawing at the sky in defiance, and, as if in answer, the sky split open once more in an incandescent flash that almost blinded him.

'Arddu!' he breathed, clinging desperately to the saddle as the horse reared in terror once more. The lightning forked towards him, then divided in two as if a boulder had been flung in its path and passed harmlessly to either side of him, the wash of light silhouetting a figure crouching beneath The Devil's flailing hooves. The horse squealed as Corwynal sawed viciously at the reins to bring the animal down to one side of her. Air thundered around them, a crack of sound and a crashing roar that drowned out his cry of relief that, a moment later, turned into suffocating anger.

'You stupid, *stupid* woman! What in the God's name are you doing here?!' He jumped from the saddle and jerked her to her feet. Her face was white, her eyes dark wells of terror. The jagged light still burned at the back of his vision, and the thunder must have deafened him, for though Brangianne's lips moved he couldn't hear what she was saying.

'Get up!' He picked her up and threw her into the saddle. 'And hold on!' The Devil, objecting to this new rider, bucked and cavorted, but Corwynal twisted the reins in his fist and dragged the horse away from the path. They had to get off the moor. It didn't matter in which direction as long as it was down.

There was a glimmer of brightness to the west, slopes falling away. He hauled the reluctant horse downhill, through streams and wet places, past peat-hags and over tussocks of wiry grass and sodden heather that deepened as the slope steepened. Eventually, they reached a deer track that flanked a stream, and the going eased. He followed the swollen stream, the water foaming and rushing beside him, the banks overflowing. The storm still rumbled on the moor, but the clouds had dropped and they rode through a streaming grey mist driven by the wind. It was colder now, and Corwynal was shivering despite the effort it took to drag the horse down the hillside. Brangianne was even colder, her face white, her lips quite bloodless, and she barely had the strength to cling to the horse's neck. They had to find shelter, and soon.

Arddu wasn't a God who welcomed the prayers of men, but Corwynal prayed to him now, and perhaps he listened. Perhaps, more surprisingly, he took pity on them, for the stream he'd been following tumbled over a lip of rock and vanished into a shallow ravine, in which, sheltered from the wind, was a little birchwood. And there, in a clearing close to the stream, stood a building.

'Thank you!' Corwynal breathed as he picked his way down the slope, no longer having to fight The Devil who, anticipating oats and a warm blanket, pushed forward. For his own part, Corwynal was thinking of a fire and food, of dry clothes and somewhere to rest. He lifted Brangianne from the saddle and half-carried her to the door. It opened at his touch, and his heart sank, for the place was little more than a cold and deserted hut that smelled of earth and damp and long abandonment. Arddu had always been grudging of his gifts.

But grudging or not, gift it was. The roof was intact, and the hut wasn't entirely empty. There was an old heather bed in one corner and dry firewood next to the hearth. Leaving Brangianne there, he went out once more, led the horse into the adjoining stable, and brushed him down with several handfuls of straw. A mouldy horse blanket hung from a peg, but he judged his own need to be greater than that of The Devil and took it back to the main room of the building.

Brangianne hadn't moved, hadn't even tried to light a fire. She just stood there, her arms clutched convulsively about her, looking . . . lost. Something softened inside him. He wanted to take her in his arms but knew he mustn't.

'Here!' He tossed her the cloak he'd stuffed into his saddlebag. It was mostly dry. 'Take your clothes off first.' She looked up at him, her eyes wide with apprehension. 'Don't worry!' he added harshly 'You're quite safe from me. In case you don't realise it, you look about as appealing as a drowned rat.'

He turned his back on her and busied himself with the fire. His flint and tinder had been buried deep in his saddlebag, and everything was dry, so it wasn't long before he'd coaxed a flame from some dry grasses and had it licking at the kindling. The flames threw out light, if not yet heat, into the abandoned building, and he looked around to see what might be of use. There were some rotting hurdles and a couple of cracked pottery cups. He pulled the hurdles towards the fire and draped Brangianne's skirt and tunic over them.

'We'll stay here until the storm has passed and our clothes are dry.' He turned his back to strip off his sodden shirt and leggings, conscious of her eyes on him and knowing she was staring at his body as most women did, repelled and fascinated by his designs and scars. He covered himself quickly with the stinking horse-blanket and crouched as close to the fire as possible, on the other side from Brangianne. Only then did he allow himself to look at her.

'You're angry with me,' she whispered, like a frightened child. But she wasn't a child, hadn't been in a long time.

'Of course I'm angry! What in the Five Hells were you doing on the moor in a thunderstorm?'

'Thinking.' She stared into the fire, shivering.

'Thinking?! What about, in the name of all the gods?'

'You.' She looked up, her expression unreadable and, despite himself, his heart lurched.

'Me?'

'About why you'd come here.'

'I came because of Drust. I stayed because of him too.'

'And you'll leave because of him.'

Unless you give me a reason to stay. But she wasn't going to do that. 'Yes. I'll leave because of him. I'm grateful for your care of him, but I think I've earned it. I've paid your price, and that of my God.'

'What . . .what price?'

'Yours? A summer of . . . of being of use to you. My God's? That's between me and him.' He thrust a birch log into the fire. The bark crackled and flared blue, throwing a strange light around the room, but it was still cold. Their clothes dripped sullenly from the hurdles. It was going to be a long night, he thought, and suddenly, after all the days and weeks of unhappiness, he couldn't keep his silence any longer.

'A heart,' he said abruptly. 'That's what I promised, not believing I had one to lose. But I've lost it now, and you hold it in your hands, whether you wish to or not, and whether I wish it or not. I don't have a choice in the matter. If I did, do you think I would have chosen you? You're not young, and your temper's ungoverned. You're stubborn and indecisive and infuriating, and you make me do things that make no sense, stay when I should go, hope when I've no reason to. You make me feel things I've not felt in eighteen years, and I was a fool then, so how much more of a fool must I be now? I don't like being in love with you. It doesn't feel good, and everything I've ever believed in tells me it ought to. Eighteen years ago, I felt as if I was king of the world. The woman I loved was young and beautiful and sunny-tempered, and I thought she loved me. Surely it should be that simple? Not like this! And do you know what the worst of it is? I've begun to wonder if that was love at all.'

She stared at him. She must think him mad. But he was cleansed of the words that had been beating behind his tongue. It was as if some infection had burst, the foulness flowing out of it, leaving the truth behind. And it hurt, as truths usually do. Even so, he was surprised to see tears well into her eyes and trickle slowly and silently down her cheeks.

'What are you crying for?' he asked with a kind of numbed exasperation. He should be the one who was weeping.

'I'm cold,' she said miserably.

So was he. The fire had taken hold of some of the larger branches and there was a smoky sort of warmth in his face, but the hut still held the bone-deep cold of a long winter. He got up and pulled the heather bed closer to the fire.

'Lie down,' he said and, when she'd done so, climbed in behind her, his chest to her back, his knees behind hers, the mouldy horse-blanket over them both. 'Don't be afraid,' he said, as she stiffened with apprehension. 'I don't make love to reluctant women. Allow me some pride.'

She relaxed a little as warmth grew between them, but with it came the awareness that only the thickness of his cloak lay between them, and he was glad when she began to talk, for it distracted him from the closeness of her body.

'Before you came, I was thinking of leaving Carnadail, so I asked my God for a sign to tell me if I should stay or go. Then I saw your boat and brought you back to life when you'd drowned. So I assumed my God had sent you. At first, I thought it was to make me go into the Longhouse because I'd been afraid to before, certain I'd find nothing but death, though that wasn't what I found. But I knew there had to be more to it than that, though I couldn't see what it could be. I was afraid of you at first and . . . didn't like you much. But you said something to me, the day Ferdiad came – that you'd become fond of Carnadail and . . . something. And I cared about what that was. I thought it might be me, though I'd given you no reason to like me, and I was confused, because I was still afraid of you, even after you saved me from the raiders. Then this morning I believed it was you who was leaving, not Aelfric, and I . . .I couldn't bear it.'

Corwynal's heart leapt as the world shifted. She turned to face him. It was an invitation, he assumed, and leant forward to kiss her, but she put a hand on his chest and pushed him away, her expression serious, her eyes distant.

'So now I know what I feel and think, but I don't know how to *be*, because the world hasn't changed. In my world, I was given a choice: to take my vows and live my life behind the walls of a monastery, or marry a man I don't like. I came to Carnadail to make that decision and still haven't made it, but I know there isn't a third choice. Not for me, not for us. Not in this world.'

He closed his eyes. The eyes were the gateway to the soul, or so they said, and he didn't want her to see what he felt in that moment. The God was always grudging of his gifts, and this was as two-edged as any other, a gift given with one hand and taken away with the other. She cared for him, against her will, against all the instincts that told her how much of a liar he was. *Not in this world*. Not in a world in which he was Corwynal of Lothian.

Eventually, having mastered himself, he opened his eyes and looked into hers. There were strange green lights there, a rain-washed forest pool shot through with sunlight, wide and dark.

You could take her, Arddu whispered in his blood. *You gave up your heart, as you promised, but I'm minded to be more generous than you think me. So take her. She won't fight you.* It was true. She was as aware of him as he was of her. He could let desire break down her resolve. His hands tightened on her shoulders, and she shuddered against him, but when he pulled her towards him, it was to draw her head against his shoulder, her hair against his cheek.

'In this world, we're both cold and tired. So sleep, my heart. You're safe with me, and always will be.'

She gave a small sigh, turned over once more, and let him pull her closer, for warmth now and nothing more. He lay very still, feeling her breathing ease, her heart slow, her body relax into sleep, but he remained awake. This night had to last for a long time, and so he lay beside her, thinking of a promise and a price, a boy won back from death, his own life won back from the sea, a dead heart brought back to life, a heart not taken but given. He thought of a woman eighteen years dead, a woman whose death he'd caused, and of all the women since, slaves and whores, princesses and queens. He'd wanted none of them as much as he wanted this one, though she had little to recommend her, neither beauty nor temperament, neither brains nor birth. Or so he kept trying to tell himself, but without success for none of these things mattered; she'd touched his soul as none of the others had.

Finally, he allowed himself to think of love. It had more facets than he'd imagined. It came unlooked for, like a storm from a clear sky, to shipwreck the heart. He thought of how fragile love could be, how defenceless in the face of a word, a look, a lie. And yet how strong, how elusive, how difficult to grasp, to hold, especially in the world he'd made. It was safer, he decided, not to try.

She was running along a track through a dense forest, a storm pursuing her, lightning flashing behind her, washing the night sky to silver. The trees, black pines, clawed at the light until they scratched it from the sky. Behind, tree after tree was struck by

lightning, and fires crackled through their branches until a red
flickering light followed her too, and so she ran faster and faster
into the darkness that would lead her to safety. The track forked
ahead of her, but she took neither path. Instead, she plunged into
the wood that lay between, thrusting her way through bush and
briar, past stands of black holly, through sunken pits full of
nettles. But the storm and the fire were still following her, and
when the forest came to an end, disappearing abruptly in front
of her, she found herself teetering on the edge of a cliff with
nothing but black night below . . .

'I brought you breakfast, such as it is. And an apology.'

He was kneeling beside her, a cracked pottery cup of water in
one hand, a few raspberries in the palm of the other. The door
stood open, letting a slant of sun fall into the room. A thrush was
singing outside, and she heard The Devil snort as he tore at a
clump of grass somewhere close by. The stream that had roared
throughout the night now chuckled sleepily between its banks.
Inside the hut, the fire was crackling merrily and her skirt and
blouse, draped over a hurdle, were dry. The hut no longer smelled
of mould, but of pine resin and smoke, and the world was a very
different place. The berries were sweet, the peat-dark water cold
and clear. She was acutely conscious that she was naked below
Talorc's cloak. He'd dressed and laid the horse-blanket over her
while she'd slept.

'Apology for what?'

'For some of the things I said last night.'

Stubborn and indecisive and infuriating.

'Some of them were true,' she said ruefully and watched his
lips curve into a smile. Those lips had almost kissed her the
previous night, but she'd pushed him away. She could still feel
the pricked designs on his chest and a desire she hadn't known
in years fluttered inside her, together with the first stirrings of
the joy she'd been robbed of, the joy she'd never expected to feel

again. She'd wanted to trace those patterns, to move from one to the next, to touch her lips to each of them . . .

'We should be going,' he said, as if nothing had happened between them, as if nothing ever would. *Not in this world.* But she knew what the dream meant, what everything meant.

'I don't want to be safe,' she said as if in answer to the last words he'd spoken before she'd fallen asleep. 'Not from you.'

He'd been getting to his feet. Now he knelt down once more. His expression was tightly controlled, but his hands were trembling.

'I wasn't really afraid of you,' she went on quickly, her voice breathless, her lungs constricted by her heart, thudding against her breastbone and making her whole body shake. 'Not even at the beginning. It was myself I feared.' She hadn't desired anyone for over seventeen years. Desire led to death. So when she'd felt it the previous night it had frightened her. It frightened her still, but the dream had given her an answer. 'If I was to leap from a cliff, would you catch me?'

His eyes widened, and she knew he understood, but he shook his head. 'No, my heart, for I'm standing on the same cliff, with the same fears, the same doubts. Nothing has changed. The world is as it is.'

'The world can be what we make of it. Time can be what we take from it. I was promised a summer of freedom and it's not over yet. You took my hand at the Longhouse, Talorc. Take mine now.'

She held out her hand, watched the colour drain from his face then rush back. His pupils were wide and dark in those storm-coloured eyes. He hesitated but clasped her hand in his, his grip firm and sure and very certain, then uncertain once more as she drew him towards her, drawing him over the threshold they'd both been too afraid to cross the night before, too afraid to leap from the cliff into whatever lay beyond. He traced her face with his fingers, and they trembled a little as they moved to touch her lips, her throat, her shoulders.

And then there was nothing between them anymore, no cloak, no blanket, no past or future, just skin and fingertips and lips. She was falling in truth, her fingers laced with his. She was falling down and down, then swooping upwards once more, a dark swan taking flight at last, beating her wings into the air in which, finally, she was flying free. The sea was glittering beneath her, empty of everything but the wind under her wings and the powerful beat of the air. Then she was falling once more, in a singing spiral, down and down to the sea that rushed up to meet and overwhelm her. The sky beat down to crush her, and the earth shuddered inside her body. She began to weep, holding him tightly, her head buried in his shoulder. She wept as if her heart had broken, because she'd found something she couldn't keep, because she was alive once more, and living was glorious and surprising and full of hazards. She wept because she'd found a man she couldn't have, an enemy and a liar, a warrior and a Steward, a man with beasts on his skin and the touch of Gods in his hands.

SECRETS AND LIES

Corwynal woke to the sound of Trystan's little white dog barking from the steading yard. He was lying in the barn, on a pile of fresh hay. The sun shone through the broken place in the roof where their weapons had been hidden, which meant it had stopped raining, though water still dripped in one corner. There must be yet another gap in the thatch. *Later*, he thought lazily. *I'll deal with it later.* For the moment, he was content to lie in the sweet-smelling hay, his arms spread wide, the heat of summer flowing over his skin as he watched dust motes dance in the sunlight. Brangianne's head was on his chest, and her eyes were closed, but she wasn't asleep. How could anyone sleep with that cursed dog barking? Then the dog fell silent at a sharp command and, moments later, he heard a harp being plucked. Trystan, who'd taken to limping along the beach to strengthen his muscles, had returned to the Longhouse.

Brangianne stretched herself languidly and propped her head in one hand to look down at him.

'He won't come into the barn,' he said, meeting her eyes and losing himself in their warm grey depths.

'Good,' she whispered, bending to touch his lips with her own.

Not again! he thought, half in the now-familiar longing, half in a despair that was new.

They ought to be in the fields. They'd barely begun harvesting the barley when a sudden downpour had forced everyone into shelter, and he and Brangianne had run back to the Longhouse. But that had been over an hour before.

'We should get moving,' he murmured, but didn't move. He was too intent on the feel of her lips against his, the trail of her fingers on his chest, and he was falling again, into her, through her. All it took was a look, a touch, and he was lost. Gradually, however, he'd become conscious of the rocks lying in wait for them in their rapidly approaching future. One day they'd have to talk, properly for once, and he wanted that more than anything: to tell her of his past and his hopes for the future, to share his life with her. But that would mean telling her who he was, and so he'd said nothing. Instead, ignoring both past and future, they existed in this seemingly endless present in which their conversations were not of voices but hands and skin. Time had been too precious for talk. *A summer of freedom*, she'd said, and there was little left of the summer.

Everyone knew, of course. Brangianne had insisted they be discrete, but she was the only one to believe that what had grown between them had gone unnoticed. Trystan, predictably, was both furious and concerned.

'Are you mad?' he'd demanded. 'Have you stopped thinking entirely?'

But Corwynal couldn't think anymore. All he could do was feel, and this was something he hadn't felt in over eighteen years.

'Please, Trys. Allow me this. It won't be for long.' But Trystan had just shaken his head in despair.

Oonagh, equally predictably, didn't approve either and glowered at Corwynal even more than usual. Uncharacteristically, however, she kept her silence, unlike the rest of the women of

Carnadail who approved because they thought he'd remain as their Steward beyond the summer. More and more, he dreamed of doing just that. But that's all it was – a dream. One day he was going to wake up – they both were – but that lay in the future. For the moment, all that mattered was the increasingly urgent demands of his body.

Then the dog began barking again, and a girl spoke from outside in the steading yard, a girl with a clear carrying voice and a refined accent, a girl who was less than pleased.

'What are you doing with that harp? It's not yours!'

Brangianne sat bolt upright, pushed Corwynal away and scrambled for her clothes.

'Get dressed! Quickly!' She pulled on her dress, fumbled at the laces, then made for the yard.

'It *is* my harp.' Trystan's voice was equally clear. He must have moved to the Longhouse door. 'It was given to me by a man who had no further use for it.'

'Actually, that's true.' The third voice had Corwynal reaching frantically for his own clothes. Those drawling tones, threaded through with malice and amusement, told him the dream was over.

Ferdiad had returned.

The girl was quite astonishingly lovely, her auburn hair tumbling down her back, waves of it framing a heart-shaped face. Her eyes were green, a warmer green than Ferdiad's, but there nothing warm about her expression, which was one of astonishment, as she looked at Brangianne and, when she turned to Corwynal, outrage.

'Lady Brangianne...' Ferdiad bowed, his lips twitching. Brangianne's blouse was only half-laced up and her hair was full of hay, her bare arms brown with the sun and none too clean. Corwynal knew he looked equally disreputable, and it must have been obvious to everyone what they'd been doing in the barn. 'I'm so sorry to have . . . inconvenienced you,' Ferdiad went on with a sly smile. 'There was no possibility of sending word in advance, but, as you see, I brought Ethlin with me. I've matters to attend to in the north, but Ethlin prevailed on me to put her ashore at Carnadail. Your brother's business in Dun Sobhairce is taking longer than he'd anticipated, but he expects to follow on in ten days or so and will collect you both on his way to Dunadd.'

Brother? Ten days? Corwynal glanced at Brangianne, but she was still staring at the girl in something very like horror.

'But I was to stay here for the summer!' she said in a strangled voice.

'I think you'll find that summer's almost over,' Ferdiad pointed out.

'It can't be, not yet!'

The Fili shrugged. 'I'll leave it to you to persuade your brother of that. He'll be travelling in the King's ship.' He gave her a merciless smile. 'Yes, indeed. It's a great honour, so if I were you, I'd endeavour not to keep him waiting when the ship arrives.'

'Your brother?' Corwynal asked, unable to keep the accusation out of his voice.

'My father,' the girl, Ethlin, cut in sharply, clearly unused to being ignored. 'I'm Ethlin, Brangianne's niece.' She regarded him with evident distaste, letting her gaze drift deliberately to his open shirt, but when she saw the patterns, the wolf and the stag, the hints of others, her gaze faltered a little, though not for long. She lifted her chin in defiance, her eyes cold. *I don't like you*, she was telling him. He smiled thinly, not giving her any of the things she expected: wonder and admiration, even a simple recognition of her beauty. *This girl's trouble*, he decided, and glanced at Trystan to see what he made of her, but he wasn't looking at the girl. He was standing in the door of the Longhouse, Ferdiad's harp in one hand, his face set and pale.

'What's wrong?' Corwynal asked. Was his wound troubling him again?

'Nothing. The sun blinded me for a moment.' He gave Corwynal a quick reassuring grin, smiled at Brangianne, nodded at Ferdiad, and went back into the Longhouse, having ignored Ethlin completely.

She stared after him as if she couldn't quite believe it and went on staring after the door was closed quietly but firmly in her face.

'Well!' she exclaimed, tossing her head defiantly, a hint of angry tears in her eyes, and would have said more had Brangianne not intervened.

'Well, this is a surprise ... Ethlin.' Her smile was distinctly forced. 'But a welcome one of course! Now let me show you Carnadail, and you can tell me all your news ...' She grabbed the girl's wrist and dragged her away from the Longhouse, leaving Ferdiad and Corwynal alone in the steading yard.

'What in the Five Hells are you up to now?'

'Why should I be up to anything?' Ferdiad leant back against the wall of the Longhouse and crossed his arms. 'Apart from off-loading an extremely trying young woman; quite how trying you'll no doubt find out. It wasn't my idea to bring her, I assure you, and I apologise if our arrival was ... ill-timed.' He grinned at Corwynal, who felt heat flood his face.

'I hope she can work. We're in the middle of harvest here in Carnadail.'

'Oh, I imagine you can persuade her to tuck her skirts up and get her hands dirty. She's a cattle-lord's daughter so it ought to be in the blood, though she's inclined to give herself airs, as you might have noticed. Fancies herself with the harp too, which accounts for her rudeness to young Drust. I gave her a few lessons once – she has some talent or I wouldn't have bothered – so she probably thought that if I was to give my harp away it ought to be to her.' He spread his hands apologetically. 'A spoiled child, but pretty enough if you like that sort of thing. Can't say I do. Clearly you don't either, your tastes running to the more mature woman ...' He tilted his head to one side and regarded Corwynal narrowly with those cold green eyes. 'You haven't told her, have you?'

He didn't have to explain what he meant.

'Not yet. Are *you* going to?'

Ferdiad had kept his silence on his last visit for his own mysterious reasons, but why should he continue doing so? There was so much more to ruin now, and what better revenge could Ferdiad have than by doing exactly that? But the man just smiled that infuriating smile of his.

'I'm tempted, of course, especially since it's now common knowledge – except in Carnadail – that The Morholt was killed by Trystan of Galloway, aided by Corwynal of Lothian. Nevertheless, I think I'll hold my tongue for a little longer. Feargus, who for some reason doesn't regard me as his favourite person, has sent me north once more, though not, thank the gods, on yet another abortive attempt to find Ninian. You were right, you know; it's impossible to get into Atholl. I gave up in the end and returned to Dun Sobhairce, and now I'm on my way to Loarn's court at Dun Ollie, which might be a worse punishment than looking for Ninian.' He shivered faintly. 'So I'll leave you to tell the Lady of Carnadail who you are – or not. The choice is yours, but you only have ten days or so in which to make it, so I'd advise you not to waste your time.'

'Father won't let you marry that man.' Brangianne and Yseult were walking along the beach towards the stepping-stones that led to the settlement on the other bank of the river. 'If that's what you're planning.'

'It's not,' she said, because Yseult was right. Feargus wouldn't allow her to marry a man with no gold or alliances and an enemy at that. And so she'd tried to convince herself that what had happened between her and Talorc wasn't something that would last, that it would fizzle out like a summer storm. As each day passed, however, she wanted him more, not less. Even so, she hadn't thought of marriage until now. 'But never mind me. Tell me all the news from Dun Sobhairce.'

The news was both good and bad. Yseult remained unpromised to anyone as yet. And while the second tribute demand hadn't been pressed, nor had it been renounced, which left Brangianne still betrothed to Eoghan.

'. . . and the man who killed my uncle is dead, or so Ferdiad says,' Yseult went on with a scowl. 'So I won't get my revenge after all.' Then she brightened, and laughed. 'Except on Ferdiad himself. I've been horrible to him ever since I got to Dun Sobhairce so, to rid himself of me, he agreed to leave me here rather than take me on to Dunadd. He told me you needed to be rescued, you see, but I didn't think it would be from anything like this!'

'It's none of your business, Yseult.'

'Ethlin.'

'Ethlin? What *is* this nonsense?'

'Ferdiad said you were pretending to be someone else, so I'd have to pretend to be someone else too. I'm trying to help you, but if you *want* me to say who I really am . . .'

'No,' Brangianne said weakly, wishing Ferdiad hadn't come, or brought Yseult to complicate everything. 'It's simply that . . .' She tailed off, because it wasn't simple at all. But if she could explain it to Yseult, she might be able to explain it to herself.

'I'm not pretending to be someone else. I'm just . . . not going into unnecessary detail. Here I'm Lady of Carnadail, and a healer. No more than that.'

'So why can't I be your niece, Ethlin, and no more than *that?*' '

They'd reached the stepping-stones by then. Yseult jumped lightly onto the first one and turned to face her. 'It's those men, isn't it? You're pretending to them. Who are they?'

Brangianne sighed. Better to tell her now than let her find out for herself.

'Britons,' she admitted. Yseult's eyes widened. 'Shipwrecked Britons,' she went on hurriedly. 'I had no choice but to take them in. I didn't trust them at first, which is why I didn't say anything about who I was.'

'Do you trust them now?'

Of course she did. So why didn't she say who she was? It wasn't as if it was a shameful thing to be the sister of a King. It would just be embarrassing to have to confess she'd been afraid Talorc and Aelfric might take her hostage. Drust, certainly, would find it hilarious. But Talorc wouldn't. She trusted him with her life, her heart, her body and her honour, but that last was the difficulty. He might be nothing more than a Steward of a few acres in a place called Manau, but he had his pride. A man of his status couldn't aspire to the sister of a King. Not in this world. She'd come to Carnadail to make a choice, and she'd chosen Talorc, but if she wanted to keep him she'd have to fight with Feargus for the right to make that choice, and couldn't risk telling Talorc who she was until she'd won that particular battle.

'Ferdiad didn't tell me there were Britons here.' Yseult danced onto the next stepping-stone. 'He didn't tell Father either. I wonder what he's playing at?' Brangianne wondered that too, but it was too late to find out, for the ship had left, taking Ferdiad with it. 'But it doesn't matter,' Yseult added with a shrug. 'It's a good game.'

'It's not a *game*,' Brangianne said crossly.

'Why not? Are they dangerous?'

'Not to anyone in Carnadail. Drust was badly hurt when he arrived, and I've been treating his wound. There was another, Aelfric, but he's gone back to the Britons' lands. He and Talorc have been helping me in Carnadail. We're shorthanded.'

'He's a Caledonian, isn't he? There was a man like him in Dun Sobhairce, talking to my father, who has some new scheme in mind by the way, so I'm free, at least for the moment. Unless . . .' She stopped, frowning. 'Unless he's planning on marrying me to some Caledonian.' Then her brow cleared. 'But that seems unlikely, given what happened in the war last year. That man here and the one in Dun Sobhairce must be from the same tribe. Those markings . . .' She tailed off, shivering. Everyone found Talorc's designs disturbing.

'He's half Caledonian, but he comes from a place called Iuddeu. Now listen, Yseult—'

'Ethlin.'

'All right, Ethlin,' Brangianne said, giving in, because what choice did she have? 'If you want to play this game, you'll have to remember you're not a Princess, not here in Carnadail. If Drust was rude to you it was because you gave him no reason to be polite. You'll have to earn the way you're treated, but I warn you; it isn't easy being ordinary.'

Yseult grinned, danced back over the stepping-stones and threw her arms around Brangianne's neck. 'I've always wanted to be ordinary, even just for a few days. Don't worry! I can pretend, better than you perhaps. Isn't it lucky I brought my oldest clothes?' Her eyes were sparkling with delight. 'I'm so glad I came, Brangianne. This is going to be so much *fun!*'

'. . . and my father has six clients who owe him allegiance, and one hundred head of cattle of his own.'

Corwynal and the others had gathered in the Longhouse for the evening meal Oonagh had prepared. She was a good cook and the fish stew, scented with thyme and thickened with barley, smelled delicious. Nevertheless, no-one, with the exception of a glowering Oonagh and a drooling dog, had any appetite.

'Indeed?' he replied, unimpressed, for that number of clients and cattle meant Ethlin's father, Brangianne's brother, was no more than a minor landowner.

He glanced at Brangianne, sister to this cattle-lord, and wondered why she was so ill at ease. He hadn't seen her all day, hadn't had a chance to ask about this brother, and now she was avoiding his eyes and twisting the ends of her sash together as she listened to Ethlin's naïve recitation.

'. . . . and he has land in Ulaid as well as close to Dunadd,' Ethlin went on.

'Really?' He wasn't surprised. Everyone in the Lands between the Walls had heard of the King of Dalriada in Ulaid who'd taken Ceann Tire and the lands to the north and moved his court and family to Dunadd. Many of his clients would have gone with him and taken lands for themselves in the new territories.

'Yes, really!' she said, ice in her voice. She didn't like him, but that was no surprise. Most women didn't, and in other circumstances he might have been amused by this young girl, so full of her own importance, the over-indulged only child of a man who'd never re-married after the death of the girl's mother. That much he'd gathered from her artless boasting. He glanced at Trystan, expecting him to share his own amusement, but, rather than finding this funny, Trystan was visibly irritated and barely holding himself in check as he struggled with his own deception. *I'm the heir to two Kingdoms!*

Corwynal hadn't trusted the girl at first, because he didn't trust Ferdiad. He'd suspected the Fili of bringing her to Carnadail out of a malicious desire to complicate their situation. She was very lovely, and Trystan, lacking companions of his own age, was bored. However, to Corwynal's relief, Trystan and Ethlin had taken an instant dislike to one another, so if this was Ferdiad's idea of revenge on Trystan, it had failed.

'My aunt tells me you were a Steward in a place called Manau.' The girl turned to him, her tone telling him her opinion of a place calling itself Manau.

'I had that honour,' he replied, suppressing a stir of annoyance. 'They weren't as extensive as your father's lands, of course, and we had more sheep than cattle,' he added for good measure, knowing how much store Gaels placed on cattle. 'Wouldn't you say, Drust?' he asked, hoping Trystan would rise to the challenge of this fabrication. He did, but not in the way Corwynal expected.

'I've no idea, I've little interest in cattle or sheep.' *I'm above all that,* he was saying, *as anyone of breeding should be.* The implied criticism roused a glitter of fury in the girl's eyes.

Corwynal's heart sank. Warfare had been declared.

'So, what are you?' she asked sweetly, with a deliberate glance at Ferdiad's harp. 'A bard?'

'No.'

'Of course not,' she agreed with a small smile of satisfaction. Bards were trained musicians, part of a brotherhood with mysteries of their own, men who crafted their own instruments, composed their own songs, and were infinitely superior to itinerant singers, such as Trystan appeared to be. 'So you won't know the songs of the Dalriads.'

'My own people have songs enough, though I do know the songs of Dalriada. I learned many from—'

'Drust—' Brangianne cut in.

He'd been about to say 'Ninian', before Brangianne stopped

him. Which meant the girl knew Ninian too. *A girl I couldn't have,* Ninian had said. Had it been this one?

'—perhaps you could sing something for us all,' Brangianne continued. 'Something from your own lands.'

He frowned at the request, clearly reluctant. Ethlin smirked, making clear her low opinion of songs from anywhere other than Dalriada.

'Very well,' he said, stung by that smirk, and reached for his harp, his eyes glittering dangerously. Corwynal thought he'd sing a song of battle, something to match the anger in his eyes, something loud and rousing to the blood, a song for a warrior rather than a woman, a song of pride and danger, where life was short and death was glorious.

But what he gave them was quite different, and it was then that Corwynal understood how far music, or Ferdiad's harp, had taken him, and how much he'd matured in the past year, for though he sang of war it was not as young men sing of it. His war was a bitter thing where bright heroes were cut down in their prime and women and children left to weep. He sang of lands plundered, kings overthrown, rivers running red with blood, peoples harried. He sang of comrades lost and men and women divided by the banners of different armies. *Too close, that!* Corwynal felt danger stir.

Brangianne was brushing away tears, but it was Ethlin for whom Trystan sang, holding her eyes with his, a challenge in their depths, controlling his voice and his fingers, but not the emotions that lay beneath. Perhaps, self-taught, he was already half-way to being a bard, but there was more to bardic training than learning a tune or two. A bard had to learn to restrain the power of his voice, for it could be as much of a weapon as any blade, and Trys had yet to learn restraint. Now Ethlin was the target of Trystan's unshielded voice, and she stared back at him, mesmerised, a hare in the gaze of a weasel. She was weeping unashamedly, tears trickling unheeded down her face, as he sang of a champion slain in a fruitless challenge. He was singing of The Morholt now, taking the song into even more dangerous territory.

'That's enough, Drust!' Corwynal snapped, and Trystan fell silent on one plucked chord, the breath rasping in his throat as if he'd been fighting. Then he gave himself a shake and returned from whatever place the music had taken him.

'I apologise, Lady,' he said, turning to Brangianne. 'It was a sadder song than I'd intended.'

'I've never heard that song before,' Ethlin said in a strangely distant voice.

'No-one has.' Trystan picked up his harp, got to his feet with the aid of a stick, limped out of the house into the moon-washed night, and didn't come back.

Yseult apologised to Drust in the morning, much to Brangianne's surprise, for she'd wept a great deal the previous evening once she and Brangianne had retired to the women's room. In part, it was because of the song, but mostly it was due to humiliation. She'd expected Drust to be an indifferent singer, but he'd proved her wrong, and Yseult hated being wrong. Nevertheless, the next day she told him she'd misjudged him, a harder admission than he realised, and his own apology lacked grace.

'I shouldn't have sung that particular song,' he said stiffly.

'Nicely said, Drust.' Talorc's voice, heavy with irony as he came into the Longhouse from the barn, set Brangianne's heart lurching. Seeking to avoid the inevitable questions, she'd stayed with Yseult in the women's room the previous night, rather than joining him in the barn, and his temper, never at its best in the morning, was evidently fragile.

'Perhaps you could demonstrate your contrition by showing Ethlin around Carnadail,' he suggested, ignoring the fact that Brangianne had done so the previous day. 'And take that cursed dog with you,' he added, jerking his chin at the little white dog that, desperate for attention, was jumping up at Yseult. 'Brangianne and I have . . . matters to discuss.' He didn't call her Lady. He wasn't going to pretend.

She followed him in silence to the beach, to the place he'd been washed ashore. She thought that was probably deliberate.

'Are you ashamed of what has happened between us?' he asked.

'If you mean yesterday, then no. I was embarrassed.'

'There's a difference?'

'Of course there's a difference! I'm not ashamed of anything.'

'You didn't come to the barn last night.'

Surely he understood why she hadn't? The world outside their dream had come to Carnadail, and nothing could be the same anymore.

'I didn't know you had a brother, or a niece,' he went on.

'There's no reason why you should. I came to Carnadail to escape my family, particularly my brother. But, despite everything, I care about my family. We were rich once, but now my brother's in trouble because of the war and the tribute. Because of Britons like you.'

He flinched at that. 'Then you'll go back with him when the ship comes for you?'

'I have no choice. I was only ever here for the summer. You knew that. A ship will come for you too, and you'll leave Carnadail, as will I.'

He folded his arms over his chest and looked out over the sea that had brought him to Carnadail and would take him and Drust away once more. 'I've no reason to stay.' He was silent for a moment. 'You've not given me one.'

Her heart shuddered. Once more, she was standing on the

edge of a cliff. He would stay for her if she asked him, if she said the words she'd kept locked inside her. *I love you.* Yet she hadn't said them, afraid of what the saying might begin, of truths she didn't want to hear, even though loving him was the deepest truth of all. But she couldn't tell him so, not yet. More was required of her than the simple choosing of one life over another. She had to make the life she wanted possible, had to construct a world other than this dream of an eternal present, one crafted out of the past and future, of grief and joy combined. She would have to act, even though she knew that by acting she'd risk losing him. Yet if she didn't act, she'd lose him anyway.

'Come.' She held out a hand. 'There's a place I want you to see.'

They walked in silence along the edge of the water. The tide was half-out, and the beach stretched ahead of them, a broad sweep of sand and pools shimmering in the sunlight. The high tide line was a ribbon of rotting weed, clouded with flies. The rocky peninsula to the south was black against the glitter of the sea. Arainn beyond was a blue mass, the distant island of Carraig Ealasaid a blur in the haze. Little waves curled and hushed at their feet, and it was hard to believe that breakers had once pounded these sands, that they'd washed ashore a drowned man. She'd given him back his life, and he'd repaid the debt in kind.

There were patterns in the world, she thought, threads of gold binding the chaos. One life was given, another returned. It was a balancing the old priests understood when they spoke of souls abiding for a time in a place of mists before returning once more. The new priests said little of these things, but that didn't mean they weren't true. *You must learn to forgive yourself,* Ciaran had said. *And there's only one place you can do that.* He'd been right. She'd forgiven herself for the death of a man, had almost forgiven herself for the death of a child.

The rowan still clung to the ruin of the old wall as it had on the day she'd buried her son, but now it was in full leaf, bunches of fruit swelling and beginning to blush. The berries of the previous year, shrivelled red globes, lay scattered about the grass like spots of blood, as if to remind her of what she'd done here: her knife cutting through frozen soil and root, the hole so small for all her effort, the pile of soil, black on the green grass.

'What is this place?' Talorc asked, sensing something but not knowing what it was. He was closer to the Old Gods than her.

'It's a grave.'

It was an appropriate place for an ending, here beneath a witch tree, beside a grave. *I should tell her and be done with it.* He thought of bones crumbling away to nothing in the roots of the tree, flesh transforming into bark. He shivered, wondering if it was the grave of her husband, the Lord of Carnadail, the man slain by Galloway raiders, the man whose place he'd taken. Was that why she'd brought him here? Was this the place to tell her it was he who'd inadvertently brought defeat to her nation, that it was he and Trystan who'd turned the tide of the battle, and how Trystan, with his help, had killed The Morholt?

Yet the words had to be said. It was why Ferdiad had come, not to tell Brangianne the truth, but to force Corwynal to destroy his own happiness. How satisfying that would be for the Fili, how fitting, and how surprising he hadn't stayed to witness the destruction.

'Why did you bring me here?' He let her hand go and leant back against the ruined wall.

'I wanted to ask you for something – a name.'

'Mine?' he asked. It was an admission, he supposed, that he had others. *Talorc's the name my mother gave me.* He hadn't been Talorc of Atholl for a long, long time, but before he could tell her so, she shook her head.

'The name of a child. A son.'

So this quiet place beneath the tree wasn't the grave of a man, but of a child. She'd spoken of a son, hadn't she?

'Yours?' But once more she shook her head. And smiled.

The world shifted. His throat, suddenly, was dry. His skin went cold as all the blood in his body drained back into his heart, making it swell inside his chest.

'Ours?' he breathed. It hadn't occurred to him that they might have made a child. Surely it was too soon to tell? Yet women knew these things. Had it been at Lughnasadh? Had the Night of Gifts, the night of storm, given birth to life, as a sunlit dawn of Beltein, eighteen years before, had done? Would that gift of life lead to yet another woman's death?

What have I done? His flood of joy was swamped by a wave of terror. But Brangianne shook her head at his fear and stepped towards him, put her arms around him and leant against his shoulder. He could feel her heart beat powerfully against his. She was a strong woman and a healer. Why shouldn't she survive it?

'Ours,' she said. 'Is that reason enough to stay? Or reason enough to come back? For we have to leave Carnadail, you and I. You have to take Drust back to his own lands, and I have to make peace with my brother and win the right to make my own choice.' She pushed herself away and looked at him, her grey eyes clear and certain. 'That choice is you – if you'll have me.'

He closed his eyes and held her hard against him.

'I want you, more than I can say. But I can't have you.' His voice wasn't quite steady. He wanted everything she was offering him – a woman, a child, a land, a future. Yet he could accept none of them.

He thought about all the women whose lives he'd touched – and damaged. Gwenllian whose death he'd caused. Ealhith whom he'd tried to protect but had given away to a man even colder than himself. Essylt whom he might have loved but had chosen not to. Gwenhwyvar who'd needed his help but whom he'd deserted. He'd walked away from them all.

And now there was Brangianne, a woman he loved and had lied to. Was he going to walk away from her too? Could he consign her to his endless past of unfinished business, his hopeless *one day, perhaps*? What would she think of him when he'd gone? Would she believe the lies he was about to tell her? Would she wait, allowing the love between them to curdle into the hatred he deserved?

He let her go and pushed her away a little, hardening himself against the flare of hurt in her eyes. 'It's not me you want. Not the truth of me. My heart, there are things I have to tell you—'

No, not yet. Was that Arddu's voice in his head, or his own? Whichever it was, it made him pause long enough for her to make her own protest.

'No.' She placed her fingers over his lips. 'This is the only truth that matters. The past lies behind us, and we can do nothing about it. It's the future that matters, the future we've made between us. Names don't signify, only what we are and what we do together.' She laced her fingers in his hair and pulled him towards her, her lips taking away any truths he might have spoken. Together, they fell to the ground beneath the tree, among the fallen berries that lay on the grass like spots of blood, and tore the clothes from one another until they were naked beneath the wind. It seemed to him then that she was wiser than he, that she knew him more truly than he knew himself, that he need not tell her who he was or what he'd done because she already knew and had forgiven him. Maybe she was right; only the future mattered, and the present. It was still summer in Carnadail, and there was time to lie in the shadow of the rowan, clothed in nothing but sky and wind. There was still time to love and be loved.

Until the ships came to take them away.

THE CHAMPION'S SWORD

The King's ship, despite the previous days' light wind, arrived earlier than expected, which, Oonagh reckoned, was probably for the best.

She'd thought the madness between Brangianne and Talorc would come to an end when the Princess arrived, for surely the girl wasn't going to stand by and see her aunt – sister to a King no less – make a fool of herself over a foreigner and an enemy. What Oonagh hadn't expected was for the girl to play the same ridiculous game as Brangianne and pretend she too wasn't anyone important – as if you couldn't see she was simply by looking at her.

Aristocrats! Mad, the lot of them!

She'd expected Brangianne to weep when the ship arrived, but she was suspiciously calm, as if nothing was going to change. She'd said her goodbyes to the people of Carnadail, and to Talorc and Drust, that morning, although no doubt things had been said privately to the Caledonian in the course of the previous week, promises made that couldn't be kept.

It was Yseult, rather than Brangianne, who wept as they stood on the shingle beach of the fishing bay where the King's ship had moored. A coracle had been dropped over the side and one of the men was rowing through the surf towards them. Yseult was holding the little white dog in her arms, a gift from Drust.

'Here, take her,' he'd said curtly, having pushed his way through the crowd. 'She likes you better than me.' Then, having pressed something else into Yseult's hand, he'd limped off and vanished.

The Flame of Dalriada had turned out to be as beautiful as they'd all said, and what with Drust being as handsome as the morning, Oonagh had expected trouble, so she'd kept an eye on them to begin with, concerned their shared passion for music would lead to other passions, for there was much to admire about both of them. Drust could be amusing when he chose, and he was certainly clever, as was Yseult. And though she might behave like a spoiled Princess at times there was more to her than that; she was spirited and not afraid of anything.

Nevertheless, neither got over their initial dislike of one another, a dislike that deepened with each passing day. Each took to goading the other in cruel and vicious games, Yseult being hurtful and Drust sarcastic, and Oonagh wasn't surprised when neither emerged the winner. Even when they sang together it wasn't for pleasure, or love of music, but as some sort of challenge. Once, coming back to the Longhouse, Oonagh had heard them singing a lament together and might have thought it the most exquisite thing she'd ever heard had she not been certain each of them was trying to drive the other to tears.

Perhaps Drust's graceless gift of his dog was the consequence of a defeat he'd suffered earlier that day. He and Yseult had been playing Fidchell on the beach, the squares marked out on the sand, with stones and pieces of driftwood as the pieces. After a long hard game, Yseult had won, and she'd leapt into the air in triumph and went running across the sands, her hair flying behind her, Drust's little dog chasing after her. Drust had watched her go, his face rigid, before turning on his heel and limping back to the Longhouse.

'Can I help it if he can't run after me?' Yseult said later to Brangianne when she took her to task. 'I'm tired of men – and boys – running after me. I had enough of that in Dunadd.'

But now she was to return to Dunadd and could no longer pretend to be a peasant, would no longer be allowed to help with threshing and winnowing, or gather shellfish along the shore, or berries and nuts to store for the winter. During her time in Carnadail, her hair had bleached in the sun, her skin had browned and her feet were filthy. But now she'd have to be a Princess once more, and that, Oonagh reckoned, was reason enough for tears.

Actually, she felt like crying herself. She *liked* Carnadail. Every stone of it held memories, every timber of her house. Its soil was beneath her fingers and in her blood. She'd buried children in Carnadail, and a husband, and had expected to grow old there, to die in her stead, her bones becoming part of the earth as the earth was part of her bones. She should be waving goodbye to all these foreigners and getting on with her old life. But she no longer wanted it. *Don't you have a family?* Brangianne had asked her. *No-one I'd care to make a claim on.* It hadn't really been an answer.

It was all that Angle's fault, of course, and her own weakness for a strong arm and an easy laugh. What had she been thinking of at Lughnasadh? *I don't make promises.* Even if he came back, would it be for her? She didn't think so. Nevertheless, she hoped it might be, and there was nothing as pathetic as hope, so she'd decided to leave Carnadail and go to Dunadd at Brangianne's invitation. And then . . . ? Had the time come to discover if the one remaining member of her family was alive – or dead? She didn't know how to find out, but she'd worry about that when she got to Dunadd.

'We'll be back soon,' Brangianne said as the coracle reached the beach, and it began to rain. But Oonagh didn't think they would. Nothing could ever be that simple, not for Brangianne, or Yseult. Or herself.

She'd sworn she wouldn't cry when they left and had remained stony-faced when the coracle beached on the shingle and the three of them were rowed to the ship. Once aboard, they made their way to a position near the stern where Oonagh clung tightly to the strake as if her life depended on it. *I won't weep*, she told herself as the anchor stone was hauled up, the oars run out and the sail raised. Gradually, Carnadail slipped away behind them, growing smaller, and vaguer until it was nothing more than a blur of smoke and rain, and the smell of the land – of home – was banished by the stink of the ship and the salt smell of deep water. Only then did Oonagh allow herself to cry. For a dream ended, for everything that had happened and hadn't happened, for all the things that might have been.

'I see a summer in Carnadail has suited you.' Feargus frowned at Brangianne in his usual critical fashion, but she just smiled.

'Thank you, it did.'

She felt amazingly well, actually. She hadn't cried when they'd left, and her eyes were entirely dry as she watched the land slide away in a smirr of rain, taking Carnadail and Talorc with it. *I haven't lost him*, she told herself. They'd promised one another they'd return at Beltein, and she was sure she'd have a child to show him by then, the child she'd used to bind him, a child to set her free. She'd let him think it would be a Lughnasadh child, and that might not be a lie. But it didn't matter where and when it had been conceived. All she needed to forgive herself, as Ciaran had demanded, was a living child to replace a dead one.

Feargus would be furious, of course, since no matter how ambitious he was, even Eoghan would balk at marrying her if she was carrying another man's child. Feargus would probably send her back to Carnadail in disgrace, and she and Talorc could be together, living openly as man and wife. There would be nothing then to prevent her from telling him who she was: the disgraced sister of a king, exiled to Carnadail and grateful for any man willing to marry her.

'And what, in the name of God, was Yseult doing in Carnadail?' her brother demanded, breaking into her thoughts. 'I thought Ferdiad was taking her to Dunadd.'

'Don't blame *me*, Feargus. It wasn't my idea, but I believe she's survived the experience.' She spoke lightly, hoping Feargus hadn't noticed the colour of his daughter's feet, but he scowled at the gently weeping clouds, the sail, hanging wet and heavy, and the steel-grey sea tilting to an oily swell from the south, before returning to the covered shelter at the bow where the passengers were huddled: guards and priests, servants and minor functionaries of his court, all of them trying to keep out of the rain while the oarsmen, oblivious to the weather, kept up the steady beat and sweep that would take them north to Dunadd.

Brangianne pulled the hood of her cloak over her hair and moved to the stern to join Yseult who was soothing the little white dog.

'Drust warned me she'd be sick,' Yseult said.

'Shhhh!' She'd told Yseult not to mention Drust or Talorc and glanced around to see if anyone had heard. To her horror, a man in a black habit, whom she'd taken for a priest, had turned his head at the sound of Drust's name.

'It's him!' Yseult whispered as he made his way towards them. 'The Caledonian I saw in Dun Sobhairce.'

The breath caught in Brangianne's throat, for she thought she was looking at Talorc, but when he pushed back the hood of his habit and she saw him clearly, the resemblance was less obvious. This man was older by ten years or so, ten years that hadn't been kind. His hair was shot through with grey, and there were lines of bitterness about his mouth. His eyes were the same stormy blue as Talorc's, but there was a watching and judging in them she didn't much care for.

'Lady Brangianne.' He bowed to them both and smiled. It wasn't Talorc's smile either. This was a colder, self-mocking thing, the smile of a man amused by life but separate from it. 'Lady Yseult,' he said, turning to her. 'You spoke a name a moment ago, one from my homeland, a name I've not heard in some time. Do you have news of . . . of this man?'

'No,' Brangianne cut in, before Yseult could speak. The man eyed her narrowly as if, like Ciaran, he could see into her thoughts.

'Good,' he said. 'This man of whom you have no news – was he alone, I wonder?'

She didn't reply, but her silence seemed to be answer enough.

'Good,' he repeated, nodded to them both, glanced at the little dog and moved quickly back to the shelter. At their feet, Drust's parting gift to Yseult howled apologetically before depositing her half-digested breakfast all over their shoes.

'Stomach problems, Blaize?'

Ciaran was sitting on his favourite bench, watching Blaize pace back and forth across the little bridge that spanned the stream at the bottom of the water-meadow below St Martin's. 'Have you consulted one of our healers? Brangianne, for instance?'

'Of course I have.' Blaize abandoned his pacing, lowered himself onto the walkway of the bridge, and dropped his feet over the edge to dangle them above the water. 'She told me it's a bleeding in the stomach, common in men of my age, apparently. *Men of my age!* She gave me some cursed powder to take in milk twice a day. Tastes like shit,' he complained then, after wrestling with himself, humphed and shrugged. 'But it seems to help.'

What she'd gone on to tell him, however, hadn't helped at all.

After Blaize's visit to Ciaran earlier that year, he'd returned to Iuddeu with news of what was happening in Dalriada. Arthyr had been sympathetic but unwilling to provide assistance without the promise of something in return. He had, however, sent Blaize to Galloway to get Marc's side of the story – a drunken incoherent tale, which nevertheless confirmed Blaize's suspicions. Trystan, with Corwynal's assistance, had indeed defeated The Morholt, but had been so badly wounded he'd had to stay on The Rock in the care of the healer-priests. Then he and Corwynal had disappeared. Blaize had travelled to The Rock himself, an unpleasant journey that had left him none the wiser. Corwynal and Trystan, together with that Angle of theirs, had set off into a storm in a fishing skiff, and everyone assumed they'd perished at sea.

But Blaize didn't think so. Trystan had a destiny Blaize had glimpsed at his birth, a destiny as yet unfulfilled, and Corwynal also had a role to play in the future. As for the Angle, Blaize doubted if anyone or anything could kill him. So he hadn't been surprised to learn from Brangianne that all three were alive, having been shipwrecked at Carnadail, a village on the Ceann Tire coast.

If only it had been that simple.

What an idiot Corwynal was! He could be forgiven for making for Dalriada, but why had he allowed himself to fall in love with the King's sister of all people? It wasn't as if she was a great beauty.

The only reason the whole sorry episode wasn't a complete disaster was that he'd had the sense not to tell her who he was. And she, for some reason, hadn't mentioned her relationship to Feargus, and nor had Princess Yseult. But secrets had a habit of turning into catastrophes, and at the heart of all these secrets was Ferdiad – sleek serpent that he was – who'd kept his council for his own obscure reasons.

'Revenge, I suppose,' Ciaran said. 'If so, it's an extremely complicated revenge, but that bears Ferdiad's mark, of course. However, if he's not careful, he'll find it turning on him. I fear for him, Blaize, I really do, but Ferdiad is the least of our problems.'

Blaize looked down at the stream flowing calmly between banks heady with meadowsweet. A hawking dragonfly darted from the shadows, iridescent wings catching the light before it whirred off once more. He tried to find his own tranquillity in the gentle flow of the stream and the drone of bees in the purple hearts of thistle blossoms, but it was no use; the aggravations of the past days and weeks had destroyed any possibility of calm.

'For the gods' sake, Ciaran, what does Feargus *want?!*'

'He wants what any King wants – as much as he can get for as little as possible in return.'

'Arthyr's made a good offer.'

An offer Blaize had struggled to get Arthyr to agree to, so it was infuriating that Feargus had rejected it out of hand. The offer of cavalry to help him defeat the Creonn was a significant one, given Arthyr's own shortage of men, and all Arthyr had asked was for Feargus to cease raiding Galloway and Strathclyde for that season and the next, pending a more formal treaty.

'Feargus doesn't believe he needs help to defeat the Creonn, because he doesn't believe they'll come by land, not after the last time,' Ciaran said. 'So he's concentrating on raising ships in Ulaid by promising Yseult's hand to whoever helps him win the war. A rather vague promise, I thought, which makes me suspect Feargus intends to wriggle out of it when the time comes. And he got Eoghan, Steward of Dalriada, to pledge the second tranche of the tribute in return for marrying Brangianne.'

The woman my idiot nephew loves. Blaize sighed. Corwynal had never been lucky in love, and it would be worse for him when he found out who she really was – a political pawn in Feargus' schemes, a woman who could never belong to someone like Corwynal, a man with no prospects, a man who'd given up everything he could have been. He wasn't even a Steward anymore. He was a stubborn pig-headed fool who'd fallen for a woman who'd lied to him. No, for his nephew's peace of mind, it would be best he never found out. But Corwynal's broken heart was a minor matter in the great game of kings and kingdoms, of war and peace, and the Brotherhood's hope of a future that might outlive the storms looming on the horizon.

'So Feargus believes this war with the Creon can be won at sea?' Blaize got to his feet and went to sit next to Ciaran on the bench.

'Yes, but I fear he underestimates the possibility of an attack on two fronts.'

'You still believe the Dragon-riders exist and have joined the Creonn once more?'

'They exist, Blaize. My sources confirm it. As to whether or when they'll join the Creonn – that's less certain.'

'Sources?' Blaize eyed the old man sceptically.

Ciaran sighed. 'Not sources Feargus would believe. The Forest People. Yes, yes—' he went on testily, '—I know what you're going to say. They dwell as much in the past as the present, so who's to say what lies behind their words?'

Like the Dragon-riders, the Forest People dwelt in the shadowy realm that lies between reality than myth, and few people believed in them anymore. Blaize, however, had met them occasionally on his travels, odd creatures, as slight and willowy as saplings and as easily startled as fawns. They were suspicious of everyone, and for good reason, for they were mistrusted in their turn. Alien, ancient, and speaking a language unlike any other, they'd once roamed freely over the lands of the north, hunting game with poison-tipped arrows, herding their little horses, cattle and goats, and hibernating through the winter in their earth-houses. Gradually, however, they'd begun to disappear as they were displaced by the taller, stronger, Celtic tribes, and now were only to be found in the dense woodlands that hedged the mountains of the interior, forests that had come to be known as the Ghost Woods, named for the ghosts they'd become.

'How can you rely on sources you can't understand?'

'Because I know someone who can speak with them. A man I'd like to trust, and yet who makes me question my own judgement.' Ciaran's eyes sharpened. 'As you begin to.'

'No, I—'

'Trust me, Blaize. There *is* a plan, though it may not succeed in our lifetime. But it *will* succeed. It must. And that means taking risks. This man is a risk, but I believe his information is correct.'

'Secrets are a risk, Ciaran.'

And Dalriada was awash with secrets. Sooner or later, he thought, they'd all come flooding out. He was correct, as it happened, though he thought later more likely than sooner. But in that, he was wrong.

'Not now, Brangianne. I'm too busy.'

When she'd been in Carnadail, she'd expected things to be simple. She'd return to Dunadd, have the painful but necessary conversation with Feargus, then everything would be resolved, one way or the other. But nothing involving Feargus was ever simple.

'For God's sake, not now!'

He was indeed busy, constantly meeting with this man or another: Eoghan, Ciaran, his principal landholders, emissaries from Loarn and Oenghus, Ferdiad, who'd returned from Dun Ollie, and sometimes that strange man from the ship.

'His name's Blaize,' Feargus had told her. 'He's one of that War-leader Arthyr's creatures, a druid of some sort, but Ciaran vouches for him. No, I don't know where he's from.' His eyes narrowed. 'Why do you ask?'

'No reason,' she'd said quickly. That had been her opening, but, coward that she was, she'd stepped back from telling him the truth. She'd wait, she'd decided, until she knew what the truth really was. But Blaize himself had confirmed everything she already knew.

A few days after she'd met him on the ship, he'd come to St Martin's to consult her about a stomach pain. He didn't much like her diagnosis, and nor did he like her questions about Talorc, but, unprompted, he'd told her Talorc was his kinsman, his nephew in fact, which accounted for the resemblance. He confirmed that he'd once been a Steward and had fought at the Loch of the Beacon. So Talorc hadn't lied to her, though Blaize gave her no reason for optimism.

'Forget him,' he advised her. 'And when I get hold of that idiot boy, I'll tell him to forget you too. Feargus won't let you marry him, and Talorc won't let you marry him either, whether I tell him who you are or not. He's not fated to be happy, and he knows it.'

'I don't believe in fate.'

'But he does.'

'That doesn't matter. We were happy.'

'Happiness terrifies him.'

'Nonsense! He's not afraid of anything!'

But she wondered about that conversation later. Was Blaize right? Did he know his nephew better than her? Perhaps it was these doubts that sapped her resolve for, as the days went by and she failed to catch Feargus in an approachable mood, she decided it would be best to wait. After all, if she spoke too soon, Feargus might decide to set sail for Carnadail, and, if Aelfric hadn't returned, Talorc and Drust might still be there.

She was safe from Eoghan too, at least for the moment, for he'd barely spoken two words to her since her return, and she suspected he hadn't given up his hopes of Yseult, who'd returned from Dun Sobhairce unbetrothed. So there was no urgency – except for the one secret she couldn't keep forever, the child she was now certain she was carrying. She'd have to tell Feargus about it sooner or later, but rather dreaded his reaction. *Later*, she decided. *I'll tell him later.*

Superficially, then, everything returned to normal, as if Carnadail had never happened – everything except for Yseult, who'd returned to Dunadd as the Flame of Dalriada indeed, a girl with a temper that increasingly resembled that of her father. Perhaps, by pretending to be no-one of importance, she'd realised that, stripped of family and expectations, she wasn't very important after all. Maybe she'd begun to wonder if she was as beautiful as everyone had told her, or that she sang better than anyone in Dalriada but Ferdiad. It was all Drust's fault, she insisted. 'I'll show him,' she muttered and threw herself into music in an attempt to best him, even going so far as to carve her own harp in imitation of Ferdiad's, the one she thought he ought to have given to her rather than Drust. 'I'll show him,' she repeated when finally, with bruised and bleeding fingers, she tuned the strings of the crudely carved instrument. But when Brangianne pointed out that she was unlikely to see him ever again she'd stalk off in a temper. Nothing pleased her in those days, and Brangianne, distracted by her own concerns, lost patience with her tantrums.

'If I'd known you were going to behave like this, I'd never have let you stay in Carnadail!'

'If I'd known how *you* were going to behave, I'd never have let you go there in the first place!' Yseult retorted. 'I've a good mind to—' She broke off, crossed her arms over her chest and gripped them tightly.

'What? Tell your father?'

'No,' Yseult said sullenly, biting her lip. 'I won't give you – or them – away, if that's what you're afraid of.'

'That isn't—' But Yseult was gone, running out of the hall to lose herself in Dunadd's warren of stables and sheds, leaving Brangianne troubled on Yseult's account, but not on her own, because she didn't believe Yseult would give Talorc and Drust away.

But she did.

'A new sword for a new Kingdom!' With a flourish, Feargus unveiled the Champion's sword mounted on the wall of Dunadd's Royal hall.

Blaize smiled grimly at Feargus' announcement, thinking how typical it was of the man to make political capital out of a defeat. The new sword had been forged in Ailech, in the lands of the Ui Niall, and blessed by their Christian saints. Its blade was iridescent blue steel shot through with water-sheen markings, its guard and grip set with dark jewels.

'He should have brought the body back to Dunadd.' Ciaran was sitting beside Blaize at the feast that had culminated in the dedication of the new sword.

'Who?' Blaize asked distractedly, picking at a dish of mutton seethed in ale and thickened with barley. He was wondering how much Feargus had paid for the sword, for the Ui Niall were the best swordsmiths in the Old Country, and this one would have cost Feargus a great deal. He was also curious about who would wield it, for the position of Dalriada's Champion was an honour still to be bestowed. That too would have its price.

'Ferdiad.' Ciaran reached for a jug of water and raised an eyebrow at Blaize, but he shook his head. It was wine he wanted and lots of it. Brangianne had told him wine would irritate his stomach, but he didn't care. His long-drawn-out negotiations with Feargus had finally succeeded – to a limited extent. The King of Dalriada had agreed not to raid Galloway or Strathclyde for the rest of the year, as long as neither attacked his trading fleet. Now Blaize was to take a copy of what had been agreed back to Arthyr for his approval. The other copy lay on the high table, and no doubt Feargus would make political capital out of that too. The prospect of getting away from the Fox of Dalriada was reason enough for celebration, and Blaize had already drunk enough to feel mellow. Even the mention of that cursed Fili didn't upset his equilibrium.

'He burned The Morholt's body in the old way, down on the shore,' Ciaran continued, nodding across the hall to where the light of a torch caught on silver hair and a face rigidly expressionless. 'Feargus was furious when he found out,' Ciaran went on. 'Everyone, pagan or otherwise, is to be given a Christian burial these days. He made Ferdiad go to where he'd burned the body to recover the sword – what was left of it. He forced him to sift through the ashes until he found all the pieces.'

'He missed one then.' Blaize squinted at the shards of The Morholt's broken sword, pinned to the wall next to the new blade. Beside the Ailech weapon, this one looked unimpressive, the metal dull and pitted, the hilt plain, the leather bindings scorched, and there was a shallow notch along one side. This sword had once defended Dalriada, but in the end it had let Dalriada down.

'Did he?' Ciaran turned to look at the broken sword, and he wasn't the only one giving it more than a cursory examination. Yseult was also peering at the sword, a frown furrowing her brow, one hand grasping a ribbon that hung around her neck. She pulled the ribbon out from under her dress and walked slowly over to The Morholt's sword.

'Stop her!' Ciaran grasped Blaize's arm, his fingers biting into flesh. He'd turned pale, his dark eyes black pits of fear in his white face. 'For God's sake, stop her!' Ferdiad too had risen to his feet.

But it was too late. On the end of the ribbon was not the jewel one might have expected but a rusting sliver of metal. Yseult stared down at it, her fingers visibly trembling. Then she reached up and placed the scrap of metal in the notch.

It fitted the gap exactly.

'You stupid, *stupid* boy!' Blaize muttered as he feverishly stuffed his possessions into a satchel. He was still shaking from the events of that evening – Yseult screaming out her accusations, Feargus rising to his feet in anger and turning first to Brangianne then to Ferdiad in furious condemnation. Names were whispered about the hall. Trystan, Champion of Galloway, Morholt's Bane – they were calling him that, apparently – then that other name, more hated even than Trystan's: Corwynal of Lothian, the man the Dalriads believed had betrayed them at the Loch of the Beacon, the man who'd come close to killing Feargus. The names grew from whispers to mutters, then to shouts and demands. *Kill them! Kill them all!*

'Time to leave, Blaize,' Ciaran had murmured, loosening his grip on his arm. But Blaize was frozen into immobility by the enormity of what had happened, and was still sitting when Feargus looked over and transfixed him with the spear of his glittering green eyes.

'You!' he spat. 'The deal's off!' He strode over to the high table, snatched up the agreement and tore it into shreds of parchment. 'Get out of Dunadd! Get out of Dalraida! If you want to live, get out now!'

He should be grateful he'd been allowed to leave with his life, Blaize thought as he bundled up his cloak and stuffed it into his bag. The ship he'd intended to take to Alcluid, The Goose, was already at Loch Gair, thanks be to the gods, but he'd have to persuade its captain, Maredydd, to leave earlier than he'd planned.

'It's not true, is it?'

Blaize's nerves were on edge, and he reacted instinctively. He lunged at the figure standing in the doorway, slammed them against the wall and reached for his knife, but it was barely out of its sheath when he realised who it was. If he'd been thinking straight, he would have expected this particular visitor.

'My dear woman, of course it's true.' He released his grip, stepped back and sheathed his knife once more.

The Lady Brangianne moved unsteadily into the little guest hut and sat down abruptly on the pallet as if her legs had given way. She looked up at him with so much appeal in her eyes that his irritation changed its target. Trust Corwynal to fall in love with this particular woman!

'You said he was called Talorc and that he was a Steward.'

'Both those things are true. Talorc is what they call him in Caledonia. And he is, or was, Steward – of Lothian. He didn't lie to you, though he didn't tell the whole truth – but then neither did you.'

She coloured briefly at that but shook her head in denial. 'I didn't conceal anything important. What he didn't tell me matters. He betrayed Dalriada. He brought that message from Ninian—'

'—and believed it to be true.'

'He tried to kill Feargus and would have done if one of his household warriors hadn't stopped him.' She raised a hand to her mouth in horror. 'There was a scar, on his shoulder . . .'

'I know,' Blaize said. 'I sewed it up. Now, if you'll forgive me, your brother's ordered me to leave Dalriada, so I'd better be going before he changes his mind.'

'He said he cared for me,' she whispered.

Blaize turned in the doorway. 'If he said so, it will be true. He's not a man who loves lightly. But that doesn't matter. What matters right now is whether he and Trystan are still in Carnadail.'

'They might be,' she said doubtfully.

A spurt of acid swirled around his stomach. As if things weren't bad enough!

'Then I need to get there. So make up your mind. Do you want me to help them or not?'

'Yes – no – yes! But what—'

'Then I need gold. As much as you can find. I have to persuade a ship to sail south rather than east, and that will be expensive.' He took her by the elbow and hauled her to her feet. 'Gold. Now.'

He hefted his gear, pulled the hood of his cloak over his head, marched her to her chamber, then stood over her while she unearthed a small box of jewellery. It wasn't much: a few chains, a string of river pearls, a couple of plain brooches. 'Not enough,' he muttered.

'Perhaps this will help?' Ferdiad appeared in the doorway, holding a small chest.

'You!' The Fili backed away as Blaize unsheathed his knife once more. 'You're the cause of all this!'

'Yes, but—'

'And now you want to help fix it? Why?'

Ferdiad gave a thin-lipped smile. 'Who knows? I certainly don't. Maybe I just want my harp back. And I need to get out of Dunadd because Feargus and Yseult are baying for my blood. So, do you want this or not? In return, of course, for passage to wherever it is you're going.'

Blaize shoved his knife back into the sheath, snatched the chest from the Fili and threw the lid back to reveal a blaze of gold. There were chains and brooches, armlets and rings, all set with strange jewels. Ferdiad wasn't wearing any of his usual regalia; this was everything of value the man possessed.

'I was going to try for a new look,' the Fili said lightly in answer to Blaize's open-mouthed astonishment. 'Silver. What do you think . . . ?'

Blaize snapped the lid shut and shoved the chest into his satchel. It would more than do. With luck, he – they – would reach the ship before anyone realised they'd gone.

'My thanks, Lady.' He turned to Brangianne, his hand on the latch. 'And Corwynal's thanks also. Is there anything you'd like me to tell him?'

'I'll tell him myself,' she said with decision, reaching for her cloak. 'I'm going with you.'

For the first time in her life Brangianne, born of a line of sea-faring men and woman, felt seasick. The stench of ropes and rowers, and barrels of salted beef, was as much of an assault to the senses as Ferdiad's presence. She wanted to kill him. He'd known all along who Talorc was and had said nothing, yet now he was helping her and Blaize reach Carnadail before Feargus. Why?

'Row, you bastards!' The captain's voice roared out over the wind, which had swung around to the northwest during the night, strengthening as it did so. Brangianne clung to a rope and peered anxiously ahead but couldn't make out Carnadail through the blur of rain and was afraid they wouldn't reach it before Feargus' ship caught up with them. The trader's vessel was sleek and fast, but though they'd got away from Loch Gair before Feargus and his war-band put to sea, Feargus' warship was larger, and it was gaining on them.

'The price just doubled,' the captain Maredydd had announced when he'd seen the other ship at first light the following morning. Nevertheless, he'd shipped another pair of oars, and for a time it looked as if they might draw ahead of the other ship, but by mid-morning he started muttering about turning east and making a run for it.

'There!' Brangianne exclaimed, catching sight of the promontory that lay north of the fishing bay at Carnadail. 'It's not far now!' Her heart thudded sickeningly in her chest and she wondered, not for the first time, what she was doing. What was the point of coming all this way to ask him if it was true? She *knew* it was true.

The ship rounded the promontory and swept into the bay. A small boy, playing by the shore, jumped up and ran along the track towards the settlement.

'Come along, if you're coming!' Blaize swung himself into the coracle that had been dropped alongside the ship, Ferdiad following, and held up a hand to her. 'There's no time to waste!'

Let him have left already! she whispered as Ferdiad paddled the short distance to the beach. Once ashore they ran up the track that led over to the Longhouse. Behind them, Feargus' ship rounded the northern point, headed into the bay and grounded itself on the stony beach. His war-band jumped into the shallows and splashed towards the shore.

'Quickly!' she shouted to Blaize, though she knew it was too late. It was a conclusion the Briton captain must have come to also, for he cut the anchor rope free, and his men backed water and pulled up the sail. Moments later, the trader's vessel was speeding out of the bay and heading east.

'Maredydd, you motherless cretin! You stinking short-arsed toad, you—'

Brangianne left Blaize to his cursing and ran on, Ferdiad close behind her. Back at the bay, Feargus' warship extracted itself from the shallows and set off after the trader, but his warband had remained ashore and were chasing after her and Ferdiad. Brangianne reached the crest of the hill, Blaize pounding behind them, but once there she pulled up short. At anchor in the southern bay was yet another ship, this one flying the raven of Galloway. Two coracles were beached on the shore, four men standing beside them. Brangianne knew three of them. A storm had brought them to Carnadail. Now a Galloway ship waited to take them away once more.

Aelfric didn't return for over a month, and Corwynal had stopped believing he ever would, just as he'd stopped believing in anything that mattered.

I should have told her. He woke to those words every day, fell asleep to them, and bore their insidious whispers for all his waking hours, which, since he didn't sleep well, were very many. Why hadn't he told her? The answer was simple. He'd lacked the courage. He'd rather have faced ten – twenty – fully armed Galloway raiders than the woman to whom he had to say the words that would change everything. And now she'd gone to Dunadd and would find out for herself, one way or another, what a coward he was.

There's something I have to tell you . . . How often had those words risen to his lips? How often had he begun to say them? But she'd always stopped him with words of her own, or a look or gesture. *Later,* he'd thought until it was too late entirely, and the ship from Dun Sobhairce sailed north, taking her away. She'd waved once, dark hair blowing on the wind, a faded blue cloak, that arm waving. *I'll never see her again.* The certainty was an absence inside him, a lack in the world so strong, so powerful, it had a heart-shaped form of its own.

Satisfied? he'd whispered as the ship vanished into the north. But if Arddu was satisfied he didn't say so, and Corwynal was forced to fill the silence with his own thoughts, and what he thought about was love. Of how it wasn't a matter of lips and skin, the curve of a shoulder, the scent of hair falling about him – but of what was no longer there. She was a silence in the Longhouse, one less person in the fields. A hand had waved, and she was gone.

So, this was love, this ache as if a limb had been torn away. *The other half of my soul.* He'd said the words, had even believed them, but hadn't felt them in the core of his body until now. And so he'd waited for Aelfric in a daze of misery. He'd been curt, irritable, impatient of the tolerant looks, the smiles he sensed behind his back, the pity.

Would Aelfric never return? Had he failed to make it to Strathclyde? Had he been unable to find Kaerherdin, or a ship? What would he and Trystan do if Aelfric didn't return? Trystan was right. The plan had been too complicated. Trystan had held on to his patience all summer, had even put up with that girl, but with the departure of the ship taking Brangianne, Ethlin and Oonagh to Dunadd, his patience had come to an end. Would Aelfric *never* come? Trystan became difficult to live with, as short-tempered as Corwynal himself. He took to haunting the promontory with the Dun and the rowan, searching the seas for a ship, but Corwynal never joined him there; the place had too many memories. It was where he'd failed to tell Brangianne the truth, where he'd failed to give her a name for a child. But that no longer mattered because he'd stopped believing in that too.

'He's coming!' Trystan limped back from the Dun, having sighted a ship. His eyes were shining for the first time in weeks. 'It's a Galloway ship!'

'Raiders?' Corwynal ran out to the dunes to see a ship heading into the bay.

'No, look!' Trystan pointed not at the raven sign on the sail, but at a big man helming the ship towards the beach, a man who raised the blade of an axe above his head so it caught the light. Aelfric had come at last.

It didn't take long to get their gear together, for they'd come to Carnadail with nothing more than their weapons. They'd already said goodbye to the people of Carnadail, and to The Devil, which had hurt more than Corwynal expected. The ship moored close to the shore in the channel by the river, and two coracles splashed into the water and were paddled ashore by Aelfric and Kaerherdin. Other Selgovians could be made out hanging over the side of the ship, waving.

'It hasn't been easy,' Aelfric complained. 'I ended up having to go to Galloway, and Marc took some persuading you were alive, but now he knows it others will too. So, best not hang about . . .' As he spoke, he was searching the beach, the tracks from the village and the Longhouse. 'Is she . . . ?' he began, colouring.

'Gone,' Corwynal said dully, before realising Aelfric meant Oonagh. But she'd gone too.

'Women, eh?' Aelfric said after a moment. 'Let's get out of here.'

He shoved one of the coracles off the beach, waded out and held it for Trystan to get in. Kaerherdin pushed the other off and

Corwynal turned to take his leave, not of a person, or a horse, but a place. *I've become fond of Carnadail.* Brangianne had promised to send another Steward, one of her own choosing, so Carnadail would survive without him. But still . . .

Then, amazingly, he saw her on the crest of the hill above the Longhouse. It was too far to make out her features, but he knew her as he would always know her. She caught sight of him in the same moment and ran towards him. Two men were running behind her, but he only had eyes for her.

'Corwynal . . .' Kaerherdin urged, but he ignored the Selgovian and raced back towards the dunes. Trystan shouted after him, struggling with Aelfric who was trying to force him into the coracle, but Corwynal ignored him too. He'd thought he'd never see her again, yet here she was, coming towards him. It wasn't too late after all; he could tell her now. He *had* to tell her now.

One of the men caught up with her and tried to stop her, but she wrenched herself away and kept on sprinting across the dunes and the beach. Corwynal opened his arms, his heart and his soul, and waited for her to run into all three, but she stopped a pace from him, lifted an arm and struck him hard across the face.

Everything stopped, his heart, his blood, his nerves, the breath in his body. But this wasn't the timelessness of battle, for in battle he could act. Here he was frozen, able to see, to watch, but unable to move.

The man who'd followed Brangianne pounded past him, and Corwynal recognised Blaize with neither surprise nor interest. On the crest of the track the other man had stopped, his silver hair lifting on the breeze. *Ferdiad, come to witness his revenge.*

'Trystan – get in the bloody boat!' Blaize yelled, racing to the water's edge where, with Aelfric's help, he forced Trystan into the coracle, jumped in after him, and Aelfric paddled strongly towards the ship.

'Corwynal!' Kaerherdin called out in alarm. He looked up, past the angry glitter of Brangianne's eyes; at the crest of the hill behind the Longhouse, behind Ferdiad, was a score of men, Dalriada's war-band, sun glittering on their spears.

'You know, then,' he said woodenly.

'Is it the truth?'

'Yes.'

'You *liar!*' She struck out at him again.

'Not about the things that matter. Brangianne, my heart—'

'How dare you call me that!'

'Let me explain—'

'No! Get off my land. Get on that cursed ship and go!'

'Run, Corwynal!' Kaerherdin was calling more urgently now. The war-band had reached the Longhouse and disappeared into the dunes beyond. Trystan was yelling from the coracle, but still Corwynal didn't move.

'I'm staying. I'd rather stay with you hating me than never see you again.'

'I don't want you to stay!'

'Then come with me. Please.' He held out a hand towards her, and she half-raised her own. For a long moment he thought she might take it. She'd taken his hand once before, and he'd taken hers. But now she snatched it back.

'No! Go now. They'll kill you if you don't.'

'Corwynal!' Kaerherdin gestured frantically towards the dunes from which the spearmen were emerging. Behind him the Galloway ship rocked on the swell, a bowshot from the beach. There were flashes from the ship as arrows were nocked and bows drawn back, but Corwynal held his ground. There was something to be said. Not everything of course. She'd know most of that by now. But not the one thing that mattered.

'I love you. Whatever I've done or said, that's the truth.'

'Go!' she screamed at him.

'Did you ever love me?' He waited for what seemed an eternity, but she didn't answer and turned her face from his. His heart emptied and absence rushed in, like a boulder falling into deep water and, with her silence, he was able to move once more. He whirled and sprinted towards the sea but turned back before he reached it. 'Did you?'

There was a flash of metal from the dunes as spears were raised.

'No!' she screamed. The war-band took aim, and Corwynal spun around and made for the coracle. The spears flew towards him but none of them struck. Nevertheless, he stumbled as if he'd taken a blow to the body. Kaerherdin reached for him, dragged him into the little boat, then paddled desperately out towards the ship. More spears flew, but all fell short, and they clambered unharmed into the ship. The anchor stone was hauled up, and the oars thrashed the water, driving the ship along the bay, yards from the beach. Then the sail was raised, and, as it caught the wind, the ship began to pick up speed and turn, making for deeper water. The spears fell away, as did the beach. And the woman. Corwynal stood by the gunwale at the stern, clutching a rope and looking back, hoping for some sign, a wave, a lift of the head. But she remained standing on the beach, unmoving, watching the ship take him away. Then she turned on her heel and walked back to the Longhouse, her back straight, her head held high, her neck long like a swan's. He watched, over and over, as she didn't look back. Over and over, not looking back.

PART II

DUNADD AND IUDDEU,

SAMHAIN TO MID-WINTER 486 AD

9

THE FORT AT THE END OF THE WORLD

In Dalriada, in the stronghold of Dunadd, the night that marked the onset of winter was called the Night of Souls. But in the country, among the stones of the ancient ones and the oak groves and carved figures of the Old Gods, the night of Samhain was known as the night of the dead, the Night of Endings.

There was an ending too in a little cell in St Martins, that most Christian of places. But no walls of stone or bells in their tower, no chapel, or oratory, or the simple– or not so simple – prayers of monks and priests could keep out the night, or the dead, or death itself.

Brangianne lost her child that night, despite everything she'd done: the tonics she'd drunk to strengthen her womb, her retreat to this place of calm where she'd curled herself around the little scrap of life and tried to protect it. But she'd failed. Did she lose the child because she hated its father? Or because she didn't know who its father was – the man she'd loved, or the man who'd lied to her?

She turned her face to the wall and brooded about those two men, Talorc of Atholl and Corwynal, Steward of Lothian. Of *Lothian!* Not a few acres on the other side of the world, but an entire country! He was the son of a King, and thus her equal.

She slammed her fist against the wall of the little cell. He'd let her treat him like a servant. How he must have laughed at her pride. Lady of Carnadail indeed! By now, that uncle of his, Blaize, would have told her who she was, so he'd know she'd lied to him too. Not that it mattered anymore, because she hated Corwynal of Lothian as much as Yseult hated Trystan of Galloway, and with more reason. She never wanted to hear his name again. He was a Briton and an enemy, and one day . . . one day . . .

But she had as little prospect of revenge as Yseult. All she could do was brood over her hatred as the Night of Souls slipped into the past and winter took hold of Dalriada. She lay in the dark in her little cell for days that turned into weeks, listening to the life of the monastery go on around her, the bells ringing out the offices, the slap of sandaled feet, the murmur of talk, voices lifting in song, the scent of burning herbs, all of it drifting away as the world abandoned her.

'Let it,' she muttered to the dark.

Feargus didn't come to see her, though he'd been told she was ill, if not the reason. They were no longer friends, but his initial fury had diminished with the rescinding of the second amount of tribute and the somewhat astonishing return of the first. Despite that, Brangianne was still betrothed to Eoghan, but she suspected that was simply to punish her. Eoghan, perhaps suspecting it too, stayed away also.

'Let him,' she muttered.

As for Yseult, she wasn't friends with her either. She'd stormed into Brangianne's cell on the morning after that dreadful night of blood and loss, her eyes spilling angry tears. 'It's true then! You were carrying his child, that murderer's brother, that deceiver! How could you!' she'd raged. 'Better it should die than the King's sister, my own aunt, should bear a child to a man like that! He tried to kill my father!'

Brangianne had leapt from her pallet and struck her hard,

then doubled up in agony as pain shot through her, and curled herself into a ball, whimpering.

'I'm sorry,' Yseult had said in a curiously detached voice before whirling away, banging the door behind her.

She'd apologised the next day, standing very straight, a red mark on her cheek where Brangianne had hit her, her eyes dry, her hands clenched into fists at her side. She'd looked very like her father, a proud princess who wasn't inclined to be humble, who demanded rather than asked for forgiveness. Then her face had crumpled. Tears welled and spilled down her cheeks, and Brangianne opened her arms for the girl to step into, but Yseult pushed past her and ran off, crying as if her heart had broken. She hadn't come back to St Martin's since.

Only Oonagh remained constant, coming to the monastery to tell her all the gossip from Dunadd, coaxing her to eat, to get up, get dressed, and visibly restraining her irritation when Brangianne did none of these things. Oonagh understood the loss of a child but couldn't understand everything, so Brangianne ignored her and stayed in her cell as the days shorted and the nights lengthened, nights riven with dreams of a ship disappearing into the mist, a man standing in the stern watching her turn her back on him.

In those dreams she'd run, weeping, along an endless beach, her wings beating and beating. But she always remained earthbound. Then one night the dream was different. In this dream her wings lifted her into the air and she rose and rose until the earth fell away and there was nothing ahead of her but high mountains, nothing beneath her but fields of snow and ice, and, far below, a lone wolf with storm-coloured eyes into which she fell, thunder all around her. She tilted her wings and banked steeply, flying low over a great whale-backed mountain, white with snow and glittering where the sun caught it, patterned with shadows the colour of slate. A man knelt on its summit, half-naked and shivering, his skin so white the patterns looked black, the wolf and the stag, the serpent and the salmon. She watched as snow began to fall, light flakes at first that melted on his skin, then heavier and heavier, whipped into a blizzard by the rising wind. She watched the snow rise to his knees, his thighs, his chest. She watched him disappear as if he'd never existed.

'. . . forgiven me?'

Corwynal looked up, aware that Trystan had been talking for some time, but the one word to have penetrated his thoughts was 'forgiven'.

'Who?'

Trystan sighed. 'You haven't been listening, have you? Arthyr, of course.'

'For what?'

'For going off to Galloway after he was chosen as War-leader. What else?'

'That was a long time ago.' A lifetime ago. Corwynal had been a different man then.

They were riding north as part of Marc's entourage, heading for Iuddeu for the Midwinter celebration, The Night of Names. There was snow on the high ground, and the low-lying farmland through which they travelled was hard with frost after a cold, clear night.

'A long time ago,' Trystan echoed, saying it with such regret that Corwynal looked at him sharply. What did Trystan have to regret? Perhaps it was simply because he was no longer a boy. He'd turned into a man shadowed by his past, by mistakes as well as successes.

'Do you still mind that Arthyr was chosen as War-leader

rather than you?' Corwynal spoke carefully, given his own role in that, but Trystan gave a bark of laughter.

'God, no! If it had been war, then maybe I would have minded. But this . . . ?' He waved a hand to indicate the slow progress of Marc's party, hampered as it was by the enclosed wagon bearing Garwyn, Bishop of Caer Lual, who'd become Marc's principal advisor. Marc was just one of the kings who'd be making their way to Iuddeu for 'discussions' – whatever that meant. 'All this diplomacy!' Trystan spat in disgust. 'I wouldn't be any good at it. Being a War-leader means having all the responsibilities of a King and none of the power.'

'Much like a Steward then,' Corwynal said with feeling. Trystan laughed, and Corwynal smiled at his amusement, but his face felt tight and unyielding, and only relaxed when he let the smile fade. He'd lost the knack of smiling.

'You don't really want to be a Steward, do you?' Trystan said, lowering his voice. 'Not in Galloway.'

'But Marc asked me—'

'You know why, don't you? He thought you didn't want to live any more. We all did.'

Corwynal shifted uncomfortably. He'd hoped no-one had noticed.

The past few months had been difficult, and he still flinched away from certain memories, the passage from Carnadail to Galloway being one of them: Blaize yelling at him that he'd ruined everything, being sick, Ceann Tire a long grey edge on the western horizon disappearing into the past, the hiss of rain and the achromatic wallowing heave of a swell, being sick again, everyone telling him to forget Carnadail, that it was over, silence from the God who'd taken what he'd wanted and abandoned him, and finally, a line of land on the larboard beam, the Rhinns of Galloway . . . Blaize had stormed off as soon as they'd berthed, and had left Galloway. Kaerherdin had gone too. But Corwynal hadn't cared because he'd begun to develop a fever, the effects of which remained long after the fever had gone. He was cold all the time, tired and unable to concentrate, unable to care about anything except a future that no longer existed.

It hadn't been until Samhain, The Night of Endings, that he'd begun to recover. Samhain had arrived on a storm, and the Feast of the Dead had been a cold affair despite the great fire pits in the middle of the Mote's feasting hall, for the doors had been thrown open to let the spirits of the dead enter and take part in the celebration. But none of Corwynal's dead came to the feast, not even Gwenllian. Perhaps her spirit lingered in Lothian, or by that pool in the forest. Corwynal was haunted rather by the living, by Brangianne and the child. A son, she'd said, but she could have lied about that. *She's to marry Eoghan, the Steward of Dalriada. He's very rich . . .* Blaize had told him. *Forget her; she's already forgotten you.* She'd hardly marry this Eoghan if she was carrying another man's child. But she might have purged herself of it; healers knew how to do that. Yet women could die of that, just as they could die in childbirth.

Morbid thoughts for a cold Samhain, but Samhain was for endings and so, at dawn the next day, he'd saddled Janthe and ridden into the forest, taking no path but letting her pick her own way. Eventually he'd come to a clearing with a stream, and there he'd cut his palm with a knife, dipped an arrow into the blood, nocked it to his hunting bow and aimed into the eye of the sun, allowing it to fall wherever the God decreed. Once, a lifetime before, Arddu had sent him a boar in answer to a blood-soaked arrow, and so he'd tensed, waiting for the God's response. But the woods had remained still, and the silence sank into his bones to join the silence that was already there. Arddu no longer dwelled in the pulse of his blood. He'd taken what he wanted, then abandoned him, leaving an empty husk behind.

'Marc's changed,' Trystan observed, bringing Corwynal back to the present. Behind them a long line of riders and wagons travelled north into the cold white hills, a ribbon of colour snaking its way towards Iuddeu. Marc was riding a spirited chestnut alongside Bishop Garwyn's wagon and appeared to be in deep discussion with the Caer Lual priest. His new tolerance, encouragement even, of the church of Chrystos was only one of the changes Corwynal had seen in Marc since arriving back in Galloway. He looked younger and fitter, and his eyes were clear, his skin firmer and his hands no longer shook. He'd changed *back*, into the man he should have been, the one promised in the young man Corwynal had known all those years before. Marc was no longer a drunkard. Now he was a King.

'I had a bad spell in the spring,' Marc had confessed. 'When I got word about Trystan. Thought I'd lost him, and you too, and I knew it was all my own fault. I should never have agreed to that challenge. I was too proud, too greedy. When word came that you'd all disappeared in a storm, I took to drink. And not for the first time, you'll be thinking. But sometimes a man needs to forget. I've done some terrible things in my day – crimes against God - and I've been punished for them. I needed an heir, but I was cursed. I couldn't . . . well, you don't want to hear the details. That uncle of yours, Blaize, told me to stop drinking. I didn't though. Then one day this summer, after I thought I'd lost you both, I got talking to a priest of Chrystos. Told him something of my problems – don't know why. Expected him to say the same thing as Blaize, but he didn't tell me to stop drinking. He asked me why I drank, and, God help me, I told him everything. Haven't touched a drop since . . .'

And this new sober Marc had plans for Galloway, good plans, things he should have done years before: the fleet to be re-fitted, relations with Strathclyde to be improved, a treaty made with Rheged and, as for Dalriada, he'd written to Feargus to tell him

Galloway wouldn't claim the other half of the tribute. Indeed, he'd decided to send the first lot back. It was, Marc insisted, the right thing to do.

Corwynal had looked at him in astonishment, wondering if some fairy spirit had stolen the old Marc away and replaced him with this one: a man who did the right thing. A King. A man Corwynal would willingly serve.

'And it's time I was married,' Marc had gone on. 'Past time. I need to get myself an heir.' The curse, Corwynal had assumed, was over now. 'Trystan won't mind, will he? He'll have Lothian and Selgovia. He doesn't need Galloway too.'

'Do you have someone in mind?'

'Not yet. Suitable princesses are thin on the ground. Pity Arthyr got that Gwenhwyvar. She would have done. Had an offer from the King of the Dal n'Araide – tried to foist his daughter on me but I'd heard she was a shrew so I turned him down. Still, there's plenty of time to look around. I'm not old, Corwynal. Neither of us is old.'

Which had been Marc's way of telling Corwynal he'd survive the loss of the other half of his soul and the whole of his heart. He'd doubted it, but had nodded and pretended, then went on pretending, which pleased everyone, so that was something. Trystan's fitness improved as his wound continued to heal. He began to ride again, then to spar with the war-band, but was careful not to overdo things. A summer in Dalriada had taught him caution, and that was something too. Trystan was growing up; the fire of his youth, which had been in danger of consuming him, was settling to a steady flame. Marc wasn't the only one who'd changed.

'What we need is action,' Trystan said now with decision. 'So I'm going to swallow my pride and ask Arthyr for a command, fighting on the border, something clean and straightforward. And I want you with me this time, as troop commander, supplies officer, whatever you want to be.' He gripped Corwynal's arm. 'I was a fool before when we were in Iuddeu. I shouldn't have left you behind. But it'll be different this time. A troop and a fort, no complications.'

No women, Corwynal understood. No wife Trystan didn't want to go back to.

Trystan's eyes brightened at the prospect of action, and he grinned at Corwynal, who smiled in return, a real smile this time. How odd to have forgotten the other sorts of love a man could feel, the love a commander feels for his men, for his brother, the love between a father and son. He began to laugh. The sharp winter air hurt his chest and made him cough, but he kept on laughing like a man who'd faced death and survived. He'd survive without a heart. He'd even survive without a god, because he didn't need Arddu anymore and would never again ask for his help.

But what Corwynal forgot was that the Old Gods don't suffer themselves to be ignored. Love, to them, was nothing more than a weapon to carve open the heart and lay it bare beneath the sky, a sacrifice on the stone of their insatiable hunger for worship, and that his own sacrifice hadn't been enough. Nothing was ever clean and straightforward, for thresholds loomed at every turning of the track.

'So, you want to fight, do you?'

Arthyr leant back in his chair and regarded Corwynal and Trystan thoughtfully. He'd kept them standing like raw recruits while Trystan had given his version of what had happened in Dalriada – an uncharacteristically colourless statement of the facts. This had happened, then that. Certain people weren't mentioned at all. Arthyr would know all about it already of course. Blaize, no doubt in furious detail, would have told him everything, and maybe that was why Arthyr looked so grim. Or perhaps it was for another reason, for they hadn't been in Iuddeu for long before they heard the rumours about Gwenhwyvar, Arthyr's wife and Queen of Western Manau, and Bedwyr, Arthyr's best friend. Corwynal was saddened rather than surprised, given the last conversation he'd had with Gwenhwyvar, but Trystan looked troubled and was keener than before to get out of Iuddeu and back to the frontier.

'We'll fight anyone, anywhere,' he told Arthyr.

'And why should I trust you to carry out any of my orders? Wait!' He held up a hand to still Trystan's protest. 'Let me remind you of all the ways in which you've failed that pledge you made to me so publicly. Firstly, you disappeared off to Galloway without the courtesy of giving me your reasons. Secondly, once there, you encouraged Marc in a number of pieces of foolishness. You led raids into Strathclyde, which resulted in extensive, and understandable, complaints – to me, Trystan – from Dumnagual. Thirdly, you refused to go to Selgovia for Hoel's funeral, a request made not by me but by one who has a greater claim on you, a woman – no, a wife – whom I understand you haven't seen since . . . When was it, Trystan? Last summer? And now, perhaps because of your absence, Selgovia has cut herself off from the rest of the Britons once more. Fourthly, you involved yourself in a pointless feud with Dalriada. And, fifthly, you went to Dalriada itself, and effectively destroyed the delicate negotiations I, through Blaize, was conducting with Feargus. All of which might be understandable but are not forgivable.'

'That's not fair!' Corwynal burst out, but he wasn't given a hearing either.

'You say you want to fight,' Arthyr went on. 'So let me put some possibilities to you . . .'

'Anything! Anywhere!' Trystan insisted.

'Then return to Dalriada, annexe this place Carnadail and march on Dunadd.'

Corwynal stared at Arthyr, sick at the thought.

'We can't do that,' Trystan said.

'No? Then are you willing to go back to Selgovia to be King-consort and husband of a valued ally? What about that, Trys?'

Trystan said nothing.

'Then to Lothian, to be a King in waiting?' Arthyr suggested. Corwynal glanced at Trystan, but he pressed his lips together and, once more, had no reply to give. 'So, not that either? But you want to fight, don't you?'

'Of course! Anyone—'

'Anyone? But not the Dalriads who are my enemies but seem to be your friends. Then what about the Angles? Or is there a difficulty there too in the form of the estimable Aelfric? Which just leaves the Caledonians.' Arthyr allowed his gaze to drift to Corwynal, who stiffened, knowing what was coming. 'Shall I send you to fight the Caledonians of Atholl?'

'I'm not leaving Corwynal behind,' Trystan said flatly.

'Trys, you don't have to—' Corwynal began.

'I said I wouldn't, and I won't.' Trystan turned to Arthyr. 'Keep us here, in Iuddeu then. We can train your new troops. We're both good at that.' But his voice had lost its bright optimistic edge.

Arthyr regarded them steadily for some time before allowing himself a faint smile. 'Very well,' he said with a nod of dismissal.

He let them get as far as the door. 'Wait. It was a test. Do you think I'd trust a man willing to fight his friends, or who's prepared to put his own brother in the position of fighting his kinsmen? So sit down, and take a look at this map.'

The map was covered with flags and markers, but the frontier was clear enough, the long line, dotted with forts, that ran northeast from Iuddeu, following the line of the mountains. Arthyr pointed to a fort at the far end of the line, one that lay beyond Atholl, almost beyond Circind, and might even be within sight of the sea. This, he told them, would be theirs to command.

'They call it—' Arthyr said, '—the Fort at the End of the World.'

'That was unpleasant,' Trystan said cheerfully as they crossed the courtyard. In truth, he'd had worse dressing-downs from Corwynal himself. 'But we got what we wanted in the end, so we'd better start thinking about mounts and supplies. Let's go to the horse-lines and find out what they have.'

'You go ahead. I'll see the armourer and meet you at the horse-lines later.'

Trys nodded and ran off down the cobbled way that led to the lower town, but Corwynal didn't head for the armoury. Instead, he made his way up the wooden stairs that led to the ramparts. He wanted to think about what Arthyr had asked them to do.

It made sense, he supposed. The distance of the fort from Iuddeu meant Arthyr needed men who could be relied upon to act independently. The fort had been torched and was badly damaged, so someone would have to direct the rebuilding, someone who knew about supply lines and signal stations. There would be fighting, of course, but the local Caledonian tribe, the Venicons of Circind, were old enemies of Atholl, and Corwynal would have no hesitation in fighting them. He and Trystan were the obvious candidates. So why did he feel as if a cloud had settled on his shoulders? Was it the fort he was afraid of, or the Venicons? Or was something else looming in his future?

It was cold on the ramparts. There was a smell of snow on the north wind mixed in with half-imagined scents of smoke and heather and the sour reek of frost-gripped bogs thawing in the brief winter sunshine. To the north, the hills they called 'The Heights' formed a hard sharp horizon, their summits dusted with snow. To the south, the lands of Selgovia layered grey on grey, the hills merging into the clouds. To the west, the sky blurred into the Great Moss, suggesting it might be snowing there too. Only the east was free of winter. The river, widening to the estuary, was a flat clear blue, the low-lying lands russet with the remnants of autumn. In the distance, the fortress of Dun Eidyn, half-imagined, was dark against the horizon. Further still, hidden in the haze, Dunpeldyr would be lying like an old wolf sleeping in the sunshine – much like its King, Corwynal's father.

Arthyr had told them Rifallyn hadn't replied to his summons. Corwynal hadn't been surprised by that. Others had responded, of course. Lot had arrived the day before. Marc was there, naturally, and Dumnagual of Strathclyde was due the following evening. Caw, King of Eastern Manau, was expected that day, and indeed, a small party of wagons and horses on the road from Dun Eidyn suggested he'd arrive within the hour. To Trystan's relief, Essylt, Queen of Selgovia, had refused to come, but politely enough, blaming the weather. The coalition of the Kingdoms between the Walls appeared to be holding.

He was alone on the ramparts but for a couple of sentries, huddled in the shelters overlooking the gates, who were more interested in the arrival of Caw's party than him. So he remained, shivering in the bitter winter wind, brooding on the north, on the future, until the snapping of the visiting kings' pennants on the flag-poles above him made his head ache. He glanced at them before turning to go, noting Arthyr's rearing bear, Lot's boar and Marc's raven. Gwenhwyvar's hart was missing; he'd heard she was away from Iuddeu, much to his relief, given the argument they'd had before he'd left the year before and the rumours he'd been hearing. But Caw's stag was flying from the rampart, which meant Caw must already be in Iuddeu. So, who'd just arrived from the east?

A shadow fell over him, the shadow of a man who blocked his retreat from the rampart, as he'd – all Corwynal's life – blocked everything he'd ever desired or needed.

'Well, Corwynal? Have you no word for me after all this time?' The voice was as light as the first snowflake of winter, and twice as cold. 'Have you no word for your father?

10

EYES THE COLOUR OF A STORM

Corwynal hadn't seen his father in over a year, but the old wolf didn't appear to have aged even a month since then. He, on the other hand, felt ten years older. It was as if his father had stopped in time and was waiting for his son to catch up with him and realise how similar they were. Both, after all, were men disappointed in love.

'I thought you weren't coming to Iuddeu,' Corwynal said.

Rifallyn had been leaning on the edge of the wall looking out over the winter-gripped hills and the darker misty lowlands, narrowing his amber eyes against the gleam of sun on waters in the east. But now his father turned to look at him to make the same assessment of his son's features as Corwynal had made of his father's. Eventually, giving no hint of his conclusions, Rifallyn raised an eyebrow.

'Why should you have an opinion one way or the other? No-one knew my intentions. Neither Arthyr, nor Blaize – who will no doubt claim credit for my presence. I go where I choose when I choose and for my own reasons.'

'Which are . . . ?'

'Amusement. I'd heard you were to accompany Marc. I thought it might be interesting to see how the world's been treating you.'

'Who told you I was with Marc?'

'Marc himself. Oh yes, we've corresponded. Yes, you may well stare. I was as surprised as you. He wrote to me when you returned to Galloway in the autumn. In his own hand, I believe, judging by the errors in the Latin. He invited me to thank God for your safe return, and Trystan's naturally. I didn't reply, of course. The mention of God by a man like that failed to move me.'

'Marc's changed, and for the better.'

His father gave him a long searching look but didn't pursue the subject. 'You've been busy I hear, since last we met. You went to Galloway, as I advised.'

'As you requested. To protect your heir.'

Rifallyn snorted. 'You call it protection to allow him to become Galloway's Champion and almost get himself killed?'

'You know nothing of the matter.'

'Oh, but I do. Marc told me everything, in that rather over-blown way he always had, but I managed to glean the salient details. You went to Dalriada, I hear, but now you're back among the Britons. So, what are your plans?'

'We – Trys and I – have a posting to the frontier. We leave in a few days.'

'Then I'm pleased not to have missed you. And there's someone else in my party who'll be equally delighted.'

Corwynal frowned, wondering who that might be. Madawg, perhaps? But he'd never been particularly friendly with Lothian's warband-leader.

'Ealhith,' his father said. 'The Angle slave you gave away. She's no longer a slave, however. I gave her her freedom, but for some strange reason she fails to appreciate it. I suppose it's to do with the boy. You remember that Ealhith was to have a child?'

'Of course!' Corwynal replied feelingly, remembering how Aelfric had half-killed him when he'd discovered Ealhith was with child by the King, since he blamed Corwynal for having abandoned her. Why, he wondered, had his father chosen to bring the girl, and her child presumably, all the way to Iuddeu in the middle of winter? Particularly when he must have known Aelfric would be here, Aelfric who'd wanted her for himself. Then it occurred to him that Ealhith's child was his own half-brother. He might even be heir to Lothian if his father carried out the threat he'd made the year before of disinheriting Trystan. 'How did you name him?'

'He's been given no name. That's a father's role.'

'Then why haven't you—'

'Oh, he's not *my* son!' Rifallyn exclaimed with his wolf's grin of malice. 'Although I'm aware everyone thinks so, and I don't disabuse them of the notion. At my age, to father a son . . . Sadly, however, such pleasures lie in the past. He's not my son. He's yours.'

'Ealhith?'

Ealhith stiffened at the sound of Corwynal's voice and laced her fingers tightly together as she turned to face him. But she barely recognised the man standing in the doorway of the guest hut set aside for the Lothian party. He looked so much older; a frown was deeply etched into his forehead, and there were drawn lines around his mouth. His shoulders were hunched as if he was carrying some heavy burden, and his eyes were troubled.

Yet she'd changed too and wasn't a child anymore, or a slave. In place of her slave's rough woollen tunic she was wearing a dark green linen dress trimmed with fox fur and scented with rose-petals. Her hair was elaborately plaited and coiled around her head and no longer concealed the livid scar that ran down one cheek, though, out of habit, she half-turned away to hide it from him.

'My Lord,' she murmured, giving him a slight curtsey.

He looked back at her, neither pleased nor displeased. Not caring, she thought. Dismay fluttered in her stomach.

'You look well,' he said eventually. 'And your child?' He nodded at the little crib in which her son, almost a year old now, lay sleeping. He had her colouring; his hair was the light gold of barley ready for the reaping, his skin milk-pale and scattered with freckles.

'He's well too.' She bent over her child to smooth back a lock of hair from his brow. When she looked up, Corwynal's frown had deepened.

'Why did you tell my father he was mine? Who got you with child? If you're afraid of him, tell me who it was, and I'll deal with him.'

'Why should you care?' She spoke more sharply than she'd intended. 'Because I once belonged to you?'

'Because you were under my protection. No-one touched you while I was Steward of Lothian.'

It was the worst thing he could have said.

'Oh yes, you protected me from all the others. But you couldn't protect me from yourself!'

'What?!'

'He *is* your child, Lord Steward.'

'That's ridiculous! I didn't . . . I would have remembered . . .'

'You don't, though, do you? I was nothing more than a slave, so why should you bother to remember? You were so drunk you could barely stand! Don't you recall weeping in my arms? Evidently not. All that mattered to you that night was a stupid promise you'd made in the hall! One hundred men by nightfall!'

The child, woken by their raised voices, began to wail, and she picked him up to soothe his fears away.

'I would have remembered!' Corwynal jerked her around to face him, but it was the child who caught his eye. Silent now, her son, safe in her arms, looked solemnly at the stranger with his wide blue eyes. They weren't the same as her own eyes, the rain-washed blue of a spring morning. Rather, they were the colour of slate, of steel, of storm-clouds. Corwynal took a breath and held it, and a pulse beat in his throat as he went on not breathing, not even when the boy stretched out a chubby hand towards him.

'You see?' she said, gently now. 'He knows you. Your son knows his father.'

The trouble with oaths, Aelfric thought sagely, was that they never turned out to be as simple as you'd thought they were going to be. Long ago, in Bernicia, he'd made Ealhith a promise, one he hadn't kept. Then he'd made more promises in Dunpeldyr, but hadn't kept them either. Now, apparently, she was in Iuddeu and, sooner or later, he'd have to face her. It was enough to turn a man to drink. Actually, that wasn't much of a hardship and, having met up with Madawg, Lothian's warband leader, in Iuddeu's main hall, he was well on the way to forgetting that uncomfortable feeling of guilt.

'Aelfric!'

What did the cursed Caledonian want now? Couldn't the man see he was busy? Aelfric lifted his mug of ale to his lips and was about to take a deep swallow when something large, sharp and very familiar was slammed down on the bench in front of him.

'That's my axe,' he said stupidly.

With another crash, his seax joined the axe.

Madawg gave a whoop of excitement. 'A fight!' he shouted, and other men gathered around, but Aelfric stared at his weapons and wondered if he was drunker than he'd thought. But no, he definitely wasn't, so that just left one explanation. Corwynal was glaring at him, his eyes glittering, and there was a wash of colour along each cheekbone. His hands, still gripping Aelfric's weapons, were quivering like a hound at the leash.

'You've gone mad, haven't you,' Aelfric observed tolerantly, having expected this since they'd returned to Galloway. The Caledonian had come pretty close then, and though he'd recovered he'd never really been the same. Now, finally, the man had cracked. 'Listen, you idiot,' he said firmly. 'I'm not fighting you. It wouldn't be fair.'

'Afraid?' Corwynal turned his back and walked out of the hall, sliding his twin swords from their scabbards as he did so.

Aelfric bristled at that. No-one, mad or otherwise, called him afraid to his face, then turned his back on him, especially in front of the massed warbands of the Lands between the Walls. 'All right. If you want someone to thrash some sense into you . . .' He snatched up his weapons, left the smoky midwinter warmth of the hall and followed Corwynal out into the icy air of the yard, where it was sleeting. *Typical!*

'What the fuck is this?' he hissed, falling into step beside the Caledonian as they walked towards the muddy practice ring in Iuddeu's main courtyard. 'What have I done?'

'You swore an oath.'

'I've sworn several oaths,' Aelfric said with feeling.

'And one of them was to kill me. Have you forgotten that?'

'It was a long time ago. Forget it. I have.'

'Have you forgotten Ealhith too? Have you forgotten *why* you wanted to kill me? You were childhood sweethearts, weren't you? You came to Dunpeldyr to rescue her. Well, you were too late. I'd already had her—'

The blood rushed to Aelfric's head and fountained in a red mist behind his eyes. 'You told me you hadn't!'

Corwynal stepped back and dropped into a fighting crouch. 'I lied,' he said. 'Or maybe it slipped my mind. Does it matter? She was mine, and her child's mine, and I'm going to keep both of them unless you fight me. It's what you wanted and what I promised. I might be a liar and a . . . a despoiler of women, but I don't break my promises.'

Aelfric launched at him with all his weight behind the first two blows, a hammer-blow of his axe and a low sweeping scythe of the seax. The Caledonian blocked the first on his crossed swords and leapt out of reach of the second, but it was close. Aelfric stamped forward, scything the axe low this time, but once more Corwynal sidestepped. He was fast for an old man, Aelfric thought, realising the Caledonian wasn't going to let him beat him down. The red mist began to dissipate, and he was able to think more clearly. What was this about? Something had changed. *Ealhith!* he thought. *She's told him!* Then the further realisation. *But not everything.* He should have known, he thought, probing Corwynal's defences and finding them ragged and mistimed. The man really had cracked. Something Ealhith had said had made him disgusted with himself and sent him to force this confrontation. Aelfric had felt the same self-disgust the previous Samhain when he'd allowed this man to beat the crap out of him. Now he was expected to return the favour. *Think again, you stupid bastard!*

'Is this the best you can do?' he jeered, easily parrying a thrust on the right, a backswing to the left. The men standing around the practice ground were cheering, most of them for himself. They thought the outcome certain, but it wasn't. Aelfric had seen the Caledonian fight, brilliantly at times, and had wondered what would happen if they ever fought one another properly. But now he was disappointed. All Corwynal's fire had gone, all his grace and speed. He was labouring for breath, slow to recover from each blow, and parrying with more desperation than skill. 'Come on, man! Have you no pride?' Aelfric taunted him. 'You're going to lose, but you might as well lose well.'

Corwynal's eyes flashed, and he blocked the next downward

hack of the axe but didn't fall back this time. Instead, he ducked, rolling over one shoulder to come up behind Aelfric, forcing him to pivot on one heel. He nearly slipped in the mud but managed to sweep his axe up to block Corwynal's backswing. Faintly, Aelfric thought he heard horns and, beating through the ground, drums that set a rhythm for the battle that, finally, was turning into what it ought to be – a fight worth watching. Aelfric began to grin, and a hint of pleasure kindled in the other man's eyes. A crowd had gathered in the yard. and people were cheering for both of them, but Aelfric and the Caledonian ignored them, even when Arthyr himself tried to intervene.

'Stop this, both of you!'

Aelfric was enjoying himself too much to stop, and the Caledonian wasn't about to give up either.

'Try to be less of an idiot, Corwynal!' Corwynal's druid uncle was there too, but his scorn had no effect. Even Trystan, screaming at them both, was ignored. One voice alone had the power to break the Caledonian's single-minded concentration.

'Do stop this ridiculous disturbance,' King Rifallyn drawled in a bored tone. 'You're frightening the child.'

Corwynal fell back. One of Arthyr's men, braver than most, stepped between them, and the fight was over. Aelfric lowered his weapons. *I'm for it now*, he thought ruefully, for if the child was there so was Ealhith. Aelfric dropped his axe and seax to the ground and stepped over to Corwynal, wrenched his swords from his slackening grip and let them fall too.

'What in The Five Hells was that about?' Trystan was white in the face. He'd missed the beginning of the fight and it must have looked more serious than it had been 'You *fool!*' he yelled at his brother.

'Took the words out of my mouth,' Aelfric said. Blaize grunted in agreement, then turned and walked away. Arthyr snapped a command, and most of his men, realising the fight was over, wandered back to the shelter of the hall, leaving Trystan in the pocked mud of the practice ground together with the Caledonian's father – and Ealhith.

She was standing beside the King, the boy in her arms, and was taller than Aelfric remembered. She was dressed like a lady, her hair piled on her head like a crown, but he didn't like the look of her expression as she lowered the child to the ground and came over to him. He stepped back, but it was too late to avoid the full weight of her hand as it struck his face.

'You promised! You *promised!*'

Which, considering what he'd been through, was hardly fair. She drew back her arm to hit him again, but he caught her by the wrist and held off the blow. 'And didn't I keep that promise? He's alive, isn't he?' He glowered at her before letting her go. 'I should never have made that promise. Do you know the situations that madman has got me into? All for the sake of a girl stupid enough to fall for an enemy who's a piss-poor liar into the bargain!'

Ealhith flushed, glanced briefly at Corwynal, and dropped her eyes. Aelfric and Ealhith had been yelling at each other in Angle, so he wouldn't have understood, but still, you'd think the man could have worked it out by now!

Rifallyn bent down to the boy who was sitting on the ground, playing with a pebble. 'Come along, child,' he coaxed, holding out a hand, but the boy got to his feet without help, toddled across to Trystan, and looked up at him. Trystan glanced down in irritation, but his gaze was caught and held by that of the child, and he stared at him long and hard before shifting his gaze to Corwynal, his eyes wide with disbelief.

'He's your son?' he asked in a strangled voice.

'So it appears.' Corwynal looked around at them all. 'He *is* my son. I claim him as my son in front of these witnesses, Aelfric and Trystan.'

'Don't!' Trystan said, still with that strained voice. 'Don't claim him!'

He turned on his heel and strode away from the practice ground.

'Leave him,' Aelfric recommended when Corwynal called after him. 'He'll get used to the idea. It's a shock at his age, becoming an uncle. It's a shock at mine.' He grinned at Corwynal's bewilderment then bent to scoop the child up. He was a sturdy little thing, his hair the same colour as Ealhith's and his own. 'This young man is my nephew.' He put his other arm around Ealhith's shoulders. 'If you'd taken the trouble to look, you might have seen the family resemblance. She's not my childhood sweetheart, you fool. She's my sister.'

'You fought like a girl.'

Corwynal and Aelfric were in the hall by then at a table in the corner, a jug of ale in front of them and two cups. People were giving them odd looks and keeping well away, but that was fine by Corwynal because there were things to be said between them.

'I know,' he said, recalling the fight in the practice ring and how, to begin with, the music had deserted him. The world had remained slow and sluggish, his limbs as fluid as rock, and he'd wondered if he'd die there, in Iuddeu's courtyard. Perhaps it was what he'd wanted. He was tired of being unhappy, and, when it came down to it, what reason did he have to go on living? Only one person would care if he lived or died, and Trystan was a man now. He didn't need him anymore.

Now, however, someone else needed him – a boy with slate-coloured eyes, a boy who, like himself, was of two nations but belonged to neither. Who, apart than Corwynal, could explain that to him? Perhaps that was why the music had come back, horns wailing from a high moorland, drums echoing from vast cliffs, beating harder and harder, faster and faster, into a rhythm into which he moved, the dance in which he knew the steps, and, with the heady scent of oiled steel and blood in his lungs, he'd found the old joy once more. Then the voices had broken in, Arthyr, Blaize, Trystan and, ultimately, his father. Then Aelfric saying the one thing he was struggling to accept.

She's my sister.

His father had taken the child from Aelfric and held him as if he'd done so many times before.

'My grandson,' he'd said, amused by Corwynal's surprise. 'He may be half-Angle and quarter-Caledonian, but he's still my grandson. Come along, Ealhith. I reckon these men have a few things to say to one another.'

But now they sat in silence, Aelfric drinking steadily, Corwynal toying with his cup despite the dryness in his throat.

'That fight wasn't to do with my oath, was it?' Aelfric asked once he'd drained his cup to the dregs. 'Or about Ealhith?'

'No.'

'Well, it was for me. I'd made her promises, then broke them. I should never have left her in Bernicia when I went back to the old country. But there was good fighting there.' He scratched at his beard and cleared his throat. 'Truth be told, I was getting away from the wife. Oh, yes,' he added mournfully at Corwynal's incredulous stare. 'I'm married. Attractive enough woman—' He gestured with his hands to indicate the nature of that attraction, '—and all smiles before we were wed, but no sooner had we walked around the fire—' He snapped his fingers, '—she turned into a shrew. Should have expected it, I suppose; her mother's a shrew. But marriage isn't about love or happiness. It's about children, and I gave her two, both strapping boys. So I reckoned I'd done my duty and took off. Promised Ealhith I'd be back in half a year, but it was nearer two, and by the time I'd returned she'd gone. Our family had betrothed her to that bastard who rules the pirates of Bebbanburgh – you lot call it Dun Guayrdi – and the ship taking her there was wrecked, so I thought she was dead. I didn't know she'd survived until a slave escaped from Dunpeldyr and made it back to Bernicia. He told me where she was and that she was slave to a Pict, a royal hostage refused ransom.'

'Royal?'

Aelfric gave him an aggrieved look. 'Don't tell me you haven't noticed the nobility of my features! Our father was Herewulf, Eorl of Gyrwum in Bernicia.'

'Eorl? Ealhith's an Eorl's daughter? Why didn't she say so?'

'Because she was afraid you'd ransom her back. Slavery in Dunpeldyr was apparently better than marrying a pirate. At least that was the reason to begin with. I didn't know that, of course, so I raised a raiding party and headed for Lothian. The rest you know.'

But there was something more, something important, and he frowned at Aelfric, trying to puzzle it out.

'Woden's balls, man!' Aelfric slammed his cup down in exasperation. 'Have you still not worked it out? The silly chit's been in love with you for years!'

Ealhith was in love with you and you didn't notice, Trystan had told him in Galloway, but he hadn't believed it.

'But she said . . . She let me think . . . The boy's mine, isn't he? So I must have—'

'—forced her?' Aelfric supplied. 'I doubt it. At the time though, I thought you'd enchanted her somehow.' He took a gulp of ale and scratched his beard in embarrassment. 'Stupid idea. Realised it later when I got to know what a fool you are with women. They're complicated creatures, Corwynal.'

Corwynal took a long swallow of ale. He hadn't eaten much that day, and it swirled pleasantly around his stomach but didn't clarify anything.

'I could have killed you just now.'

'Didn't stand a chance! I wasn't really trying, not once I calmed down. You never came close, though you left yourself wide open, and there were moments when I was tempted . . . But I'd promised Ealhith I'd bring you back to her. And I have.'

Aelfric poured himself another cup of ale and stared into its depths for a long time before lifting his head, his expression uncharacteristically thoughtful.

'Do you remember, on the Rock, you offered me anything I wanted if I'd take you to Dalriada? I nearly asked you to go back to Lothian and be kind to Ealhith, but it's as well I kept my big mouth shut because now, after Brangianne . . . ?' He spread his hands. 'I don't know if you've got it in you to make any woman happy.'

It was a little thing to ask, yet at the same time a great thing, an impossible thing, perhaps. But some impossible things were worth striving for. Happiness, Corwynal had come to realise, was transitory, and maybe it was time to stop thinking about himself. He had a son now. He'd been the son of an unhappy mother and a father who didn't want him. But things would be different for Ealhith's son; of that he was determined. So, at the beginning of the Midwinter feast, on The Night of Names, he named his son in front of two royal, if reluctant, witnesses, Marc and his father. He named him Caradawc, after the grandfather he barely remembered, a name that shocked his father out of his urbane disdain for the whole proceeding.

'That was my father's name! Have you forgotten that I killed him?'

'How can I forget it when you never allow me to? But I've heard – though not from you – that you had good reason. And it seems to me you must have cared for him once.'

That silenced his father, but what Corwynal did next silenced everyone. He asked Ealhith to be his wife. Marriage, as Aelfric had pointed out, wasn't about love or happiness or anything impossible like that. It was about children, and now he had a son.

And so, in his thirty-eighth year, Corwynal became husband to a girl he didn't love and father to a son he didn't know, thereby putting all prospect of happiness firmly behind him, killing it in the sight of the gods by oaths as binding as any he could imagine.

My husband. She couldn't think of him as that. He was just *him* – an impatient voice, dark hair falling into slate-blue eyes, ink-stained hands gripping the bridle of one of those terrifying horses, a rare smile that was rarely for her, the scent of leather and ink. Fragments of a man. Not *her* man. He made that clear that Midwinter night in the private chamber they'd been given.

'Why did you marry me?' she asked him.

'For the child,' he said evenly. 'Why did you agree?'

'For the child,' she retorted, and turned to the sleeping infant. He was called Caradawc now. She'd have to get used to that too.

'Shall I leave you alone?' he asked.

'Do you want to leave me alone?' In the flickering light of a beeswax candle, she could see nothing in his face but a profound weariness.

'I don't know. I'm not sure what you want from me, or if it's in me to give it to you, but I'll give you what I can.'

It wasn't what she'd been hoping for. She should send him away – it was clearly what he wanted – but if she did, she might never see him again. She began to unbraid her hair to hide how much her hands were shaking.

'You offer me the little that remains of you,' she said, turning from him to comb through her hair. When she finished, she put the comb down and took a deep breath. 'I suppose that's better than nothing, so explain to me how much is left. Tell me about the woman you left behind in Dalriada, then we need never speak of her again.'

'How do you know about that? Did that cursed brother of yours tell you?'

He had, actually, but she shook her head and lifted her hand to her scarred cheek.

'My dear Lord! It's as clear to me as this scar is to you.'

He slumped onto the pallet and dropped his head into his hands. Tears trickled through his fingers, and she remembered how he'd wept once before, so she sat beside him and put an arm about his shoulders. He turned to her and gripped her hard against him. Eventually, the shuddering of his body eased, and he moved away from her and lay down on the bed. She blew out the candle, lay beside him, and covered them both with the bed-furs. Then, in the dark of the longest night of the year, she listened while he told her everything.

A little after dawn she woke to find him lying next to her, watching her sleep. He didn't say anything but touched her face, the back of his fingers brushing the scar on her cheek, the line of her jaw and the curve of her brow. Her lips trembled as he touched them, and his hand drifted to rest on her throat, lightly, hesitantly. She was shuddering like a deer about to flee, and yet it was he who seemed poised to run. One wrong move on her part and he'd be gone, but she didn't know how to keep him, how to *be*.

She closed her eyes and thought back to the last time, so different from this. His hands had been sure then, uncaring of her response, his fingers hard in her flesh, insistent and demanding, the weight of him crushing her down. There had been pain too and something else that had made her cry out, half in terror, half in something she didn't have a name for. Now that same something was rising inside her, loosening and uncurling, his hesitant touch drawing it to life. This time there was a giving in him when that other time had been a taking of something long on offer, though he hadn't known it then.

Now he did, and perhaps it made a difference, for his hands, touching her, were leading her somewhere, pausing from time to time to see if she followed. And she *was* following. Then she was beside him, shoulder to shoulder, thigh to thigh, lip to lip, racing ahead like her heart. 'Wait,' he murmured. 'Wait . . .' But she couldn't wait. It had been too long, and the fire – for surely it was fire? – burned out of control, flaming right through her, in her breasts and belly, and she was crying out but not, this time, in pain. She was crying because she knew it couldn't last.

Nothing like this could ever last, neither pleasure, nor warmth, nor the slick of sweat between their bodies, nor the arch of her spine, nor his shuddering into her. But love could. She'd curl herself around it and keep it alive until he came back to her, because even as he slipped from her, turned his back and pretended to be asleep, she knew he'd leave. So she wept silently, unmoving, pretending she was asleep too, and in the end was so indeed. He was gone when she woke, leaving her with nothing but a cooling space at her back and a spill of seed in her womb – gone to the Fort at the End of the World.

PART III

DALRIADA

SPRING 487 AD

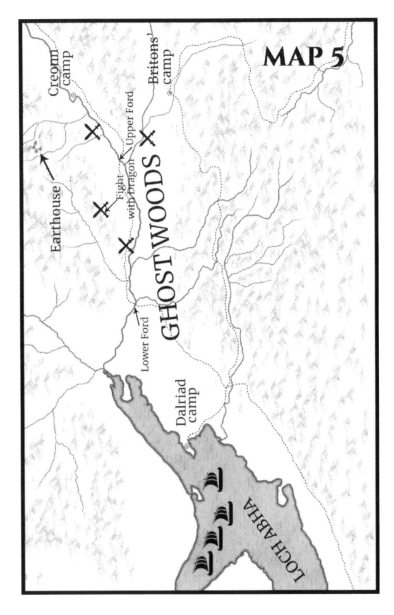

**THE BATTLE WITH THE CREONN
AND DRAGON-RIDERS**

THE RISE OF THE DRAGON

'Curse it, woman! Can't you give me something that works?!'

Brangianne ducked as the cup flew across Feargus' chamber and shattered against the wall behind her, splashing her with its contents and filling the room with the smell of hyssop.

They glared at one another, for they still weren't friends and hadn't been for the whole of that dreadful autumn, the bitter winter that had followed, and the long grey days of early spring.

'It *is* working,' she insisted crossly. 'A week ago, you didn't have the strength to throw things at me.'

He snorted and would have replied if a fit of coughing hadn't robbed him of breath. When it was over, he lay back against the pillows on his pallet, gasping for air. The lung fever that had swept Dunadd in the wake of unseasonal Beltein storms had reached into the royal chambers to strike at the King himself. But he was strong and stubborn, and Brangianne reckoned he was over the worst.

'If you'd swallow my medicine instead of throwing it at me, you'd soon be well enough to lead your army. I suppose that's what you're worrying about.'

'Navy,' he corrected her. 'This war will be won at sea, not on land.'

War. Such a little word for such a monstrous thing, and yet it was that little word that had brought her back to life.

Your brother's ill, Brangianne. Ciaran had sounded concerned but, floating in the grey cloud that had engulfed her since Samhain, she hadn't thought it mattered.

My father's really ill. Yseult's voice had cracked with fear, and still she hadn't cared.

The King's dying, Oonagh insisted. But Brangianne was dying too and didn't see why she should concern herself about a King.

War. The word had seeped into her cell, stealing through the shutters like a draught of icy air and penetrating the fog of her indifference. It had woken her from her sleep and set her feet on the long climb back into the light.

'Give me some more of that cursed stuff then!'

She poured Feargus another cup of the medicine she'd made him, a herbal infusion of hyssop and mallow sweetened with honey to soothe his cough. He took it with his usual scowl and, this time, drank it down, glowering at her over the rim as he did so, but he didn't fool her. He might be the man who'd schemed her life away, railed at her for her stupidity the previous summer, and threatened to send her to St Martin's with a demand that Ciaran confine her to the smallest cell he could find, but he was still her brother. He cared for her, as she cared for him, and she was about to tell him so and make them friends once more when the door from the hall opened and someone swept in, someone who smelled of salt wind and uncharacteristically stale clothes, a man who looked as if he hadn't slept in days.

'What are you doing here?' Feargus demanded, for he'd sent Ferdiad to Dun Ollie, stronghold of his foster-brother, Loarn, and told him to stay there until summoned.

'Bringing the King news. That's my role, isn't it? As your Royal Messenger?'

'A Royal Messenger who speaks on my behalf when it suits him.'

Despite the return of the tribute, Feargus still blamed Ferdiad for the death of The Morholt and his failure to capture Corwynal of Lothian, an act of treachery he hadn't forgiven Brangianne for either.

'Not on this occasion.' Ferdiad's normally mobile face was rigid.

'Well, out with it, man! If you've news about my foster-brother, let me have it.'

'Not about Loarn. News from further north. I went to Creonn territory—'

'I sent you to Dun Ollie—'

'—to spy on Loarn. But he's not important right now. The Creonn are.' Ferdiad had been standing over Feargus, but now he crouched beside his pallet. 'Listen, Feargus – Sire . . .' His voice was soft and persuasive, but though he tried to smile he failed, which unnerved Brangianne more than it should have. 'I was at their Beltein celebration,' Ferdiad said. 'I saw the Crann Tara go out among the clans and warriors begin to muster. I saw their fleets. They're gathering all along their coasts. It was rumour before, but now it's certain. By summer Dalriada will be at war.'

War! Brangianne's breath caught in her throat. Feargus had brushed the rumours aside, but now he smiled grimly. 'You tell me nothing I don't already know.'

Ferdiad rose to his feet. 'Then let me tell you this new thing.' There was something in his voice, a reluctance that turned her disquiet to fear. 'The Creonn spoke of old allies.'

The two men's eyes met, some understanding passing between them, but Brangianne didn't know what or who they were talking about.

'Old allies? Which old allies?'

Feargus didn't reply and, after a moment's silent regard, it was Ferdiad who answered. 'Dragon-riders.'

'But they're just a story!' Weren't they? Hadn't Feargus destroyed them twenty years before? It was what he'd always claimed. Had he been wrong?

'They're still a story,' Feargus said. 'A story compelling enough to convince a credulous Royal Messenger.'

Ferdiad's head snapped back. 'You can, with justification, accuse me of many things, but credulity isn't one of them, so please take me seriously. If the Dragon-riders are back, that means the Creonn will attack by land as well as by sea. Which means you need an army at the head of Loch Abha, because that's where they'll try to break into Dalriada, as they did once before.'

Feargus scowled at him, not believing Ferdiad, not wanting to believe him. But he wasn't a fool.

'Very well,' he said reluctantly. 'As a precaution, I'll send an army to the head of the loch to block the routes south.'

'An army with cavalry.'

'I don't *have* cavalry. And I won't need cavalry to defeat the Creonn. As for these Dragon-riders, did you see them with your own eyes?'

'No, but—'

'Then when you have, come back and tell me. Now get out!'

Ferdiad didn't move. 'You need cavalry, Feargus,' he said softly, but Feargus' eyes blazed.

'I don't, but if you're so convinced of it, then find me some!' he snarled.

'Is that an order or a suggestion?'

'I'm King of Dalriada, as you seem constantly to forget. I don't make suggestions. But do what you want. Go where you want. As long as you get out of my sight!' Then his furious gaze fell on Brangianne. 'Both of you! Get out of my sight!'

He might have said more, but his burst of temper had caught in his throat, and he began coughing once more. Ferdiad jerked his head at the door out to the terrace.

'Talk to him,' he said once the door slammed behind them and they were out in the open, away from anyone who might overhear. 'Make him believe in the Dragon-riders. You know why he doesn't, don't you? Because if he didn't defeat them as comprehensively as he likes to think, his rule of Dalriada is on uncertain foundations, and Loarn will take advantage of that. Remind him. He listens to you.'

'No, he doesn't,' she said sourly. 'Not anymore. Not since last summer. And that's *your* fault.'

It was the first time she'd seen Ferdiad since that desperate journey to Carnadail the previous autumn. When she'd returned, she'd secluded herself in St Martin's and had only recently emerged, and Ferdiad had been away in the north. So now she had a few things to say to him, and he must surely have expected her recriminations. Nevertheless, his mobile eyebrows shot up in mock surprise. 'I concealed certain secrets, yes, and the satisfying outcome was the tribute being returned. Everyone seems to have forgotten that. And I did as you asked – I let you have your summer of freedom.'

'And deliberately allowed me to . . . to . . .'

'Fall in love with an enemy?'

'I'm not in love with him! I hate him.'

He shrugged. 'He's in love with you.'

Was he? Could he be? Still? She pushed the thought away, but another took its place, something that hadn't occurred to her until now. 'Was that what you wanted? Was it your punishment for The Morholt? Did you *use* me to punish him?' Ferdiad spread his hands in mock apology, and blood pulsed behind her eyes. 'Feargus told you to get out of his sight. Now get out of mine!'

He smiled a smile of quite acrid sweetness. 'Willingly. But talk to Feargus. I hope I'm wrong, but if I'm right, he really does need help.'

Like her brother, she didn't want to believe the Fili, so scowled and turned her back on him. He said nothing more, and when she looked around, he'd gone, slipping from the Royal Terrace as softly as the snake he was, leaving her to pace back and forth, her skirts brushing the herbs she'd planted between the outcrops, thyme and hyssop, weld and self-heal. It was almost exactly a year since Yseult had paced this same terrace, furious at not being included in Feargus' council, while Brangianne had huddled against the wall, beset by nothing more alarming than a vague apprehension.

Now everything was different. *She* was different. *You need to begin living once more*, Ciaran had said that day a year ago. So she'd done just that, and what a life it had been, full of joy and sorrow and everything in between. But it wasn't over; she had more life to live, and there would certainly be sorrow, if little joy – she no longer believed in joy – but there might be quiet satisfaction in becoming the woman she'd always intended to be, with taking life in her quite capable hands and wresting from it something for herself.

There, on Dunadd's Royal Terrace, beneath a duck-egg blue sky streaked with the feathers of high white cloud that presaged a change in the weather, with the scent of healing herbs all around her and the horns of war blaring in her future, Brangianne finally knew who she truly was. The woman who'd lain herself down on the hard pallet in the little cell at St Martin's and dreamed away the winter was gone, leaving behind the woman she was meant to be – not lover or mother, not sister or daughter or aunt, but herself, Brangianne the Healer. And this time, in this war, no-one, especially her brother, was going to stop her being that woman.

'He said no,' Ferdiad announced, after strolling into Blaize's draughty little room in Iuddeu's citadel and throwing himself on the pallet.

'Of course he said no!' Blaize retorted, poking the brazier into life. It was always cold in Iuddeu, even in summer. 'I told you you were wasting your time.'

Ferdiad had arrived close to nightfall on a wet and blustery day in the middle of May, sodden, exhausted and stinking of horses, but determined to speak with Arthyr as soon as he arrived.

'I don't suppose he believed you,' Blaize added.

'Oh, he believed me! I haven't entirely lost my touch,' Ferdiad said with a hint of asperity.

To Blaize's annoyance, Arthyr had wanted to see Ferdiad alone, but he knew how it would have gone. He could hear Ferdiad's honeyed compelling voice, see his sweeping gestures, and imagine himself caught up in the sheer poetry of his story. Blaize had his own skills in telling a tale and could paint a picture in words. He could show men the blood and the colour of the sky, make them hear the cries and the birdsong. But Ferdiad had the power to force men to *feel* what had happened too. In the end, however, it had made no difference. Arthyr had no desire to see Dalriada fall, but he couldn't spare the men. With the ending of the Beltein truce, the Caledonians had begun to raid all along the frontier, and so, as Blaize had warned Ferdiad, Arthyr had said no.

'Are you sure you're right about the Creonn?' he asked the Fili.

'Of course I'm sure! Two months up and down the whole of the western seaboard when I swear it rained every single day.' He shuddered at the memory, and Blaize didn't blame him. He'd travelled into the Creonn lands himself many years before, but they wouldn't have changed. Mountains swept scree-strewn slopes down to dark sea-lochs that thrust long fingers of water deep into the mountainous country. There were few landing places, and many rocky peninsulas, dangerous reefs and raging currents. It was a land lived on the margins, where, as in Dalriada, people travelled by sea rather than land, for the forests were ancient and impenetrable, and the only way to move about the interior was by trackways on the ridges where pine and juniper woods were more open, but those were blocked with snow for half the year. Small wonder the Creonn coveted the rich lowlands of Dalriada.

Blaize sighed. 'Once the Creonn came to terms with the Carnonacs, I suppose it was just a matter of time.'

'Agreed. But that isn't all. Not this time. They spoke of old allies . . .'

A cold hand took hold of Blaize's guts and squeezed. So it was true. He shouldn't have discounted Ciaran's fears of the previous year.

Ferdiad eyed him sharply. 'You knew about the Riders?'

'Ciaran heard rumours last spring,' Blaize admitted. 'But I didn't believe him.'

Ferdiad rolled to his feet, his brows snapping together. 'And no-one thought to tell me? What am I, Blaize? Some little boy who can't be trusted to keep a secret? Feargus may treat me like a messenger, but I'm rather more than that. I'm Dalriada's Fili!'

'You haven't always behaved like Dalriada's Fili! That business with Galloway last year—'

Ferdiad's face turned white; his lips were bloodless, his eyes glittering balefully. 'If you mention The Morholt—' he said softly, '—you will regret it.'

Blaize looked up at the younger man, twenty years his junior, unarmed perhaps, but still dangerous. Nevertheless, certain things had to be said. 'I hadn't intended mentioning him but, since you bring it up, I'll remind you that in the wake of that whole sorry episode you were in no condition to be trusted with anything. All that concerned you was some stupid oath of vengeance you'd sworn. Well, you've had your revenge, so perhaps you could turn your attention to more serious matters.'

'Have I, Blaize?' Ferdiad asked narrowly. He subsided back onto Blaize's pallet and leant against the wall, linking his hands behind his head. 'Do you really think I've had my revenge?'

'If you wanted to break Corwynal's heart, you've done it.'

Ferdiad snorted. 'He did that himself. All I did was stand aside and let him do it.'

'If you'd told him who Brangianne was, it wouldn't have happened.'

'Which is why I didn't. But he'll know who she is by now.'

'He doesn't, because I didn't tell him. There didn't seem any point, given that he'll never see her again. Anyway, the idiot boy's married now.'

Ferdiad smiled. 'So I heard. A child too. Fast work for a man with a broken heart or . . .' He paused and narrowed his eyes. '. . . could it be this marriage was a mistake? Is that why she's here in Iuddeu and he isn't?'

'Leave him alone. Be satisfied with what you've done already.'

'But I'm never satisfied. It was Trystan who killed The Morholt, so by rights I ought to break his heart too.'

Blaize laughed at that. 'Trystan doesn't have a heart to break! Oh, yes, I know you tried. That was why you took Yseult to Carnadail, wasn't it?'

Ferdiad shrugged. 'Maybe. If so, I misjudged her powers of attraction and his susceptibility. It doesn't, however, mean I've given up.'

'For the gods' sake, Ferdiad, there are more important matters to think about! Does Feargus know about the Dragon-riders?'

'Yes, but he didn't believe me, or didn't want to. He flew into one of his passionate rages and told me he wasn't going to listen to rumours and that I should go and see for myself. So I did.'

Blaize stared at him. 'You went to their old lands?' That would have been no easy journey. The Dragon-riders' lands, long since abandoned, lay in the high moorland of the interior, west of Atholl and east of the Creonn mountains, north of Dalriada. A hard land for a hard people.

'I did – and they're back. I got close enough to smell their cooking fires and the dung of their horses, close enough to hear their smithies beating out weapons.' He dropped his voice to a whisper. 'Close enough to see The Dragon himself.'

The Dragon himself! The fabled leader of the Riders, a man who, unlike his men, whose helmets were crowned with the horns of animals, stags, boar, ancient cattle, wore a gold-washed helmet in the shape of a creature that didn't exist – a beast with wings of leather, a beast that breathed fire.

'You're sure it was him?'

The younger man threw up a hand in disgust. 'You doubt me too? Feargus accused me of credulity, but I'm not making this up because I like a good story. I saw the Riders, and I saw the Dragon. I recognised him.'

'You recognised him? From where? When?'

Ferdiad leant back into the shadows, his face closed. 'Why should I tell you when you don't believe anything I say? When no-one trusts me?'

There was a bitterness in his voice he'd succeeded in keeping out of his face. So when Ferdiad got to his feet and announced his intention of relieving Blaize of his unwelcome presence by leaving immediately, he felt a wave of sympathy. The man was swaying with exhaustion.

'It's a long way back to Dalriada. You'll make more speed if you wait until the morning and find yourself a better horse than the spavined creature you rode in on,' he said irritably. 'You can take mine, and my bedchamber too. I'll make do with the hall.'

'Why Blaize, how generous! Despite that gruff exterior, you care after all! Who'd have thought it?'

Blaize watched Ferdiad sink back on his pallet and stretch out his legs, his green eyes already flickering into much needed sleep. He stood for a while, looking down at the younger man, at Ferdiad the Snake – charming, fickle, dangerous and enigmatic, a man impossible to trust, impossible to love, impossible to hate.

'It was a good day, wasn't it?'

Trystan pushed his platter away, leant back in his chair, put his feet up on the trestle table in the fort's hall and stretched wearily, stifling a yawn as he did so.

'For a change,' Corwynal agreed.

There had been times when he'd wondered if the garrison at The Fort at the End of the World would make it through the winter, but the laggard spring had finally arrived, and now the trees were almost all in leaf, the fields thick with young shoots of barley and rye, and the woods were perfumed with drifts of bluebells. Days were lengthening and birds sang through the long still evenings. The fort had been rebuilt, the new recruits trained to defend it, and not before time. The Venicon of Circind had begun raiding across the frontier, and it could only get worse as the year went on.

But that was for the future. For the moment, a successful day's hunting was reason enough to celebrate, especially since the long-awaited supply wagon-train had arrived from Iuddeu with a draft of horses and, more importantly, a couple of barrels of ale.

'Let's hope the Venicon don't attack us now,' Corwynal observed, for few of their men were entirely sober. On one side of the fort's draughty hall, a dog fight had begun, and Kaerherdin and some of the recruits had waded in to break it up. On the other, two men were wrestling, with Aelfric adjudicating, and bets were being taken. Someone, sooner or later, would ask Trystan to sing, and tonight he might even agree, for he was in a better mood than he'd been in all winter.

'They won't if our sentries are doing their jobs, and—' He looked up, eyes narrowing, as the door to the hall opened, banishing, for a moment, the warm fug of smoke, ale, grease and the stench of damp clothes. But it wasn't a sentry come to warn them of an attack. It was a single man, a traveller by the look of him. 'Oh, good!' Trystan exclaimed. 'I won't have to sing after all.'

The traveller had a battered harp under one arm, a ragged cloak over his shoulders, and a greasy cap pulled down over his hair. He was a disreputable looking fellow but was greeted with enthusiasm by the men in the hall, dragged to the fire and pressed down onto a stool, and a platter of meat and a horn of ale were thrust into his hands. But the harper barely had time to swallow a few mouthfuls before the chanting began. 'A song! A song!' The man held up a hand and, once silence had fallen, plucked a single chord on the harp. The notes rippled around the hall, and when the echo faded away the man began to sing. He had a good voice, but Corwynal knew the song, and he stopped listening. There were other matters to think about, matters he'd avoided all winter.

I have a wife and a son. Sometimes he'd forget, and then, without warning, it would come rushing back, rocking the world as it did so. His marriage to Ealhith, the impulse of a moment, had been a mistake, and he'd known it almost immediately. Now he was going to have to live with the consequences.

I'll never see her again. But he was thinking of Brangianne rather than Ealhith. It was over, and he should try to forget her as she must have forgotten him.

The hall was revolving gently around him, but he wasn't so drunk he didn't know he'd regret it in the morning if he had any more. He decided to slip away while the harper was still singing and got to his feet. Only then did he notice that the song had changed, that the language was different.

He was moving before he knew it, but Trystan was ahead of him, vaulting across the table and striding over to the harper who, seeing him approach, laid his harp down and pulled off the cap to let his silver hair cascade over his shoulders. And so Corwynal knew it wasn't over after all.

'What in the Five Hells are you doing here?!'

Corwynal hauled the Fili to his feet and would have demanded an explanation there and then, but Trystan forestalled him.

'Not here!' he hissed and jerked his head at the door that led from the hall to his own quarters. They were cramped, uncomfortable, and cold, but had the advantage of privacy. Ferdiad pulled himself out of Corwynal's grasp and strolled towards the door. Once in Trystan's chamber, he sat on the pallet and crossed his legs.

'What was I doing?' His expression was one of wounded innocence. 'I was entertaining you and your men, until I was interrupted so rudely.'

Trystan closed the door behind him, leant his shoulders against it, and folded his arms across his chest.

'Answer Corwynal's question. What are you doing here?'

'Perhaps I came to get my harp back,' Ferdiad said with a shrug. 'This one—' He gestured to the battered harp he'd laid beside him. '—is useless. You might have noticed.'

'You didn't come all this way for a harp,' Corwynal said, leaning on the back of the single chair in the room.

'All what way?'

'From Dalriada, I imagine.'

'Then your imagination is faulty. I didn't come from Dalriada. I've been in the north. The Crann Tara has gone out among the Caledonians, by the way, but I expect you know that already.'

'We do. So if you came to bring such old news you've wasted your time.'

'Why does everyone worry so much about how much of my time I waste? It's my time, after all. But I haven't come to bring you that particular news. I've been further west and north.' He threw Corwynal a glinting smile. 'Not Atholl. Not yet. No, I was in Creonn country, and they too are gathering for war.'

'Against the Carnonacs? That's hardly news either.'

'Creonn? Carnonacs?' Trystan asked, puzzled.

'Caledonian tribes from the western seaboard,' Corwynal explained. 'They've been fighting one another for generations.'

'And are fighting no longer,' Ferdiad said. 'So now the Creonn have turned their attention to the South – to Dalriada, to avenge a twenty-year-old defeat. Already their ships have put to sea, and the clans are on the move. Only the weather can hold them back now. Feargus defeated them before, but he can't defeat them this time, not without help.'

Ferdiad leant forward, his green eyes glittering. 'Because they're not coming alone. They have allies who won't be content with a summer's plundering. Allies who also want revenge for that twenty-year-old defeat. Allies who'll push on south for Dunadd, burning and slaughtering as they go, allies who'll leave nothing behind but a wasteland of ash and wailing women.'

Brangianne! It was Corwynal's only thought. Brangianne was in danger, and Trystan must have understood it too for he paled, and his voice, when he spoke, was urgent.

'Who are these allies?'

But it was to Corwynal that Ferdiad looked. 'Dragon-riders,' he said softly.

'I thought they were all dead!'

'So did everyone in Dalriada. But some must have survived the defeat Feargus inflicted on them, and I assume they've been in the North ever since. Now, however, they're back in their old lands, with The Dragon himself leading them.' He met Corwynal's appalled gaze and dropped his voice to a whisper. 'I've seen the gold armour and the dragon helmet. I've seen the man's face.'

The years fell away. Trystan's cramped room vanished, and Corwynal was back among the mountains, the black peaks echoing to the sound of steel on steel, the smell of oiled weapons at the back of his throat. *The Dragon!*

'It can't be the same man!'

'It is.'

'What are you talking about?' Trystan demanded. 'What are Dragon-riders? Who's the Dragon?'

Corwynal didn't know where to start, and it was Ferdiad who explained.

'The Dragon-riders are horsemen, armoured cavalry, mercenaries. Their origins are forgotten, except by themselves, but they have strange names and customs, and mark their faces with beasts no-one has ever seen. Twenty years ago the Creonn bought their services to fight Dalriada, but Feargus destroyed them, a surprise attack in a place that wasn't easy for horsemen. He drove them into Loch Abha and most of them were killed, though not The Dragon himself. It's said he can't be killed except by himself, and that's what happened. Once defeat was inevitable, he took his own life by drowning himself in the loch, rather than give Feargus the satisfaction of killing him. But there's always a new Dragon to replace the old, and he leads the Riders now, a man who's never been defeated in single combat, except once and that wasn't by a man. It was by a boy. How old was he, Corwynal, do you remember?'

'Fifteen,' he said, understanding now why the Fili had come to the Fort at the End of the World.

Trystan was frowning at him. 'How do you know about this? Who was the boy?'

'Me,' he said resignedly. 'It was me.'

'You can't be serious! Not *Eoghan!*' Brangianne objected, but not, on this occasion, to Eoghan as a potential husband. This time it was because Feargus had decided to give command of the land army to his Steward.

All his experienced men and commanders, his personal household guard, everyone who'd survived the war two years before against the Britons, were to join Feargus' navy that, even now, was mustering in Crionan and other harbours up and down Dalriada's west coast. Those that were left, old soldiers and untrained boys, had been put under Eoghan's command, a man with no experience of war.

'He's a good organiser. That's half the battle.'

'What about the other half? Can you imagine Eoghan actually fighting?'

Feargus' lips had twitched at the image of Eoghan – who'd had some rather fancy armour made for himself – getting his flashy sword dirty. 'A good commander delegates. I expect Eoghan to do the same. There are sufficient men of experience to advise him.'

But would Eoghan take that advice? She'd regarded Feargus narrowly, suspecting him of being up to something, as he so often was. 'Why Eoghan?'

She'd tracked Feargus down to Dunadd's lower terrace where

he'd been watching some of his household warriors sparring. Now he turned to her and scowled but didn't reply.

'I'm going to keep asking you – very loudly – until you give me an answer,' she warned him, whereupon he jerked his head at the rampart and leapt up the stairs, leaving her panting in his wake.

'Because I need him, as I needed him before,' he replied once they were alone. 'For his men, this time.'

'Tribute-gatherers,' she pointed out. 'Not warriors.'

'But loyal to Eoghan. It's numbers I need, a substantial-looking army to occupy the river valley at the head of Loch Abha and make the Creonn think twice about attacking Dalriada from the north. However, if it comes to fighting, I'll expect Eoghan to get word to me so I can come and deal with the Creonn myself, though I'm likely to be hard-pressed all along the coast.'

'And the price? Eoghan won't be doing this for nothing. What have you promised him this time? Not me again, I hope.'

'You're still betrothed to Eoghan until I say otherwise,' he said sharply, but she met look with look.

'You know there's a rumour that you'll give Yseult to any man who wins this war for you?'

Feargus' eyes slid away, so she knew where that rumour had originated.

'Eoghan can choose to believe it if he likes,' he said curtly. 'Although it's ridiculous, of course. Only one man will defeat the Creonn, and that's me. Only one man has ever defeated the Dragon-riders, and that's me too.'

'Then deny the offer.'

'I will, once I no longer need Eoghan. And once I no longer need him, I'll deal with his misplaced ambition. Sooner or later, he'll make a mistake he'll regret. Now, have done, Brangianne. This war has nothing to do with you.' He gave her a quick piercing look. 'Nor will it.'

'I know your opinion on the matter,' she assured him. 'But I assume I'm permitted to pray for your victory?'

He'd regarded her thoughtfully but nodded his assent, and so she'd gone to St Martin's, though not to pray.

'Eoghan's army – I want to go with it,' she told Ciaran. 'And, no, I don't have Feargus' permission. I wasn't stupid enough to ask for it. I'm going whether he likes it or not.' They were in Ciaran's private orchard where a blackbird was singing from the branches of a cherry, and a little wind had got up, shaking the blossom and carrying with it the green smell of spring, of new beginnings. It didn't feel like a day to talk about the brutalities of war.

'I don't expect you're going to ask Eoghan either.'

'Of course not! But I have to go, and please don't tell me it's dangerous. I *know* it is, and I'm terrified. Feargus insists there won't be any fighting, not on land, but I have a bad feeling about this, and I'm not going to be left behind. If men are hurt, I can only help them if I'm able to treat them immediately, not weeks later when sickness has got into their wounds. You know that.'

Ciaran nodded, but not, she thought, in agreement. His dark eyes were distant and thoughtful, and seemed to be looking into the future and searching for a pattern there. Eventually, he got to his feet and moved over to a small table, on which stood a board scattered with counters, an unfinished game of Fidchell.

'Do you play, Brangianne?'

'Badly.'

'Even so, take a look at this game.'

The pieces were familiar, the warrior and the queen, the ship and the poet, the tree and the fortress. Half of the pieces were carved from bleached ash, half from black bog oak, but the board, normally made of alternate squares of those two woods was a single sheet of pale birch marked with what looked like deep scratches.

'Do you recognise it?'

Brangianne shook her head; she'd never seen a board like this before.

'It's a map,' he explained, 'and this—' He touched a fortress piece. '—is where we are now.'

It was a moment before she understood. The fortress with the swan sign was Dunadd, and what she'd taken for scratches were coasts, rivers and mountains. Other fortress pieces were positioned on the board in places that now made sense – Loarn's stronghold of Dun Ollie, marked with the gull, Oenghus' stronghold of Dun Bhoraraig on The Isle with its sea-eagle sign. North of Dunadd was the long finger of Loch Abha, and it was at the west of this loch, near the southern end, that Ciaran set a piece that, unlike the rest, was made of silver. The druid piece normally bore the sign of the snake, but in this particular set the snake had legs and wings and a tongue that forked like a flame. Ciaran rested his fingertips on the piece, his face grave and stern. Outside in the courtyard the blackbird went on singing, and the life of the monastery murmured away as it always did, but Brangianne felt as if a bell had begun to ring, impossibly far away but insistent in its summons – or warning.

'You understand the value of the Druid piece?'

'Of course. It's a wild piece and can be played by either side.'

He picked up the silver disc and turned it over in his fingers.

'This token will call such a piece into the game. So, yes, I'll help you go to war, Brangianne, and without Feargus' knowledge, but I expect you to help me in return. I want you to travel to the monastery of St Torran on Loch Abha and find a man who calls himself Father Adarn.'

An odd name for a priest, she thought, for it meant one who was proud.

'A priest? Not a druid?'

He smiled gravely. 'I'm not sure what he is.' He held the silver disc out to her. 'Give this to him and tell him that sanctuary is over and the world awaits.'

'That's all?' She was oddly reluctant to take the silver piece from him, as if by doing so the world would change.

'That's all, but make certain you have the words right. "Sanctuary is over and the world awaits." He'll understand.'

'What will he do?'

Ciaran leant back in his chair, a bleak expression of fear and doubt flickering across his face and, as she took the disc, Brangianne heard once more the plangent warning of a bell swinging in the wind.

'I don't know,' he said grimly. 'Kill someone? Save everyone? Both? Neither? I wish I knew.'

They'd come for them at Samhain, the Night of Endings, which was fitting, since as the old year died so had they. The boys they'd been were gone, the men they'd become not yet born. For the whole of the night that lay between one year and the next, one life and the next, they'd been nothing. In the morning, in the dawn of the first day of the New Year, all over the Kingdoms of the North, boys like him had begun their journeys, travelling by winter to the Island of Eagles to become the men fate had decreed them to be – warrior or bard, priest or king. They'd have no choice in the matter, he'd been told.

They took away their names first of all, then their countries, their futures, their histories, their memories, and any reason they had for pride. All of that would have to be won back, to be fought for.

I'm Corwynal, son of Rifallyn, King of Lothian. You can't take that from me. *But he didn't say it aloud. He stood in silence with the others, in the training ring of the Island camp, shivering in the thin unbleached tunic he'd been given, and felt the mountains, black and riven with water and cloud, loom over him. He was eight years old.*

Wolf. That was the name they gave him. Other boys were given the names of different creatures – hare or otter, salmon or sea-mew. 'The Wolf of Lothian', he'd thought, satisfied with his new name until he discovered he had to earn that too. Until then he was nothing more than "boy" They were there to work, to learn, to become whatever the gods had chosen for them. But Corwynal had already chosen for himself. I'll be a warrior. I'll return to Lothian and lay my sword and skills at my father's feet, and this time he won't send me away. *As yet, however, he had neither skill nor sword. All he had was a wooden foil sheathed with so much lead he could barely lift it.*

'But you will *lift it. You* will *fight with it. You'll fight with wood and lead until you're ready for steel, and it's I who'll decide when you're ready.' The fighting master was a tall young man with a face patterned with swirling tattoos unlike anything Corwynal had seen among the Caledonians. He had the glittering brown-gold eyes of a sparrow hawk, a great beak of a nose, a crest of stiff red hair, and, marked across his face, the tattoo of a beast Corwynal didn't recognise. He had the name of a beast too, but it wasn't Eagle or Hawk or anything else Corwynal might have imagined. This man had the name of a creature he'd neither seen nor heard of. 'I am called The Dragon.'*

'. . . and I'm tired of it! Do you hear me? Corwynal? Are you listening?'

Abruptly, he was back in Trystan's little room at the Fort at the End of the World, and they were alone now. Ferdiad had been sent back to the hall, Aelfric and Kaerherdin told to guard him, and Trystan was pacing back and forth ranting at Corwynal.

'You've done this to me all my life! Kept secrets about things you must know I'd want to hear about. You say this man taught you to fight, as you taught me. Didn't you think I might have been *interested* in that?!'

'It was a long time ago,' Corwynal said weakly. He'd told Trystan no more than the bare facts, that The Dragon had indeed taught him to fight, and in one of their practice bouts he'd managed to defeat him, to everyone's surprise, including his own. It wasn't the whole story, of course.

'Yes, over twenty years ago,' Trystan agreed. 'And you're, what, almost forty now? You're *old*, Corwynal. You can't fight that sort of battle anymore. Whatever Ferdiad's come here for, it's not you, at least not just you.'

'I'm not going to fight – not that I couldn't or wouldn't if I had to – but because The Dragon owes me, and, if he remembers, it could make a difference. So I'm going with Ferdiad. I have to. A threat to Dalriada is a threat to Brangianne.'

'A woman who hates you.'

'It doesn't matter.'

Trystan smiled grimly. 'No, I suppose not. But Ferdiad didn't come here for just one man. He didn't say so, but I suspect he's already been to Arthyr, who would have turned him down. Arthyr has no reason to help Dalriada, but we do. You love Brangianne, and I owe her my life. And there are other people in Dalriada we care about, people who'll be in danger if Dalriada is defeated. Oonagh, for example, and that silly girl Ethlin. None of them deserve what happens to women when a stronghold is sacked.' He stopped abruptly, his fists clenching. 'Which is why I'm going too.'

Corwynal stared at him, aghast. 'You can't strip the fort of men, not at a time like this! Arthyr trusted you with this command. Your reputation would be ruined and—' He stopped, understanding. 'That's what Ferdiad wants. Don't you see? He doesn't do anything for only one reason. He's here to tempt you to make this mistake.'

'No, Corwynal. He cares about Dalriada, perhaps as much as you care about Lothian. Even what happened with The Morholt was for Dalriada. Whatever lies in the past, and whatever he may plan for the future, Ferdiad needs our help because Dalriada needs our help. As for my reputation, such as it is, I'm not such a fool as to weaken Arthyr's frontier. Between us we've made a strong fort and trained the men to defend it, to fight when the time comes, and to lead. They don't need us here, but Dalriada does.'

'You just said Ferdiad didn't come for one – or two – men.'

Trystan smiled for the first time, the light of battle in his eyes. 'No, of course not. Ferdiad came for horsemen to fight these Dragon-riders, and where are the best horsemen in the Britons' Kingdoms? Kicking their heels in Selgovia because Essylt won't let them join me – unless I go in person and ask her.' His smile faltered a little. 'So that's what I'll do. I'll go to Selgovia and get down on my knees to . . . to my wife. And I will beg.'

12

THE BLACKSMITH OF ST TORRAN'S

O nce she got used to the sheer number of people, Oonagh grew quite fond of Dunadd. She liked the bustle of the place and how she, as the Princesses' companion, was treated with the respect she'd always thought she deserved. She was happy there, except when she allowed herself to think about a certain Angle. But she didn't do that too often. He was in the past, like all the men in her life.

The news that there was going to be a war with the Creonn had come as a shock. *Not again!* It had been her first thought. She didn't talk about it, but she was from the North and had lived through the first war. News of this new war had unleased a floodtide of memories she thought she'd forgotten – the settlement on the river, the isolated farm on the high ground, thatch burning, stock slaughtered, a smell of charred flesh in her lungs as, with her mother, she'd fled from the smoking ruin of her home. She'd only been a girl at the time, a girl who'd turned into a woman who didn't want to remember anything about that time, especially one person in particular. *I'll never forgive you!*

'Do you still have family there?' Brangianne asked.

'No-one has family there.' Everyone had fled that war, and the settlements were deserted now, only ghosts remaining to wander the ruins.

She and Brangianne were in the infirmary at St Martin's, rolling bandages, rather a lot of bandages, Oonagh had thought to begin with. Now she wondered if there would be enough.

'I'm going with the army, Oonagh, one way or another,' Brangianne said, laying down her roll.

A choice was being given, Oonagh understood, but she didn't hesitate. Her son had died without someone to hold his hand, and she wasn't going to let that happen to other mothers' sons. 'So am I.'

'It won't be easy,' Brangianne warned her, but Oonagh didn't expect war to be easy. 'I mean getting away. My brother . . . I haven't asked him. He thinks I'm going to St Torran's Sanctuary on Loch Abha to pray for victory. I've a message to deliver to someone there, and then we'll join the army. Ciaran has an idea of how we can do that . . .'

Ciaran! She meant the Abbot, a man Oonagh didn't trust. Always smiling, always reasonable, endlessly understanding and forgiving. But Oonagh thought there was steel inside him, and those eyes . . . She felt as if he could see into her soul, that he knew everything there was to know about her. Ridiculous, of course. Nevertheless, she was unnerved when he drew her to one side later that day.

'I've asked Brangianne to deliver a message to a . . . a colleague. I'd very much like you to be with her when she does so.'

'Why?' Suspicion came easily to Oonagh. 'Is this colleague dangerous?'

The Abbot smiled his usual gentle smile. 'In his own way. As you are in your own way, Oonagh.'

She flushed at that, more certain than ever that he knew more than he ought. That raider in Carnadail, the one she'd killed so . . . comprehensively. It still haunted her.

So she'd agreed, and a few days later she and Brangianne

travelled north with that toad of a Steward's army, heading for St Torran's, together with a couple of healers from St Martin's, a wagon full of medical supplies, and an extremely uncooperative addition to their party.

'I don't know why you had to bring that animal,' Oonagh complained as they approached the ford over the river that flowed into the southern end of the loch, grateful they wouldn't have to persuade The Devil to enter the shallow but fast flowing water, since he'd objected to everything for most of their plodding journey north from Dunadd.

'He's a warhorse, and this is a war. He'll be useful.'

Oonagh didn't agree. She suspected The Lady had had him shipped from Carnadail – at great expense, given the damage not only to the horse-transport but the horse-handler – because the animal reminded her of that cursed Caledonian. Right then, the animal was more of a hindrance than a help, though he tolerated Brangianne because the Caledonian had trained him to do so, and Oonagh because ... well, just because. But he'd let no-one else ride him.

Yseult, predictably, had been furious when she'd seen the horse in Dunadd. Unlike Brangianne, she didn't want to be reminded of Carnadail, and was even more resentful when she learned that Brangianne and Oonagh intended joining Eoghan's army.

'*I* should be going. *I* should be leading this army, not Eoghan. Instead, I'm stuck in Dunadd.'

'Leading your father's Council,' Brangianne reminded her, for this last moment concession by the King had reconciled Yseult to being left behind, if only a little.

'But not making decisions,' she complained.

'Not yet, but if you do well, things will be different once the war's over.'

Things are always different once a war's over, Oonagh thought, *but rarely for the better*.

It was late in the day and the sunset was flaring across the loch by the time the small party from St Martin's approached the Sanctuary of St Torran, having left the army, which had crossed the ford to camp further east. Oonagh had been quietly satisfied. Not for them a tent in a wet meadow. Instead, they'd have comfortable beds and a hot meal, for surely St Torran's would be like St Martin's, a place of order and cleanliness, noisy with all those bells they insisted on ringing, but peaceful nevertheless, a gracious place, not luxurious of course, but somewhere with beds free of bedbugs, and food that was edible. St Torran's, sadly, was none of these things.

'This is going to be fun!' Oonagh looked around the cramped and dusty guest hut they'd been given and wasn't impressed. No fire had been lit, and the walls were bare, the floor covered with stale rushes. The pallets were lumpy and smelled of mould and old sweat.

'We're not here to have fun. And it's just for one night. Once I've found this Father Adarn and given him the message, we'll re-join the army.'

Oonagh didn't think it would be that easy; surely someone would notice if a Royal Lady went missing? But once she met the monks of St Torran's she understood why Ciaran had been so confident about their ability to escape detection. The monks were old, for the most part, and silent too, shaven-headed sterile old men whose thoughts were on the afterlife they all went on about. They barely looked at the two women, their reluctant guests for the night. The Abbot of St Torran's was like his monks, a painfully thin old man in a dirty habit who looked through them as if they weren't there. Women, Oonagh understood, had no place in the monks' world and so were invisible. Getting away from St Torran's to join the army was going to be easy after all. First, however, they had to find this Father Adarn.

'Father Adarn?' the Abbot said vaguely. 'Father Adarn . . .' He seemed unable to call a face to the name. Was he senile? Blind? Then light dawned, slow and reluctant, and he scowled, but eventually, as if some long-forgotten manners had flickered into life, he relented. 'He's our blacksmith, so I expect he's in the forest.' He waved a dirty hand towards the woods beyond the northern gate. 'With his children.'

Oonagh snorted. Not so sterile after all, these shaven-headed priests! They were still men under their filthy robes, and this Father Adarn was nothing more than a man with children. How dangerous could he be?

On a bright spring evening with the birds singing, it was easy to feel confident, but when they left St Torran's the following morning after an uncomfortable night, Oonagh didn't feel so sanguine.

The Sanctuary of St Torran dissolved behind them into the early morning mist; ahead, the forest loomed, part of the Ghost Woods that clothed the shores of Loch Abha. Oonagh was unnerved by the shifting grey shadows between the trees, but a little trodden path ran into the wood from the Sanctuary, a path trodden by men, not ghosts. Nevertheless, the forest was unsettling, the trees festooned with beards of lichen that moved fitfully in a little wind that brought with it the smell of smoke – and other things. A strange foxy scent pervaded the wood, and, ringing through the trees, came the cries of birds Oonagh hadn't heard in years, odd little fluting notes. As they edged their way along the winding narrowing path, she was convinced eyes were watching them from the shadows. She heard Brangianne swallow hard, and her own heart banged against her breastbone.

'Don't be such a coward!' she scolded herself, and Brangianne laughed weakly, but the laughter fell heavily into the silence and died away, dulled by the mist, as if the forest – or those watching eyes – didn't approve of laughter.

Don't these priest's children laugh? Oonagh wondered, as they moved on along the path and into a little clearing where, to her relief, the shadows drew back – but only to allow something else to enter. Between one moment and the next, the empty clearing was peopled with the very children Oonagh had been wondering about, children dressed in skins decorated with twigs and feathers, and strings of dried berries, children who bore themselves proudly, and who carried weapons too – wicked little spears, bows of polished yew, and quivers of arrows tipped black as if dipped in poison.

'God in Heaven!' Brangianne murmured. Oonagh stared at the creatures who'd emerged not from the wood but from memories she was no longer sure about. They must be the Forest People, the Children of the Ghost Woods, but though they came no higher than her shoulder they were certainly no children. She'd always thought of them as nothing but a story, but clearly they were real for there was no mistaking their smell, that foxy scent, or the fluting sound that must be their speech, which grew animated as they drew closer, pointing at them and muttering to one another as they did so.

We should run! she thought. If this Father Adarn was one of them, Oonagh wanted nothing to do with him. But it was too late to run. The Children of the Ghost Wood had closed in behind them, and the only escape was onwards, deeper into the wood, towards a building that appeared out of the mist in a wider clearing, a building open on one side, and in which a fire belched smoke and heat and red-hot metal was being beaten. The hammer was wielded by a blacksmith, a tall man, broad across the shoulders, a great deal bigger than the little Forest people. He was wearing the habit of the monks of St Torran's, the hood drawn up despite the heat of the forge, though his arms were bare, powerful sweat-streaked arms whose muscles rippled in the flamelight as he worked. And he was humming.

That was when Oonagh knew she'd been tricked. By her assumptions, by the past, by Abbot Ciaran.

You evil old man! You knew!

She hadn't been ready for the Children and she wasn't ready for this. *Run! Before it's too late.* But she was rooted to the ground and, when he lifted his head to look at her, she saw from within the hood's shadows a gleam of the golden eyes that had glimmered through a lifetime of nightmares.

The humming stopped abruptly. *Why that song?* Oonagh wondered. Then the man threw back his head and laughed.

Her feet freed themselves, unlocked by that laughter, the harsh cawing croak of a raven, and she whirled and ran, pushed past the little people and sprinted along the path away from the forge, away from a past that was the past no longer, away from promises that had never been kept, nor ever would be.

'So,' Essylt began. 'Tell me about the woman who healed Trystan.'

She and Corwynal were in Hoel's private apartments at the back of Meldon's hall, a room once full of fire and light, with richly woven tapestries on the walls and tables on which had stood gold-rimmed cups filled with the deep red wine Hoel had loved. The place used to be scented with apple-wood burning on the braziers, and the earthier perfumes of the various large-breasted women Hoel had enjoyed as much as the wine.

Now the hangings were gone, as were the braziers and tables, leaving an austere and empty room that smelled of nothing more than dried-up pleasures. All that was left of Hoel was his chair, set on a raised platform. Now it was Essylt's chair, and though it dwarfed her, and her feet barely touched the ground, she still looked imposing in her grey unadorned tunic and skirt and a veil caught back with a thin fillet of silver. She looked like a queen, rather than a woman, and Corwynal cleared his throat nervously, wishing he could speak to her as a woman, rather than a queen. But he'd forfeited that privilege the previous Imbolc, and, in any case, he'd never been much good at talking to either.

'There's little to tell,' he said. 'Nothing Trystan hasn't already told you.'

When they'd arrived in Meldon, Essylt had looked up from her place by the fire in the hall, and her face had softened and glowed with delight. As Trystan talked, however, that glow had faded, leaving something cold and inflexible behind, and she'd listened to his tale of how he'd been healed in Dalriada with visibly growing suspicion. He'd told her he owed Brangianne his life, that he could only repay her by helping the Dalriad people fight the Creonn clansmen and their allies. He respectfully asked leave to take the Selgovian troops to war.

'Please, Essylt.' Trystan had smiled his best smile, but instead of softening she'd stiffened and couldn't be persuaded either by reason or appeals to her charity. Not even when Trystan got on his knees and begged her.

'You'll have to persuade her,' Trystan said to Corwynal the following morning. He looked haggard and sleepless, as if he'd spent the night not making love to a girl who adored him but fighting with a woman who had every reason to mistrust him. 'And don't say "I told you so". I know it's my fault. I know I've neglected her, but I always thought . . .'

You always thought she'd come running.

'Trystan told me nothing,' Essylt replied later that day, after Corwynal had been summoned to attend her. Her voice was as sharp as a blade and just as unforgiving. 'Only that she healed him, but am I not a healer also? Why didn't you send for me?'

'It was a long way, Essylt.'

'I would have come no matter the distance! You knew that, yet you took Trystan to Dalriada. So tell me about this woman. What does she look like?'

'She's not tall,' he began awkwardly. 'Or short. Her nose is long and straight, and her mouth is wide when she laughs. Her eyes . . .' What colour were her eyes? He'd never been certain. '. . . are grey, but sometimes brown or green. She has long hair that tangles in the wind. It's brown, dark brown, with strands of silver and—'

'Silver?' Essylt interrupted him. 'Is she old, then? And plain?'

'She's my age. I suppose that's old to you, but not to me. And I don't think her plain.' What had he said to make Essylt think she was?

She laughed then, the bright bubbling laugh he remembered from that Beltein morning two years before. 'You're in love with her! *You!*' And so he understood. Essylt had thought Trystan had fallen for the woman who'd healed him. Her amusement didn't last long, however, and, once her laugher ebbed away, she gave him a long searching look.

'So Trystan has come to Meldon because you love this woman, and he loves you.' She rose to her feet and looked down at him from her elevated position. 'So tell me, Corwynal of Lothian, why should I help you save the woman you love? Why shouldn't I punish you for all the things unsaid and undone?'

He supposed he deserved that.

'Because we share something, you and I, as we could have shared a life. Because you love Trystan and all he loves is fighting and glory. Because I love Brangianne of Dalriada, but she feels nothing for me but hatred. But love doesn't have to be returned or deserved. You would have travelled any distance to help Trystan. And I too would do anything to help Brangianne, no matter what she thinks of me. So I too will beg, Essylt.' He stepped towards her and knelt in front of her, reaching up to take her hands in his and holding them firmly when she tried to pull away. 'I'm begging now. Is this enough punishment for you? Do you need more? Do you want to know how much worse my life is? The one woman I care about hates me, and even if she didn't, there's no hope for me in this world, because I married another woman as foolishly as Trystan married you.'

'Let me go!' She pulled her hands away. 'And get up.'

'I'm sorry, Essylt, but I'm desperate.'

'Why did you marry her, this other woman?'

'Because there was a child.' He got to his feet, too weary to think what he was saying.

'You have a . . . a child?' Her voice broke on the word and he cursed himself for his stupidity. *Give me a child!* she'd cried out to him that Imbolc night over a year before, words that had broken her spell over him. Now, the mention of a child had broken something else.

'Yes. A son. I . . . I'm sorry.'

Her face was a frozen mask as she turned and walked away, slowly to begin with, then more quickly, stumbling in her haste to get away from him.

'Please, Essylt!' he called after her. '*Please!*'

She paused in the doorway, half-turning, and he could see tears pouring down her cheeks. Then she was gone, the door slamming behind her.

And so, like Trystan, he'd failed.

'Father Adarn?' Brangianne wished she'd asked Ciaran more questions about this hooded figure who found the situation so amusing. And who were these little people?

'Who seeks him?' The Blacksmith strode to the entrance of the forge. A sword hung by his side, hardly the accoutrement of a priest.

'I bring a message from Abbot Ciaran of St Martin's.' To her annoyance, Brangianne's voice wavered. The hooded figure regarded her in thoughtful silence before laughing his raven's croak once more.

'Has the old man fallen so far as to send a message by a woman?'

She glanced around. Oonagh had vanished, and she wished she'd run too, but she'd come here with a purpose. Best get it over with.

'Who brings the message is irrelevant. Come, put that sword down and show yourself. I won't give a message to an armed and hooded man.'

He tossed the blade to the ground, and Brangianne could see it was rusted and pitted. 'Well? Give me your message, then leave me alone.'

'Not until I see your face.'

'You won't like it,' he warned her, but she'd seen men disfigured by wounds and disease, so the prospect didn't alarm her.

'I insist.'

He pushed back his hood, and Brangianne stared at the strangest face she'd ever seen. His skin was marked in the Caledonian way with a tattoo in the shape of a fearsome beast with jaws and wings and claws. His eyes, glittering balefully, were those of a predator, and his head was shaven, except for a strip along the crown where the hair had been allowed to grow long and was woven into a thick grey braid. She stared at him with a mixture of horror and fascination, and the man laughed once more. 'I warned you! Your companion was wise to flee. Now, give me the message.'

She pulled out the silver druid piece, untied the ribbon from which she'd hung it, and handed it to the man, repeating Ciaran's words as she did so. *Sanctuary is over and the world awaits.*

The Blacksmith had been reaching for the disc, but at her words he froze, his hand outstretched.

'What did you say?' he breathed.

She repeated the words, and the man's face slowly hardened until he looked like one of the old ones, carved into stone. He stared at the disk for a long time before taking it from her, his fingers visibly trembling. Then he tied the ribbon around his neck to join a little silver cross that already hung there and tucked it beneath his habit, but not before she'd seen another marking. This one wasn't pricked out with dye; it was a purplish weal that ran around his throat, indented into the flesh. At some time in this man's past, someone had tried to strangle him.

'What does the message mean?' she asked.

He gave her a hard, unreadable look. 'It means what it says. Sanctuary is over. Clearly, since I find myself plagued by an impertinent young woman. As for the world awaiting, it's waited thus far, so I believe it can manage very well without me.' And with that, he turned his back on her.

'You'll ignore it?' Brangianne asked in astonishment, for no-one ignored a summons from Ciaran. 'You're supposed to help Dalriada!'

'Am I? Is that what everyone expects? No, my work is here, among my people,' he said over his shoulder, gesturing at the strange little people who still ringed the clearing. 'The old Forest People, what's left of them. I call them my children because they need a father. So tell Ciaran I refused. He won't be surprised. He may even be relieved.'

The Blacksmith turned away once more to return to the forge, but someone stood in his way. The woman who'd fled had returned. Oonagh stood facing him, her hands on her hips. The expression on her bone-white face was an odd mixture of terror and fury.

'Recognise me?' she demanded. 'Remember me? Remember a promise you broke? The gods know I never wanted to see you again, and I ran away just now, but at least I came back. I came *back!*'

'Dear God!' the man whispered, stumbling back from her in something close to horror.

'You know Father Adarn?' Brangianne asked her stupidly.

'Know him?' Oonagh's eyes were glittering with anger and unshed tears. 'Yes, I know him! But his name isn't Adarn. It's Azarion, and if he can help Dalriada, then he'll do it.' She stepped towards him. 'Won't you?!' she hissed, holding those glittering feral eyes with hers until eventually, like a man accepting a death-sentence, he nodded. Oonagh turned to Brangianne, a strange mixture of defiance and shame in her face. 'You see these markings? This man, calling himself a priest, is a Dragon-rider. And he's my father.'

'Women!' Aelfric thought in disgust as they climbed steadily to the watershed that marked the edge of the Dalriad lands. The four of them, Aelfric, Corwynal, Trystan and Kaerherdin, were driving their troops hard, but Corwynal was the worst, and he was impatient and short-tempered whenever they stopped to rest the horses. And all because of a woman.

Not that Aelfric blamed Brangianne. Woden's balls, he *liked* her! And he didn't blame Oonagh either. They couldn't help being women, couldn't help being clueless when it came to war, and he knew neither of them could stop themselves from getting involved. He didn't blame them for that either.

No, who he blamed was Essylt, who'd kept them kicking their heels in Meldon while Trystan had negotiated – unsuccessfully – for the release of the Selgovian archers. It was clear Essylt was jealous of the woman who'd healed Trystan, and thought he'd lost his heart to her. Aelfric could have told her Trystan didn't have a heart to lose and, let's face it, Brangianne was *old*. You'd think Trystan might have had the sense to mention that at the outset. Essylt didn't listen to Corwynal either, though Aelfric couldn't blame her for that. The man had made an arse of himself with her the previous Imbolc, so it wasn't surprising.

In the end it had been Kaerherdin who'd got things moving by going behind her back and talking directly to the men. He'd told them whom they were going to fight – Creonn, whoever they were, and Dragon-riders, whatever they were. Corwynal had been characteristically unforthcoming on the matter, but Kaerherdin had pressed him for details.

Yes, they wore armour. Yes, some of them wore red cloaks. Yes, they carried pennants in the shape of some flying beast, pennants that droned. Aelfric didn't know what to make of that particular detail, but he could tell it mattered, that it meant something to Selgovians. 'Selgovia remembers,' Kaerherdin had said more grimly than usual.

And so the Selgovians were riding not to fight for the army they'd fought against the previous year, nor to save the lives of the one or two women who were bound to get caught up in the fighting, but for revenge on an old enemy. Essylt hadn't been able to stop them, so she'd given them permission to go, but not before she'd extracted a promise from Trystan.

'You'll come back,' she'd insisted. 'When this war's over?'

'Of course,' he'd said stiffly, and Aelfric knew he'd rather not have made that promise. Their marriage had been a mistake, but it was too late now, and they'd both have to live with it.

'Come on, you laggards!' Kaerherdin yelled at his troop. 'Do you want these Dalriads to start this war without us?'

It was a real possibility, for it was almost a month past Beltein, and armies generally took to the field as soon as the

Beltein Truce was over. But they'd ridden hard from the Fort and had ridden even harder since leaving Selgovia. Now, only a handful of days later, they were a long way from Meldon and had reached a watershed between two river valleys where they'd stopped to rest the horses once more and survey the way ahead. The mountains all around them still held a little snow along their crests and in the shadows of north-facing gullies. Ahead, to the northwest, the land fell away into yet another of the forested twisted valleys through which they'd been riding for days in weather that had been wet and unpleasant. For the moment, however, it wasn't raining, and the wind was picking up, tearing the clouds apart to reveal, in the distance, even higher mountains, a range that scraped the sky. *Cruachan*, Ferdiad called the highest of them. *The old one,* he said it meant.

Aelfric didn't trust the Scot. Hadn't he been their enemy back in Carnadail? 'We're on the same side now,' Corwynal told him, but Aelfric wasn't so sure. That Scot was trouble. Yet he'd guided them north surely enough, through forests, across rivers and high passes in the mountains, heading for yet another loch where he said the Dalriad army would be encamped.

'You're sure they're down there?' Trystan asked Ferdiad, nodding at the woods that were still wreathed in cloud. *The Ghost Woods*, they were called, apparently. Aelfric didn't want to know why. Below the forest, in a fog-bound river valley, they were to join up with the Scots army. The previous night, Ferdiad had drawn a map for them in the muddy ground of their camp. To the northeast was another river valley through which the Dragon-riders and the Creonn would have to pass. To the west was a long narrow loch, into which the river below them ran, and at the head of which the main Dalriad army would be camped. It made sense. Aelfric would have put his army there too. Yet there was no sign of them, no smoke from campfires, no sound of horn or horse, no lookouts. Aelfric, had he been in charge of that army, would have put lookouts on the heights, something that had also occurred to Trystan, who looked doubtful.

'You think I'm leading you into a trap?' Ferdiad asked. 'If I'd wanted to, I could have done so days ago and saved myself the trouble of riding all this way in the rain.'

'He's right, Trys,' Corwynal said. 'Let's get moving before it starts raining again.'

Which went to show that being in love was not just inconvenient but dangerous too, for Corwynal, with his finely tuned sense of danger, must be as aware as Aelfric that something wasn't quite right, that something was waiting for them, something hostile. But, after a moment, Aelfric reasoned away his unease. The Scots in that valley had very likely fought Selgovians in the battle the previous year and, even if they hadn't, they'd have relatives and comrades who had, and some of them would have died with a Selgovian arrow in the throat or been cut down by one of their long cavalry swords. They were bound to be hostile, for the Selgovians had proved themselves enemies to be reckoned with. Now, however, they were intent on proving they were allies worth having, better warriors than the Scots, stronger and more resolute.

So they rode down from the watershed and into the valley, proudly aware of their own hard-learned competence and determined to prove themselves worthy of respect. And so, in the end, it was only through pride that they were riding fast enough to avoid the worst of what was lying in wait for them.

Brangianne was quite pleased with her disguise. The monk's habit she'd put on over her clothes might be hot and heavy and useless at keeping out the rain that began to fall later that morning, but it concealed not only her identity but her sex.

Oonagh was equally unrecognisable. Or would have been if only she'd stop complaining.

'That old man!' she snarled, referring, Brangianne gathered, to Ciaran. 'He should have warned me!'

They were on their way, with the St Martin's healers, their supply wagon and The Devil, to re-join the army that was crammed together at the southern end of the loch waiting for the transports to return from the northern end over twenty miles away.

'What a shambles!' Oonagh grumbled, looking around in disgust. What they'd both suspected as they'd journeyed north from Dunadd was now painfully evident. This wasn't a proper army. 'Have you seen them? Most of them are that Steward's bullies and, as for the rest, half of them are old enough to be my grandfather. The other half's younger than my son was and, for all their bluster and bragging, I reckon they're just as frightened.' She scrubbed quickly at her eyes. Did monks cry? Brangianne wasn't sure.

'I expect all armies are this chaotic,' she said, reassuring herself rather than Oonagh. 'Eoghan's in charge and he's a good organiser.'

Yet even an efficient Steward couldn't organise the wind, which had blown from the southwest and taken some of the army north, had strengthened, stranding Eoghan, his men, and the bulk of the supplies at the southern end of the loch, for the transports, unable to row into such a powerful headwind, were stuck in the north until the wind eased once more. And who knew when that would happen?

Eoghan's troops were wearing the sign of the Swallow, she noticed, wondering when Eoghan had awarded himself a family sigil, but it didn't make his men any more popular than they'd been, since they were the ones who enforced the annual tribute demand. Now, bored with waiting, scores were being settled as the old hands quietly ignored their orders, and the younger ones were openly defiant. It wasn't a good beginning, and Brangianne wondered if the Steward of Lothian might have handled this war better than the Steward of Dalriada.

But no, she refused to think of him, so turned to more immediate concerns.

'Is that man really a Dragon-rider?' She still wasn't sure she believed in them. In all the stories, they were fearsome young warriors, not tired old men with grown-up daughters. 'I thought you said you didn't have a family.'

'I said I didn't have any I'd care to make a claim on,' Oonagh reminded her, speaking through her teeth. 'And I'll not make a claim on *him!* You delivered your message, so now we can forget about him, given that he's gone.' It was true. After Oonagh's astonishing declaration, the man had vanished, the Forest People with him, but Brangianne couldn't forget him so easily, or Ciaran's concern about what he might do. *Kill someone? Save everyone? Both?*

Right then, however, Brangianne's most pressing concern was getting herself, Oonagh, her supplies and The Devil to the far end of the loch before anyone discovered she was missing. But getting away still wasn't possible. The wind, which had died down during the night, sprang up again not long after dawn, driving away the fog, and it wasn't long before a full gale was gusting out of the south. Which meant there was no prospect of the transports returning any time soon, and so the bulk of the army settled down, complaining, to wait.

A few of the more enterprising men set off along the track that ran along the eastern shore but it was narrow and boggy and the carts soon got stuck, and those on foot or horseback returned, saying the way was cut through by streams or blocked by fallen trees or landslips.

'I suppose we'll just have to wait,' Brangianne said resignedly.

'You give up too easily.' The harsh voice came from behind her. Oonagh gave a cry of dismay and Brangianne whirled about to find a tall man standing there with two ponies, his eyes gleaming from within the shadows of his raised hood. 'Take all the supplies you can carry.' Azarion handed her the reins of one pony, untied The Devil from the back of the wagon and leapt into the saddle. To Brangianne's astonishment, the horse didn't even flinch.

'Well? Do you want to go to war or not?' Without waiting for a reply, he set off for the track along the eastern shore. Brangianne and Oonagh looked at one another. Oonagh shrugged and mounted one of the ponies while Brangianne unearthed the more essential of her supplies – bandages, moss, poppy, her knives, needles and thread – stuffed them into a satchel and scrambled onto the back of the other pony.

At first they rode along the track by the loch-side, but it wasn't long before they were forced to abandon the muddy trail and take to the hillside, dismounting to lead the horses up dizzyingly steep slopes tangled with trees and vegetation, and cut by rain-swollen streams that fell in sharp little waterfalls down to the loch. The straps of Brangianne's satchel cut into her shoulders even through the thick fabric of the habit whose frayed hem kept catching on brambles and branches, but she struggled on up the slope with the wind rushing and moaning in the swaying tree-tops, bringing with it the scent of high moorland, bogs and bog myrtle, sphagnum moss and deer grass.

Eventually, they reached a higher trail. It was little more than a deer-trod, but it ran along the crest of the hills, following the line of the loch in more open pine woods, and the going became easier. The Blacksmith pressed on, as if desperate to be rid of his unwelcome responsibilities, and didn't stop until what felt like the middle of the night, to light a little fire in a stony hollow ringed by pines. The wind had dropped with the falling of dusk, and a pair of owls hooted to one-another through the treetops. Oonagh, muttering, strode off to the other side of the hollow, as far from her father as possible, wrapped herself in a blanket and went to sleep. Brangianne was exhausted too, and the man doubtless thought she'd be too tired for questions, but he was sadly mistaken in that.

'Azarion is a strange name.'

'All my people's names would be strange to you.'

'Are you really a Dragon-rider?'

'I was, a long time ago.'

'I thought they'd all died.'

'Not all. But those who were left changed,' the man said. 'They moved north, but now they've come back, and they're riding to war.'

'*You're* riding to war,' she accused him, remembering that the Druid piece could be used by either side. 'Are you going to join your people?' He smiled, a feral gleam of teeth from within that concealing hood, then threw back the hood, revealing his face in all its animal strangeness, and tugged loose the lacing at the neck of his habit to reveal the odd purple scar she'd noticed before. 'My people did this. Have you heard of the three-fold death?'

Her stomach turned over. Yes, she had, but only in the oldest of stories. It had meant something back then, but no-one did that anymore. Did they?

'They stunned me with a rock, tried to strangle me and succeeded, almost, in drowning me,' Azarion said with a shrug. 'My people. My family. That's not something I'm likely to forgive.'

'So what *are* you going to do?'

He regarded her seriously. 'I don't know.'

He'd replaced the ribbon on the druid piece with a narrow strip of leather and had hung it around his neck. Now, as he leant forward to poke at their miserable fire, the medallion fell free, twisting back and forth in the firelight, the strange embossed beast writhing in the flames, matching the marks on his face. She knew what it was now, a creature she'd never seen, a creature she'd never believed in. A Dragon. Maybe the beasts didn't exist anymore, if they ever had, but the Riders clearly did. And this man was one of them.

'I've been many things in my life.' He saw her staring at the silver disc and pushed it back beneath his tunic. 'Father, brother, warrior, teacher, outcast, priest.' There was a pause. 'And traitor,' he added, raising the hood to conceal his face and leaning away from the fire so all she could see of him was the glitter of his hawk-like eyes. 'Maybe that's why I'm here . . .'

13

I WILL LEAD THE ARMY

'**K**aer – hold the line! Aelfric – drive them back to the woods!' Trystan's voice rang out across the clearing in the forest.

They'd had no word from their scouts, and fog still wreathed the main river valley in thick grey streamers, and so they rode without warning into the ragged line of spearmen. There was dense woodland to the left; to the right the ground fell away to a smaller river that plunged in a series of rocky falls down to more open country. There was nowhere to go except back, but they were riding too fast to pull their mounts to a halt before they reached the line of men. Horses reared and screamed, terrified of the spears. Men were screaming too, in challenge and agony, but then they were through, more by luck than judgement. They'd been riding too fast for the spearmen to close ranks, and most of the Selgovians shot through a narrow gap by the river, drawing and firing as they did so, sending arrows whistling past Corwynal's ear. On his left, a horse went down, squealing and thrashing, but its rider leapt clear. To his right a face swam into his vision. Without thinking, he struck out, and it dissolved in a shattering of blood and bone, but not before he'd seen the ram's head mark on the man's forehead – the black ram sign of the Creonn.

He wheeled Janthe to look back. Beside him, Trystan was cursing as he hauled on his stallion's reins, pulling him in a tight curve. On his far side, Aelfric was shouting at his mount. Most of them had made it through the gap. The rest, Kaerherdin's troop, were trapped and trying to break free; Kaerherdin was yelling at his men to get them into formation, ready to punch their way through the line of Creonn.

Then a figure emerged from the fog, a stag's head catching the light.

Arddu? But there was no answering pulse in his blood, no distant mocking laughter. This was no god, but a living man, armoured in steel and horn, mounted on a similarly armoured horse, a man whose iron helmet was crowned with the tines of a stag. He lifted a pole from which flew a long narrow standard, and a strange droning signal echoed through the trees, a noise he'd never heard before, half-beast, half-ghost, but he knew what it meant. The Creonn were led by a Dragon-rider.

'Corwynal! Aelfric!' Trystan called out, signalling to the men who'd broken through to move back. 'I want that man's head!'

Aelfric grinned, a flash of white in a blood-spattered face and, with a yell, plunged back into the battle. Trystan was close behind him, but Corwynal hesitated. The grip of his sword was sticky, though he hadn't been aware of using it. Everything had happened too fast. There had been no slowing of the world, no dance or pattern, no music or joy. He felt acutely vulnerable and strangely alone.

You're never alone.

The voice came from inside him, as sardonic as ever, sweeping Corwynal's uncertainty away in a hot flood of anger.

You abandoned me! I sent an arrow but you didn't come.

I do not come at the summons of a mere man. Arddu sounded stern and saddened, and unnervingly like Corwynal's father.

Then why come now?

Arddu just laughed.

'I want nothing from you!' Corwynal yelled.

Janthe was dancing with impatience. Trystan and Aelfric and their men had reached the line of spearmen who were turning, beset on both sides now and beginning to scatter. Then a horn rang out, drowning out the eerie wailing of the dragon standard, a signal for the spearmen who moved together once more, forming a shield wall that bristled with spears and separated the two wings of the Selgovian horse.

The Dragon-rider moved down the hillside and, when free of the trees, kicked his mount into a trot that became a canter, then a gallop, aiming for the remaining men Kaerherdin commanded. Corwynal, helpless on the far side of the Creonn line, watched as the combined weight of rider, horse and metal crashed into the Selgovian horsemen.

I want that man's head. The man who controlled the Creonn.

Corwynal would have to fight his way across a battlefield and kill a man who was better armed, better armoured, probably younger and certainly less doubtful.

Are you sure you want nothing from me? The voice thrilled through his veins, taunting him, tempting him.

'Curse you, yes!'

He could die here. Yet that was why he'd come, wasn't it? To die for a woman who hated him.

You'd do better living.

He kneed Janthe into a gallop. He could do this. He didn't need Arddu because, this time, he had something else: the nightmare he'd dreamed every night since Ferdiad had come to find them. He heard fires raging, saw a monastery burn and men – priests in torn and bloodied habits – dying in their own blood. He smelled the stench of spilled guts, tasted iron in his mouth. There was a woman, her back pressed against a wall, a horned creature reaching out to tear her dress away. But now, in reality, Corwynal was with her, as he hadn't been in his nightmares. This time he wasn't too late, and, snarling his defiance at both the Dragon-rider and Arddu, he plunged into the fog-wreathed battle. His sword grew red in his hands, his palm slick with blood and brains, his shield smashing at any upturned face, and Janthe, screaming her challenge, was lashing out with her hooves and driving him on until he was within reach of the Dragon-rider.

A blade hacked down. He caught it on his shield, but the blow shivered up his arm and sent Janthe stumbling. She recovered and danced away, but her stumble robbed his backhanded slash of much of its power, and the tip of his sword clattered feebly against the man's breastplate. Then, before he could recover, another impossibly heavy blow bore down on him, but this time he didn't try to catch it on his shield. Instead, he pulled Janthe around, and the blade whistled past his shoulder to strike the rear saddle-horn. It drove Janthe to her haunches and tumbled him out of the saddle. He rolled to his feet, but now he was unhorsed beneath an armoured mount and its rider, and the world was still moving too fast. Battle raged all around him, deafening with the screaming of men and horses, and Trystan yelling his name as the Dragon-rider drew back his blade for the killing blow.

I'm going to die here! His body, however, refused to believe it and, instinctively, he threw away his shield and twisted to one side as the blow fell. Then, instead of falling back, he stepped forward, grasped the mailed fist and struck with his own sword, not at the armoured thigh or the protected underbelly of the man's mount, but the saddle-girth, which tore and snapped. The man, weighed down with all that armour, toppled to the ground, the one weakness in his armour, under the arm, exposed to Corwynal's blade. It slid through muscle and lungs and the man screamed, throwing his head back, exposing his throat.

Corwynal's sword hammered down once more, stifling the scream in a fountain of red. Then he was hacking at every point of weakness until the Dragon-rider was lying in a pool of blood in the courtyard of the burning monastery of his nightmare. But when Corwynal looked up, both Brangianne and the monastery had gone, and Trystan stood there, staring at him.

'I think he's dead, Corwynal,' he said gently. Aelfric came to join them both, his face bloodier than before, and raised an eyebrow at the mutilated corpse at Corwynal's feet. Beyond, the Selgovians, what was left of them, were riding in pursuit of a scattered band of fleeing Creonn.

'They're getting away,' he said.

'They're running away,' Trystan corrected him, his face grave. One of his men rode up then, leading Rhydian, and Trystan swung into the saddle, reached for his horn and blew the signal, but not for advance. He called for retreat. 'We can't afford to lose any more men.' He turned to the Selgovian. 'Find me Ferdiad,' he said. 'Find me that Gaelic snake.'

So that's a Dragon-rider. Aelfric looked curiously at the bloody mass of meat and metal that was all the Caledonian had left of the man with the stag's head helmet and oddly patterned face.

It had been a bad moment when he'd first seen the rider coming out of the fog like one of the Old Gods or a ghost, for didn't they call these the Ghost Woods? But the rider was neither ghost nor god, just a man, as big as Aelfric himself. And he was impressively armoured, or so it had appeared from a distance.

Now, however, when he looked more closely, he saw that the armour was old and corroded, dented and much repaired, the leather fastenings worn through, the metal thin. The Dragon-riders the Selgovians had spoken of with such awe and bitterness had been formidable, but this one at least was neither unstoppable nor invincible. And nor were their allies, these Creonn spearmen who fought on foot, trusting not to armour but to some tribal mark on their foreheads. Several lay dead, slain by Selgovian arrows or swords. The badly wounded had been killed, and there was a small group of prisoners, but most had run away and probably wouldn't come back now the Dragon-rider who'd led them was dead. Nevertheless, Aelfric thought it would be wise to move back up into the woods, perhaps as far as the watershed where the rocks and cliffs would give them some protection from further attack. First, however, there was the Scot to interrogate.

'Where in the Five Hells are the Dalriads?' Trystan demanded. 'How did the Creonn get past an entire army?'

'How should I know?' Ferdiad had been bound and forced to his knees but wasn't intimidated. 'Dead? Mistaken? Believe me, it's a question I want an answer to as much as you. You don't trust me, I know, but you can trust me in this; when I get my hands on whoever's leading this army, I'll personally tear his guts out through his nose.'

Aelfric, looking at the man's expression, didn't envy the Dalriad leader, especially when the Fili smiled, for it wasn't a comfortable smile. 'But that's a pleasure for the future,' he went on. 'For the present, you – we – have to decide what to do, and I suggest that what you need right now is someone who can think, and that's my skill. Make use of it, because, like it or not, we're in this together. Now, please, I understand your need to blame someone, but this—' He held up his bound hands, '—is humiliating, and I don't think well when I feel humiliated.'

Corwynal stepped forward, cut through Ferdiad's bonds and dragged one of the prisoners over.

The man was limping from a wound in the thigh, and his naked chest was splattered with blood, which meant it was

Selgovian blood. Kaerherdin, wounded himself, growled some curse and stepped forward to strike the sneer from the Creonn's face, but Corwynal beat him to it, hitting the man so hard he fell to his knees. Then he jerked him to his feet and pulled apart the lacing of his own shirt to reveal the designs Aelfric had first seen in Selgovia. Corwynal snarled something in Caledonian at the Creonn that wiped the contempt from the man's face and made him fall to his knees once more. Ferdiad laughed at that. The Fili, in Aelfric's opinion, laughed a great deal too often.

'You make claim to Atholl when it suits you?' the Scot asked Corwynal.

'When it suits me, yes.'

'Ask him how many of his people there are,' Trystan said. The answer, spat in a defiant torrent of foreign, wasn't encouraging once it was translated; the troop they'd run into was an advance party, and the man knew of at least three other war-bands marching west. More were to follow, all led by Dragon-riders. The Dragon himself commanded a troop of his own horsemen.

'And the Dalriads?'

The man shrugged. There were no Dalriads.

The Scot's eyes hardened at that, and a muscle flickered in his jaw but, before he could speak, to deny it perhaps, one of the Selgovian scouts returned from a sortie to the river valley and confirmed what the Creonn had said, and what, from the absence of smoke, Aelfric had suspected. The place was deserted.

Trystan looked thoughtfully at the prisoner, still on his knees, his hands bound as Ferdiad's had been, and drew his sword. No-one enjoyed the killing of prisoners, but Aelfric understood the necessity, so watched stoically as Trystan put the tip of his sword under the Creonn's chin and lifted it, forcing the man to stand, to let him die on his feet. Then Trystan dropped his sword to cut through the man's bonds.

'Go.' He gestured to the woods. 'Go!' he repeated as the man hesitated, then, as a growl of disapproval rumbled from the Selgovians, the Creonn took to his heels and ran. 'Let the rest go.' Trystan turned to Aelfric and jerked his head at the cluster of prisoners.

'Why? They'll take word back of where we are.'

'Exactly.' Trystan glanced at Corwynal. 'I assume that gesture wasn't for nothing? No, I thought not. Setting those men free means they'll return to their people and tell them that Britons ride against them and that a man of Atholl rides with them too. Let the rumours gather. It may give them pause, and us a breathing space.'

'A breathing space for what?' Aelfric asked, but it was to Ferdiad that Trystan turned.

'Well, my Lord Fili, you claim to be a man who can think. So, give me the benefit of your thoughts.'

Ferdiad pursed his lips and looked around at them all. 'We have to assume my people are still at Loch Abha,' he said eventually. 'If they're anywhere. Hopefully, they're at the north end, by the ferry crossing, but they may be in the south if there's been some delay, or if they've decided to make their stand there. Either way, we can't stay here.' He glanced about the clearing, with its pile of corpses and stench of death, and shuddered. 'If that party of Creonn truly was just an advance party, the rest of the river valley may be clear, but we can't risk it, not in this fog.' The clouds still clung stubbornly to the lower land. 'We should go back to the watershed, then head west over the high ground to the loch. But it's hard country, particularly if we have to travel to the southern end of the loch. And that means we can't take the wounded.' He spread his hands apologetically, and they all understood. Those who couldn't ride would have to be left behind.

Aelfric didn't like that, but he understood the realities of war.

They all did. Nevertheless, he wasn't surprised when Kaerherdin objected.

'Selgovians don't abandon their own. I'll stay with the wounded.' He probably felt responsible for letting his men get separated from the others, and his offer would make the decision easier for Trystan. But Trystan didn't need anything to be made easy.

'Don't be an idiot! Do you think I haven't noticed the blood dripping down your arm? How much use are you if you can't draw a bow or wield a blade?'

'I can still wield a blade,' Kaerherdin replied hotly. 'The wound's in my shield-arm, not my sword-arm.'

'You *are* my shield-arm, Kaer,' Trystan said. 'And I've a harder task for you – to go west with Ferdiad, as he suggests.'

'Just the two of us?' Ferdiad objected.

'It should just take one of you, only you, to find your army and get it moving up the river valley as planned. Because this war isn't over. Your people may have given up, but I haven't. I don't care how you do it, but it must be done quickly. You've failed me once. Don't fail me again.'

Ferdiad looked long and hard at Trystan, then nodded. 'Why the Selgovian?'

'Because I don't trust you. And because he's hurt, and I know that wherever your army is there will be healers among you.' He gripped Kaerherdin by his good arm. 'Find someone to treat your wound and persuade them to come back with you to tend the rest of our own wounded. I won't abandon them, so don't fail me, Kaer.'

Aelfric wondered how, with the limited Scots Kaerherdin had picked up on the journey, he'd be able to persuade anyone of anything, but the Selgovian nodded, and Trystan turned back to Ferdiad, his eyes narrowing as he did so.

'Bring your army, and take this warning to those you serve,

that, whatever reasons we have to be here, we'll fight, with or without you. But if we fall and die alone, then all the Kingdoms of the North will know of it, and Dalriada's dishonour will be a thing of song for generations to come.'

Then, without waiting for an answer – for what, after all, could the Scot say in response to that? – Trystan turned to face those of his men who remained of the one hundred who'd set out from Meldon half a moon before.

'The Lord Ferdiad advises us to flee, to leave our wounded and fly to the west to cower with the army of the Dalriads, if it's even there. That's what any sensible commander would do: retreat to lick our wounds and, God knows, there are enough of them. But that's not what we came for.' His voice rose, pitched so everyone could hear. 'We came to fight the Dragon-riders, and that's what we're going to do.'

Brangianne wasn't impressed by the camp at the northern end of Loch Abha. It was set out on a narrow promontory crowned by the ruins of an old fort, but had neither plan nor order, and was nothing more than a sprawling mass of men, each trying to find a place for himself in the absence of tents and supplies, still wind-bound at the other end of the loch.

Nevertheless, the chaos worked to Brangianne's advantage, because everyone was too busy complaining to pay any attention to three monks and a bad-tempered horse. The only interest anyone had in her was because she carried a healer's bag, and she quickly found herself employed, for wherever men gathered there were fights and wounds and worse. It wouldn't be long, she reckoned, eyeing the dubious sanitary arrangements and smelling the stink of badly positioned latrine pits, before the camp was riddled with fluxes.

By the end of the day she'd arrived, however, the wind eased and the following morning the transports, able to row south once more, began to return, bringing Eoghan, his sizable entourage, his personal baggage, and a very large command tent that was erected in the shelter of the ruined fort. Brangianne was more interested in being reunited with the healers from St Martins, her precious medical supplies, and the tents that would provide shelter for the wounded. Not that there were any as yet, not that day, nor the next, nor the day after.

She'd expected the army to march north to guard the river crossings and routes south into Dalriada, but everyone remained resolutely by the loch shore, in easy reach of the boats in case they had to retreat. It was as if the war they'd expected to fight had turned out to be nothing more than a rumour. But maybe it was. Maybe Feargus was right and this war would be won at sea, not land. Still, surely it would make sense to send out patrols? No-one was sent, however, and the army settled down to enjoy itself. The women of the camp – for many had followed their men to war – busied themselves with cooking and washing, while the men and their dogs made up hunting parties or arranged races and mock fights.

Perhaps it was because there was no fighting, but Brangianne discovered, to her surprise, that she was happy. She was being who she was meant to be at last. Talorc, the man who didn't exist, was still a wound in her heart, but the wound was scabbing over. She even found herself smiling at the chaos of Eoghan's army and—

'Out of my way, priest!'

It was as if she'd called him to life; Eoghan himself barged past her, almost knocking her over, and she thought, for one terrifying moment, he'd recognised her. But he continued on his way without apologising, making for his tent; all he'd seen was a healer in a rather too-long habit.

'Is that man a complete fool?' The derisive voice from behind her made her jump. She hadn't expected to hear that harsh raven voice again, for Azarion had disappeared as soon as they'd arrived at the camp.

'I thought you'd left.'

'To join the Dragon-riders? Not yet. I've been in the camp, listening to the rumours.'

So had she. In the absence of any fighting, there had been little for the army to do but gossip and speculate. Dragon-riders? The old hands, those who'd fought for Feargus twenty years before, spoke chillingly of their old adversaries, but most folk dismissed them as a story out of the old days. As for the Forest People, the ghosts of the Ghost Woods, what nonsense! Brangianne, who knew both rumours to be true, wondered what the army was doing there, enjoying itself, when the Creonn might already have slipped past them to strike at Dunadd itself.

'Listen . . .' Azarion cocked his head. From somewhere in the tents a boy was singing in a high clear voice, a song of Feargus' twenty-year-old defeat of the Dragon, a song to stir the blood. But, as they listened, the singer stopped abruptly in the middle of a verse.

'That was before,' Azarion said. 'This is now. And it's not your King who leads this army this time, but a man who's afraid to move. Nevertheless, there seems to have been fighting further west,' he went on, 'which makes me curious . . .'

He stalked off in the direction of Eoghan's tent. Brangianne didn't want to risk another meeting with Eoghan, but her own curiosity overcame caution, so she pulled her hood closely about her face and followed the tall priest to the tent, beside which two lathered horses were tethered.

'What now?' she whispered, for the entrance to the tent was guarded by a couple of Eoghan's men. Then the door flap was swept open, and a servant emerged, caught sight of her and her healing satchel, and jerked his head.

'You, there! The Lord Ferdiad needs your assistance.'

Ferdiad? Here? Brangianne had only just recovered from her encounter with Eoghan, and her pulse began to race once more. Had he come from Feargus? Had Yseult betrayed her and told Feargus her plans? Had he sent Ferdiad to bring her back?

'A messenger's hurt,' the servant explained.

Her panic subsided and, with a thrill of devilment, she knew she could do this. A man sees what he expects to see, and all Eoghan and Ferdiad would see would be one of Ciaran's monks with a healing bag slung over one shoulder.

And so it proved. Neither Eoghan nor Ferdiad, engaged in an acrimonious argument, paid her any attention. 'In there.' Ferdiad jerked his head at an inner section of the tent, Eoghan's private sleeping quarters, where the wounded man lay.

Perhaps a woman also sees what she expects to see, for the first thing she noticed was the wound in the man's arm, which was a bad one. A spear thrust, she thought, having seen such wounds before. The muscle of the upper arm was torn, and the bandage, a filthy piece of fabric, was saturated with blood, the sleeve below the wound dark with a visible seepage of fluid. The man's skin was unnaturally pale, his face—

Her heart thudded once, then stopped. The man had dark hair and grey eyes, a coldly handsome face, a mouth that seemed unused to smiling, and a brooding reserve she could have reached out and touched. Then he was gone, the man she refused to think about, and a stranger sat on Eoghan's camp bed, his hair longer than that of the man she remembered, his eyes paler, his face narrower, his mouth wider, his skin grey with exhaustion and loss of blood. He wasn't the same man, yet he was familiar, and he was staring at her, as if he too felt the same puzzling recognition.

'You are healer?' His voice was deeper than that of the man she'd feared he was, his accent that of the Britons, his words carefully considered. A Briton then, one who spoke little Gael, a swordsman and an archer, judging by the callouses on his palms and fingers. How odd that the first wounded man she'd encountered in this war between Gaels and the Caledonian Creonn was a Briton. She wondered what he was doing with Ferdiad, but that was a question for later. She pushed back the hood of her habit and smiled her calm professional smile; it was important that her patients see nothing but confidence. His eyes widened when he saw she was a woman, but he said nothing as she opened her satchel and took out clean bandages, swabs and surgical needles, and began to probe the wound. He kept his eyes on her face as she worked, narrowing them a little when she caused him pain. He didn't cry out, though his body shuddered as he fought to stay conscious. *Let yourself go; it will be easier for us both,* she wanted to tell him, but had the feeling that to this man, like the man he resembled, control was everything.

She cleaned, sewed and bound the wound, listening as she did so to the raised voices from the other part of the tent. Ferdiad was arguing with Eoghan about some troops, and spoke of a battle, men and horses lost, though a victory of a sort. But she wasn't really listening, too intent on binding the Briton's wound in clean linen. The man's face was paler than before, but he was still conscious.

'Rest now.' She made a gesture of sleeping, but he shook his head and, for the first time, smiled at her. He had an oddly charming smile, one that lit up his grey eyes and made him look younger, the smile not of a patient to a healer, but of a man to a woman. Her heart thudded to a stop once more, and the young Briton's face blurred and shifted as his smile unlocked memories of another man's smile and what it had promised. The blood rushed to her face, and a hollow place inside her trembled.

'Kaerherdin,' he said, bringing her back to the present. 'My name.'

Then she was back in a different past, on a sandy beach where a ship lay anchored in the shallows, a coracle pulling for the ship, another waiting by the shore, one dark-haired man calling to another.

Run, Corwynal! Run!

'He asked me find you,' the man Kaerherdin said now, less than a year later. 'He want me bring you him.'

Did armies have moods? Oonagh hadn't thought about it before, but this army certainly did, one that had swung from excitement to impatience, then from boredom to rebellion.

It had been fine to begin with, everyone pulling together to get the army to the northern end of the loch, then make camp on this little promontory, which she'd thought strange when there was a whole valley to camp in further north. The men had squabbled cheerfully as they'd found themselves somewhere to pitch their tents, then settled down to do what men normally did when they were away from their families: drinking, gambling, hunting, and generally making fools of themselves.

Yet as the days went by and nothing warlike happened, the army's mood began to change. *Why aren't we moving?* was the refrain, whispered at first, then voiced more openly. *If we don't move now, we'll never move.* Oddly, no-one suggested going home, despite some doubt about the existence of a Creonn army and the dismissal of rumours of Dragon-riders. The army, both old or young, arthritic or inexperienced, wanted action.

Eoghan the Steward didn't, however, and Oonagh thought he'd lost his nerve, but didn't blame him. The northern end of the loch felt a very long way from Dunadd. The loch itself, deep and cold under a sullen sky, was oddly malevolent, the Ghost Woods, that spilled down to the shore in a dense tangle of vegetation, even more so. Small wonder the Steward had pitched his enormous tent as close to the boats as possible and refused to leave the cramped position on the promontory. If even a single Dragon-rider put in an appearance, he'd be off, she reckoned, and wondered what he'd do if he discovered a real Dragon-rider was stalking about his camp. Soil himself, probably.

The only order Eoghan had given was for his men to find 'that cursed bard', for the army, which had brought its women and dogs to war, had also brought its singers, and one in particular was going about the camp singing songs of battle, songs that dwelt more on the glory of it all than the very real possibility of dying unpleasantly. Oonagh thought it was one of the reasons the army's mood had changed. But the bard escaped capture and continued to circulate about the camp, trailing discontent in his wake. *We should be moving*. Eoghan ignored the whispers. *Not yet*, he'd been heard to say. *Not ever*, Oonagh suspected.

'Things are about to change.' The voice came from behind her. 'Do you want to be part of it?'

Her whole body went rigid, and she couldn't have turned to face him even if she'd wanted to. She'd seen him in the distance, a tall figure striding about the camp, ignored by everyone, including herself. Now, however, she could ignore him no longer.

'Why are you still here?'

'You insisted I help Dalriada, and I've not yet done so. But now I know what has to be done. This army needs another leader.'

'So you'll kill the present one and take his place?'

'What a blood-thirsty young woman you've turned into! No, there are other ways. And I've no desire to take this Lord Eoghan's place. Anyway, it's time I left because my people need my help too. I have debts to pay, promises to keep.' He hesitated, irresolute. 'I'm sorry I didn't keep the one I made to you, and I owe you an explanation. I was in danger and didn't want you and your mother to share it. I might have shared a life, but not death, and I *did* die, Oonagh. The man you remember is dead. The return of a ghost would have done no-one any good.'

They were just words, but nevertheless something hard and rigid in Oonagh's heart began to soften, and she turned to face him.

They were alone in a little hollow not far from the old fort where The Steward's gaudy tent stood. In a crowded camp, the man who used to be her father carried solitude with him, a space around him everyone avoided, and it rendered him invisible. He'd thrown back his hood, revealing the dragon mark on his face, the one Oonagh remembered. The mark had faded with the years but was still disturbing, encircling his golden eyes. Those eyes were the only thing of colour about him, for his dark red hair, once the same shade as her own, was now a mess of grey strings, braided into a plait that fell half-way down his back. His shoulders were still broad, but seemed burdened with more than his years. *He's an old man!* she realised with a sense of shock, for in her memory he was still the vigorous young man who'd disappeared, whistling, into a sun-shot morning and never returned. Not this ghost, this half-corpse. *He needs looking after.*She brushed this surprising and unwelcome thought away. He was still her enemy, and owed her more than excuses.

'What are you going to do?' she asked.

'What are *we* going to do?' he corrected her. 'That's the question, Oonagh. Now, let me tell you the answer . . .'

He want me bring you him.

Brangianne stared at the Briton. *He? Him?* A hundred questions rose to her lips, but she could voice none of them, for the man called Kaerherdin, if she'd got the name right, spoke as little Gael as she spoke Briton.

'I still don't understand why Feargus put you in charge of this army!'

Ferdiad's voice, from the main part of Eoghan's tent, was crisp, clear, derisive, impossible to ignore, and a welcome distraction from all Brangianne's questions. She moved closer to the hanging that divided the main part of the tent from the sleeping quarters in which she'd tended the Briton and eased it aside.

Ferdiad, looking travel-worn, was towering over Eoghan, his green eyes flashing, and barely listening to Eoghan's blustering excuses.

A holding position, importance of supply lines, operational decision, no positive sightings of Creonn—

'No sightings? You're not going to see them, Eoghan. The first sight you'll have of them is when they come charging out of the woods. The last sight you'll have of them is of some grinning tattooed clansman as he rams a spear through your belly.'

Brangianne's lips twitched as Eoghan turned green.

'Have you actually sent out patrols?' Ferdiad demanded, and, when Eoghan didn't reply, since he hadn't, the Fili sighed. 'Well, in the regrettable absence of someone who knows how to manage an army, you'll have to do it, because I have bad news for you, Eoghan. The Creonn are heading your way. They might already have been here, might already have outflanked this ridiculous position, had it not been for the cavalry I brought to aid Dalriada—'

Cavalry? Whose cavalry? His? His and Trystan's?

'—men who expected the Dalriad army to be occupying the river valley, men who didn't therefore anticipate being ambushed by a Creonn war-party,' Ferdiad went on.

Ambushed? Hurt? Kaerherdin had been hurt. Were there others? Him? Was he dead? No, he couldn't be. *He want me bring you him.*

'And that's not all,' Ferdiad continued remorselessly. 'This Creonn war-party was led by a Dragon-rider.'

'Oh, yes, very amusing,' Eoghan retorted. 'You're always so full of stories, aren't you, Fili? Creonn, Dragon-riders—' He stepped sharply back as Ferdiad grasped his tunic in one hand and twisted, forcing Eoghan to look up into his murderous green eyes.

'Dragon-riders. Who are cavalry. Who can only be defeated by cavalry.'

'We have cavalry,' Eoghan squeaked, struggling in vain to free himself from Ferdiad's grip.

'You have a few horses, and a few men who can ride them. That's not cavalry. The one hope you had of defeating the Dragon-riders rode into an ambush, and now there are less of them than there were.' He shook Eoghan as one might shake a rat, then, with a grunt of disgust, let him go. 'But if you move now—'

Eoghan, his face purple, straightened his tunic with an angry yank. 'This army will not move until I say so! And I will not say so until I have my own information on the movements of the enemy from someone I trust. And that's not you, my Lord Ferdiad. I know what your game is!'

'Do you? I wonder. Do you know what Feargus' game is? I doubt it. But I know what yours is. I know what you want and how close you think you are to getting it. What a pity Galloway renounced the rest of the tribute! What a disappointment that must have been – Feargus no longer beholden to you, Yseult slipping out of your grasp, the consolation prize of the Lady Brangianne at risk.'

'Brangianne?!' Eoghan snarled. 'I never wanted her, you fool!'

A red mist washed behind Brangianne's eyes, and she swept

the hanging aside and stormed into the main part of Eoghan's tent.'

'Don't think for one moment I would ever have married you, you small-minded craven, you useless toad, you—!'

'My . . . my Lady—' Eoghan stared at her, his face draining of colour. 'What. . . what are you doing here?'

'What am I doing? I'm here to treat the wounded, of course! Except there aren't any. None but that man in there – and he's a *Briton!* ' The Briton in question had got up and moved to the opening, and was watching and listening in some bemusement. Ferdiad, who'd grinned when she'd revealed herself, was now helpless with laughter, but Brangianne didn't share his amusement.

'Am I to believe what I'm hearing, Eoghan? That you're letting Britons fight your battles for you while you sit here skulking in your tent?'

'I'm not skulking!'

'You're giving a very good impression of it!' she said tartly. 'And what's more—'

She did indeed have a great deal more to say to him but was interrupted by the arrival of one of his men. He was dragging a dirty-faced boy wearing a shapeless red cap and carrying a harp-bag over his shoulder.

'This is the one, my Lord. That singer you've been looking for.' He kicked the boy and sent him sprawling into a corner of the tent. The bag dropped at Eoghan's feet, and he glared at the boy then stamped on it, shattering its contents to pieces.

The boy gave a mew of distress and scrabbled across the ground to cradle the ruined instrument in his arms as if to bring it back to life.

'Oh dear!' Ferdiad's voice quivered with hilarity. 'I don't think you should have done that!'

'I can do what I like!' Eoghan snarled. 'And I will not be

dictated to by a . . . a messenger and a woman who has no right to be here. War is the business of men.'

'Men?!' Brangianne exploded. 'Are you seriously calling yourself a man, Eoghan? For I see no evidence of it. You make me ashamed, all of you. The entire Dalriad army is sitting by this loch, letting Britons fight their battles for them.'

'No-one asked them to fight for us,' Eoghan complained.

'Someone did.' She turned to Ferdiad. 'You, I suppose?'

He shrugged. 'Why not?'

'I can think of a number of reasons.' She narrowed her eyes at him. 'It's them, isn't it?'

'Of course,' Ferdiad replied with one of his sharp smiles. 'Who else?'

The boy, still crouched in the corner of the tent, clutching the ruined harp, stiffened and looked up, but Brangianne had no interest in a bard with a broken harp.

'Who else?' she echoed with a bitter laugh. 'Anyone else, I would have thought. Anyone but them!'

'They felt indebted to Dalriada, for some reason or another.'

'And now we're indebted to *them*.' She rounded on Eoghan once more and jabbed a finger at his chest. 'You will get this army moving to support these Britons. Immediately.'

'I will not be goaded into an ill-considered move!' he insisted. 'I need more information – numbers and dispositions. There are supply routes to be thought of, lines of communication, and—'

'Quite,' Ferdiad cut in. 'You make a passable Steward, Eoghan, but a Steward like you can't lead an army. So who will?'

'I will.' The boy, unnoticed by everyone, dropped the shattered harp and got to his feet, still clutching his ribs where Eoghan's man had kicked him. He pulled off the filthy red cap – and out spilled a torrent of shining auburn hair.

'I will lead the army,' Yseult said.

THE GHOST WOODS

After the fight with the Creonn, Corwynal and the rest of Trystan's men made camp further up the narrow valley, by which they'd descended, and left the wounded there. Then they moved back to the deserted river valley. From time to time, they came across old clearings where crops had been planted, but the dwellings were abandoned, and most were just a rickle of stones on which the forest had encroached. Eventually, they reached a stony ford and crossed to the far side, then rode into the woods beyond until the sound of the river faded behind them to a rush and hiss that came and went with the wind.

Ghost Woods, Ferdiad called them, part of the lands of the ancient Forest People, hunters of deer and hare, tenders of crops in scattered clearings, and herders of little ponies on the open moorland beyond the forest. Corwynal had heard tales of them but, never having seen them himself, had doubted their existence, though Ferdiad had assured him they could still be found in the dense forests that lay between the Dalriads to the south and the Creonn to the north. But the Forest People were friend to neither, and their gods were of earth and stone, of root and branch, oak, alder and fern, gods who stirred with the seasons, half-asleep, half-dreaming, as sap rose and fell. Perhaps it was these gods who drifted like mist between the trees, carrying with them the stink of fox-earths, but Corwynal thought it more likely living men kept these rides open, burned the clearings, and tracked strangers within their woods. For they were certainly being tracked. The wind moaned through the trees, but beneath its deep boom could be heard a thin fluting that was the call of no bird he recognised, a faint ringing that might have been the chiming of little brazen bells, and a drumming that beat through the earth itself, and which grew stronger as they moved slowly through the woods.

Eventually, however, they emerged from the trees, and the sense of a watching presence eased as Corwynal, Trystan and Aelfric dismounted and crawled to the edge of a cliff that fell away to yet another valley in which a river ran southwest to join the one flowing into the loch. And there, in a bend further up the river, they could make out the camp of the Creonn army.

'So many,' Trystan breathed, his eyes narrowing in calculation. 'Five hundred at least. And more coming.'

He jerked his chin towards the north where the land rose to the trackless, uninhabited sodden moorland that lay between the mountains. Clouds hung low there still but, on the very edge of sight, a darker patch moved against the wind, a shadow that crawled over the ground, glinting with spear-tips.

'What do you want to do?' Corwynal asked. 'Fall back and join the Dalriads?'

'It would make sense.'

Corwynal agreed, but he didn't want to retreat, defeated, didn't want to see Brangianne again, defeated, and Trystan didn't much like the taste of defeat either.

'The men won't stomach that,' Aelfric pointed out. 'They're angry.'

'If we're going to fight that many Creonn, we'll have to be clever about it,' Corwynal said.

Trystan nodded. 'Once they reach the valley between here and the loch, they'll be out in the open and vulnerable to horsemen. So we strike them from the woods. They're spearmen, as are the Dalriads. They won't be expecting bowmen. If we move in small groups, avoid direct engagement, strike and disappear so they don't know where, or how many, we are, we should be able to hold the valley until the Dalriads join us – if they ever do.'

'Your Selgovians came to fight Dragon-riders, not Creonn,' Corwynal reminded him. 'Defeat the Riders and we defeat the Creonn. And there they are. Look!'

The Creonn army was a jumble of smaller encampments, each with a cluster of tents and fires, each clan flying its own symbol as well as the Creonn sign of the ram. Within the chaos, however, there was a different camp, this built on a raised platform beside the bend in the river, neat lines of tents set apart from horse-lines, and protected, even within the greater encampment of their allies, by a ditch and wooden palisade built on the bank that surrounded it.

'Good God!' Trystan exclaimed, impressed. 'Kaer insisted they were a relic of some Roman troops, but I didn't believe him, because how could they be after all this time? But now I'm wondering if he was right.'

Trystan might be intrigued, but to Corwynal there was something chilling in that rigid arrangement of ditch and bank, in the symmetry of the tent-lines, something implacable that made him shiver with more than the cold of the rock on which he was lying. He could make out the flutter of pennants on the palisade, could hear, distantly, the wind-blown droning of the dragon-banners, and see the movement of horsemen as they left the camp by a guarded gateway, a gleam of gold within their midst as a shaft of sunlight picked out the armour of one of the Riders.

'That must be The Dragon himself,' Trystan said. 'The man Ferdiad saw. But who is he?'

A good question. Anyone could wear golden armour. Was it the man Corwynal remembered? Could it be?

With that thought, he was back among the mountains with horns echoing, drums beating, his heart thudding, his pulse jumping as spears clashed on shields, his name resounding from cliffs, the name he'd earned. *Wolf!* they yelled. *Wolf!* The music had swelled in great chords in his head until he was the music itself, not flesh or metal, not muscle or blood, but air and wind and the leaping light of an island's summer's dawn, numinous and transcendent. Then his opponent had come, and the voices stilled, the music falling away as he remembered that light failed with each gathering night, that darkness held all the weight of stone and earth, that he still had everything to learn. He hadn't known quite how much.

He'd expected to fail that day, but he'd fought hard, believing he was fighting for his freedom, seeing himself still as music and light, as a flame that refused to gutter and die, and he whispered his true name in his head as the crowd yelled out the name of the man he was to fight. *Dragon!* they'd shouted. *Dragon!* Only after he'd won did he learn that the price of his triumph was the very freedom he'd fought for. He'd been used, and hadn't won after all.

Now, twenty years later, a lifetime of folly behind him, he knew why he was here – to defeat the man who'd taught him to fight all those years before. It was why Ferdiad had come for him, to re-enact an old victory, except it hadn't been a victory. The world was circling to its beginnings, taking him back to the threshold he'd turned away from. It loomed darkly in his future, closer and closer, and as he squinted at the distant gleam of gold, at the man this had to be, he knew that this time he wouldn't be allowed to win.

'Don't be ridiculous!'

Brangianne and Eoghan spoke as one. It was the first time they'd ever agreed on anything.

'You can't lead an army, Yseult,' Brangianne insisted.

'It isn't seemly,' Eoghan said.

Yseult's eyes flashed. 'Someone has to lead this army, seemly or not.'

'My dear . . . my Lady, it's not safe. You must return to Dunadd for your own protection. Your father would never forgive me—'

'That's right!' Her voice was relentless. 'He won't. And I won't forgive him for putting you in charge. What was your price? No, don't answer that. I know what it was, but if you think he'd ever make good on that promise you're more of a fool than I'd thought. A fool and a *coward!*'

Ferdiad was standing to one side, arms folded across his chest, laughing softly, and Eoghan's man just stood there, his mouth hanging open. The Briton frowned, not following the words but understanding the tone as Yseult gave full rein to her frustration, anger, and embarrassment.

Eoghan bore it for a while, but his face, which had paled when the bard turned out to be Yseult, gradually suffused with blood. Finally, he snapped and stepped towards the entrance to the tent.

'Guards!'

But no-one came running. Instead, Eoghan gave a squeal of terror and stepped slowly back from the doorway, urged on by the tip of a rusting sword that prodded him backwards, a blade borne by a tall man wearing a priest's habit, the hood thrown back to show the dragon tattoos on his face.

Behind Brangianne, the Briton, Kaerherdin, muttered a curse and drew a knife, but before he could throw it, Azarion grabbed Brangianne and swung her against him, making her body a shield against the Briton's throw, then snapped out some command in the man's language.

She was more puzzled than frightened. She didn't believe Azarion would hurt her, but wondered whose side he was on now. The Briton glanced around the tent, looking for support, but none was forthcoming. Ferdiad just stood there, a wary reserved expression on his face, and Eoghan and his man were still cowering by the entrance, afraid not so much of that rusting sword as of the Dragon-rider himself. Eventually, with another curse, the Briton dropped his knife, and Azarion let her go then turned on Eoghan and his man to quickly and efficiently bind them at ankle and wrist and silence their mewling protests with a couple of rags. Neither put up a fight.

Ferdiad was staring at Azarion as if he was a ghost from his own past. Maybe he was. 'Who are you?' he breathed, with the look of a man re-evaluating everything he knew.

The Dragon-rider gave him a long appraising gaze that made Ferdiad shiver. 'Who knows?' Azarion said lightly. 'We'll just have to wait and see.' Then he turned to Yseult. 'Well, girl, don't you have an army to lead?'

She grinned and strode from the tent, pausing only to kick Eoghan's man between the legs. Azarion laughed his raven croak and followed her, leaving Brangianne with Ferdiad and the Briton.

'She can't be allowed to do this!' she protested.

Ferdiad shrugged. 'I doubt anyone can stop her, and I'm not about to try, but I suppose I'd better go with her . . .' He turned in the tent's opening. 'Give Corwynal my regards. Or Talorc, given that they're the same man.' He raised an eyebrow. 'I assume you're going back with Kaerherdin? Then tell Trystan I've done what he asked, and the Dalriad army is finally moving.'

With that he was gone, leaving Brangianne with Kaerherdin, together with the moaning Eoghan and his man, neither of whom mattered.

He asked me bring you him.

'You go back?' she asked the Briton. He ought to rest. He'd lost a lot of blood and shouldn't be travelling, but she didn't have the words to say these things and doubted if he'd listen if she did. He had the same stubborn expression as another dark-haired, grey-eyed man.

'You come?' Kaerherdin asked, trying, and failing, to make it sound as if it was no more than a casual invitation. It wasn't, not to her. It was the call she'd been waiting for without knowing it, a call to the woman she'd decided to be, Brangianne the Healer. There were men in the Britons' camp who'd been hurt because her people's army was led by a coward. And so, no matter who awaited her, the man she'd tried to forget or the boy she'd come to love, her answer wasn't in doubt.

'I come.'

Oonagh wasn't a woman given to regrets but, right then, she wished she'd never met Brangianne. If she hadn't, she wouldn't have ended up walking back into the life of the man who'd walked out of hers over twenty years before. She closed her eyes and prayed to all her Gods that when she opened them she'd be back in Carnadail, dull boring Carnadail, dull safe Carnadail. But the gods had never listened to her prayers before and didn't do so now, because she was still standing behind the big tent in the ruin of the fort, with two of the Steward's guards lying unconscious at her feet, and a wriggling little white dog in her arms.

She hadn't been surprised to see the dog, actually, since she'd never trusted Yseult's promise to stay in Dunadd. *The first chance she gets she'll be off,* Oonagh had thought at the time, and so had a good idea of the identity of the bard they were looking for, the one singing those songs of glory. She'd seen the singer herself, wearing a red cap to hide her hair, and had recognised her crudely-carved harp. Now that same singer had just been dragged into the Steward's tent by one of Eoghan's bullies.

Oonagh felt bad about that, for it had been she who'd given the bard away, though the idea had been her father's. The unconscious guards were his doing too. *Things are about to change,* he'd said. They certainly had.

'Oh, well done, Oonagh!' Yseult declared, marching out of the tent and seeing the guards at Oonagh's feet. There was a bruise across her cheekbone, and she'd lost that ridiculous cap, but her colour was high, her eyes wild and excited. 'I'm going to lead the army,' she announced, bending to pat the ecstatic little white dog that Oonagh had let go. 'I'm over-ruling Eoghan.' She laughed at Oonagh's expression. 'Yes, you may well stare! And, yes, he would very much like to object, but he can't.' She threw back her head and laughed. 'He's tied up and gagged and is going to remain that way until I've got the army moving, and—' Her expression darkened as someone else emerged from the tent.

'Lady.' The Fili, Ferdiad the Snake – where had he come from? – bowed mockingly to Yseult. 'Or should I say 'Commander'?' Nevertheless, despite his attempt at irony, he had the look of a man who'd lost control of events.

'How dare you?!' Yseult turned on him. 'How could you bring *him* of all people to Dalriada? How could you let him humiliate us by fighting our battles and laughing at our cowardice?'

'He's not laughing,' Ferdiad said. 'As for cowardice, that's for you to determine now.'

'I will!' she said, her eyes flashing. 'And, since you're here, finally, where you belong, you can help me.'

'You can't lead an army,' Oonagh protested, wondering what the girl was talking about. Who was 'him'?

'No?' Yseult lifted her chin in the way Oonagh knew meant trouble. 'Just watch me . . .' she said and strode off into the camp.

'I rather think she might indeed be worth watching . . .' Ferdiad murmured to himself and turned to Oonagh. 'Are you coming?'

'Not yet,' she said and watched him follow Yseult who was making for the tents of the troop commanders. There was someone she had to speak to first.

'That was your idea of helping Dalriada, was it? Persuading a girl she could lead an army?'

Azarion was standing not far from the tent, his hood shadowing his face once more, waiting, she thought, for this confrontation.

'She'll do better than that old woman.' He nodded at Eoghan's tent. 'All I did was facilitate the inevitable.'

'And now . . . ?'

'Now I need to find a horse and, much as I'd like to take that black devil, I believe your Lady will have more need of him than me.'

'So, you're leaving.' She wasn't surprised. He'd left before, and she hadn't seen him for over twenty years. 'Don't go,' she said abruptly – and that did surprise her.

'I must.' He hesitated. 'Come with me.'

For a wild moment, she wanted to say yes, for he was the only family she had left, and she was half-Dragon-Rider. But the other half of her, the half that wanted roots and certainty, remembered her new family, those two silly women. She cared about Dalriada too, as once her father had cared about her. Perhaps, despite his talk of death and denial, he still cared about her enough not to betray the land that had given her shelter. But that meant she would have to stay.

'I can't,' she said, fighting back tears.

He smiled, pulled his hood more closely around his patterned face, tightened the belt from which hung that long rusty sword, and walked away, merging into the growing shadows between the tents as if he'd never existed at all. Suddenly, without warning, it started to rain, a heavy drumming downpour that drowned out both sight and sound of the camp until she was no longer in the camp at all. She was standing in the doorway of a house watching a man walk away, and she was a child, unaware that the world contained anything as terrifying as death and betrayal. She didn't understand why the man was leaving, or know where he was going or why. But she knew he'd come back. He'd promised, hadn't he, and he'd smiled at her. The child hadn't understood the smile, but the woman did – the smile that gave the lie to the promise, for it was a smile of farewell.

'Hold the light steady . . .'

The flame of the rush-lamp wavered and Brangianne looked up. For a moment, she was in Carnadail and another man was holding a lamp, his head close to hers, a dark-haired man, his face ravaged with fear and exhaustion. Then the light steadied, and she was back in the present.

'Sorry.' Kaerherdin moved the lamp so its light fell more evenly on the wound in the man's leg. An arrow was deeply embedded in the thigh, tearing the muscle, but the bone, though chipped, wasn't shattered, and none of the larger blood vessels were cut. It was a different wound from the once she'd faced in Carnadail, and her patient was a man rather than a boy, this one grimly conscious and fighting to remain so.

'Tell him nearly done,' she said to Kaerherdin, giving the wounded man her calm confident smile as she probed for the last chip of bone.

She and Kaerherdin had reached the Briton's camp around

midday on the day after they'd left Loch Abha. It hadn't been far, but the going had been difficult, despite the long afterglow of the June night and the occasional light of the waxing meadow moon. Eventually, they'd taken shelter in a hollow in the rocks on high ground, and she'd woken stiff, cold and hungry. *I shouldn't have come*, she'd thought more than once, not least for the sake of the Briton who was still weak. But when she tried to persuade him to rest, in a mixture of Briton, Gael and gestures, he shook his head, and so they'd pressed on, crossing high broken moorland riven by gorges in which sharp little streams plunged through granite outcrops. Later, in the early dawn, they'd descended into the green gloom of the trackless Ghost Woods. *I should have stayed with Yseult.* She felt guilty that she hadn't, but Yseult had Ferdiad now, and he, no matter what he'd done or why, could be relied on to support her against Eoghan. The thought made her smile. *Goodness! Relying on Ferdiad! Whatever next?* They wouldn't let Yseult lead the army of course – the troop commanders weren't fools – but they might use her as an excuse to rebel against Eoghan's caution. So maybe Yseult absconding from Dunadd had turned out for the best after all. Chances were to be taken, and Yseult had taken one. Now, in coming with Kaerherdin, Brangianne was taking a chance of her own.

The Britons' camp, when they finally reached it, was in a clearing dominated by a huge ash in a narrow steep-sided valley that ran up into the hills to the south of the main river valley. Her heart had thundered behind her ribs as they'd dismounted, but the place was practically deserted. She'd expected to find it much like the camp by the Loch of the Beacon, with its flies and stench and chaos, but here there was order. Tethered horses grazed quietly downstream, and a handful of dark-haired men, all wearing the symbol of the tree, guarded the camp, in the centre of which was a shelter that had been set up beneath the spreading branches of the ash for the more seriously wounded.

And that was why she was there, the only reason. So she rolled up her sleeves, pinned back her hair, unpacked her supplies and got to work. Kaerherdin, despite her insistence that he should rest, remained beside her, pale-faced but determined, while she worked. He was quiet and efficient, and between his broken Gael and her few words of Briton, they were able to communicate.

The light wavered once more, and she looked up to see him staring out into the dark. As she'd worked, a whole day had passed, and dusk was falling. The leaping flames from a campfire drew shadows out of the evening, and the wood crept closer, as if the trees were stretching out their branches for warmth.

'Listen!' Kaerherdin said. 'They coming.'

In the distance, muted by oak and pine, she heard the plangent notes of a horn. Moments later, another answered and the echoes rang through the still June evening.

Her heart pulsed in her throat, and her fingers shook as she sewed the man's wound closed and bound it with clean linen. Her smile was rigid now, and her knees trembled as she got to her feet and went to stand by the entrance to the shelter.

Talorc still didn't appear, though others came, dark-haired men like Kaerherdin, all of them wearing the sign of the tree. All were weary, but they tended to the needs of their horses before themselves. Only once they'd done so did they come to the shelter to visit hurt companions, or with wounds of their own and, understanding she was a healer, nodded to her with the grave courtesy they all seemed to possess.

There had been a fight, apparently, a running battle in the forest, the Creonn driven back. Some of the Britons had died, Kaerherdin told her after talking with those who'd returned. Her heart went on banging, harder and harder, as, over and over, Talorc didn't come.

Then, out of the growing night, there he was, walking slowly towards her, carrying a wounded man over his shoulder. He didn't see her at first, for the light was behind her, and the crowd around the fire threw the shelter into temporary shadow. Then he caught sight of her. She saw shock shudder through him, watched the colour drain from his face, saw him stagger beneath the weight of something heavier than the man he carried.

Her heart lurched to a standstill, solidifying into a cold stone within her chest, and her body hardened into immobility. A muscle in her neck spasmed as the desire to flee warred with her inability to move. Her smile was still frozen to her face.

'Put him down there.' She pointed to a place beside the entrance to the shelter, her voice short and clipped out of a dry breathless throat. It was as if she stood outside herself, watching her own reaction as he, in his turn, watched her. She heard the chill in her own voice and felt as if she was no longer stone but ice and, like ice, she could move, if only sluggishly. She watched herself fold her arms across her chest to protect her heart and to stop herself from reaching out to him, for she knew she'd meet ice there too, a rigid shell of it, thick and translucent, well beyond the power of a single hand's warmth to melt.

'What ... what are you doing here?' His voice, the remembered cadences that plagued her dreams, was barely controlled. That, she supposed bleakly, was something. But not enough.

He asked me bring you him. Clearly, that was a lie. Whoever had asked for her, it hadn't been him.

'I was told some Britons had need of a healer. So, if you could put him there ...' she repeated, calmly, professionally, coldly.

He lowered the wounded Briton onto the pallet, then rose to his feet, slowly and awkwardly for a man who'd once moved with such grace. His face, when it turned to her, was as bleak and set as her own. He hadn't greeted her, hadn't said her name. Or she his, but by what name should she call him? Not Talorc, the name she'd whispered to wake him on summer mornings or cried out on summer nights, the name of the man she'd wept for when she'd lost her child. Talorc had gone, as if he'd never existed, leaving behind Corwynal of Lothian, betrayer of her people, an enemy and a stranger.

'Why are you here?' she asked. Her throat was aching with the need to weep, and it turned her voice harsh and angry. He didn't answer and made a gesture with his hands that could have meant anything, incomprehension, indifference, regret, and so silence settled between them, ice thickening, so palpable that she shivered and was glad when someone called out her name.

'Brangianne?!'

A young man, glittering with mail and with a long cavalry sword at his side, a quiver of arrows at his shoulder, and a bow in one hand, was striding towards her. He was graceful in the way the man standing before her had once been graceful, and that, more than anything else, told her who this must be long before she recognised his features.

'Drust?'

The name caught at his stride as once his wound had done, and a little of the openness left his expression. Like Talorc – Corwynal – he looked older by more than the year since she'd last seen him. But in Drust – she couldn't help but think of him as Drust – it was less of an ageing than a coming into a maturity that fitted him like his mail, and she sensed in him the power of a commanding presence and the separateness that comes with leadership and responsibility.

'Not Drust.' His voice was apologetic, still with a hint of laughter behind it, still music. 'Here I'm Trystan. And Corwynal is . . . Corwynal; I think you must know that by now.' He glanced at Talorc, a frown cutting between his brows, and when he looked back at her, his welcome was gone. 'I asked Kaerherdin to bring us a healer from the Gael camp. I didn't imagine for one moment . . .'

He asked me bring you him. So there *had* been a truth there, but one she'd misunderstood.

'It's not safe here,' Drust – Trystan – went on. 'We drove the Creonn back today, but tomorrow there will be more of them, and we'll have to retreat, unless your people come as they promised.'

'They'll come!' she snapped, furious with Eoghan for his procrastination, for shaming Dalriada. Yseult, at least, would make sure that promise was kept, from pride and anger if nothing else.

Trystan looked at her steadily. 'Good,' he said eventually, not believing her and, after a glance at the older man, still standing motionless two steps from her, an impossible distance away, he walked off to join the men around the fire.

Hardly a welcome! she thought but didn't appreciate how grudging it was until she caught sight of another familiar face, one that, unlike that of the boy and his father, had always been open and easy to read. It was far too easy now, and all she saw in Aelfric's face was hostility.

'You shouldn't be here,' he told her bluntly, and Talorc, as if that truth had finally freed him from his frozen immobility, strode into the darkness beyond the fires. 'He'd forgotten you,' Aelfric added. 'It was best that way for everyone.'

Including me, she thought. *I'll leave in the morning.* She didn't know the way, but if she set her face to the west surely she'd reach the loch eventually? No-one wanted her here. She badly needed to cry, needed, like Talorc, to walk into the dark of the Ghost Wood, to lean her suddenly aching head against the cool bark of a tree and weep her heart out. But she couldn't. Not yet. She straightened her spine, aware that she'd been standing hunched over as if to protect herself from a blow. *Too late for that,* she thought bitterly. She rubbed at her eyes, blinked tears away, swallowed to clear her throat of the appalling need to wail, and turned to the tent where the wounded lay.

'Well,' she said, smiling rather too brightly at Kaerherdin. 'We seem to have more work to do.'

He didn't smile in return, as he might have done earlier that day, and was looking at her with the same expression as Aelfric, less easy to interpret but no less disturbing for that. His glance slid past her into the forest where a man he knew had fled, and, when he looked back at her, his dawning understanding and bitterness were more than she could bear.

But it had to be borne, so she crouched beside the man Talorc had brought. He'd regained consciousness but was confused as she examined his hurts on account of a blow to the head. He had a flesh wound of some kind in the arm, but he'd live. Others wouldn't. And she realised she couldn't run away from any of this. These men, these strangers, were why she was there. She wasn't Lady of Carnadail, sister of Feargus, and not, absolutely not, lover of the man who'd forgotten her. She was Brangianne the Healer, and she'd bear her inner wounds – they wouldn't kill her – and be what she'd decided to be. So she worked by torchlight with the help of the now silent Kaerherdin, and bound the man's wounds, checked those of others, dispensed poppy or smiles as required, and brought ease back into a painful world, at least for these men, if not for the one who'd fled into the wood. She was back in her old dream – the line of men, her own exhaustion, the longing to lie down with them – and so at last she did so, lying in the one space that remained, with a bleeding gap in her chest. But in this reality no-one came, no dark-haired man with a storm in his eyes, and there was no-one to give her back her heart, and nothing, in this wide world, neither poppy, nor salve, nor sweet remembrances, to ease the pain of that.

15

DON'T LET HER WEAKEN YOU

'**A**re you thinking about Brangianne?' Trystan asked.

Corwynal had thought of nothing else since he'd seen her in the camp, and the familiar clench in his chest had turned into a sick pulsing ache.

He was lying, wrapped in his cloak, between Trystan and Aelfric, trying to sleep. He'd watched the constellation the Caledonians called The White Stag arc across the sky, tracked by a waxing moon, then disappear behind a bank of cloud that slid across the sky from the north. An owl called out, another answered and, from further down the valley, a dog fox barked. He heard the scream of something dying in the night and thought of all the other deaths there would be that day.

'This is no place for a woman!' Trystan said irritably. 'But she'll have to stay here now. I can't spare anyone to escort her back. I'll have Kaer guard the camp, and her. He won't like it, but it will be his own fault. He should have had more sense than to have brought a woman, and he knows it. He's not thinking straight, but I suppose that's my fault. I shouldn't have sent him with Ferdiad with that wound in his arm, or asked him to come back, but at least we know the Dalriad army's on the move at last . . .'

Corwynal stopped listening. He was thinking about Brangianne, about her coldness. Yet what had he expected? He'd known she must hate him, and yet part of him had hoped ... What had he hoped for?

'... so you win,' Trystan said, cutting into his thoughts.

'Win? What about?'

'About fighting separately, of course. But I don't like it.'

Corwynal had been trying to persuade Trystan that they should split the troops up so they could cover more ground, but that wasn't his real reason. He'd sent a message via the Creonn to The Dragon, that Talorc of Atholl fought for Dalriada. Surely The Dragon would remember him from the Island and recall an unpaid debt. Even if he didn't remember, and they were to meet as enemies, he wanted to meet the Dragon alone. He didn't want Trystan anywhere near him. Now, because Kaerherdin couldn't fight, he'd won that argument. The plan was for them to attack in small groups without warning, break up the Creonn spearmen before they could form a line, strike and vanish, and tempt the Creonn into the woods where they'd be at the mercy of Selgovian archers. It wasn't ideal; woodland was poor terrain for horses, but the little Selgovian mounts were used to moving about in forest. They were quick and clever and would come to a call if their riders chose to fight on foot.

As for the Dragon-riders, singly they could be dealt with; they'd proved that. A whole troop of them, however ... ? Corwynal wasn't so sure. The key would be the man who led them, and that was why Ferdiad had come to find him, so Corwynal could fight and kill their leader and thus demoralise the others. But the prospect terrified him. The Dragon might be twenty years older than the young weapons-master of the Island, but so was he. The outcome was far from inevitable. He hoped, fervently, it wouldn't come to a fight.

'Kaer's men will follow me,' he assured Trystan.

'That's not what I'm worried about.' Trystan gripped his arm for emphasis. 'Don't let her weaken you.'

'Of course not.' Trystan sighed and turned on his side, his back to him, and Corwynal knew he wasn't convinced. He hadn't even convinced himself.

He slept in the end and woke in the pale green glow of a summer's dawn, disorientated and exhausted. Beside him, Aelfric was yawning and rubbing sleep from his eyes. Corwynal's cloak was furred with moisture, for a faint mist had risen in the night and was drifting like ghostly banners about the clearing, torn open here and there by spears of light from the rapidly rising sun.

'The Scots? Any sign of them?' Trystan stood a little way apart, talking softly with a Selgovian scout. The man shook his head, and Trystan looked over at Corwynal, saw he'd heard, but didn't say anything. There was no need. Both knew what it would mean if the Scots failed them. They'd have to retreat, and their losses would all have been for nothing. They hadn't come to Dalriada to fight the entire Creonn nation, but to strike at the force that controlled them, the Dragon-riders.

The camp came to life quietly, the men making their preparations without their usual banter, buckling weapons to saddle or waist, slipping mail, cold from the night, over tunics, checking the slide of a sword in a scabbard, the number of arrows in a quiver. Horses were watered, fed and saddled, and water-skins were filled from the pool above the horse-lines. Mouthfuls of food were swallowed as the sun rose through the trees, its warmth and light impossibly precious, a benison from the gods.

Taranis and Camulos, the gods of war, drew close on the morning of a battle, and Corwynal was aware of their presence in everything around him: the singing of the birds high in the canopy, the sway of grasses on the lifting breeze, the soft blowing of Janthe's breath and the faint quiver in her muscles, the green summer smell of growing things, of fern and bilberry. And in the woman standing by the shelter, her hair disordered from sleep, shading her eyes against a sun that washed her in gold.

Why are you here? Brangianne had asked. He hadn't given her an answer, but now he spoke his reasons to himself, knowing she wouldn't hear them, but hoping that somehow, in the long day of battle, she might come to understand.

To fight for you. To fight anyone who might harm you. To kill and maim and make widows and orphans for you to weep over. To spill blood and tear open flesh for you to make whole once more. To risk my life for you, perhaps to die. If I'm hurt, you'll bind up my wounds with no more thought than you'd give to the wounds of any other man, even my enemy. If I die, you'll grieve for my death no more than you would for other deaths. And you'll not thank me for any of it.

Someone handed him a skin of water and a bannock fresh from the fire. It tasted of smoke and ash and settled like cinders in his stomach, but he forced himself to eat and drink, knowing he'd regret it later if he didn't. The cold of the water made his teeth hurt, but the ache was as nothing to the one inside him, the scraped hollow in which his heart had once lain, a heart that belonged to the woman standing in the sun. He looked at her for a long time, then touched his heels to Janthe's flanks, turned her head and trotted down the track towards whatever waited for him in the shadowed woods beside the river, carrying stillness within him.

It lasted only as long as it took to reach the main valley and the forest beyond, where the trees thinned to birch scrub and the grass was clumped with reeds, loud with the burbling song of curlews, and where the Creonn, first of many, came screaming towards them through the golden mist of a battle morning.

She knew from that long unsmiling look, from the set of his shoulders as he turned away, riding from the sunlight of the camp into shadow, the answer to her question. *Why are you here?* He hadn't replied because she ought to have known the answer. Now, too late, she did.

He wasn't here simply to fight. He wasn't like other men in that. Nor was it pride, or gratitude, or recompense for an imagined wrong, though those would be part of it. His reasons were deeper and stronger, sourced in the core of his soul. This was something he couldn't have lied about if he'd tried.

He was here for love. But it wasn't for Trystan, though that would be part of it too, for man and boy were bound by ties stronger than blood. Yet for all that Trystan appeared to lead these Britons, it hadn't been him who'd come to Dalriada, the man he thought of as his brother following him. It was the other way around. Talorc – Corwynal – had brought these men to Dalriada for her.

Behind her in the shelter a man moaned in pain, but she remained standing by the entrance, her attention on the woods in the valley and the slopes beyond. Were they fighting already? She could hear nothing but birdsong, the calls piercing the stillness beneath the trees. But still she listened, turning her head to the west, hoping to hear her people's army, the unmistakeable heartbeat of marching feet.

We'll have to retreat unless your people come. But surely they'd come now? Yseult would make them, or Ferdiad. They'd prevail against Eoghan's caution. She listened in vain, however, hearing only the birds, the distant bark of a stag, and closer, almost beneath hearing, the faint ringing of little bells.

The wounded man moaned once more, breaking into her thoughts, and she turned back to the shelter. Kaerherdin looked up at her when she came in, his eyes narrowing, as if he'd seen a change in her. *That man sees too much*, she thought, bending to the man who'd cried out, and when, some time later, she looked back at Kaerherdin, lines of resentment marred his handsome features. They'd left him to guard the camp, to protect it – and her – from any attack, and he blamed her for his enforced inaction.

She turned to the wounded man, laid a cool palm on his forehead, and did what she could for his pain before moving on to the next, checking bandages and bindings, murmuring a reassuring word here, smiling a reassuring smile there, and blinking away the sun in her eyes. It would be hot later, a day of blood and screams and the smell of terror, and impossible things for her to deal with. Later, she'd be busy. It was the reason she was here, but only part of the reason. She was a healer, and there was a man who was hurt, a man *she'd* hurt, and she'd have to heal him too. And so, having done what she could for the men under her care, and prepared as much as possible for those still to come, she went to the horse-lines, saddled The Devil and pulled herself into the saddle. Kaerherdin wouldn't like it, but he could hardly leave the camp unguarded to chase after a single woman when all she was doing was following her man into battle, as so many women had done before her. She had to know he lived, had to watch him fight, share his fear, and feel the hurts of his body as if they were in her own. Perhaps she'd see him die, but better that than learning of it from another and never knowing the true manner of his death. She had to be there at the end, whatever the end might bring, to say the words he might not even hear, far less understand. She had to take back the lie that had saved his life in Carnadail.

Did you ever love me?

No! she'd screamed, not at him but at the men her brother had sent to kill him. Yet she *had* loved him, even then, no matter who he was, no matter what he'd done. She understood that now. She loved Corwynal of Lothian, and she could say his name at last because who he was and what he'd done didn't matter anymore. Because he was the other half of her soul.

Reaching the valley and the ford across the river, she paused, listening, but all she heard was a horn ring out, half-imagined and impossibly distant. Nearer, on the other side of the river, in the thinning woods that rose to the hills to the north, she heard shouting, the unmistakable clash of weapons, then screaming. He was there, fighting for her. Her heart raced, robbing her of breath, and she was sick with something beyond terror. She wanted to flee, to head west for the safety of her own people. But she didn't. She flicked the reins and gave The Devil his head, releasing him to a battle joy she couldn't feel for herself, and the horse surged across the river and into the woods. *I love you, Corwynal of Lothian. I forgive you for everything.* It was the reason she'd come to the camp and the reason she'd left it. Now all she had to do was find him and make him believe it.

'Look out!'

The warning came almost too late. Corwynal dropped to a crouch and lifted his shield as the Creonn spear streaked towards him. It splintered the edge of the shield and fell harmlessly away, but the force of it threw him to one side, and he scrabbled desperately at the ground for purchase. Finding a tree-root, he grasped it and used the leverage to pull himself around. His damaged shield swung with him to take the full force, near the boss, of yet another Creonn spear that embedded itself in the leather-covered birch, its weight dragging the shield down. He flung the shield away, scrambled behind the tree, a big elm, and heard the thud of two more spears strike the trunk on the far side.

'Corwynal!' The cry was from further away now. He shook sweat-soaked hair out of his eyes as the last of Kaerherdin's men disappeared into the undergrowth beyond a clearing near the edge of the forest. 'Corwynal, come on!'

The Selgovians were retreating. It was what they were there to do – to fight then vanish once more, only to burst out of the tree-gloom somewhere else. In these woods, they were the huntsmen; at least that was how it had begun. Now, more and more of the Creonn were moving west along the river valley, still to the north of the river. Family was travelling with family, clan with clan, and it was becoming harder to engage them. All the Britons could do was lure them westward into the arms of the supposedly advancing Dalriads. As yet, they hadn't seen any Dragon-riders, not even with the Creonn. Corwynal wasn't sure if that was a good sign or not.

'Come on!' The voice was irritated now. If he didn't move, they'd have to leave him. Trystan's orders had been clear. Yet they also knew Trystan wouldn't forgive them if they left Corwynal behind. It was a contradiction, and war was no place for contradictions.

Corwynal knew that if he left the safety of the elm, he'd be hopelessly exposed, and could imagine all too vividly the whistle of yet another Creonn spear as he made a break for it, the thud of it striking his spine. He wished he was wearing mail, but he'd chosen to fight bare-chested, not only because it was lighter and cooler but to allow the Creonn to see the designs that would tell them who and what he was. It might make them pause, if only for a heartbeat, and today he'd need every heartbeat's delay he could find.

'Corwynal!' A warning this time, but he'd already heard footfalls on the other side of the elm. There were two of them, their bodies the only shields he was likely to have against the spears from the far side of the clearing. It was time to leave the shelter of the tree. Corwynal's palms were sweating, but he brushed them against his leggings, gripped his sword tightly and slid the other from its scabbard on his back. Then he was moving into the sun, screaming his challenge, coming in low to rise with a sword in each hand, one arcing upwards from the ground. It cut deep into the abdomen of one of them, the man's scream horrifying as, his innards spilling, he folded himself over the blade, the weight of his maimed and dying body dragging at Corwynal's arm.

It was the weight that saved him, the pull of death granting him life, as a hand-held spear thrust past him. He felt the wind of its passing, and the bright blue jay's feathers bound behind the blade flicked along his cheek like the kiss of a lover as the spear was drawn back for a second thrust. It never came. An arrow fletched with the feathers of a white goose whined past his ear. There was a dull thud, a cry, and a body fell into a patch of sunlight.

Then he was running, the skin on his back crawling, imagining a spear bursting through his stomach as he ran. He jinked like a hare from one shaft of sun to the next, from shadow to light, from light to shadow. One spear missed him completely. Another struck him on the metalled shoulder scabbard and skittered harmlessly away, but the force of it sent him tumbling forward, his shoulder hitting the ground, the jar of it right up his arm as he rolled, out of control, through a patch of nettles and into the relative safety of a thicket of hazel.

'Nice!' The voice, half-amused, half-sarcastic, was Selgovian. They'd waited for him after all. He'd have to reprimand them for that. But not now. Not until he could breathe.

'Where now?' another asked. They'd gathered the horses together in a hollow, Janthe among them, in preparation for riding on and striking somewhere else at the tide of Creonn heading west.

'Give me a moment,' he gasped, sinking down, his back against a rock. His heart was hammering so hard he wouldn't have been surprised if it burst through his breastbone like the spear he'd imagined. His breath rasped painfully as he dragged great lungsful of air into his labouring chest, and his hands were slick with sweat, his whole body streaming with it. He felt old.

You are *old.*

As ever, Arddu came to him when he was at his weakest. He was close enough for Corwynal to smell his breath and see antlers meshed with the branches of the trees.

'Go away,' he breathed. The Selgovian nearest to him gave him an odd look. 'I don't need you.'

But he did. He'd been fighting badly all day. That he was still alive and relatively unhurt was due more to luck than anything. His skills were still there, as were his instincts, but he was used to having more. Once, not so long ago, he'd had the fire of the gods in his blood, their music ringing in his ears. Once, he could have ignored the ageing of his body.

Don't let her weaken you. They were Trystan's words, but it was the God's voice he heard in his head.

'I won't.'

Too late. You already have.

Then Arddu was gone, leaving behind the faint smell of rutting stag and a fear deep in Corwynal's' belly, because the God was right. To the east of them, not far enough away, Brangianne was in the Selgovian camp, guarded by a man with a useless arm and a handful of men just as badly wounded. Corwynal had been conscious of that all day, his thoughts forever turning east to where she was, imagining some of the Creonn finding the entrance to the narrow valley, imagining them screaming into the camp and then . . . and then . . .

Further up the slopes of the Ghost Wood Trystan and the others would be pushing west as they'd planned, but behind him, to the east, was Brangianne. So, west or east? Trystan or Brangianne? A man shouldn't have to make a choice like that.

All men have to make choices.

Inevitably, the God was back, crooning over Corwynal's struggle to choose, but before he could make that choice he heard the drum of hooves on the track coming from the east. *Something's happened at the camp!* He reached for Janthe's reins to mount up and meet whoever it was who'd come, but the rider, going too fast, rode into the clearing they'd just left. A horse screamed, but it was a scream of fury rather than pain, a scream Corwynal recognised since he'd taught The Devil to do it. Then he heard other screams and recognised those too.

'Ah, Oonagh! The very person I was looking for . . .'

In normal circumstances Oonagh might have been flattered to be sought out by such a handsome man, but this was Ferdiad, that snake of a Fili, and he hadn't come to find her because of her charms.

'I'm busy,' she told him.

'Stealing a horse?' Ferdiad had found her in the horse-lines near the loch where she'd been eyeing the unclaimed horses. 'In case you were thinking of taking mine—' He nodded at a dark bay with white socks, '—I need it.'

'Why? To escape if things go badly?' she asked, her lip curling.

He smiled cheerfully, unmoved by her disdain. 'Exactly! But I'm here for information, not to admit my lack of courage. I saw you talking with that Dragon-rider, so, tell me, Oonagh, who is he, and what is he to you?'

She shrugged. 'He's someone I knew twenty years ago. I haven't seen him since, so whatever it is you want to know, I can't tell you.'

He narrowed his ice-green eyes at her. 'Not good enough, Oonagh. I need to know what that particular Dragon-rider is doing in the Dalriad camp and why he helped Yseult take over the army.'

'I don't know,' she said, wishing she did. 'But I've questions of my own. You've been with Britons, haven't you? Which Britons?'

'I think you can guess.'

'It's Drust and that Caledonian, isn't it?' *And that oaf of an Angle.* 'Is Aelfric—?'

'There you are, Oonagh—!' Yseult could have chosen a better time to interrupt. 'Oh, it's you!'

Yseult was as put out to see Ferdiad as Oonagh had been, and no wonder, for she was dressed for riding and leading not only a spirited little bay mare Oonagh recognised from Dunadd, but a wall-eyed roan.

'Yes, it's me,' Ferdiad agreed. 'And you, if I'm not mistaken, and in complete disregard for the conversation we had earlier, are intent on joining what everyone is laughably calling the cavalry.'

'They *are* cavalry!'

'They're men riding horses; that isn't the same thing, as I already explained to Eoghan. Anyway, you did your bit when you over-ruled him. You share your father's courage, and clearly have the heart of a warrior, but you don't share your father's guile and you've no experience of war.' He twitched aside her cloak to reveal that over her boy's garb of tunic and leggings she was wearing mail, its weight accounting for the stiffness of her bearing and the smell of oiled steel. 'Not that you don't look magnificent,' he added with a sly grin. 'I can't understand why that boy didn't fall for you in Carnadail.'

Yseult's eyes flashed as she forced her mass of auburn hair into a leather cap. 'How can you *speak* of him!'

'Easily. He's the reason you're here.'

'That's not true!' But the colour had risen into Yseult's face. 'Well, maybe it is. Someone has to show that liar we're not all cowards. Are you coming, Oonagh?' She turned her back on the Fili. 'I brought you a horse.'

Ferdiad looked from one to the other and sighed. 'What a troublesome pair of women you are! I suppose this means I have to go too.'

'Why?' Yseult asked.

'Because I'm the King's messenger,' he said dryly. 'As such, I'll be expected to take Feargus the news that his daughter wilfully rode to her death.'

On which discouraging note, the rabble of Dalriad riders set off in advance of the foot soldiers, leaving the safety of the loch to head upriver. And riding with them were two women, a snake, and a little white dog.

'Get out of here!' Corwynal thrust Janthe's reins at one of the Selgovians. 'I'll catch you up! Leave Janthe where I can find her.'

Distantly, he thought he heard horses, felt rather than heard the thud of their hooves, and half-imagined the jingle of their bridles. Had the Dalriads come at last? Or was it the Dragon-riders? Then a horn rang out, Trystan's horn call of three rising notes that signalled they should all retreat and regroup. The Selgovians were reluctant to leave him behind but they wouldn't disobey the horn call. 'Tell Trystan the Creonn have the Healer. He'll understand. *Go!*'

The man nodded and melted into the trees, and Corwynal scrambled his way back through the hazel thicket to the clearing, a grassy meadow backed by high ground crowned with oak and ash and dense scrub willow. The Devil was on the far side, plunging and rearing, still screaming his defiance, but the

Creonn had managed to get a halter about his neck, and two of them had dragged him to a tree and tethered him there. Of Brangianne, there was no sign, but he could hear her screaming. Then, abruptly, it stopped.

Gods, no! Was she hurt? Stunned? Dead? Or were the Creonn, even now, taking their pleasure of her? It didn't occur to him to wonder why she was there at all. He was frozen, unable to think, unable to move. Then Brangianne, alive and unharmed as yet, was pushed forward by a Creonn warrior. Her hands were tied behind her back and a gag was strangling her screams. The man held her by the hair, a knife in his other hand, using her body as a shield.

'We have your woman!'

My woman. A truth there, the only one that meant anything.

So, man of Atholl, or Lothian. Do you need me now? The voice came from inside him, low and amused, but Corwynal shook his head. There was always a price to pay for the God's help; he'd learned that to his cost. He didn't need Arddu's help because he wasn't going to fight. He couldn't risk it because he couldn't tell how many there were. He might defeat one, maybe two, three if he was lucky, if he took them on one after the other, but if there were any more the last of them would kill Brangianne before he could get to her. So he couldn't risk fighting them.

'Let her go!' Corwynal called out. 'Have the Creonn sunk so low that they fight women?'

He spoke in Caledonian, as they did. They knew who he was, and that gave him an opportunity – if there was time. Because, through the sound of the rising wind in the trees, he could a low droning that grew louder as it approached until it was a high wailing shriek, a sound that came not from the east but from the west. Which meant the Dragon-riders, in force this time, had got behind them and were now between them and the Scots.

'You hear that, man of Atholl?' the Creonn called out, jerking his head towards the sound of the still distant but approaching Dragon-riders. 'Shall we give her to them?'

'She's just a woman!' Corwynal protested. 'You think The Dragon will thank you for a nameless woman when you could give him Talorc of Atholl?'

'You'd exchange yourself for her?' The voice was incredulous.

'I would,' he said. 'Let her go.'

They'd pass in the centre of the clearing. He'd have a few moments only, but they would be enough. *I love you. Forgive me.*

'No.'

No? Their refusal fell like a stone on his heart. 'You know who I am? You know what I'm worth?'

'We've heard of you, Talorc of Atholl. They say many things of the Creonn, but not that we'd take a man of your reputation without a fight. If you want the woman, fight for her.'

The Creonn warrior dragged Brangianne to a sapling birch that stood on the edge of the clearing and bound her to it, then stood over her with a knife in his hand, as another couple of clansmen emerged from the trees. He could smell the rank stink of the sheep's tallow with which they stiffened their hair.

'Don't think you're up to it, old man? Can't get it up anymore? Perhaps your woman would welcome a fine Creonn buck between her thighs.' The man with the knife reached for the neck of Brangianne's dress.

You still don't need me? The voice was mocking now.

'Wait!' Corwynal called out, stepping out into the clearing. 'I'm Talorc of Atholl, and I'll give you the fight you want. However many of you there are, I'll fight you – all of you, all at once. Now get away from her!'

The man laughed, exchanged a few words with one of the others, nodded, and then, with a smile, lowered his knife. More Creonn emerged into the clearing, thrusting spears in one hand, battle shields in the other, daggers at their waists. First one, then

another, then a third and fourth—

He couldn't do it without help. *What do you want this time?*

For you to make a choice. The boy or the woman.

I . . . I can't make that choice!

a fifth, sixth—

What if I promise both will live?

—and a seventh.

I will help you save her, but you will lose one of them.

He'd already lost Brangianne, and a price already paid was worth the paying if it meant she'd live.

I choose Trystan then. He reached for his swords, and the God thrilled through his veins and nerves. But, in his heart, all Corwynal felt was despair.

'Kill them! Kill them all!'

Yseult was yelling like a demon as she watched the Creonn being slaughtered, but Oonagh was sick to the stomach. Some of them were little more than boys, and though she knew they'd come to kill Dalriad boys in their turn they were still boys, still no older than her son, no better equipped, no better led.

The Dalriad horsemen had run into a troop of them out in the open, in the river plain, not far from the northern end of the loch. Even Oonagh, no strategist, had thought that a mistake on the Creonn's part. Against foot-soldiers, they might have had a chance of escaping, but against horsemen they had none, especially in the absence of their so-called allies, the Dragon-riders.

'Where are they?' Ferdiad muttered, peering into the woods that swept down to the river from the higher ground, woodland that could have concealed anything, Britons or Dragon-riders. Oonagh, however, was glad the Dragon-riders weren't fighting alongside the Creonn. She'd been afraid of seeing her father on the other side of a battle and knowing he'd made a choice that wasn't her. But maybe they wouldn't come. Maybe her father had some influence. Maybe he'd persuaded his people not to fight at all.

'They're falling back!' Yseult screamed. 'They're running away!'

She was right. The Creonn had fallen back in some sort of order, but now they were fleeing in disarray, heading back east along the river. The fight had become a rout.

'Come on!' Yseult shouted, kicking her mare forward.

'No, you fool!' Ferdiad made a grab for her bridle, but it was too late. Yseult had gone, still yelling as she rode to join the mass of horsemen pursuing the fleeing Creonn, then pushed her way through them until she'd outstripped the pack. Her cap had fallen off, and her hair streamed like a banner as she galloped along the river track, the little white dog in close pursuit. 'For Dalriada! For Dalriada!' Men cheered and kicked their own horses into a gallop to follow her.

'Shit!' Ferdiad muttered, his horse sidling beneath him, catching his rider's indecision, but Oonagh didn't hesitate.

'I'm going after her.'

'It's too late. Look!'

From the trees flanking the river, figures emerged, a troop of riders who were mailed and helmeted, whose horses gleamed with armour and who moved slowly to begin with but gathered speed to crash into the stretched-out and vulnerable Dalriad horsemen.

'Is he there?' Ferdiad demanded as Oonagh, open-mouthed with disbelief, watched as her countrymen were slaughtered by her father's people. But if her father was there, she couldn't see him, or make him out, for many wore elaborately horned helmets that obscured their faces. 'It was a trap,' Ferdiad said bitterly.

'This is what he wanted when he helped Yseult lead the army. I should have seen it.' He turned his horse to head back to the loch.

'Where are you going? We have to save her!'

'That's what I'm doing. I'm going for help.' He kicked his mount into a canter and disappeared back along the river to safety.

But Oonagh knew he'd be too late. The Dragon-riders were between Yseult and the few riders who'd held back from her impetuous charge. Yseult looked back once, saw what lay behind her and took off, galloping east, away from the slaughter. But as Oonagh watched, one of the Dragon-riders caught sight of her and kicked his mount in pursuit. Yseult fled, but the Rider caught up with her, dragged her from her horse and over his saddle in front of him, then rode off with her.

So, like Ferdiad, Oonagh turned her horse and rode away from the battlefield. She too was going to find help.

The music crashed through him, fire burning in his veins in the old sweet agony, and the light changed. The mists of the forest vanished, leaving everything hard-edged and silver, glittering with possibility. Corwynal could see properly once more, and the pattern of what would happen was clear in his mind. The first Creonn would come in high, the second low; the third and fourth would circle around him, and the others would hang back. And so it was easy – his right blade flung up to block the first blow, then sweeping back to parry the second. Then he was whirling, cutting in on the right, stamping forward on the left, his sword red as one man went down. His heart was beating like a Caledonian war-drum, strong and clear, his breath surging into laughter in his throat. He was Talorc of Atholl and, with the God in his blood, he was invincible.

His sword hacked deep into the neck of another. A low thrust was met and parried, but his blade slid along the length of the Creonn's into the man's groin, and his opponent fell back with a scream of agony. The others bunched together, as cattle before a wolf, because here he was the wolf indeed, the Wolf of Atholl, the Wolf of Lothian, and he was snarling his defiance. His twin swords dripped red in the green of the forest. He didn't wait for the rest of them to attack. Instead, he plunged forward, screaming, scattering them apart, pulling away from a spear thrust and ducking beneath another. Then he was through and turning, leaving a body behind him.

Old man, am I? He came back at them before they could turn to face him, and he cut one down, his blade shattering ribs, before hacking to the left, deep into the man's side. Then there were only two left, edging back, shields held low, spears trembling in their hands. Behind him in the clearing, the bodies of the Creonn lay scattered, one still alive but panting with the desperation of a mortal wound. In front of them was the old man, Talorc of Atholl, who'd once had a reputation, the man they'd mocked and laughed at. They weren't laughing now. He stamped forward, feinted to the left, was blocked by a shield, then thrust in on the right, and another was down. And so there was only one of them left.

The music, no longer needed, began to fade, and the God's breath was no more than a taste in his throat, the smell of incense-smoke in his lungs. Arddu's presence no longer crashed through him, but instead pulsed at the root of his nerves. He became aware of a thrush singing high in the spreading branches of an ash, the piercing calls of goldcrests flitting through the canopy, and The Devil's bridle jingling as he jerked at his tether. He could hear the rasp of air in the lungs of the Creonn facing him. The man was spent, expecting to die, but, whatever they said of the Creonn, they didn't lack courage, so Corwynal would make it a clean kill. The moves formed ahead of him, the stabbing blow the man would block with his shield, the way Corwynal would fall back then strike forwards, above the returning blow, straight into the man's breastbone. He took a single breath and—

'No!' Brangianne had worked the gag away from her mouth. 'No, don't! Let him go!'

Let him run off and bring others? Even as the thought formed, the man whirled and disappeared into the willow scrub.

'Let him go!' Brangianne yelled as Corwynal moved to follow the Creonn. Her voice pulled him back, and the man crashed deeper into the woods and vanished.

'Why?' he asked, sheathing his swords then going over and untying her bonds. She wouldn't look at him at first. All her attention was on the carnage in the clearing, her eyes wide with horror, and when she finally looked at him and took in his blood-sheeted body, her expression was one of disgust.

'Did so many men have to die?'

'Would you rather only one man had died?'

She pushed past him, went over to the wounded Creonn and knelt beside him, laying a hand on his forehead and smiling – *smiling!* – down at him. Corwynal strode over, grasped her by the elbow and jerked her to her feet.

'Come on, we have to go. The one who got away may come back with others.'

'No!' She shook off his hand and crouched beside the man once more. 'I can help him—'

'He's going to die.' He crouched beside her and, ignoring her cry of protest, slit the man's throat. 'You were wasting your time.' The aftermath of the fight was hitting him hard by then. His body was aching, and there was a dull sickness in his belly as he understood that, despite saving her life, all she felt for him was loathing. But that was the price he'd agreed to pay. *You will lose one of them . . .*

'Get up and let's get out of here,' he said, holding out a hand.

She didn't take it. 'Why did you come here?'

'For you.'

She looked around the clearing in horrified disbelief. 'You did all this for me?'

'Why else? But I wouldn't have had to do it at all – or for you to see it – if you hadn't left the camp. Why did you do something so foolish?'

'Because I had to speak to you, to tell you . . .' Her eyes had been on the bodies in the grass, but now they lifted to his, tears welling. 'You could have *died!*'

'And you would have been glad of it,' he said bitterly. 'I don't blame you.' He gestured around the clearing. 'This is who I am, and I know what you must think of me. I tried to tell you the truth in Carnadail but lacked the courage. You can't hate me any more than I hate myself.'

'Hate you?' She stared at him. 'I don't hate you. I should, but I don't. I tried, but couldn't. And I've never, ever, wanted you dead! You're as much a part of me as I am of you. How could I want part of myself to die? Who you are and what you've done isn't important.'

She took a few steps towards him, and without thinking, he opened his arms. She'd struck him the last time he'd done that, but now she walked into his arms and put her own around him. They clung to one another, heart to heart, and the wound in his soul, the one he'd lived with for almost a year, began, finally, to close. He pressed his lips to her hair, breathing in its scent.

She pushed away from him a little to look up at him. 'Can you forgive me?'

'Forgive you? For what?'

'For letting you leave Carnadail believing I hated you. For never telling you I loved you. Then and now. Always.'

Love. Always. He pulled her hard against him once more, as if to crush her into his body where she'd be safe. The world brightened – until he remembered. Until he understood how the God had tricked him. *You will lose one of them*. And, believing he'd already lost Brangianne, he'd chosen Trystan.

He let her go. He had to allow her to hate him as he'd believed she already did. He had to tell her the truth. 'We have to talk, my heart. There are things you don't know. But not here, not now.'

He whistled for Janthe, but there was no answering whinny, no beloved horse moving towards him from where the Selgovians had left her. Instead, from behind him came a low whickering snort and the thud of a heavy hoof. Brangianne's eyes widened and he whirled around, drawing his swords, putting himself between her and whoever had come. But this was no Creonn, not this time. This man was mounted on a massive war-horse, bigger even than The Devil, a horse as armoured as its rider. The man's armour glittered with gold, and a gold-washed helmet hung from his saddle, but it was the face that drew his gaze, the patterned face he remembered, the face with the eyes of an eagle. This was The Dragon himself, the man who'd taught him to fight, who'd taught him to win, and who'd come to the Ghost Woods to teach him to die.

'Run,' he whispered, desperate to get her away from what was about to happen. 'Take The Devil and go.'

But Brangianne, staring at The Dragon in disbelief, didn't move.

'Go!' he snarled.

She turned and made for the tethered horse, but it was too late. Other Riders had moved into the clearing, and two of them dropped to the ground between her and The Devil, who whinnied and reared, snapping the weakened Creonn tether, and whirled off into the forest.

'Take her.' The Dragon's speech was an odd form of Latin.

Another of the Riders dismounted and gripped Brangianne by the wrist, stifling her protests with a mail-clad hand across her mouth. He twisted her arm behind her back and forced her to her knees.

'Let her go!' Corwynal demanded, but with little hope. 'For the sake of our friendship on the Island.' Whatever they'd been, it hadn't been friends, but The Dragon owed him. Would he remember? The other man looked down at him, his eyes glittering in the old familiar way, but with less warmth in his gaze. Twenty years could do that to a man.

'Your name escapes me . . . ?'

'Talorc of Atholl, Corwynal of Lothian. You taught me to fight on the Island of Eagles.'

He spoke in Latin, his words as much for the Riders as The Dragon and, sure enough, there was a frisson of interest from The Dragon's men. There were few in the North who hadn't heard of the old Caledonian training camp on the Island and of those who'd trained there. They looked around the clearing at the fallen Creonn with renewed respect, murmuring to one another as The Dragon dismounted and stepped towards Corwynal.

'Talorc of Atholl . . .' He nodded, sheathed his drawn sword and held out his hand in greeting.

Relieved, Corwynal sheathed his own weapons and stepped forward to take The Dragon's hand in the warrior grip, hand to elbow. The man moved closer, as if to embrace an old friend, his other hand gripping his shoulder, squeezing painfully. Something wasn't right, but Corwynal couldn't see it. Something about The Dragon wasn't right. This was no greeting. This was—

The Dragon stamped forward, hip crashing into Corwynal's side, twisting his left shoulder away, and Corwynal's right arm, still in the other man's grip, was wrenched forward. Then he was falling, all his weight, and the weight of his assailant, on his right shoulder. Horrifyingly and agonisingly, he felt his arm being wrenched out of its socket.

Then he was on his back, winded, fighting darkness as pain flared through his whole body. All he could see was a circle of sky where a drift of cloud was moving eastward, driven by the rising wind. Then the cloud was blotted out by The Dragon, his armour glinting in the wan sunlight – the last of the sun, impossibly precious. The sword swung high, catching the light before it descended towards him. Corwynal closed his eyes and tried to think of Brangianne, to fill his thoughts with her so he could take an image of her on his journey beyond the veil. He heard a loud inhuman scream of denial that must have been his own, then the crashing splintering sound of his skull shattering. But how was it that he could still hear the screaming? And who was yelling obscenities, yelling his name?

'Corwynal! Get up! Come on, get up!'

Trystan reached down to him from the back of The Devil. The Dragon backed away as Trystan threw his damaged shield at him and jerked The Devil into a squealing rear, making him strike out with his hooves. Corwynal rolled onto his good side, scrambled to his feet, reached up with his left arm and let Trystan pull him behind him. The other Riders had kicked their mounts forward into the clearing, but there was a gap to the north and Trystan wheeled The Devil, made for the gap, and then they were free. But Brangianne was still struggling in the grip of the Dragon's men, and so Corwynal slipped back to the ground.

'What in the Five Hells are you doing?!' Trystan reined The Devil in savagely. 'We have to get out of here! I can't fight them all!'

But Corwynal couldn't leave Brangianne, couldn't lose her like this, didn't trust the God's promise that she'd live. Behind, in the clearing, the Riders threw her to her knees in front of The

Dragon, who drew his sword, took it in both hands, swung it to one side and—

'Look away, Corwynal!' Trystan reached down to grip his shoulder.

—and held it there, the long blade glinting in the sun. Brangianne's eyes, wide with terror, were on Corwynal. 'I want a death here!' The Dragon shouted. 'Is it to be this woman's? Or another's?'

From the far side of the clearing another prisoner was dragged forward, a prisoner wearing men's clothing and swearing like a man too, a prisoner with a torrent of auburn hair.

'Ethlin?!' Trystan exclaimed, and Brangianne groaned in horror as the girl was down flung beside her.

'This one was with the Gael cavalry,' The Dragon said with satisfaction. 'The cavalry who won't be riding to your rescue since they rode into our trap. Since all of them are dead. Except for this one, so now there has to be another death.'

Trystan's grip on Corwynal's shoulder loosened, and he let him go, slid to the ground also, and stepped towards The Dragon and the two kneeling women.

'Another death, you say? Then let it be mine – or yours.'

16

THE PAST AND THE PRESENT

*P*lease let me wake up! Please, God! Let this be just a
nightmare...

But prayers, in Brangianne's experience, were rarely
answered, and this was no exception. And so the nightmare
continued, becoming more and more terrifying by the moment.
If only she'd never left the Britons' camp in the forest, or her own
people's camp by the loch, or, indeed, Dunadd. She even wished
she'd never met Corwynal of Lothian, for he was the reason she
was here, kneeling on the ground, a sword – a *sword!* – so
terrifyingly close to her neck. And what, dear God, was Yseult
doing there, kneeling beside her? And why had Trystan called her
Ethlin? Surely he knew who she was by now?

But why was she worrying about stupid things like that? She
ought to be preparing herself to meet her God. Right then,
however, she couldn't prepare herself for anything. All she could
think about was what a fool she'd been to trust Azarion, despite
knowing he was a Dragon-rider. Ciaran had sent her to him, and
he'd helped her reach the camp and threatened Eoghan, but all
that had clearly been for his own ends. He'd *wanted* Yseult to
lead the Dalriads into a trap. Yet hadn't Ciaran been afraid of this
very thing? *What will he do?* she'd asked. *Kill someone?* he'd

suggested. She hadn't imagined that someone might be herself. Azarion's sword filled her vision – long and lean and dreadfully sharp. He'd cleaned the rust from it, she noticed, and part of her was relieved; infection often followed a blow from a dirty weapon. As if that was likely to worry her.

'Seize them!' Azarion, who seemed to be The Dragon himself, snapped an order at his men, pointing at Corwynal and Trystan and speaking in a mangled form of Latin, the language of civilisation, of Christianity, though he was clearly neither civilised nor Christian. Corwynal had fallen to his knees as if all his strength had left him. Trystan, however, far from trying to escape, walked back into the clearing, past The Devil who bared his teeth at any Rider who tried to approach him. The two men could have escaped, but they were surrounded now. Yet neither seemed to care.

She stared at Corwynal, knowing he might be the last thing she ever saw. She wanted to emblazon his features on the back of her eyes, but not looking like this, defeated and broken, his right shoulder deformed, almost certainly dislocated, his skin an ashen grey, pain etched in the lines of his face, despair in his eyes. She'd never seen him afraid before, but he was now, though it wasn't for himself. He believed his son was going to his death, and must have looked like this when he'd watch Trystan fight The Morholt.

'Are you afraid to fight me?' Trystan called out, his Latin accented but understandable. 'They say The Dragon can't be killed, except by himself. So why should you fear me?'

Trystan opened his arms wide so everyone could see how little armour he wore: light mail that only came to mid-thigh. Apart from some silver arm-rings, more decoration than protection, his arms were bare, and nothing sheathed his lower legs except for light leather boots. He wore no helmet and was armed only with a long cavalry sword and a damaged shield. But he smiled as he circled the clearing, showing himself to the Riders, before leaping effortlessly onto The Devil's back. The animal reared, snorting and lashing out with his hooves, but could be seen to be unarmoured also.

'—or is the contest too unequal for you?'

'Why should I exert myself to fight a boy?'

'Because this boy is the man who fought and defeated The Morholt. Because this boy was trained to fight by the man who defeated you on the Island of Eagles. I am Trystan of Lothian.'

Yseult smothered a cry, but Trystan barely glanced at her. His attention was on the circle of Riders. 'And because this boy is the man who leads the troops who drove back your Creonn paymasters.'

He's playing to the Riders! Brangianne realised when none of them moved to do the Dragon's bidding. They were more interested in seeing Trystan fight their leader, unequal though that fight would be.

Azarion swept his tawny gaze around the clearing, frowning at his men, but then he shrugged.

'Very well. I don't expect this will take long.' He pulled his helmet over his head, heaved himself into the saddle of his huge stallion, and hefted his heavy sword.

'Set the women free first,' Trystan insisted.

The Dragon threw back his head and laughed. The helmet covered his face except for his eyes. Side pieces, hinged to protect his jaw, were decorated with teeth and gave the appearance of the snout of a beast. From inside the helmet, his voice had a harsh hollow sound. 'Why should I fight anyone when there's no prize for the winner? When I defeat you, boy, I'll take the girl. The older one will serve for my men.'

Brangianne's insides liquefied at that and, beside her, Yseult swallowed hard and bit her lip. Trystan's brows snapped together, but it was Corwynal who protested.

'Have the Riders, under your leadership, fallen so far as to make war on women?'

An ominous resentful silence fell at that, but The Dragon's men didn't move. They stood around the clearing, their mounts as still as their riders, as still as the old stones in Dunadd's valley, as old as history itself, watchful and judging. The power here wasn't Azarion's alone; he ruled the Riders by consent, and they weren't pleased by that slur. Brangianne's nightmare lifted a little, until Corwynal got slowly and painfully to his feet.

'If my brother loses you *will* have a prize. Talorc of Atholl is more valuable than two worthless women.'

Worthless? Why had he said that? The honour-price of the sister and daughter of the King of Dalriada was considerable, and Azarion would know it. *Ethlin*, Trystan had said. Did neither of them know? Had Ferdiad kept a secret that no longer mattered?

'No, I—' she began.

'Don't!' Trystan's protest came too late. Corwynal had already pushed his way past The Devil to stand beneath The Dragon, his right arm hanging uselessly at his side.

'I'll submit myself to you—' Corwynal told The Dragon. '—if you win.'

'You're in no position to haggle.'

'No?' Corwynal glanced around the clearing, at the six dead Creonn warriors. One arm might be useless, he was saying, but he could still fight. He had a knife at his waist, another strapped to his thigh, and he wouldn't let himself be taken alive. Dead, he was worthless. 'Let the women go. If you do so, and if you win, I'll submit myself to your men without a fight. I give you my word, as Talorc of Atholl.'

Azarion stared down at him, his eyes glinting from the shadows of his helmet, then swung his head to look at Trystan, whose face was ashen.

'Brother, eh? I had a brother once – until I killed him.' He shrugged. 'It's the way between brothers. So, choose, boy. Two women? Or a brother?'

Doubt dulled Trystan's bright assurance, and Brangianne could see indecision in his face, in the grip of his hands on the reins, the muscle that flickered in his jaw, and the way he flung his head back and stared at the sky as if he might find the answer there. Perhaps he too longed to wake from this nightmare. For a moment, in a lull in the ever-present wind, it was quiet in the clearing, but for the soft jingle of harness, the stamp of hooves, and the birds, indifferent to the affairs of men, singing their hearts out from the trees. It was so quiet Brangianne could hear her heart beating and might have thought it her own had it not been so slow and steady. She looked at Corwynal, wondering if it was his, but it carried on beating just as steadily when Trystan looked down, met Corwynal's eyes with his own, and nodded.

'Let the women go.'

'No!' Brangianne protested, but Azarion ignored her and snapped his fingers. The two men who'd forced her and Yseult to their knees now jerked them to their feet.

'Let me stay,' Brangianne begged Azarion as Corwynal tossed his remaining weapons to the ground. The two men kicked his feet from under him, making him cry out as he fell on his damaged arm. 'He's hurt. Let me help him.'

The Dragon helmet swung towards her.

'To what end? He's going to die, if not at my hands. I'll sell him to his Caledonian kinsmen, and they'll see to that. So go, woman. Take the girl and go.' He bent down, gripped her arm and pulled her towards him. 'You won't get far,' he hissed before thrusting her away. Then he grasped Yseult and threw her after her, sending the two of them sprawling at the Devil's feet.

'Go,' Trystan said softly, after dropping to the ground to help them up. 'Find our horses. They're not far. Rhydian's winded, but he'll get you to the river. Head west as quickly as you can.'

'You can't do this!' Yseult exclaimed. 'You don't have the right!'

It was as if she'd slapped him. His head snapped back, and his face hardened. 'You'd prefer someone else to fight for you?'

'I'd prefer *anyone* but you!'

He smiled, but it wasn't a pleasant smile. 'I'm sorry, Ethlin, but I appear to be the only one . . . available. Now go, or all this becomes meaningless. Brangianne, take her away.' He turned his back on them, leapt back into the saddle and trotted The Devil towards The Dragon, raising his voice as he did so.

'So, shall we begin . . . ?'

'He *what?!*' Aelfric demanded of the Selgovians, originally Kaerherdin's men, but now Corwynal's troop. 'And you just left him to it? To single-handedly fight how many Creonn?'

'But Trystan's orders—'

'Don't talk to me about Trystan's orders! It's not like that mad bastard obeys his own orders when it doesn't suit him!' Aelfric had just learned, from one of Trystan's men, that Trystan had abandoned his troop to go in search of that idiot of a Caledonian, leaving Aelfric in charge. Normally, that wouldn't have bothered him but here, in these Ghost Woods, he felt at sea. No, not at sea, because that was the point. At sea he could navigate by the lift of the waves and the feel of the wind on his face, but here there were no waves, and the wind, smelling of death and foxes and loam, was making the trees sway and groan as if they were possessed by pitiless wights. The forest hated him as much as he hated it, and it closed in on him, sucking the air from his lungs. *What am I doing here?* An Angle in command of Britons, fighting Caledonians and

Woden knew what else, on behalf of a bunch of Dalriads who couldn't be arsed to turn up to fight their own war.

Women! Aelfric thought in disgust, not for the first time. This was all Brangianne's fault. One look at Corwynal's face when he'd seen her in the camp had told Aelfric there would be trouble. And look how right he'd been about that! If she hadn't taken it into her head to leave the camp and ride into danger, Corwynal wouldn't have abandoned his men to fight for her. Now Trystan had gone after the bloody man. What a balls-up! *What am I supposed to do now?* Advance or retreat? Head west to join the Dalriads? If there were any left, since a scout had brought news of a fight and a slaughter, and he'd heard horn-calls that weren't their own. Dragon-riders? Creonn? Where had the bastards gone? Should he look for them or blunder about these cursed woods, searching for two madmen who were very likely dead already? *What do I do? You tell me that, Woden!* he demanded of his God, shaking his fists at the small circle of sky he could just make out through all those fucking trees. And maybe Woden was listening for once, because, just then, when Aelfric needed someone to take out his frustrations on, one of his scouts turned up.

'Found this one at the edge of the forest,' the Selgovian scout announced as he dragged a prisoner into the small clearing. A fodder bag had been thrown over the man's head, and his hands were bound in front of him and tied with a rope, which the scout jerked, sending the prisoner sprawling across the clearing to land at Aelfric's feet.

Whereupon all the Five Hells broke loose as something small and fierce exploded from the undergrowth and launched itself at Aelfric, growling and barking and nipping at his ankles.

'What the—?'

He was too busy fending the thing off to notice that the prisoner had got to his feet and dragged the bag from his head. But he noticed when he was kicked firmly in the balls.

No-one knew where their new weapons-master, The Dragon, had come from. He spoke both Caledonian and Gael but belonged to neither race. 'Not a Briton either,' the other boys said with provocative glances at the only one of their number who was. Corwynal ignored them, remaining silent and contemptuously apart, which wasn't easy when they had to share a crowded roundhouse and there was only one fire. When he did draw closer to the others, it wasn't for warmth or companionship, but because he was curious about the man teaching them to fight, a man who appeared to be as much of an outsider as Corwynal felt himself to be. Yet, whatever they whispered about the man's origins, one thing was evident; his skills with every kind of weapon were breath-taking. And so his pupils fought desperately for his praise, flinched from the lash of his caustic tongue, and dreamed of being just like him. But Corwynal didn't worship The Dragon like the other boys. People you worshipped sent you away. So he watched from his habitual distance, learned what was offered, and practiced on his own when he could. Things were easier that way for an outcast, for someone who preferred to be alone or, failing that, to be invisible. But he wasn't as invisible as he'd imagined . . .

Past and present mesh until Corwynal's no longer sure if he's a boy on the Island or a man watching another boy fight the same opponent. Miraculously, Trystan's still holding his own. His lack of armour allows him to duck and weave and, beneath him, The Devil, equally unencumbered, is spinning on his hocks, dancing forward and advancing, an extension of Trystan's will as Corwynal had trained him to become. The Devil is a fighter, and he's snapping at the Dragon's mount, a big roan, rearing to lash out with his wicked hooves, and turning and kicking back with all his strength, but to little effect, given the other beast's armour. A spear struck hard and at close quarters might take the roan down, or a man brave enough to slide between those murderous hooves with a knife and skilful enough to hamstring the creature. But Trystan has neither of those options. All he can do is attack the horse, rather than the man, with his own mount.

The two men are still probing one another's defences, whether they be of metal or speed. Corwynal had taught Trystan that, had learned it himself from the man Trystan's fighting, and standing there, watching, his throat dry with fear, his shoulder throbbing with each agonising beat of his heart, Corwynal's vision falters once more, and he's back in the past . . .

'Why here?'

Corwynal dropped his weighted wooden practice sword and turned to face The Dragon, who'd found Corwynal's private place, the corrie beyond the waterfall where he'd gone to perfect the moves he'd been taught.

'There are practise rings at the camp,' The Dragon pointed out.

'I prefer it here,' Corwynal replied stiffly. It was true, as it happened; it wasn't just because of the privacy. It was because there was music here, as if horns and drums echoed from every cliff.

'You'd do better with an opponent and a real weapon.' The Dragon had been leaning against a boulder with his arms crossed, but now he straightened, drew one of his two swords, borne on the back in the Caledonian manner, and tossed it to him.

'But we're not supposed to—' Corwynal stared at the gleaming weapon in his hand, the first time he'd ever held a real

*sword, since they'd been forbidden to use anything but the
wooden practice weapons.*

*'I say what you're supposed to do.' The Dragon drew his other
blade. 'Well, little wolf? Do you want to learn or not? Get into
position . . .'*

*The metal blade was light and responsive in his hand after
his weighted wooden practice weapon, which, of course, was
the point. Yet there was more to it than that. The sword had a
life of its own, its vitality and spirit calling to his, and it flowed
into his muscles until he felt light and deft and the practiced
moves came as smooth as burnished silver. The ring of steel on
steel, echoing from the cliffs, rang like bells, and the little
hollow filled with music. Corwynal lost himself in the dance, in
the joy of it, and something coiled tightly inside him began to
unwind.*

'Slow down, woman!'

Aelfric had been accused of thinking with his balls, and
maybe he did, for right then he couldn't think at all for the pain
in his testicles. What was Oonagh, of all people, doing in this
gods-forsaken forest?

'You're with the Scots? And you're telling me there's been a
battle?' That at least made sense, since the scout had confirmed
it. 'How can I think when you're shouting at me? And can't you
keep that fucking dog quiet?'

Aelfric's men were grinning, clearly enjoying the
confrontation between their leader and the red-headed woman.
She was calling him an oaf and making no attempt to calm the
little white dog, who was jumping up to lick Aelfric's hands, still
clamped firmly to his throbbing balls.

'I'm not shouting!' Oonagh yelled at him. 'I'm just trying to make you understand! We have to save her from the Dragon-riders!'

'Brangianne? I thought it was the Creonn who had her.'

'What are you talking about?' Her eyes flashed, and Aelfric stepped back smartly in case she decided to kick him again. 'Where's Drust? Where's that Caledonian? It's them I came to find, not you, you oaf!'

'I don't know where they are,' Aelfric said with feeling. 'Corwynal went chasing after Brangianne, and Trystan went chasing after him. They could be anywhere.'

'Then we'd better find them.'

'How?' He looked pointedly around at the fucking trackless woods.

Oonagh gave him a look in which derision and pity were combined, turned to the little white dog and clicked her fingers, whereupon the beast sat down and wagged her tail.

'Good Dog!' she said in warm tones to the creature who'd half-savaged him. The dog cocked her head and barked. 'Find Drust. Go on, find him.'

The dog barked once more, got to her feet and sped off into the undergrowth, heading east.

'That's how,' Oonagh said.

'I'm going back,' Brangianne announced.

It hadn't taken long to find the horses. They were hobbled in a little hollow beside a stream, a chestnut mare and a big grey drooping with exhaustion. The stream ran down the hillside, cutting a groove through the mossy forest floor. It was their route to safety, and Brangianne regarded it with a mixture of longing and regret as she turned to Yseult. 'You go on,' she said. 'Get help.'

'It's too late for help.'

'You don't know that. You have to try. Drust's fighting for you. It's the least you can do.'

'Then you go,' Yseult said mulishly. 'I only came this far to make sure you'd get away. And he's not fighting for me. Nor is his name Drust.'

'He's fighting to save your life! *Our* lives! Are you going to throw that away?'

'Are you?'

Yes, she was, because a man Brangianne loved was watching the death of another man she loved, and she couldn't let him watch it alone, even if it meant giving up everything he'd done for her. 'My place is with the Britons,' she insisted. 'Yours is with the army.'

'They don't need me. They'd have done better without me. All this is so *wrong*, Brangianne! He shouldn't be doing this. I didn't ask him to.' Yseult shook her head fiercely. 'I don't want my life if it's at the hands of Trystan of Lothian!'

'Is your pride all you can think about?'

'It's not pride! Oh, you don't *understand!* He's fighting for Dalriada, when we should be fighting for ourselves. Dalriada's honour is at stake. He can't be allowed to fight with no-one to represent what he's fighting for. You do what you want. Go back, or go for help: I don't care, but I'm going back. I have to see, to bear witness, to tell him . . . I don't know what, and it's probably too late anyway. But I have to go back. I . . . I can't help it.'

And because Brangianne couldn't help it either, she sighed and, with one last regretful look at the horses, walked back the way she'd come to watch a man die.

The Devil is tiring. His spirit is strong, his anger fervent, but he's labouring now, falling back and turning more slowly, his screams of defiance less confident. It's hardly surprising, considering what Trystan has asked of him and what the horse has already given. But a time will come when he won't be able to dance out of the way or dodge the snapping teeth of The Dragon's heavy mount. And so Trystan does what everyone knows he'll have to do eventually. He drops smoothly to the ground, slaps The Devil away, discards his shield and reaches for a knife. Then he moves in closer, sword in one hand, knife in the other, and readies himself to plunge between the big roan's hooves to try and hamstring the beast. But he doesn't go low enough or fast enough, and The Dragon bends in the saddle, swinging his sword at Trystan's unprotected back. Perhaps Trystan has anticipated this move because The Dragon, in his turn, is too late to change the direction of his heavy swinging blade as Trystan twists away and up, rising from his crouch to leap up and grasp that outstretched arm. Unbalanced, The Dragon slips from the saddle and tumbles down with a crash of metal, crushing Trystan beneath his armoured body.

'Enough!' The Dragon stepped back, sheathed his sword and gestured for Corwynal to hand back his weapon. It was a wrench, giving it up, but he did so. Only then was he aware he was breathing heavily and his tunic was soaked with sweat. The sun was dipping towards the rocky island that guarded the horizon. How long had they fought? The Dragon, however, had barely broken sweat, and his breathing was light and even, his demeanour more amused than anything, and his gaze, falling on Corwynal, was speculative.

'You have the makings of a warrior, given the right training—'

Corwynal glowed at this unlooked-for praise. It was all he'd ever dreamed of.

'—*but you won't get it,*' *The Dragon went on. 'I came to tell you myself. You're to leave the warrior-school to train as a druid.*'

It was as if he'd been dashed with cold water. The glow faded, and the coiled thing inside him wound itself tightly once more. '*They can't make me. I'll run away.*'

'*And what would that achieve?*'

'*They can't make me learn.*'

'*You'll learn nothing if you run away.*' *The Dragon crouched in front of him, his yellow eyes piercing Corwynal's own, topaz meeting slate. 'So stay, learn the lore of the druids, and I'll teach you to fight—*'

'*But you said—*'

'—*in secret.*' *The Dragon swept his hand around the empty corrie, dark now as the sun sank below the horizon. Corwynal eyed the man warily. Nothing was given for nothing.*

'*Why?*'

He didn't intend to say it in quite that way, and there was something in the Dragon's topaz eyes he didn't much like. But then it vanished. 'I have my reasons. One of them is that we're more alike than you realise. Which is why I know you could defeat even me.'

There's silence but for the sound of metal on metal, and Corwynal is dragged into a different past – to a clearing in Lothian and a boar. Arddu had intervened then, and perhaps he does so once more in the clearing in the Ghost Wood, for Trystan wriggles himself free. But he isn't unscathed; a long gash runs down his leg, bleeding freely, and he holds a hand to his right shoulder. His sword has flown out of his grip, and The Dragon, rising to his feet, is between him and his weapon. All Trystan has is the knife. The Dragon laughs, an unworldly hollow sound from inside the helmet, and draws his own heavy blade. Trystan backs out of reach, limping from the wound in his leg, the knife held in his left hand, his right arm hanging awkwardly. Behind him, lying on the ground, is his discarded shield and, as The Dragon moves closer, he stumbles back, catches up his shield with his left hand, and swings it into position to block the backhanded hammer of the sword, then falls back a little further as The Dragon steps forward – right into the path of Trystan's flung shield, shifted at the last moment from left to right, from defence to attack, whirling as it speeds towards his opponent.

'No, Trys!' Corwynal groans as he watches Trystan's shield spin across the clearing. He'd taught him this trick, had seen it used against his opponents. But The Dragon is armoured to the thighs and expects this particular attack. Why would he not since he'd taught Corwynal this move in the first place? So now he stands braced for the expected blow . . .

It was one of the many things Corwynal learned as part of the double life he began to lead on the Island of Eagles. At first, he refused to learn the priests' lore, but soon discovered that if he didn't apply himself, he was kept back and missed his secret weapons training in the hidden corrie above the fall. And so by day he learned of lands and languages, of symbols and gods, of politics and power, then, as light faded in the long summer evenings, he'd meet The Dragon and practice until it was too dark to see. Later, in the boys' roundhouse, The Dragon's voice would march through his dreams.

'Again,' he'd say. 'Not that way. Watch . . .' Gradually, Corwynal learned to beat strength with speed, power with technique. He learned the dance of the fight and the deceit of it too, all the tricks that might give a man – or a boy – an edge. And

*he learned to search out his own weaknesses and either correct
them or turn them into strengths. 'All men have their
weaknesses,' The Dragon told him. 'As does armour. Don't trust
armour, not in your opponent, and not in yourself. It will make
you feel invulnerable, but you're not. No-one is. Life makes you
vulnerable, the wanting to hang on to it, the desires it gives you,
the ties of blood.' But, for himself, Corwynal wanted to feel
invulnerable, to protect himself from death, rejection, even
friendship. And perhaps that was why The Dragon remained as
enigmatic as ever, a man who taught him for his own reasons,
taught him how to fight, and, though he didn't know it at the
time, how to live.*

Now, more than twenty years later, he watches the man
encased in the protection he'd been so dismissive of all those
years before, wait impassively for the blow he knows will be
futile. Except it isn't, because he'd been right all those years
ago. All armour has its weakness, and Corwynal had taught
Trystan this in his turn. Now Trystan has spotted a crucial
weakness in The Dragon's armour, and so the shield, spinning
across the clearing isn't aimed at The Dragon's invulnerable
legs but at his equally well-protected head, where it jams in the
metal jaws of the beast that form the side pieces of the helmet,
and wrenches it off.

A gasp of shock runs around the clearing as the Riders see
their leader exposed and vulnerable. Trystan runs lightly across
the clearing for his sword and comes up with it in his right hand,
the arm apparently undamaged, the limp gone. He's smiling, but
his smile vanishes as he catches sight of movement at the edge of
the clearing. Two women are standing there, one auburn-haired,
the other dark, the women Corwynal has given up his freedom

for, the women Trystan is fighting for, the women who've just ruined everything. And The Dragon knows it.

'Dragon! Dragon! Dragon!'

Five years later, five years of learning, of training, of growing up. Now the time to be tested had come. Those who were to return to their tribes as warriors had to prove themselves by fighting the man who'd taught them. The Dragon beat all of them, of course, but it was the manner of their defeats that mattered.

Corwynal had changed over those years. Physically he was taller, but would never be a tall man, though he was far from being the little wolf The Dragon alone called him. He was stronger too, though his strength was of sinew rather than muscle, and he lacked the broad shoulders of the warrior-school. But he was still alone, still separate, still armoured against the world, especially now, because it was time for him to return to Atholl, when it was Lothian he longed for in his heart. 'If you beat me, they won't send you back to Atholl,' The Dragon had told him. Once he was back in Atholl, Corwynal knew they'd never let him go. And so he had not only to fight well but to win, something no-one had done before. He had to prove that someone training to be a druid could also be a warrior – and no-one had done that before either.

'Dragon!' The shouts of the warriors and trainees echoed in the bowl of mountains. The clouds were high that day, and the great jagged peaks of black stone peered down with malign curiosity as The Dragon defeated the last of the young warriors he'd trained. Then he lowered his sword and looked around at the staff and pupils surrounding the training ring.

'Anyone else?' he asked, his gaze touching lightly on

Corwynal, his expression not altering one fraction as he stepped forward.

'Me,' he said. Someone laughed, but Corwynal was more conscious of the angry protests of the handful of watching druids. 'They call me Talorc of Atholl, but my true name is Corwynal of Lothian,' he announced. 'And I will fight you.'

He should be fighting him now. He's older, wiser, more experienced in the ways of battle, if not in friendship, more understanding of himself, if not of others. He's supposed to fight The Dragon as he'd fought him before. But he's not supposed to win. He understands that now. Ferdiad had brought him to Dalriada not to defeat The Dragon but to be defeated. He's still not sure why. But Corwynal isn't here for Ferdiad or Feargus, but for the one woman who matters, the woman who shouldn't be here at all. *Don't let her weaken you.* Yet he has. Everything he's done since coming to Dalriada, every mistake he's made, has been because of her, and now he has to live with the consequences. He has to watch Trystan take his place, a boy who isn't prey to the same weakness, for hadn't he tried to pull Corwynal away and leave Brangianne to her fate? Yet when The Dragon dragged Ethlin forward everything had changed. Now something monstrous begins to take shape as Trystan stares at the girl he'd believed to be safe, the girl standing with Brangianne at the edge of the clearing. *It's not the same. It can't be the same!* But whether it is or not, with his attention on Ethlin rather than The Dragon, Trystan's advantage is gone.

'Trys!' Corwynal yells, breaking whatever spell the girl has cast on him. Trystan whirls, lifts his sword into the correct position by instinct or luck, and the two blades meet in a scream of steel.

Then the fight – the real fight – begins, and Corwynal is back on the Island of Eagles once more, fighting The Dragon for himself...

...and losing. How could he have imagined otherwise? For a time, they'd called out his name. Wolf! Wolf! Wolf! But gradually the crowd fell silent. The boys' laughter stilled, and the hissed anger of the druids fell away, all of them fading into the moment, because he couldn't afford distractions. There was nothing but himself and The Dragon and the fight he had to win, and that meant using everything he'd been taught, every technique, every trick. It meant not making a single mistake. Yet even that wouldn't be enough. He had to find something he hadn't been taught, something The Dragon wouldn't expect. 'All men have their weakness.' So what was the Dragon's?

There's another crashing flurry of blades. Trystan is aiming for the patterned face, the mocking amber eyes. But it's a difficult target, and each of his blows is parried with ease. The knife in his left hand is next to useless, because he's unable to get close enough to use it. He's tiring visibly, the limp, exaggerated when he'd reached for the shield, is more evident now, his leg dark with blood from the gash in his thigh. Everything of joy in him is gone, and so he makes a mistake. He throws the knife at the man's head but misses by a hairsbreadth, and isn't ready for The Dragon's response, a little knife snatched from a scabbard on the man's sword arm and flung towards his chest. Trystan throws up a hand, then stumbles back with a cry as the hilt of the knife thuds through the back of his left hand with such force that the blade emerges from his palm. But it's not a fatal wound and Corwynal expects The Dragon to follow up on Trystan's shock. Yet he holds back, a slow smile stretching his lips in a rictus of humour before he lunges forward once more. Trystan, with that moment granted him, is able to block the blow, then curve himself away from the savage backhand that follows, but when he steps back once more, he slips on his blood-soaked heel. Throwing his sword across his body, he's able, with a shuddering effort, to ward off the downstroke. But he won't survive another.

Look away, Trystan had advised him. He wants to. He really wants to. But he can't. He cares too much. As he'd cared all those years before.

He cared about being Corwynal of Lothian, and because of that he cared about winning. Yet The Dragon had no weakness, no fear of anything, and why should he? If he won, it would be what everyone expected. If he lost – an increasingly unlikely possibility – it would be no more than a credit to his own teaching. But that wasn't going to happen, for how could Corwynal defeat the man who'd created him? Especially when he'd failed so comprehensively to be like him, to armour himself against the world. So that was what had to change. He stepped back, breathing heavily, the twin swords gripped tightly in sweat-slicked fists. 'No!' he said, rejecting everything he'd been taught, everything he'd tried to become, letting it fall away like the discarded armour he knew it to be, encumbering, masking. He felt naked and vulnerable and deeply afraid. Then he stepped forward . . .

'No!'

Oonagh couldn't stop herself. Not when she'd seen what was about to happen in the clearing. They'd heard the clash of steel from some way off and had known two men were fighting. Leaving their horses with Corwynal's and Trystan's, Oonagh, Aelfric, and his men, had moved forward to crouch behind a thicket of hazel. Aelfric had signalled to the men to surround the clearing, had grabbed the little white dog and clamped his hand about its muzzle to stop it from rushing over to join the fight, but when Oonagh saw who was fighting, she couldn't stay silent. That was her father, the man who'd been a Dragon-rider in the past, and was once more. Hadn't he said he was going to his people? Now here he was, clad in the armour of a King. *A King!* Her protest was as much at how naïve she'd been to believe anything he'd told her as at what he was about to do: kill the boy she'd come to love like her own son, the boy who was sprawled on the ground before him, hurt, winded and helpless.

She scrambled to her feet. Beside her, Aelfric cursed but, hampered by the dog, couldn't prevent her pushing her way out into the clearing.

'Don't do this! Father, please! You promised . . .'

But had he? So why did she imagine he'd listen? Yet the blade, poised to descend, paused in its downward fall and her father, The Dragon, turned towards her, his brows snapping together.

She stepped closer, her eyes on his, willing him to step back, holding out her hand, not in supplication but in demand. At first, she thought she'd succeeded, for his own hand rose to meet hers. It was then that she knew something was wrong, something about his eyes, something unfamiliar. But it was too late; the mailed fist swept her own aside then whipped back to smash across her face.

There were stars and flames as the ground flew up towards her, and darkness pulsed in from the edges of her vision. All she could see in the shrinking circle of light was the little patch of grass in the clearing in which Drust was lying. The last thing she saw before she lost consciousness entirely was the boy rolling to his feet, screaming as he tugged the knife from his hand, then driving it deep into The Dragon's neck.

Corwynal ignored The Dragon's feint to the left, the thrust on the right, and threw himself between the man's twin swords. It was an insane move born of despair and desire. Unexpectedly, even by himself, his next blow slid past The Dragon's guard, to be caught, but only just, by the hilt of the other man's weapon. Distantly, Corwynal thought he could hear music.

'What are you doing, boy?' It was the first time The Dragon had spoken.

'Winning.' It was as insane a claim as that striking desperate move and had the same effect. The Dragon fell back as Corwynal launched himself forward, thrusting and lunging, hammering his sword down, and sweeping it across his body. The music was growing. He'd heard it before but only in the distance. Now it came from inside him, and he began, for the first time, to fight to its rhythms. There was a halo at the edge of his vision, sunlight shimmering as it fell slowly through the air, leaving veils of time through which Corwynal struck like a hawk, his blade grating along the length of the other's so that they were forced together, and Corwynal found himself looking up into The Dragon's glittering golden eyes.

'You can't kill me, little wolf. No-one can kill The Dragon. Only The Dragon may kill The Dragon.'

He hadn't believed it then and doesn't believe it now. The Dragon falls back with a cry, and for one miraculous moment Corwynal thinks it's over, that he *can* be killed, but the man lifts a hand to his throat and pulls the knife from his neck. It's missed the big vein in the throat, and the wound is little more than a cut. Trystan staggers back also, doubled over in agony from the knife-wound in his hand, which is bleeding freely now. Then he gropes for his sword and staggers back, bracing himself for The Dragon's next assault. But The Dragon just stands there, staring at the little knife in his hand on the blade of which his blood is mingled with Trystan's. He drops the knife and, like a great tree, rotten in its heart, rocked by a winter storm, falls to his knees.

As Corwynal, all those years before, had fallen to his knees. But not in defeat. It had been one last desperate gamble, a risk he should never have taken against an opponent he didn't know. And he really didn't know the man with the patterned face and the eyes of a raptor. Yet it seemed he did. Somewhere in the heart of their contest, in the clarity of vision that had come with the music, he'd understood more than he'd learned.

It was still a risk, a move that would leave his right side open to a killing thrust, for the fight had gone beyond the postured display of a mock-battle. This was serious now. He was aware that he'd been hurt, that blood was trickling from wounds on arms and legs, that bruises were forming. But he had to risk it. There was too much at stake. He had to hope The Dragon would think this the mistake he'd been waiting for, that he'd fail to see the trick, the thorn within the blossom. Corwynal had to hope he could move fast enough to avoid the consequences. Could he trust The Dragon? Could he trust himself?

These thoughts rushed through him like a wave, even as he

was falling to his knees, even as the ground thudded through his bones, his right hand rising, its blade held low across his body, his left hand hidden. Time slowed as he watched the Dragon's own blade slide towards him, slicing through the veil of each moment as the chords crashed and thundered all about him. He watched as the point aimed for a place near his collar bone. He watched it come to a halt, quivering, a hair's-breadth from his skin.

The Dragon smiled wryly, believing he'd won, but, before he could draw away, he became aware of the touch of metal as the tip of Corwynal's hidden left blade kissed the skin of his unprotected flank . . .

Trystan, breathing hard, draws his blade back to make an end of it, and, as before on the Island of Eagles, time stops. Light, fixed in the moment, sharpens and shapes itself into crystals, clear and perfect. Sound ceases too, the wind in the trees pausing on a breath of air, the birds struck dumb between one trilling note and the next. Even the movement of blood and breath are unnervingly absent. It's as if the gateway that stands between each moment and the next, its threshold endlessly forming and reforming, now yawns open, and, through it, Corwynal can see two futures. He sees Trystan step forward and, with the last of his strength, smash his blade across the Dragon's uplifted face. He sees the Dragon, feigning defeat, surge to his feet, thrusting upwards. Trystan, hurt and spent, won't be able to block the blow, and the blade will strike deep in his belly. Either way, one man will die at the hands of the other, as everyone has known from the start.

What he doesn't see is what actually happens. From the shadows beneath the trees emerges something that's immune to the stasis in the clearing, a man who glides forward and comes to a halt in front of the Dragon, then drops to his knees also. The two men face each other like a reflection in a mirror, one bright with metal, the other enveloped and hooded in a dark fabric that absorbs the light. The newcomer throws back his hood, and it can be seen that the two men are indeed as one, mirror images – the same patterns, the same hawk's nose, the same feral glittering yellow eyes, one the ghost or fetch of the other.

'You,' The Dragon says flatly, his voice heavy with doom.

'Indeed,' the other replies coolly and holds out a hand to The Dragon, the third to do so that day. This time, however, the offer isn't violently rejected. The Dragon lets his sword fall to the ground and reaches out to clasp the offered hand.

'Please,' he says, holding out his other hand, as if offering a gift, though there's nothing in his palm but a smear of blood from the wound in his neck.

The dark-cloaked man looks at the other's hand, lets his amber gaze drift to the splash of red on the Dragon's throat, then at the little knife, half-buried in the grass, and finally to Trystan, still braced for attack or defence, as frozen as everyone else. It's only then that any emotion shows in his patterned face, for he frowns at Trystan, then lifts his head to gaze across at Corwynal. And there's something horrifying in those yellow eyes, so horrifying that Corwynal has to look away. When he masters himself sufficiently to look back, the man has got to his feet and is standing in front of The Dragon, holding a long rusting sword in both hands. He swings it to one side and brings it back, hard and fast.

And strikes off the Dragon's head.

PART IV

DALRIADA

SUMMER 487 AD

 **17**

THE KISS OF FIRE

ime moved once more. Eyes watched the head tumble over and over, its braid of hair twisting and coiling like a snake, until it came to a stop at Trystan's feet. Horses stamped impatiently, their bridles jingling as they tossed their heads, and birdsong pierced the silence. Oonagh got to her knees, and Brangianne, released from her frozen immobility, went over to help her. A murmur rose, like the little wind that springs up on a summer evening, as the Dragon-riders began to chant the name of their leader. *Dragon! Dragon!*

It hadn't been the Dragon's name they'd chanted on the Island of Eagles. Time moved there too, slowly at first then rushing along like a river in spate, racing into the future, taking the music with it. Corwynal became aware of noise all around him, of men and boys shouting.

'Wolf!' they were yelling. 'Wolf! Wolf!'

The two men stared at one another for a long moment. Not man and boy anymore, for Corwynal had risked everything in the place ringed by mountains and had survived it. No boy could have done that. He drew back his blade, still holding the Dragon's eyes with his own, and The Dragon drew back also, tossed his blades aside and reached down a hand to pull Corwynal to his feet.

'So, little wolf, do you think you've won?' he whispered, then threw back his head and laughed. He turned and pushed his way through the crowd as if through a field of rye, and Corwynal never saw him again. He hadn't understood that whispered question. Surely he'd won? He'd defied the druids and proved himself a warrior, so surely, they wouldn't send him back to Atholl now?

They hadn't, but nor was he free to return to Lothian. Winning turned out to be its own defeat, for he was still bound to the Island – as the new weapons-master to replace the old one. The Dragon had trained him to take his place. Corwynal had been nothing more than the key to The Dragon's freedom and he'd never forgiven him for that.

'The Dragon's dead!' the man, whoever he was, shouted in a harsh voice that stilled the Rider's speculation. 'Yet The Dragon lives,' he added softly.

Only then did Trystan emerge from his rock-still rigidity. He went over to this new Dragon, sword in hand, and Corwynal wondered if they'd begin the fight all over again. But the man raised his hands to show he was unarmed, for his rusty sword was lying on the ground beside the headless body.

'You interfered in a challenge!' Trystan snarled.

'The challenge was over,' the man pointed out as he bent to pick up the golden helmet. 'And you couldn't have killed him, for The Dragon may only be killed by The Dragon. Who is, and always has been, me.'

His voice was harsher than the other's, and a deep purple scar ran around his neck, above a narrow chain from which hung a silver medallion together with a little cross.

'Who are you?' Corwynal asked, the question everyone must have been asking.

'My name's Azarion, or Father Adarn if you prefer, but you, little wolf, know who I am.' A faint smile cracked the man's – The Dragon's – patterned features.

Corwynal glanced at the body lying in the grass. 'And him?'

'My younger brother, until he stole my place.'

'He said he killed his brother.'

'He tried, but, as you can see, he failed. It's a long story. Nevertheless, I loved him once, and taught him to fight as I taught you, as you, clearly, taught this young man.' He glanced at Trystan. 'Is he your—?'

'—my brother.'

The Dragon regarded Corwynal with something unnervingly like pity. 'I'm sorry, little wolf, because—'

A white fletched arrow alight with fire thudded into the ground close by him. More flaming arrows flew across the clearing, whining over their heads like a flight of starlings to strike the Riders on the far side. Most fell harmlessly away, skittering off the mail of horse and rider, but the fire, which caught in the wind-dry grasses, startled the horses, who whinnied and reared. A Rider cried out as a lucky shot took him in the ankle, and the rest of them turned their mounts and edged together to face this new threat. The Dragon – the real Dragon – ran for the armoured mount of his predecessor and leapt into the saddle, reined the horse savagely around, cried to the Riders to follow him, kicked his mount, and headed into the trees. The Riders streamed after him, leaving nothing behind but hoofprints, the sound of their passing, the smell of horses, and the metal-clad body of their former leader.

Brangianne had always found Aelfric peculiarly reassuring, so when he strode into the clearing with a troop of Selgovians behind him, a little white dog at his heels, she thought everything would be all right. But that feeling didn't last for long.

'What in the Five Hells are you doing?' Trystan demanded when Aelfric went over to make sure Oonagh wasn't badly hurt. 'Go on, you fool, get after them before they bring the Creonn down on us! I'll catch you up when I've had this hand seen to.'

Aelfric gave Trystan a measured look, then let his gaze drift to Corwynal, lifting his chin in enquiry, but Corwynal just looked at him blindly like a man in shock. And no wonder. Brangianne had been unable to watch Trystan fight the man calling himself The Dragon. Instead, she'd watched Corwynal, white-faced and shaking, wage a different fight, against despair and helplessness, a battle as hard as the one Trystan was fighting. Now, however, it was over, and she was free to go to him, fix his shoulder-joint, then put her arms around him and tell him all the things she should have told him before. But there was other healing to be done first.

'I'll see to your wounds,' she told Trystan once Aelfric and his troop of men had collected their horses and ridden off. Her medicine satchel, strapped to The Devil's saddle, had fallen free when he'd broken the Creonn tether, but, miraculously, most of the contents were intact, and it didn't take long to clean, salve and bind the wounds in Trystan's palm and thigh, ministrations he bore with unconcealed impatience.

'I believe I told you to go,' he said when she'd finished, looking not at her but at Yseult. His voice and expression were harsh and forbidding, and Yseult flushed and dropped her eyes. Like Corwynal, she'd watched, rigid with horror, as Trystan had fought The Dragon, her hands closed to fists at her sides. Now she relaxed her grip and opened them, half in appeal, but was speechless in the face of Trystan's fury.

'Why did you come back? Brangianne had some sort of excuse, but you . . . ? What do you think would have happened to you if I'd lost? War isn't a game, Ethlin. It isn't about dressing up and riding into battle. It isn't a *song!* War is hard and brutal and undignified and it hurts. And silly little girls can die just as easily as men who've been fighting all their lives. So what in The Five Hells were you doing, riding with the Scots cavalry? What incompetent fool let you join them? And don't try to tell me no-one knew. That disguise won't have fooled anyone. But I don't know why I'm surprised. Only a bungling idiot would have led his men into such an obvious trap!'

By the end of this tirade, Yseult was so pale Brangianne thought she'd be sick.

'Drust – Trystan –' she intervened, but that just diverted his ire towards herself.

'You were supposed to stay in the camp where you were, and probably are, needed. Not charging off through the woods after a man who doesn't even—'

'Trys!' Corwynal interrupted sharply.

'—who doesn't even have the sense to obey a simple order.' It wasn't, she thought, what he'd intended to say.

'Now look here—' Corwynal began.

'Enough!' Trystan flung up his good hand. 'I'm going after Aelfric. You stay here. All of you, *stay here!*' He bent down, picked up the Dragon's head, and tied it by its braid to The Devil's saddle, then hauled himself up with one hand. 'A trophy,' he explained grimly. 'Like in the old days. They'll probably call me Dragon-slayer from now on, though that won't be the truth.' He turned the horse and trotted towards the edge of the clearing.

'And what, exactly, am I supposed to be staying here for?' Corwynal called after him, his voice sharp.

Trystan reined in The Devil and looked back over his shoulder. 'The Scots of course. Didn't you hear them?' He lifted his head, the gesture he'd made when he'd accepted The Dragon's challenge. Beneath the sound of wind in the trees Brangianne heard once more the dull thud she'd assumed to be her own heartbeat. Now she knew it was the sound of men marching. 'Didn't you hear them earlier?' Trystan laughed harshly. 'Why do you think I fought the Dragon? For the exercise? No – I knew the Scots were coming and wanted to delay the Riders so they could surround them. But, as usual, they're too late, and we'll have to do everything ourselves. Yet again.'

'You pretended you were fighting for me!' Yseult burst out. The colour had rushed back into her face, leaving it mottled and ugly.

'I wasn't.' A muscle flickered in his jaw. 'You didn't want me to.'

Yseult swelled visibly with fury. 'And why should I? But I thought it was for honour, not to show off. You're insufferable, do you know that? You think you're so wonderful, so clever! Well, you're not! You're just a pompous big-headed boy!'

Trystan jerked on the reins and trotted back into the clearing to tower so menacingly over Yseult Brangianne thought he was going to strike her. He did, in a way, but not with a weapon; the edge of his tongue was sharp enough. 'And you're just a silly little girl who deserves a good thrashing! If I had the time, I'd do it myself!'

'Oh, you would, would you?! Well, let me tell you—'

'You can tell me nothing I don't already know! Go home, Ethlin. Go home to your farm and your cattle and stay there.'

'You don't know everything, you pig-headed spawn of a lying Briton! When my father hears of this—'

'If there's any justice in the world, he'll give you the thrashing you so richly deserve. And you can tell him from me he should keep you at home in future, locked up if necessary.'

'No-one—' Yseult was breathing hard and her voice was pitched to wound, '—has ever spoken to me like that!'

'Children, children . . .'

The voice, amused, familiar and distinctly unwelcome, came from the edge of the clearing. There, leaning on the saddle horns of a dark bay, with two other horses, a grey stallion, and a chestnut mare, tethered behind him, was Ferdiad.

How long has he been there? Corwynal wondered. Had he been watching from the edge of the clearing since the beginning of the fight? Had this been the culmination of his revenge? To see Corwynal fail, then be forced to watch Trystan die in his place? But whatever the man had seen or felt, whether triumph or disappointment, had been stripped from his face, and all that was left was mild curiosity and a hint of boredom mixed in with the all too predictable amusement.

'You're a day late,' Trystan snapped, turning his back on Ethlin, who walked stiffly away.

'*Ferdiad, how nice to see you*, would be a more appropriate greeting.' The Fili trotted into the clearing with Janthe and Rhydian. 'Because *I'm* not a day late. The Lord Eoghan, who'll join us as soon as he's established it's safe, is a day late. And he's a day, or a week, or a lifetime, earlier than he, in his military wisdom, considers necessary. You owe it to me that he's here at all.'

'Then you're absolved,' Trystan said curtly. 'Now, if you'll excuse me, it seems I've wasted my time fighting the wrong man, and the right one is getting away . . .'

'Wait, Trys.' Corwynal caught The Devil's bridle. Something was wrong; Trystan's barely controlled anger at Ethlin was uncharacteristic, and his fury extended even to himself, for

Trystan kicked The Devil into a vicious rear that tore the reins from his grip.

'No, but *you* will wait, and this time it's a direct order! Stay here until the Scots arrive and make it clear to this Lord Eoghan how many of my men have died on account of his cowardice. Ask him why he let his cavalry ride into an ambush. Perhaps you could also explain that the Creonn are far from defeated and that the Dragon-riders might have lost one leader but now they have another. What the Selgovians and I have done – and suffered for – must be followed up by these laggard Scots. It's their country, after all, so you might remind them of that too. But you'll say all this as diplomatically as only you know how – because I've lost all patience!'

Then, kicking The Devil into motion, he cantered into the forest.

'If anyone deserves a thrashing, it's that young man,' Ferdiad mused, watching the trees swallow Trystan up.

Corwynal agreed with him but didn't think it was Ferdiad's place to say it.

'If anyone's going to thrash him, it'll be me. At least I'm alive to do so, which must be a disappointment to you.'

Ferdiad raised a pained eyebrow. 'You think I wanted you dead? That I had so little faith in your ability to defeat The Dragon – one way or the other?'

'I think you don't know what you want.' Something flickered in Ferdiad's cold green eyes, but he didn't reply and dismounted to examine the headless body of the Dragon.

'Ferdiad's right,' Brangianne said. 'Trystan does deserve a thrashing, but you won't be doing it until your shoulder's healed. And that won't be for a long time.'

She made him extend his arm, which sent pain flaring around his shoulder, but that was as nothing compared to the agony when she gripped his wrist, braced her other hand against his chest and pulled hard. There was a horrible wrenching plop as his shoulder joint slipped back into its socket, and he would have fainted if she hadn't put her arms around him to hold him upright.

'It's over now,' she said as the waves of pain ebbed. He held her hard against him with his good arm and breathed in the smell of her hair against his cheek. He wanted to weep with relief. She was safe, and so was Trystan. That was all that mattered.

You will lose one of them . . .

Involuntarily, he glanced east, the direction Trystan had taken, frowning. Brangianne pushed him away a little and narrowed her eyes at him. 'You're not going after Trystan, I hope?'

She knew him too well, because that was what he wanted to do, though he couldn't have said why. Trystan's wounds weren't serious, and he was with Aelfric and the others. The Creonn, with the Dragon-riders retreating, were less of a threat than they had been. The last thing Trystan needed was a man with a useless arm.

'Not this time,' he said and, when she continued to look suspiciously at him, 'I promise, because we need to talk, my heart.'

Because he had to pay Arddu's price for enabling him to save her life. He had to tell her everything he'd kept from her in Carnadail, and more than that, had to give her the freedom to hate him. Or not. Deep within him, a tiny flame of hope defied a God. *Maybe I don't have to lose either of them.*

Brangianne smiled and might have said something, but was distracted by a sob from Ethlin, standing stiffly at the edge of the clearing, and went over to her.

'I think you should go after him.' Ferdiad was still crouched beside the headless corpse, but all humour had been stripped from his voice, and when he looked up his face was ashen. He got to his feet, holding, between thumb and forefinger, the little dagger that had wounded Trystan's hand and the Dragon's neck. 'It's poisoned.'

Image followed image down a long dark tunnel – the knife, flung across the clearing, Trystan crying out as if he'd been burned, The false Dragon smiling as if that wound had been more serious than it looked, the horror on his face at the sight of blood from the wound the dagger had made in his throat, then the gesture of appeal to the man who'd turned out to be his brother. *Please*, he'd begged. For the ending The Dragon had given him? What was it he'd feared more than death?

'They call it the Kiss of Fire,' Ferdiad went on. His voice was flat, but the hand holding the little dagger was trembling. 'It's very rare. Very powerful. And there's no antidote.'

Corwynal glanced at Brangianne. Healers knew about poisons. But the Fili shook his head. 'She won't know about this.

'What . . . ?' Corwynal's mouth had dried up. 'What does it do?'

For once Ferdiad's expression was completely open and easy to read, and Corwynal could see fear and panic, as if he'd become aware of a future he hadn't predicted. He didn't reply at first, then, taking a deep breath, he blurted it out. 'It makes a man deranged.'

Deranged? Had Trystan's uncharacteristic anger been the beginning of it? His own anger ran through him like fire. *You promised me both would live!*

There was no answer from the God, but he didn't expect one. He should never have trusted Arddu, never have allowed himself to hope.

'I didn't want this,' Ferdiad insisted. 'I didn't bring you here for *this!*' Abruptly, as if it had burned him, he let the little knife fall to the ground.

'You know a great deal too much about this poison.'

Ferdiad's eyes flashed murder, and a muscle pulsed in his jaw. 'I know a great deal about a great many poisons. Don't imagine that was my *choice!*' Then he mastered himself and looked down at the knife lying on the earth. 'I'll come with you,' he offered, but there was reluctance in every line of his body.

'No. You've done enough damage already. Stay here and give Trystan's message to this Lord Eoghan. That's what you do, isn't it? Deliver messages.'

Ferdiad stiffened but didn't reply, turned on his heel and strode off to join Brangianne and Ethlin.

'How are you going to ride with that arm?'

Corwynal, so focussed on Ferdiad, hadn't seen Oonagh standing close by. How much had she heard? Enough, it appeared. One side of her face was red and swollen, but the tears in her eyes weren't for herself. She unfastened her belt and used it to bind his damaged arm across his chest. 'If he was my son, I'd go after him.'

'He's my brother,' he said automatically.

'Does it matter who he is?' She laced her fingers to boost him onto Janthe's back, then jerked her head at Brangianne. 'What do I tell her?'

He glanced over at the woman to whom he'd made a promise he had to break. 'Tell her I'll find her. Somehow, somewhere. I'll come to Dunadd itself if I have to.' If he was going to lose her, he had to face her as he did so.

Oonagh gave him a steady look. 'Best not,' she said. 'For everyone.'

He kneed Janthe around and headed for the edge of the clearing but turned around before the trees could swallow him up. Oonagh was talking to Brangianne, and she'd whirled around in protest, her eyes wide. *I'll find you,* he promised himself, a promise he intended to keep. He was about to kick Janthe into a canter when he heard the jingle of horse harness, and yet another rider rode into the clearing, an older man wearing an excessive amount of mail. The man checked his horse, a nervous bay, at the sight of the Creonn bodies lying on the ground. Then, having assured himself they were all dead, and it was safe, he ponderously dismounted. Accompanying him was a small party of men wearing the sign of the Swallow, but one of them carried the Swan standard of Dalriada. The Scots' army had finally arrived.

'Find me?' Brangianne asked Oonagh. 'What did he mean? Find me where? When?'

Oonagh just shrugged.

'He's gone after Trystan,' Ferdiad told her, sounding resentful.

'But he's hurt. And he promised—'

'He'll always choose Trystan. No matter what he's promised.'

We need to talk, my heart.

She'd thought he'd meant now. She'd thought that finally they could be together with nothing but the truth between them. But now he'd gone, with so many things unsaid. And it was Ferdiad's fault.

'Why didn't you tell him who I was?'

'Because it didn't matter then, and it doesn't matter now. He won't come looking for you.'

'I'm going after him.' She needed a horse. Ferdiad's would have to do since the grey stallion had gone, presumably with Oonagh who'd vanished too.

'No!' He grasped her arm. 'He'd want you to stay here. To be safe. You can do that for him, can't you?'

'Safe?'

Ferdiad nodded at the edge of the clearing. An armoured

warrior trotted tentatively from between the trees, closely followed by a few of his men, and dismounted in a clatter of armour. Except this was no warrior. This was Eoghan.

'Safe,' Ferdiad confirmed dryly.

Brangianne would have felt safer with a man with a dislocated shoulder than Eoghan and his troop of over-paid bullies, but her lack of confidence wasn't shared by Yseult. She broke free of the trance into which she'd fallen and went running across the clearing to fling her arms about Eoghan's portly body and bury her face in his mailed chest. 'Oh, Eoghan! Thanks be to God you're here! I was so frightened! I'm so sorry about the things I said to you. And I should never have tried to lead the army. You were right!'

'Yseult, my . . . my lady!' he exclaimed. 'All that matters is that you're safe, praise be to God and his blessed angels! And . . .' He looked up, his eyes turning to stone. 'My Lady Brangianne.' The warmth in his voice had gone. 'What are you doing here?'

Brangianne had borne a great deal already that day. She'd been terrified and rescued, threatened with rape and death, then had to watch first one then another man risk their lives for her sake. She'd found the man she wanted to spend the rest of her life with and had lost him in a heartbeat. It was all too much.

'What am I doing here? I might ask you the same thing, Eoghan! No, don't answer that. I'll tell you what you're doing. You're doing nothing. *Nothing!* You've left the Britons to do all the fighting and all the dying. They survived I don't know how many attacks by the Creonn, pushed them back and defeated the Dragon-riders.'

'Defeated Dragon-riders?' Eoghan's eyes flew to the edges of the clearing as if the trees might conceal any number of enemies.

'The Dragon's dead.' Brangianne gestured to The Dragon's body. It was hardly the whole truth, but this wasn't the time to go into detail. 'The leader of the Britons killed him, and now he's pursuing them and the Creonn. And you, my Lord Eoghan, together with my brother's army, are going to help him.'

She glanced at Ferdiad for support, but he didn't seem to be listening, and had clearly forgotten Trystan's message. But she hadn't and had no intention of being diplomatic about delivering it.

'You're going to take the army east to fight the Creonn, because these are Dalriadan lands and there's no reason for any other people to sacrifice themselves to hold them. And when we get back to Dunadd Feargus will hear of your incompetence, your cowardice, your indecision. The Britons have made a fool of you, but it's as nothing compared to the fool you've made of yourself. And what's more—'

She got no further. Eoghan, who'd turned an alarming purple colour, signalled to two of his men who took her respectfully but firmly by the elbows and pulled her away.

'What are you doing? Get off, you oafs!'

'You're overwrought, my Lady.' Eoghan's voice was smooth and unctuous, his eyes malevolent. 'War is no place for a woman—'

'I'm *tired* of hearing that!'

'I'm sure your brother will be distressed to hear that you've been exposed to such . . . unpleasantness.' His gaze drifted to the body, and he shuddered. 'No wonder you're saying things that can't possibly be true.' He looked pointedly around the clearing. 'I see no Britons here.'

'There were Britons here,' Yseult said from the safety of Eoghan's arms. She'd stopped crying, and her green eyes glittered like ice. 'They were mercenaries, in the pay of The Dragon. One of them was Trystan of Lothian, the man who killed my uncle. And the other was Corwynal, the man who betrayed my father at the Loch of the Beacon. They tried to take me prisoner. But you saved me, Eoghan.'

Brangianne gaped at her, wondering if the shock of everything that had happened had robbed Yseult of her senses.

'Yseult, you know that's not true. *Trystan* saved your life.'

'He didn't,' she insisted. 'Eoghan saved me. He . . . he killed The Dragon.'

Brangianne laughed at that, and even Eoghan looked startled. His men glanced at one another; they'd know better than anyone how little Eoghan had done. But none of them said anything, and Brangianne saw Eoghan's expression change to one of calculation. It was then that she understood. Yseult had always disliked Drust, but his casual and accurate stripping away of all her illusions, his justifiably calling her a silly little girl who deserved a good thrashing, had turned dislike into hatred. Now, childishly, she was refusing to acknowledge the risks he'd taken, the successes he'd had, and had transferred his role to Eoghan, that most unlikely of heroes. And Eoghan was going to take the credit for the Dragon's defeat and death.

But, though his men might accept the lie, knowing they'd be well paid for their silence, there were others, apart from herself, who knew what had actually happened.

'Ferdiad . . . ?' But, like Oonagh, he'd vanished.

'Get that body on a horse.' Eoghan gestured to a couple of his men. 'And someone find the head.'

'The Dragon-riders took the head,' Yseult stated, looking steadily at Brangianne, daring her to contradict her.

'Yseult, this is ridiculous and dangerous! The Dragon-riders are still out there. Eoghan, you have to—'

'I don't have to do anything. If these supposed Dragon-riders have run away – and who can blame them, given the size of my army – then we need go no further.'

'But they're not defeated. Eoghan, be a man for once and—!'

A horse rode into the clearing, its flanks heaving, its rider mud-spattered.

'Ships! My Lord Eoghan, ships are crossing the loch! Creonn ships! Heading for the camp!'

And so there was no possibility of the army going east, and neither reason, nor fury, nor tears, could persuade Eoghan and the Dalriad army from turning on its heels and heading back the way they'd come, back to the camp, their boats, and their means of escape from the Ghost Woods, the Creonn and the Dragon-riders. And Brangianne, her soul straining for the east, was forced to go with them.

Corwynal heard the sounds of battle long before he could see who was fighting. He heard the screams of men and horses, and the drone of war-horns from further along the valley, echoing from the slopes above and the river below.

He'd reached the eastern margins of the forest and was heading up the river where the Creonn had camped before he caught up with Trystan and the Selgovians. The country was more open here, oak and elm having given way to scrubby birch and, on the heights where the hills loomed through the low clouds, a scattering of pines. To his right, the river tumbled steeply among rocks, impassable for a horse, but a man with good balance could leap from each half-submerged rock to the next, and that's what the Creonn had done. A howling mass of them was racing up from the river, while, from the hillside on the left, men were leaping down through the heather. Between these two groups was a milling disorganised body of Selgovian horsemen facing yet another band of Creonn on the valley floor.

Trystan should have had scouts out, scouring the hillsides and riverbanks. He should, at the very least, be retreating. But the Selgovians pressed on, a wedge of horsemen driving into the massed ranks of spearmen, a golden head at the apex of their wedge, while all along their flanks the bands from the river and the hill were sweeping in, tightening the noose around the Selgovians. Corwynal barely managed to join them before they were surrounded.

'Woden's balls, you took your time!' Aelfric's axe whistled past Corwynal to bury itself in the neck of a Creonn warrior. Janthe reared, her flailing hooves crushing another's skull, as Corwynal tried to hack down with his sword. With his right arm bound across his chest and no shield, he was unbalanced, and his blow lacked force. Nevertheless, the impact juddered through his damaged shoulder, making him cry out with pain, and he knew he'd be of little use here. Aelfric's troop, together with Kaerherdin's men, were facing the river but were buckling under the pressure of the onslaught, their line being forced back as men and horses went down. Behind them, Trystan's troop, facing the slopes, were also being pushed back, and the two bodies of horse meshed in screaming yelling confusion. They were too few of them, the pressure of the Creonn too great, the wedge driving east too far ahead. It was all too . . . uncontrolled.

'He's gone mad!' Aelfric lunged at yet another spearman, half-severing the man's arm. 'Wouldn't listen to reason. Pulled the scouts back, went screaming off on his own. Kaer's men followed him and—' Aelfric kicked his big roan forward, tramping a Creonn into the mud. '—and where are those fucking Scots? Trys said they were just behind us . . .'

But to the west there was nothing, no movement of marching men, no heartbeat in the earth. Dalriada had betrayed them once again.

'Get through to him,' Aelfric begged. 'Make him see sense. If we pull back now, we might be able to break out of this and— Look out!'

The spear only just missed him. Janthe sidestepped neatly and the thrust he would have blocked with a shield, if he'd had one, slipped harmlessly by. From behind him, a Selgovian shot the man in the throat, but most of the Selgovians had run out of arrows, and it was sword-work now. The horses, so closely bunched together, were more of a hindrance than a help, their bellies vulnerable to the Creonn's short thrusting spears. The screams of pain and terror from hamstrung beasts were heart-rending, the thrashing bodies of maimed animals dangerous obstacles to a man trying to force his way through.

Corwynal dodged and weaved, ducked a spear thrust, leant aside from another. Janthe was an extension of his own body as she stepped lightly over all dangers, shying away from dying horses, and biting and kicking out at all who attacked her or her rider. At last they were through and driving into the back of the leading wedge, Corwynal shouting Trystan's name. Men pulled aside to let him through until he reached the golden-haired warrior at the spear-point of the wedge and could see what Aelfric meant. *Mad!* he'd yelled. *Deranged,* Ferdiad had warned him, and Trystan was both. He was cursing bitterly and graphically, and there was nothing of his former grace in the hacking and maiming, or the brutal slashing of a sword thick with gore. Nor was there any beauty in a face so contorted with hatred and fury Corwynal barely recognised it.

The Devil, infected by the same insanity, was squealing and rearing, his hooves smashing skulls and trampling screaming men, his fore-hooves slick with blood, his teeth bared in challenge, his nostrils flared and foaming. Trystan and The Devil were as one, a maddened animal blind to everything but the next man to be slaughtered.

'Trys, stop! For the gods' sake, stop!'

But Trystan was deaf too and kept on cutting a swathe through the press of Creonn, sword in one hand, shield on his left arm, the one with the poisoned hand.

'Trystan—!'

A high droning wail rang out across the battlefield and, through the screaming, Corwynal heard a susurration of disquiet. The pressure of the fighting eased as the Creonn fell back to allow a new opponent to join them, horsemen who glittered in the amber light of the setting sun, their lances glinting, the wind streaming eerily through standards that wailed like the dead. The Dragon-riders had returned.

But Trystan either didn't see them or didn't care, for as the Creonn moved back to let the Riders in to the kill, he followed them, cutting down retreating warriors, then, balked of any more opponents, turned back, dropped from The Devil's back to hack at wounded and dying men. His sword was thick with blood and innards, his face spattered with mud and brains, the air around him dense with the stench of battle.

'Trys – stop this!' Corwynal dismounted awkwardly and went towards him, treading carefully through the carnage Trystan had caused. He was hacking at a body, long dead, over and over, his sword biting on bone. 'Trys, please –' At last Trystan stopped and looked up at him, his eyes wide and staring, white in his filthy face, the pupils dilated. Then, with a scream of fury, he lunged forward, his blade thrusting for Corwynal's belly.

Corwynal managed to parry the blow but, stepping back, tripped and fell onto his damaged shoulder. The world reddened with pain, then turned black and contracted to a small circle of light, and in that circle, impossibly far away, Trystan raised his sword high above his head and—

'Trystan of Lothian!'

The voice boomed across the battlefield, and everything fell silent, but for the wailing of the dragon standards in the wind. The blade hanging against the sky fell to one side, and Corwynal watched Trystan collapse into himself, as if all the strings of his body had been cut in one stroke. His sword slid out of his grasp, and he dropped his shield to fold himself into a crouch, his arms going around his shins, his head pressed into his knees, eyes grinding into his kneecaps. He began to wail wild gut-wrenching cries of terror.

Corwynal eased himself to his knees, crawled over to him and put a hand on his shoulder, but Trystan shuddered and flinched away. The sky darkened above him, and a heavy foot stamped down close by. A horse snorted heavily through its armoured mask, and Corwynal looked up to see The Dragon, still in his threadbare black garment, removing his golden helmet. Beside him was another horse, Trystan's Rhydian, ridden by Oonagh, her eyes wide with horror as she looked at Trystan and what he'd done.

No-one said anything. No-one moved. The wailing stopped abruptly, and, after a long shuddering moment, Trystan raised his face and looked around at the carnage he'd caused with something close to panic.

'What's happening to me?' he whispered. '*What's happening to me?!*'

The Dalriad army made it back to the loch before the Creonn ships, but only just. The sun was setting when they'd reached the last rise in the trackway before it dropped down to the loch. Brangianne, still 'escorted' by two of Eoghan's men, saw ships approaching the eastern shore, narrow vessels, much like their own, six oars to a side. Their bleached sails, marked with the Creonn sign of the black ram with its curled horns, caught the last of the sun and glowed like flames on the water.

'Well, Eoghan, you'll have to fight now,' Brangianne said tartly. 'And you'll have to let me go. I'll have work to do with the wounded.'

'There are monks to deal with that sort of thing,' Eoghan

retorted. 'You're sister to the King, not some peasant woman with her herbs and hearth-magic. You'll remain under guard until you're back at Dunadd.'

'Why? What do you imagine I might do?' What a pompous, pointless little man he was!

'I imagine—' he said, his stone-cold eyes malevolent, '—you might run back to that pagan of a Briton you were rutting with all last summer.'

She stared at him, too outraged to speak. Dislike she expected, for she'd failed to conceal her own dislike, but hatred . . . ? It was a moment before she understood. Eoghan had never seen her as a woman. To him she was nothing more than a symbol of the status he desired, but when she'd rejected him for a ship-wrecked enemy, a no-one, she'd rejected him not just as a social inferior but a man. Eoghan's pride turned out to be more fragile than Brangianne had imagined, and now he was her enemy.

Right then, however, there were other things to worry about. The Creonn vessels had dropped their sails and were nearing the shore, their oars sweeping the water. One of them, larger than the others, forged ahead. A tall man stood by its prow, cloak flying in the wind, light glittering on weapons and jewellery, but when the ship drew closer, it could be seen that the symbol on his tunic wasn't the ram's head with its vicious horns, but a pale curve of white on blue. The ship reached the shore and grounded in the shallows unopposed, and the man leapt lightly into the water and waded ashore. The men nearest to him sheathed their weapons and fell to their knees.

Feargus, King of Dalriada, had come to war at last.

18

THE EARTH HOUSE

'Is he going mad?' Corwynal ignored the baying yells of the Creonn and the heavy silence of the Dragon-riders who surrounded the exhausted Selgovians. All that mattered was Trystan. He'd curled in on himself, rocking on his heels, his arms about his body as if he was trying to hold himself together.

The Dragon, Azarion, dropped to the ground, tossed the reins of his mount to one of his men, and took a torch from another. The sun had sunk behind the hills that lay between the valley and the loch, and shadows lifted from the river. The carnage of the battlefield faded into a slowly diminishing circle of dusk.

Trystan flinched as Azarion crouched in front of him but suffered the man's grim scrutiny, and there was a terrible pity in the Dragon's tawny eyes when he rose to face Corwynal. 'He's on a journey into the dark, from which few men return.'

'Surely there's something ... Anything ...' His voice was breaking.

'There are only two things that can be done, little wolf.'

'Two?' So Ferdiad had lied. Corwynal was sick with relief, but Azarion's expression was grave.

'To stop the poison spreading to his mind, the hand should have been cut off—'

Corwynal looked at Trystan, still rocking on his heels. Cut off his hand? Turn him into a cripple? A cripple who, nevertheless, was alive and sane?

'—but it's too late for that. Such a thing must be done within heartbeats of the wound being inflicted.'

'And the second thing?'

'To do as I did. To spare him, because he's going to suffer, and to avoid it he may kill himself, or everyone around him.' He looked at the darkening battlefield, at the mutilated Creonn bodies beside Trystan. 'He's already begun.'

And the Creonn wanted revenge for that. Outside the torchlit ring of mailed Riders, they were yelling their demands to be allowed to move in and slaughter the remaining Britons. The Dragon lifted his head, looked to the shadows beyond the torches, nodded once, and raised his arm.

Arrows flew, darts flighting into torchlight. One fell close by them and slithered through the grass to lie at Corwynal's feet. It was a little thing, fletched with the barred feathers of a peregrine, its tip stained black. Most of the arrows fell further away, and men cried out, in outrage to begin with, for the darts of the Forest People were tiny, but the cries turned into screams as the poison with which the darts had been tipped took effect. But it wasn't the Selgovians who were dying; it was the Creonn. They were falling and screaming, some of them scattering into the dark, fleeing this unseen threat, running as if the fell spirits of the otherworld were behind them.

The Riders, disciplined to a man, didn't move, and their horses stood stoically, snorting through mailed head-covers. The ring of steel around the Selgovians remained unbroken and didn't even waver when the skin-clad bowmen slipped past them, like smoke drifting between trees, to kneel at Azarion's feet.

'My Children,' he said, his hawk-like face softening, but Corwynal wasn't interested in the Forest People or the Riders, or whatever The Dragon was to them, or had been, or might become. Only one thing mattered.

'Few recover, you said. That means some do?' His flicker of hope wavered and strengthened when the Dragon, after a moment's painful scrutiny, slowly nodded his head.

'I demand to speak to my brother!' Brangianne yelled, banging on the door. 'When he finds out you're holding me prisoner, you're all dead men, you and that slimy toad of a Steward!'

She'd been overwhelmingly relieved to see Feargus and learn that the Creonn ships were manned by his own men, for he'd sailed north and harried the Creonn navy into The Narrows at Connel, where he'd defeated them and taken possession of their fleet. Then he'd had the smaller ships portaged through the narrow defile below Cruachan to Loch Abha and rowed across to join Eoghan's army.

Now justice will be done! she'd thought. Eoghan would be stripped of his command, and the Dalriad army would march east to the relief of the Britons. If they moved quickly, it might not be too late. But far from being able to explain everything to her brother, Brangianne had been incarcerated in an old storeroom in the ruined fort by the loch, her demands and threats all ignored, and wasn't released until the following morning. Whereupon she discovered it wasn't her brother who awaited her, ready to listen to her accusations against Eoghan, but Feargus, King of Dalriada, a man unwilling to listen to anyone.

'Well, Brangianne?' Feargus was sitting in a camp chair, his hands gripping the armrests. Yseult stood by his side, her face pale, her spine rigid, looking like someone who'd just been comprehensively stripped of any illusions she might have had about her ability, now or ever, to lead an army. Eoghan stood on the other side of Feargus' chair but didn't look as if he'd suffered the criticism he deserved.

'Well, Feargus,' she countered, 'you took your time! One might almost imagine the Creonn had been defeated.'

'They have been. We fought their fleet in The Narrows and captured their ships. And they've been defeated here also.' He glanced at Eoghan for confirmation but, far from appearing embarrassed, the Steward just smirked.

'Indeed, Sire. They fled in the face of the might of Dalriada's army.'

Brangianne glared at Eoghan, but he didn't back down. Nor did Yseult contradict him.

'How do you know? Have you sent out any scouts? Because *I* saw them. Unlike you, I was *there!*'

She turned to her brother, wondering what he was up to now. It was as if he believed Eoghan and Yseult, as if he *wanted* to believe them.

'Were you?' he replied, his green eyes glittering balefully. 'I'd naively imagined you to be at St Torran's, praying for victory.'

'Praying is all very well, but I'm a physician. My place was with the army.'

'Not so much of a place that you chose to stay in it,' he retorted. 'I hear you ran off to that half-caste Briton I gather was fighting with the Dragon-riders.'

'That's not true!'

'You're right, Eoghan.' Feargus turned to his Steward. 'She's besotted with the man.'

Besotted? It was such a horrible word. 'I love him, it that's what you mean,' she said stiffly. 'And he has a name. It's Corwynal of Lothian. I know you have personal reasons to mistrust him, but I wouldn't be standing here if he hadn't saved my life. And Drust, Trystan of Lothian—'

'—The Morholt's killer,' Feargus cut in.

'Yes, Trystan killed him,' she conceded. 'But in a fair fight after a legal challenge. And the tribute was returned, which it needn't have been. Corwynal and Trystan came to Dalriada's aid when they didn't have to come at all. And what happened? They had to fight the Creonn alone, to die alone, and they might be dying even now. They thought our army would back them up, but one whiff of danger sent Eoghan running back to his boats. I've never been so ashamed of being a Dalriad!'

'You'd rather be a Briton, I take it! They've certainly filled your mind with falsehoods. I need not defend my Steward's actions to you, Brangianne, but I will point out that he returned to face a credible threat to my forces. That the threat turned out to be a false one is merely a happy circumstance. He had, though you seem to be unaware of it, already defeated the Dragon-riders and the Creonn in the east, and while pursuit might have been an option, returning to face a threat to this camp was more important.'

'He didn't defeat the Dragon-riders. The Britons did. Trystan killed their leader. Except they have a new leader now.'

'No, they don't.' Yseult spoke for the first time. 'Eoghan fought The Dragon and killed him,' she said, her voice brittle. 'He saved my life and brought the body back to prove it.'

Brangianne began to laugh; the idea of Eoghan fighting anyone was so ridiculous! No-one shared her amusement, however. Feargus regarded her with something close to compassion in his gaze. Yseult's expression was cool, Eoghan's smile sleek, and Brangianne wondered if she was going mad.

'But not the head,' she pointed out. 'Trystan took the head.'

'The Riders took the head,' Yseult stated, as she had in the clearing.

'Enough!' Feargus snapped. 'I've always been of the opinion that war is no place for women, and all this nonsense has just confirmed my view.'

'It's not nonsense,' Brangianne insisted. 'You could go east and see for yourself.'

He frowned at her. He didn't want to go, didn't want evidence of Eoghan's cowardice. Whatever he was up to, he wanted it to play out. But she knew how to deal with that. 'If, as Eoghan claims, the Creonn and the Riders have been defeated, it will be quite safe.'

'Safe?' A slur on his courage wasn't something he could ignore.

'My Lord, is that wise?' Eoghan protested, throwing Brangianne a look of pure venom. 'There might be . . . pockets of resistance . . .'

Feargus regarded him steadily. 'Perhaps. But there are times when the truth matters more than one's personal safety. So we'll go east and establish whether or not the Creonn and the Dragon-riders have indeed left our lands. And maybe. . .' He glanced from Yseult to Eoghan and back again, then smiled. '. . . maybe we'll even find the head.'

'He's turned berserker!' Aelfric nursed his left hand, which Trystan had just bitten like a woman. 'I've seen it before. Woden knows, I love that boy like a brother, but I'm telling you straight. It's him or us.'

'I don't believe that,' Corwynal insisted.

That man, Aelfric thought sourly, had an astonishing ability to believe, or disbelieve, anything he wanted. But the Caledonian had to face facts. Trystan wasn't Trystan anymore. Aelfric had seen it before; once a man turned berserker, you had to put them down like a rabid dog.

'How can you not believe it when he just tried to kill you?'

They'd taken the boy's weapons away, but he'd flung himself

at Corwynal, his hands going around his throat. The Caledonian, with his damaged shoulder, had been no match for him, and Trystan had half-strangled his brother before Aelfric managed to prise his fingers away.

'That wasn't Trystan.'

'And this is?'

After the attack, only one of many, Trystan had collapsed, his fury fading, like a fire that runs out of fuel. 'What's happening to me?' he whispered. 'Make it stop. *Make it stop!*'

'Yes.' In the darkness, lit by a few flickering torches, Aelfric couldn't make out the Caledonian's face, but he could hear his voice breaking.

What am I doing here?

He should have left with the Selgovians, headed back to the camp in the forest, and left Dalriada forever. The man leading the Dragon-riders, who, for reasons Aelfric didn't understand, were on their side now, had insisted they leave. This was the land of the Forest People, he'd said, waving a hand at the dark forests, the dark hills, the darker night. So the remaining Selgovians had left, leaving Corwynal and, against his better judgement, Aelfric, to get Trystan to shelter. He couldn't be trusted on a horse, so they were half-carrying him, half-forcing him to walk, along narrow deer tracks that ran into the hills, through woods and below looming cliffs that blotted out the night sky. For the whole of the journey Trystan fought and kicked and screamed like a wounded animal and dug in his heels. Each step became an act of will on Aelfric's part, a lost battle on Trystan's.

So why, exactly, was he doing this? Was it for Trystan? Or Corwynal? Or was it for the woman who was riding ahead, leading their horses? Aelfric had been given the choice of going back with the Selgovians, but Oonagh's raised chin had made him decide to stay, though he'd known it was a challenge rather than an invitation.

'Where the fuck are we going anyway?' He peered into the dark as the trail climbed ever higher. He didn't trust these odd little hunters with their poisoned arrows and their stink of fox. Looking back down the valley, he could see a huge fire, burning on the site of the battlefield. The Forest People had piled the dead Creonn in a heap, covered them with branches and set the pyre alight, but had treated the dead Selgovians with more respect. They'd been taken into the forest and laid out on platforms high in the tree-tops to be picked at by ravens. Aelfric shuddered at the thought, though he knew it was what they would have wanted.

But this act of respect didn't endear him to the little Forest People, and their settlement, once they reached it, was even less reassuring. It was set in a little hollow in the hills, below a cliff, out of sight of the river far below. A fire burned in the centre of the hollow, and at first he couldn't make out anything other than a few crude huts built against the cliff. Then he noticed the mounds with their dark entranceways. The Forest People's houses were underground, roofed with grass and moss, with a single low door, from which smoke oozed greasily, together with the stench of foxes and filth.

'I'm not going in there,' he said flatly, after Trystan, breaking free from his slackening grip, had bolted into the nearest earth-house.

'I thought you might not.' The Dragon had a surprisingly quiet voice for a man with such a fiercely tattooed face. 'Make yourself useful then and see to the horses.' He nodded at one of the huts. 'Oonagh and I are leaving soon, so I expect you'd like to say goodbye,' he added before going into the earth-house himself, following Corwynal.

'You're really leaving?' Aelfric asked Oonagh, feeling strangely bereft. He'd thought . . . Woden knew what he'd thought, but he'd assumed she'd be staying for Trystan, if not for himself.

'I didn't take care of that boy in Carnadail to watch him go mad now,' she said, her eyes glistening. 'Well, Oaf?' She glared at Aelfric as if everything was his fault, dispelling any suspicion he might have had that she was going soft. 'Do you want to say goodbye or not?'

'You're afraid,' Azarion said.

Corwynal couldn't deny it. Apart from a pinprick of light from a smoking tallow lamp set in an alcove in the earth wall, the only illumination came from a weakly glowing hearth in the otherwise empty centre of the dwelling place, but it was sufficient to show how low the roof was. Corwynal had always been uncomfortable in enclosed spaces, especially those beneath the earth, and this earth-house with its smell of foxes and mould, terrified him.

Trystan was barely visible in the gloom, a dark shape huddled against the far wall, muttering to himself.

'Yes, I'm afraid, but not of Trystan. So, tell me about this poison. What can I expect?'

'For him to sleep very little, and for you to get no sleep at all. But the journey's exhausted him, so I think he can be left for the moment. Dawn's breaking.' He nodded to the doorway, gradually brightening with the pink-gold light of a summer's dawn. 'Make the most of it. You won't see much of daylight in the days to come.'

That wasn't encouraging, and nor was what Azarion had to say when they'd settled themselves by the fire in the hollow, under the weight of nothing heavier than a chill little wind.

'I don't know what the poison is, or how my brother acquired it, but I do know what it does. Somehow, it untethers the darkness within a man's soul. Someone like me, or my brother –

or you – would quickly fall under its spell, but your brother's young and that might save him, though it will still be hard. There will be terrifying nightmares, illusions, a longing for death, a longing to kill. Everything of light and hope and joy will be crushed. Your boy's clinging on to reason right now, because he's a fighter. But he may lose the fight.' His gaze touched on the bruises on Corwynal's throat. 'So, if I were you, I'd kill him now while he's still the boy you know, while he can understand what you're doing and why, while he might be grateful to you. You can tell yourself it's out of love, that it's what he'd want, that he begged to die, even if no words were spoken. Tell yourself it was your last gift to him, made out of the purest of motives. Tell yourself you've no hate in your heart, no resentment, no jealousy, nothing but compassion. Tell yourself anything you like and wonder—' Azarion broke off, squeezing his eyes shut, his fists clenching and unclenching, '—wonder how much or how little of that is the truth.'

Corwynal turned away from the anguish in Azarion's eyes. He'd killed the man who'd betrayed him, his own brother. If he could kill his brother, he expected Corwynal to be able to kill his. But Trystan wasn't his brother.

'Surely there's some other way, some hope?'

'There's always hope, I suppose,' the Dragon said doubtfully. 'Keep him awake as much as you can, distract him, take him out of his own mind, out of the dark. Tell him stories. That might work, but I warn you; if he survives this, it will leave him changed.'

'In what way?'

Azarion shrugged and got to his feet, but Corwynal was afraid to be left alone with Trystan and his own helplessness.

'Wait. I want answers. About the Island. About the Riders.'

'You want my story?' Azarion looked to the light, growing beyond the hollow, but nodded reluctantly and settled down once

more. 'It's not a happy one. As for the Island, I was there for the
same reason as you – to learn. I believed that if I mastered the
druid lore, it would help me make changes to the way the Riders
lived. I'd persuaded my father, The Dragon before me, to send
me to the Island, though none of our people had ever gone
before. But the Druids would only take me if I paid their price
and served as weapons master for as long as it took me to train a
replacement. Yes, I used you, but I've more than paid that debt. I
didn't want to make enemies of the Creonn, and now, for you
and your men, I've done so.'

'How did your brother come to lead the Riders rather than
you?'

'While I was on the Island my father involved the Riders in a
misjudged war with Dalriada on behalf of the Creonn. He died in
the final battle, took his own life rather than be killed or
captured. Most of the Riders were slaughtered. The rest escaped
and, when I returned, I persuaded them we should seek our
fortune further north. I still tried to change them, but they
weren't ready for change and I paid the price for my impatience.
My younger brother, who craved more power than he'd been
given, and had spoken against me, decided to take my place. We
resembled one another closely and the markings on my face
would have been easy to copy. But he knew he couldn't defeat me
openly, so he chose the three-fold death.

'I suppose I should have been honoured, but he bungled it by
choosing a pool revered by the Children of the Forest. After he
threw me in, unconscious, and I sank, he assumed I'd drowned.
But the pool had an outflow into an underground river and the
Children tracked me to where it emerged, further down the
valley. They too knew of the three-fold death and what it means if
someone survives it. I became their God.' He smiled ruefully.
'Death and deification change a man; for a long time, I didn't
know who I was. But the Forest People took me to a Christian

healer, and that changed me too. I foreswore the world and all thoughts of revenge, of taking back what was mine by right. But I was indebted to the healer, and this year that debt was called in. Sanctuary was over, and the world waited for me to take my place in it. It wasn't a place I wanted – I still don't – but sometimes we must take up burdens we'd rather leave to others.

'So, now I must complete what I tried to do all those years ago: to make a better life for the Riders, and now also for the Children of the Forest, who have become my people too. Perhaps it will be the same life, perhaps not. But it won't be easy, and time is pressing, so I must leave you to do whatever you decide to do.' He'd been staring into the fire, but now he lifted his head and looked steadily at Corwynal, his amber eyes, hazed from the past, sharpening into the present. He got slowly to his feet, an old man feeling the weight of his years. 'And I rather fear you'll have to do it alone, since I doubt that Angle will be much help to you.'

Corwynal nodded. He'd seen the fear in Aelfric's eyes and knew he'd have to keep him away from Trystan until . . . until he was better. He looked over at the entrance to the earth-house and shivered.

'What about Oonagh?' he asked, remembering the devotion with which she'd cared for Trystan in Carnadail.

But Azarion shook his head. 'Trystan is a threat to everyone, and I don't want to risk her.' He paused, frowning. 'She's my daughter, a daughter I'd forgotten I had, so there's a debt to pay there too. I have to give her a chance at the life she believes she wants. She's wrong, but I owe her the opportunity of finding out for herself.'

He whistled, whereupon a few of the Forest People emerged from the shadows. One of them was leading The Devil. 'I'm taking him too,' Azarion said. 'I've more use for him than you, so he'll form part of the debt you owe me for the lives of your men, and for the aid my Children will give you – food and fuel for as long as you stay here. As for the rest of the debt, one day I'll call it in. As you, one day, will call on me. We're bound together, you and I, for better or worse.'

He swung himself into The Devil's saddle, kicked the horse into a trot and, after collecting Oonagh, rode off, the little people trotting at his heels, leaving Corwynal alone by the fire. To the east, the sun broke through the clouds, bathing the cliff in sunlight, but the earth-house remained in shadow, and the darkness beyond the doorway was deeper than ever. Yet that was where he had to go, so, clenching his fists and setting his face against light and hope, Corwynal stepped over the threshold and into the dark.

Brangianne shuddered at the sight of the bodies of the men Corwynal had killed. They were still lying in the grass of the clearing where Trystan had fought The Dragon, flies clustering around their wounds and faces.

'Did you kill them too, Eoghan?' Feargus looked at the dead Creonn with interest.

'My men did,' he replied, his face a sickly green.

'And the arrows?' Feargus nodded at the white-fletched shafts scattered in the undergrowth or piercing the trunks of trees. But Eoghan, with no explanation, just shrugged.

It had rained earlier that morning, but hoofprints could still be seen in the soft earth of the clearing, a trail that led back to the river valley before turning east. The four of them, Feargus, Brangianne, Eoghan and Yseult, with some of Feargus' men as outriders, followed it east until it divided. Brangianne wanted to turn towards the south, across the ford and into the narrow valley that led to the Britons' camp – if it was still there – but Feargus insisted they head northeast, following a river that ran into the main river valley, for that was where the trail of the bigger horses led.

She smelled the burning long before she saw it. When they emerged from the margins of the forest, not far from the river, a column of smoke climbed greasily into the sky and blew towards them in swirling billows. Brangianne gagged at the stench of charred flesh, for this was a pyre. The fire had blackened and contorted the corpses until they were unrecognisable, but a few had fallen free, all Creonn warriors, their bodies pierced by little darts. So where were the Britons?

Lifting her eyes from the smouldering carnage to the woods beyond, she saw yet another plume rising from the trees, black smoke that fragmented into what looked like charred scraps of parchment. It was a flock of ravens, which meant there were dead men in the forest and, as they approached, she saw they were in the trees themselves, laid out on platforms built high in the canopy.

Then a living man emerged from beneath those death-laden oaks.

'Kaerherdin!' He spurred towards her, coming close enough for her to see the grief and fury in his face. Everything else she'd seen in him – admiration, care, the beginnings of love – had vanished.

'They died for you!' he yelled.

'All of them?'

'All of them!'

Yseult gave a moan of distress, but Brangianne didn't believe him, and wouldn't until she'd seen the bodies for herself. She kicked her horse towards the edge of the forest, but Feargus came after her, grabbed her mount's bridle, and dragged her back to the others.

'Let me go!'

He didn't, and she was forced to listen to Kaerherdin yell

curses at them. She didn't know what he was saying, but she understood his meaning: they were cowards and he'd never forgive them. With one last smouldering look, he wheeled his horse and rode back towards the pyre before vanishing beyond the billowing smoke.

Then something else appeared, a creature she took to be a mountain hare in its winter plumage, for it was white. Yet it was high summer, and the blue hares of the uplands rarely descended this far, so it couldn't be a hare. It was a dog, Yseult's little white dog, which had disappeared when Aelfric and his men had ridden off in pursuit of the Dragon-riders. Yseult called out to her, but the dog ignored her, dropped her nose to the ground and picked up a scent she recognised, a scent that led her further up the valley. Then the dog vanished, the last creature to link her with Corwynal, and Brangianne, her soul straining after a man who might already be dead, was forced to return to the loch.

The earth-house stank of mould and old bones, bog-water and rotting ferns, burnt and blackened timbers, and of the little people who normally lived there. But none did now. They'd all left with Azarion.

Trystan was still crouched against the wall, his arms around his shins, rocking to himself and muttering, sobbing like a lost little boy. Corwynal reached out to him warily, but Trystan didn't flinch away for once, so he put his good arm around his shoulders and held him close.

'I can't,' Trystan mumbled against him. 'I can't be like this . . .'

He tore himself out of Corwynal's embrace. In his free hand he held Corwynal's eating knife, its point pressed hard against his breastbone. 'I'm sorry.'

Corwynal dived at him, clawing desperately for the blade.

How could he have forgotten about it! Trystan kicked out, catching Corwynal's damaged shoulder. He gasped in pain but managed to get a grip on the knife, intending to pull it away, but it was no use. Trystan was stronger than him, and he forced the shuddering knife point back against his chest until blood began to flow.

'Trys, don't do this! Aelfric! Help me!'

But Aelfric either didn't hear or refused to be summoned. Corwynal was going to have to do this alone, as Azarion had warned him. Except he was never truly alone.

You expect my help once more? The voice came from the darkness, from the earth and the rock and the deep places of the mountain. It was made of wind and water and the rush of air in the black pines of the Ghost Wood. The God had returned. *When I gave you the woman's life, I warned you you would lose one of them.*

You promised me they'd live!

No-one lives forever . . .

Suddenly, he was tired of it all, of bargaining with a God who had no interest in the lives of those he loved, other than as tools to break Corwynal to his will. A God who tempted him and tricked him and allowed him to hope, then punished him for that hope.

Enough of your empty promises! You can't force me to choose between the two people I love. But I can force you to make a choice. You want to go on ruining my life? Then give me Trystan's. Because if you let him die, I swear I'll follow him. It was the first time he'd threatened the God.

A lacuna formed in the world, a place in which Corwynal saw two images – Brangianne, a woman who loved him despite who he was, and a boy with his eyes, a child who might one day have mourned his passing. But he forced those visions away and focussed on a single image – his own hands gripping a knife, the

place on his breast below the wolf-marking, the single thrust
through muscle, past bone and deep into the chambers of a heart
that, if Trystan died, no longer cared to go on beating.

He will live, the God said, his voice echoing in that hollow in
the world, shaking with a fury Corwynal had never sensed
before. Trystan's grip on the knife loosened until he was able to
pull it away. *But one day you will wish he had not . . .*

Corwynal had thought things would be easier after that, but they
weren't, and he had to watch, impotent and horrified, as Trystan
descended into the full monstrosity of the Kiss of Fire. One
moment he was raving and furious, the next coldly savage and
hateful, but usually he was weeping in terror at monsters
Corwynal couldn't see or screaming at enemies he couldn't fight.
Yet fight he did. Corwynal watched his desperate battle against
what was happening to him, watched him clutch at the all too
brief moments of sanity as if they might avert his fall into the
dark.

Distract him. Take him out of his own mind. Tell him stories.
But he didn't know what to say and was terrified of saying the
wrong thing. It didn't help that he hadn't slept since the night
before the battle in the forest, and now exhaustion had its grip
on him, robbing him of hope, of the ability to think or reason,
until he wondered if he was going mad too. He longed to sleep,
yet knew if he did so he'd lose Trystan, so was grateful for the
pain in his shoulder that kept him awake as he told Trystan
stories from their shared past. He even told him the tale of why
he was afraid of underground places: of the curious seven-year-
old, the disused well with the hint of gold at the bottom, and his
climb down the broken shaft. Then the slick of moisture and the
slithering fall from one handhold to the next, the scream as he

fell, the thud, agony in his ankle, water closing over his head. It hadn't been deep, and he'd managed to crawl out into a little side passage in the broken ground at the bottom of the well. Then the shaft had fallen in, entombing him in a tiny chamber beneath the earth. He'd thought he was going to die there, in the cold and dark . . . This wasn't, he realised, the lightest of stories.

'But someone came in the end. Don't give up hope, Trys.'

Trystan's eyes glimmered in the light of the reeking tallow lamp, and Corwynal thought he'd reached him.

'Who came?'

'My father.'

Trystan stared at him as if waiting for more.

'He thrashed me in front of the whole fort.' Corwynal hoped Trystan would laugh, but something died in his eyes, and he turned his face to the wall.

'I hate you,' he muttered. 'I *hate* you!'

19

IN THE HOLLOW HILLS

The trouble with women, Aelfric decided, was when they said they wanted the truth, that didn't include truths they'd rather not hear. Such as that he already had a wife.

'What?!' They'd been lying in the heather not far from the little people's earth-house. How they'd got there Aelfric couldn't exactly remember. Oonagh had been weeping about Trystan, and he'd put a comforting arm about her shoulders. That was how it began, but one thing led to another, and afterwards, when he was feeling all warm and fuzzy, he'd decided, like a fool, to tell her everything.

And so, after an acrimonious exchange, involving a lot of shouting on Oonagh's part and a desperate defence on Aelfric's, she'd gone off with The Dragon.

'I was going to ask you to come with me. But not now! You stay here. You look after them!' She'd jerked her head at the earth-house then went striding down the hill and rode out of Aelfric's life forever.

That had been the previous morning. Now, a day later, sitting on a pile of mouldy straw in what passed for a stable, he was still brooding about it.

Look after them. He would far rather fight off a bunch of Creonn or a troop of Dragon-riders than do as Oonagh had asked. There were, he was forced to admit, different sorts of courage, and he didn't possess them all, because he couldn't confront the wight living in that earth-house, the one inside Trystan. Sooner or later, it would find its way into Corwynal, and Aelfric would have to kill him too. But he wasn't sure he could do that, though he didn't know why not. Granted, the man was his brother in marriage, but there had to be more to it than that. Sometime, during their long journey from Dunpeldyr to Dalriada, Aelfric had lost first his hatred of the Caledonian, then his derision. Unlooked-for, the cursed man had become his friend, and friendship brought with it certain responsibilities.

'Fuck this!' He forced himself out of the stable and shook off the rain that began trickling down his shoulders. 'Fuck you, you Caledonian bastard!'

Spirits of the earth or not, wight of madness or not, Aelfric knew Corwynal couldn't face what he had to do alone, and he was the only man around to help him. Which meant that, as the man's friend, he was going to have to face his own fears and go into that earth-house. He clenched his fists and reminded himself he was Aelfric of Gyrwum, then approached the yawning entrance. But as he reached it, something small and white – that just had to be a spirit of the underworld – rushed past the entrance and attacked him. It began to nip his ankles, which, Aelfric thought, with something like relief, was getting to be a habit.

'About bloody time you showed up!' Aelfric fought off the little white dog who, regarding this as a game, was jumping about and nipping at his shins. 'Get off, you brute!' Then he turned to the other new arrival. 'Did you have to bring this beast with you?' He scowled, pretending he wasn't overjoyed to see Kaerherdin.

The Selgovian had appeared out of the drizzle, but Aelfric hadn't recognised the man to begin with. He was filthy from travelling, stank of sweat and bog-water, and just grunted at Aelfric's question.

'Where are the others?' Aelfric peered behind him, expecting a troop of Selgovians to appear out of the murk.

'Dead, most of them,' Kaerherdin said, his voice flat. 'The rest went back to Selgovia and—'

A scream rent the air.

'That's Trystan,' Aelfric's resolve to go into the earth-house withered away completely. 'There's some wight inside him that's turned him berserker, but Corwynal refuses to accept it. Maybe you can talk some sense into him, because he won't listen to me. Tell him he has to kill the boy before he turns on the rest of us.'

'If anyone's going to kill Trystan, it's me.' Kaerherdin moved towards the entrance to the earth-house, but Aelfric stepped into his path.

'Not like this. Not you.'

'He killed my men! I don't care if he's possessed or not. *He killed my men!*'

'What in the Five Hells . . . ? Kaer . . . ?'

Kaerherdin's jaw dropped when Corwynal emerged from the earth-house, and Aelfric wasn't surprised. The Caledonian looked even worse than the Selgovian; he was dirty and unshaven, his face gaunt and hollow. His eyes had dark shadows around them, and they were dull and rimmed with red. *He looks old.* But Kaerherdin didn't care.

'What did you do to my men? What did *he* do?' He jerked his head at the opening to the mound.

'It wasn't his fault, Kaer,' Corwynal said tiredly.

'It's his fault we were here, on this fool's errand!'

'No, it was mine.'

'Then it's you who killed them, and it's you who's going to answer my questions!'

'What questions?'

Kaerherdin's jaw clenched and unclenched as if he had a thousand questions and didn't know which one to ask first.

'Is he dying?' he asked eventually.

'No. Yes. I don't know.'

To Aelfric's dismay, Corwynal dropped his face into his hands and ground his fingers into his eyes to stop himself from weeping.

'Listen, man . . .' Aelfric pushed past Kaerherdin and laid a hand on Corwynal's shoulder.

'Don't touch me!' Corwynal jerked away, his face disfigured with anguish. 'If you're too afraid to help, or too angry, I don't need you. I don't need *anyone*. I can do this alone.' His voice was breaking as he stumbled back to the earth-house and vanished into the dark.

'He can't.' Aelfric's hands were opening and closing into fists, and his voice felt raw, as if it was breaking too. 'I never thought I'd say this, but I'm not man enough to do what he's doing.'

'What *is* he doing?'

'Trying to fight a spirit of madness by talking to it, but he's losing. Woden knows what he's saying, but it's not helping Trystan, and it's killing Corwynal. Someone has to either stop him or help him.'

But Aelfric still couldn't follow the Caledonian into the earth-house and nor, it seemed, could Kaerherdin, who frowned at the entranceway before nodding curtly as if he'd come to a difficult decision.

'Then I'll find someone to help him.'

A lie and a truth, each balancing the other in this place of balance, of stone and air, past and present, life and death. Anything could alter the balance. Or anyone. The lie had been his – *I can do this alone* – the truth Aelfric's. *It's not helping Trystan, and it's killing Corwynal.*

He still hadn't slept. The little he got, snatches and never deeply, was worse than nothing, and he could feel the lack weakening him. He'd hooked Trystan with stories, and now he couldn't let go, even though his throat was raw with talking, his mind aching from turning over the stones of the past, only to find them crawling with regrets and missed opportunities. Yet Trystan, chained to life by Corwynal's voice, listened without seeming to care, and whenever he fell silent Trystan turned his face away as if, somehow, Corwynal had disappointed him.

Never again did his eyes glimmer with interest, as they had when he'd told the story of the well. His madness appeared to have reached a new phase and was no longer a thing of terror and violence or hatred. This was desolation, and he just lay there, refusing to eat or drink, refusing to talk. He heard Corwynal's voice but not his words and seemed to be existing against his own will. But Corwynal couldn't stop, though all he had to tell him about was his own past. And so he told him everything he'd avoided speaking of before: about his childhood in Lothian, then Atholl, about the Island and The Dragon, the walls of stone and the drums and mountain peaks, the bitter chill of the western sea and the longing for a home he didn't have, about a mother who'd sent him away, a father who'd banished him.

Everything?

As always when Corwynal thought he'd reached the limit of despair, the God came to remind him how much deeper he could go. *You haven't told him everything.*

'Help me . . .'

You threatened me. No man can threaten a God and go unpunished.

'I don't care what you do to me. You promised me his life.'

I didn't promise a life worth living . . .

Of course he hadn't. *He'll live, but one day you will wish he had not.* Had that day come? He could feel his resolve slipping, hope fading, failure sending him into a darkness of his own. *I can't do this!* Death was very close, here beneath the suffocating pressure of all that earth above him, in the airless stench of decay. Trystan longed for death. Aelfric thought Corwynal should kill him. Kaerherdin, coldly furious, wanted Trystan dead. It wouldn't be long before one of them steeled themselves to come into the earth-house, blades in hand.

I won't let them. Yet he knew he couldn't stop them, not in his present weakened condition. Even Kaerherdin's final words hadn't raised a flicker of hope. *I'll find help.* He meant Essylt, of course, but Essylt was far away, and Corwynal knew she could do nothing. No-one could.

But he was wrong. The little white dog – where had she come from? – trotted into the cave and curled herself beside Trystan, her hot little body pressed against his chest, her warm breath on his face and, when she gave a soft yip, Trystan opened his eyes and, for the first time since the poison had taken him, his cracked lips widened into a smile.

'She sent you,' he murmured, sighed, and passed into something like natural sleep. Corwynal held his breath, knowing that such sleep was needed, that it might mark a turning of the tide. But it didn't last long. 'She sent you away,' Trystan whispered bleakly, only half-conscious now and shivering. But he didn't push the dog away. It was progress, Corwynal thought, hope flickering into life once more. But when Trystan opened his eyes again it was to stare at him, silent and untouchable.

'Trys – help me. Tell me what to say, what to do. Talk to me.

Say something, anything!' But Trystan just turned to face the wall.

It was then, in the darkness of a snuffed-out hope, that doubt slithered beside him, and whispered in his ear. Did he have the right to deny Trystan the death he longed for, the end to a life that might never be worth living? What was he keeping him alive for? Himself?

He was beyond exhaustion now, beyond reason, sick and frightened, yet, finally, everything made sense, and he knew what he had to do. Desperately needed sleep blurred his vision like the veil between the worlds. He'd told Arddu that if Trystan died, he'd follow him through that veil, and he'd meant it. But he'd lied. No father could watch his son die, any more than he could kill him, even as a looked-for gift. He should never have forced the God to stop Trystan from killing himself by threatening to do so himself. He was tired of fighting, tired of giving in to Arddu as, bargain by bargain, he gave him power over his soul. Let there be an end to these futile bargains. Let there be an end to everything. He wasn't going to follow Trystan into death. Rather, he was going to lead him there. He reached for the dagger that, until now, he'd kept out of Trystan's reach.

'You win,' he said, and something in his voice made Trystan turn to look at him. 'I can't do this anymore. But I'll wait for you, however long it takes. When I'm gone, you can take the knife and do what you want with it.'

Trystan was staring at him now, as he lifted the dagger to his throat.

Don't!

But the God had no power over him anymore. *It's too late now.*

His blood thrilled as it pulsed beneath the skin, beneath the blade. One thrust was all it would take.

It's never too late.

Time stopped, and the music began, but this wasn't the music of battle, the horns and drums of bone and nerve. This was the faint tinkling of bells and pipes in the worlds beyond the veil. He could fall asleep to that music. He longed for sleep like a lover. But still he hesitated, the grip on his knife slackening. Wasn't there something he'd been meaning to say? *I'm your father.* Yes, that was it. But, with that distant alluring music in his ears, he said nothing. Eternity lay beyond the veil, past the knife-thrust, and there would be time in all that eternity to say everything that had to be said, explain everything that had to be explained, and so he smiled encouragingly at Trystan and tightened his grip on the knife once more – only to have it prised painfully from his fingers.

Do you think it's that simple? The voice came from a long way off and yet it was close by, right in his ears, a honeyed vicious whisper. *Do you think I'd let you escape so easily?*

It wasn't Arddu, though the God had relented and sent someone to help – the last man on earth Corwynal wanted.

He'd sent Ferdiad.

'You're a brave man. There are four men here who want to kill you.'

Corwynal changed the grip on his knife, grasped the Fili by the arm, and marched him out of the earth-house away from Trystan. In the blinding light of a windy summer morning that smelled of pine sap and the high moors, everything was different. Had he seriously considered killing himself? Had the God intervened? Death still hung about him, its sharp metallic scent the smoke of a guttering fire, but now it had a new form. It was no longer cold and bitter but hot and violent, and, whatever reason Arddu had for sending him Ferdiad, Corwynal had every intention of taking out his fury on the man who'd brought them to Dalriada.

But Ferdiad shrugged off Corwynal's threat. 'Four men? One who doesn't know who he is, two who can't agree about which of them is to kill me, and a fourth with a death wish of his own. Forgive me if I don't exactly quake in my boots.' He smiled faintly and threw a glinting, mocking glance at Kaerherdin. 'And I'm not here out of choice.'

'I found him skulking in the hills,' The Selgovian laid a hand on his bow. 'He'd tracked you from the forest.' Aelfric was fingering his axe. He'd never trusted the Fili either.

'I wasn't skulking.' But Ferdiad looked as if he'd been living rough; his clothes were filthy, his silver hair dull. 'I was waiting.'

'What for?'

'For whatever was going to happen.' He spread his hands, made an odd gesture, balancing one against the other. 'Death maybe.' His otherworldly eyes bored into Corwynal's until an image came into his head, not of a snake but a Raven, perched on a rock, waiting for a dying man to breathe his last before hopping down to pluck out his eyes.

'You came to gloat! You manipulated a boy who just wanted to prove himself to a people he thought he'd wronged. As for me, you knew what to threaten. You must have been laughing behind our backs when we fell for it! But it wasn't enough for you merely to betray us; you had to come and see the consequences for yourself.'

Ferdiad stepped towards Corwynal until they were no more than a hand-span apart. 'Then why don't you strike me down?' He glanced without emotion at Corwynal's blade as it began to shake. 'Even with a useless arm, Talorc of Atholl is surely equal to an unarmed Fili.'

The knife leapt in Corwynal's hand, as if it had a mind of its own. His longing for blood was strong but he forced the blade down. Willing or not, Ferdiad was the God's gift, and Corwynal had to make use of him. 'I'm not going to kill you.' He sheathed the knife. 'Not unless you fail.'

'Fail at what?'

Corwynal jerked his head at Aelfric. 'Bring me Trystan's gear.' When he'd done so Corwynal pulled out something Trystan always carried with him and thrust it at Ferdiad – the harp he'd given Trystan in Carnadail.

The Fili stared at it with something like horror, but his voice, when he spoke, was flat. 'You expect me to sing to a madman?' He threw his head back and laughed. 'You do, don't you? You *need* me! You actually need *me!*'

'*I* don't need you,' Corwynal snarled, because he did. 'But *he* does.' He jerked his head at the entrance to the earth-house. 'You thought to wait until Trystan lived or died? You thought it was simply a matter of *waiting?* I'm afraid you'll have to do rather more than wait if you want to live. I can't reach Trystan, but you can. So you'll play until your fingers bleed, and sing until your voice breaks.'

'Oh, my voice will break.' Ferdiad took the harp and cradled it in his arms, his long fingers touching the strings as one might touch the face of a lover. 'But so will yours. So will yours.'

Maybe it was no more than chance, or maybe the poison from The Dragon's knife was finally losing its power, but Corwynal could date the beginning of Trystan's recovery to the day Ferdiad arrived and, with it, his own growing resentment. He'd pleaded, reasoned and threatened, had talked himself hoarse as he'd scraped away at the dark places of his past, but it had made no difference. It was Ferdiad, with his casual charm, his light-hearted Dalriad humour and his mobile fingers on the harp-strings, who slowly but surely drew Trystan back to life, back to the person he'd been. It was Ferdiad who persuaded him to eat and drink. And it was Ferdiad who first made him laugh.

After that, Trystan slept more often, and though he was still plagued with nightmares and illusions they became less intense. Everything he'd been through had weakened him physically, but he was no longer violent, and it wasn't long before he could be left alone, which allowed Corwynal to leave the earth-house and rest properly, free of the weight of earth above him. Gradually his shoulder ceased to ache, though it was still stiff and he knew it would be a long time before he could fight once more, if he ever could.

But Trystan's recovery was even slower, and summer passed, the nights shortening towards the new moon of the summer solstice, The Night of Turning, then lengthening once more. The Forest People continued to bring them food and fuel, though they rarely saw them. Aelfric and Kaerherdin went hunting to keep them in meat and exercised the horses. The world contracted to the earth-house and the surrounding moors, as if nowhere else existed, and Corwynal had the oddest fancy that when they returned to the world of men they'd find that everyone they'd known had died years before, as if the days that turned into a moon's passing and more were years in the real world, as if the entrance to the earth-house was a portal into the Hollow Hills of legend where time moved differently.

The Meadow moon, which had been waxing when they'd arrived at the earth-house, waned once more. The slim crescent of the new moon of The Night of Turning, the Stag moon, swelled to the full as Trystan slowly recovered. But, as Azarion had warned him, he wasn't the same person. With Ferdiad he laughed and joked like the old Trystan, or argued about music, but with Corwynal he was distant and silent.

I hate you! He'd never said it again, but Corwynal couldn't forget it, and the words echoed along with those Arddu had spoken. *No-one can threaten a God and remain unpunished . . . I didn't promise you a life worth living.*

He'd thought the God meant Trystan's life, but he began to feel it was his own life that wasn't worth living, as if some essential part of him had been excised, leaving behind an aching hollow.

'He's improved a lot in the last week,' Ferdiad observed, coming to sit on the other side of the entrance to the earth-house where Corwynal was brooding, not long after the Stag moon was little more than a waning crescent in the morning sky. Beyond the earth-house's central hearth-fire, Trystan was sleeping, his breath slow and even. 'We should be able to leave in a few days.'

'We?'

'Trys and I.' Ferdiad raised an eyebrow at Corwynal's surprise. 'Didn't he tell you? We're off adventuring. Not sure where yet, but that shouldn't matter to you, given your own plans. I seem to remember you made a promise to Brangianne – and you haven't kept it, have you? It's been – how long now? It must be close to Lughnasadh.'

Lughnasadh? Had the summer passed already? Had it been a whole year since he and Brangianne had first made love in that hut on the moors above Carnadail? How impossibly distant that memory was now.

'You could have left half a moon ago,' Ferdiad went on remorselessly. 'It's not as if Trystan needs you anymore. Or wants you.' He glanced at Trystan, who'd turned over in his sleep. 'But I wonder if Brangianne wants you either. She'll think you're dead by now, you realise. And maybe that's for the best. She was betrothed to Eoghan, the man who failed to lead Dalriada's army. He's a horrible little man, but he's rich, and women like that sort of thing. And what do you have to offer her? Apart from a truth she'd rather not hear. Women, in my experience, don't like learning a man's already married.'

'You know about women, do you?'

'I do,' Ferdiad replied with a glinting smile. 'Which is why I think it would be better for everyone if you didn't go to find her. Settle for the damage you've already done, and don't make things worse. Because, no matter how much she might believe the two of you could make a life together, you know she's wrong.'

Corwynal said nothing. He had no defence to make, not against something that sounded horribly like the doubts that had assailed him in the long nights under that weight of earth and his own hopelessness.

'Maybe you should go back to that wife of yours,' the Fili continued. 'I'm sure she's a charming creature and might actually care about you.'

Because no-one else does. Ferdiad didn't have to say it. Not Trystan, nor Aelfric or Kaerherdin. Not his father. No-one.

Silence fell between them, a hard-edged brittle silence full of bitterness on Corwynal's part, and quiet satisfaction on Ferdiad's as, word by word, he confirmed everything Corwynal had begun to fear: that life wasn't worth living, not without Trystan, not without Brangianne.

The air in the earth-house, foetid and reeking of smoke and mould, seeped into his lungs and tried to choke him, and he turned away from the fire-lit darkness within to face the light beyond the entrance, the golden glow of a rain-washed July evening. But it was remote and unattainable, for the claustrophobic shadows of the earth-house reached out to him with fingers of roots and bones of stone.

'You're afraid, aren't you? The Fili's voice was a blade in Corwynal's soul. 'You don't like being underground.'

Corwynal tried to shrug, but the shrug turned into a shudder. 'Does anyone?'

'I do.'

'You've always been an unnatural creature.'

'Have I?' Ferdiad's eyes glittered dangerously, and he plucked a discordant note on his harp.

'You're Arddu's creature. He sent you here.'

'It was the Selgovian who brought me here, not a God. I'm no more, or less, Arddu's creature than you are.'

'Then you came for revenge. You wanted to be in on the kill, after all your efforts.'

Ferdiad's fingers stilled, allowing silence to fall. All Corwynal could hear was the faint crackle of fire in the hearth, the night-wind in the pines outside and, low and steady, Trystan breathing in his sleep. Ferdiad laid his harp down and leant forward until his face was half-lit by the shifting light of the fire, half by the bronze glow of the setting sun, and his expression was impossible to read.

'All my efforts? Do you imagine I engineered a war to get my revenge on you? I have many talents, but that would have stretched them to the limit!' Then he grew serious. 'Much as you mistrust me, perhaps with good reason, I do have redeeming qualities. I care about Dalriada. I didn't want this war, but if there was to be war, I wanted Dalriada to win. That's why I came to find you at that Gods-forsaken fort at the end of the world. Not for revenge. And I'm here, am I not? Whatever my reasons, whoever brought me here, Selgovian or God, I'm in this earth-house when I'd much rather be in Dunadd. I saved Trystan's sanity when you failed, and I prevented you from killing yourself. Would a man whose sole motivation was revenge have done any of these things?'

Corwynal felt as if he was choking. Ferdiad was wrapping him in such coils of argument he no longer knew what to think. 'So, it's over, is it? You're satisfied with what you've done?' But he'd never had a straight answer from the Fili and didn't get one now.

'I said it wasn't my only motivation. As far as Trystan's

concerned, however, maybe it is over. He's suffered enough, and I can't entirely blame him for The Morholt's death. He was the weapon who struck him down, but you don't blame the sword; you blame the swordsmith.'

'Me?'

'You made him.'

'As you made The Morholt?'

Ferdiad flinched at that, his eyes sliding away, and Corwynal might have considered it a win in their battle of words, if he hadn't been certain this was too simple an explanation. Nothing about Ferdiad was ever simple.

'No. It was always me. You knew me in Galloway. That challenge was directed at me.'

A muscle flickered in Ferdiad's jaw, but when the Fili spoke his voice was flat and unemotional. 'Yes, I knew you in Galloway, because we'd met before, though you've clearly forgotten. So think back, Corwynal of Lothian. Look into the depths of your own past, in the tomb where you keep all that is the worst of you, because that's where you'll find me. That's the place with the answers as to when and where and why.' He smiled a slow slithering smile, but there was no humour in his eyes, and none at all in a voice that dropped to a hiss of chilled venom. 'I know who you are and what you could have been, and I've begun to wonder what you did to avoid it.' He leant closer, his voice dropping to a whisper. Corwynal could feel his breath on his face and imagined, for one horrifying moment, the flick of a forked tongue on his cheek. 'One day I'll find out all your shameful secrets, the ones you've told no-one, not even Trystan, the ones you'd rather kill yourself than reveal. And then I'll use them. Little wolf.'

The shock of the name froze Corwynal's blood. Only The Dragon had called him that, and never in public. How could Ferdiad know? He must have been on the Island. Had he been one of the younger boys, one of that anonymous mass shouting his name? Yet there had been no Dalriads on the Island that he'd known of. But was Ferdiad really a Dalriad? A snake can slip its skin and become anyone.

'Who are you?'

Ferdiad laughed with real amusement.

'At last, a question of genuine insight! Keep asking it. Keep wondering.' He got to his feet, a swift uncoiling of fluid limbs, and towered over Corwynal, the light of the fire throwing his face into shifting shadows and planes of light. Then his hand dropped to Corwynal's shoulder, as a friend's might do. 'If you ever find the answer, do let me know, because I've always wondered.'

He left then, having delivered what was probably a mortal blow, for, enmeshed in his argument with Ferdiad, Corwynal hadn't noticed Trystan's breathing had changed. He was awake, listening to every word that had been said.

'Where is he?' Corwynal demanded.

The others were sitting by the fire outside the stable. There was no sign of Trystan, and Rhydian was gone. 'He isn't well enough to ride.'

'He's fine, and he won't have gone far,' Aelfric said soothingly, but Corwynal just glared at him. He still hadn't forgiven the Angle for his reluctance to help Trystan, and though Aelfric had tried to apologise, he still wasn't ready to accept his apology.

'He's gone to the Creonn pyre,' Kaerherdin said, ice in his voice. He wasn't sure why the Selgovian was so antagonistic, given that he'd forgiven Trystan for the death of so many of his countrymen, but he didn't care.

'Couldn't someone have stopped him?' He looked to Ferdiad, but the Fili's attention was on something hanging in the corner of the stable above a low fire suspended by a grey braided rope, something that swung slowly around to stare at Corwynal. A face, stretched over a skull.

'It's The Dragon's head,' Kaerherdin explained, with a measure of pride. In the way of the Selgovians, he'd preserved it over a smoking fire until the flesh had dried to leather. Most of the brains and other soft matter would have been removed, by a process Corwynal preferred not to think about, and now it was nothing more than a skull covered in the patterned skin of the false Dragon, suspended by its thick braid of grey hair. Yet it still had life. The lips were drawn back in a rictus of an enigmatic smile, and the eyes, dark hollows in the face, were impenetrable but knowing.

'Disgusting!' Aelfric complained. 'I had to share a fire with that, and if you think it's rank now, it was worse before.'

'What's it doing here?'

'Waiting.' Ferdiad poked it with a stick, making it twirl on its braid. 'Trystan hasn't decided what to do with it yet.'

'It's not his to decide about. It belongs to Azarion.'

Ferdiad shrugged. 'By all means tell Trystan what he should do with it, but I wouldn't advise it.'

'*You* wouldn't *advise* it?!'

Corwynal's increasingly fragile temper leapt through his veins. How dare Ferdiad advise him about how to deal with the boy he'd brought up from childhood!

'No,' the Fili replied, a mirthless smile on his lips, his eyes cold. 'I wouldn't.'

He doesn't need you. He doesn't want you.

'We'll see . . .' He strode into the stable, saddled Janthe, gathered her reins, then leapt into the saddle and kicked her into a trot. It was too fast for the narrow way across the cliff face, so he slowed at the first bend. Looking back, he saw that the three men were watching him go. They exchanged a look, some private wordless agreement, and Corwynal, with a cold lost feeling, understood that Ferdiad had turned not only Trystan against him, but everyone.

The pyre lay some way off, not far from the forest's edge, and, as he rode, Janthe's hooves drumming on the summer-dry earth, Ferdiad's words drummed through his head.

He doesn't need you. He doesn't want you.

Trystan wasn't Trystan anymore. The poison or the madness or both had changed him into a cold-eyed, cold-voiced stranger. Something between them had broken, a link forged from a shared history, a shaped childhood, a mutual dependence that was no longer mutual.

Yet he'd always known this day would come. He'd brought Trystan up to be a man who stood on his own and made his own decisions. But he'd always assumed there would be a place in Trystan's independence for himself, that brother would become companion, tutor become advisor, guardian become brother-in-arms. The ties between them would be weaker, no doubt, but they'd never break. Or so he'd always believed.

There wasn't much left of the pyre of the Creonn, just a burned mark in the moor that still stank of smoke, though grass and new heather had begun to sprout through the rain-soaked ash. Trystan had dismounted outside the burned area and set Rhydian loose to graze among the bee-loud heather scrub and dwarf willow while he wandered about, staring at the ground. When Corwynal reached him, he'd just bent to pick something up, the twisted remains of what might have been a silver arm-ring. He must have heard Corwynal's footsteps, but remained crouched, turning the ring over in his fingers.

'I don't want to talk to you,' Trystan said, still with his back to him.

'I don't care what you want. We need to talk. Listen, I know why you're angry with me.'

Trystan rose from his crouch and whirled to face him. 'I doubt it, but tell me anyway.' His voice was clipped and sarcastic.

'Because I stopped you killing yourself.'

'That's one reason.'

'But you were wrong. I know you didn't want to be . . . the way you were. But you're not anymore, so I was right to stop you.'

'At least I had a reason. You didn't.'

So Ferdiad had told him.

'I thought I'd dreamed it!' Trystan flung the silver arm-ring away, and it tumbled across the pyre, sending clouds of ash into the air. 'I saw you with a knife at your throat, and thought it was one of the nightmares. They were bad, those nightmares – beyond bad – but that was the worst. You'd talked to me of hope, made me cling to it when I had none, then you gave up. *You* gave up! You had no right to do that!'

'I know.' Corwynal ran a hand through his hair, unable to explain it to himself, far less to Trystan. 'I was tired, unhappy. It was—' *Madness* was the word he wanted to use. He couldn't use it any more.

'—cowardly?'

'Is that what you think of me?'

Trystan shrugged, folded his arms across his chest and looked down at the ground, scraping through the ash with the heel of his boot. 'I think you're afraid of life. And I think you always have been.'

'That's not true!'

'Is anything about you true?'

'What does that mean?'

'That's right! Answer one question with another. You always do that. But if you can't trust me with the truth, you don't need me. And I don't need you.'

It was an echo of Ferdiad's words, Ferdiad who'd whispered and laughed with Trystan. At him? Undoubtedly. He'd woven a web of lies and trapped Trystan in its mesh.

'That's not true either, but you're not listening to me anymore. You're listening to Ferdiad.'

'Why shouldn't I?'

'Because, no matter how persuasive he is, he's our enemy.'

'He may be your enemy, but he isn't mine. I can handle him.'

'No-one can handle that devious snake! And he won't be telling you the truth.'

Trystan shrugged. 'Probably not. But then, neither are you. So it's up to me to decide whom to believe. But if I choose to believe Ferdiad rather than you, you'll put it down to me still being . . . deranged.'

'No, I—'

'Yes, you will. I can see it already. You're judging me and wondering if I'm still not myself. And I'm not. Maybe I never will be.'

It will leave him changed. Azarion had warned him, but he didn't want to believe it.

'Yes, you will.'

'You don't know that! I certainly don't. I can still feel the poison, in my blood, in my mind. It makes me feel . . . angry and . . . reckless. I'm afraid of what it might make me do or say.' There was a quiet desperation in Trystan's voice, and his hands trembled as he reached out to grip Corwynal by the shoulders. 'Look at me, Corwynal. Tell me what you see. Tell me you don't see the man who slaughtered those Creonn, who hacked them to pieces and bathed himself in blood – and enjoyed every single moment. Tell me you don't see the man who destroyed a silly girl's illusions and felt nothing but triumph. Because that man hasn't gone. Look closely and you'll see him, still there, still inside me.'

Afraid, suddenly, Corwynal, tried to look away, but Trystan shook him hard, forcing him to look up into his eyes. And there it was, the shadow he'd never seen before in someone who'd once burned so brightly, a shadow of doubt and fear and violence.

'There's darkness in us all, Trys,' he said slowly, not sure where this was leading. 'In me, in Ferdiad, in everyone who lives the life we do. No matter where it comes from, that darkness is as inevitable as death. But it needn't define you. Don't let Ferdiad use it to turn you into another Morholt. Don't give up. Don't walk away.'

Trystan squeezed his eyes shut, trapping the shadow inside him, then, abruptly, let him go. 'But I have to. Not for Ferdiad. Not for me. For you. It's time, Corwynal. Time for me to let you go. Time for me to give you your freedom.'

Corwynal stared at him, at a boy who was pale and thin and slightly breathless, a boy who was a man now, a man who'd changed into someone who didn't need him anymore.

'Freedom to do what?'

'To live your own life. It's strange, but in the dark, in the fever, in the nightmares, I could see everything clearly. I saw *you* clearly, *us* clearly. I should have seen it before. Maybe I did and didn't want to believe it, but I see now how you've lived your life through me. And that has to change. So it's time for you to make a decision. Go back to Iuddeu and be a husband and a father. Or go to Lothian and be a son. But whatever you decide, tell whoever you choose to be with all the things you couldn't tell me, all the secrets you'd rather kill yourself than reveal.'

So he'd heard that too.

You will lose one of them. . . And so it was Trystan he'd lost. Much as he wanted to blame Ferdiad he knew the fault lay mainly with himself, for Trystan was right. He hadn't told him everything, hadn't told him the deepest of truths. *I'm your father.* Should he tell him now? Would it make any difference? He doubted it.

'And what, if I'm allowed to ask, have you decided to do?' He tried to sound dignified, but the words came out laden with resentment, and Trystan, hearing it, smiled thinly.

'I'm not telling you. Maybe I haven't decided. Maybe I won't until you do. I want you to make a decision based on your own wishes, not mine. But if I was to wish for anything, it would be for you to do something courageous. Be an example, if it's the last thing you do for me. I'm giving you your freedom, Corwynal; don't make me force you to take it.'

Freedom to do what? Returning to Ealhith and the child would be the honourable thing to do, taking them back to Lothian the sensible thing, allowing Brangianne to believe he was dead the kindest thing. It was the decision, goaded by Ferdiad, he'd already come to. But now he changed his mind; Trystan was both right and wrong. He *had* been a coward, in so many ways, and he *did* need to make a decision. But that decision wouldn't be based on his own needs or desires or fears, because he *was* Trystan's father and that mattered more than anything. He'd always tried to be an example and, though he'd failed more often than not, he wasn't going to let him down now. He would find the courage Trystan believed he lacked – and courage wasn't about being honourable or sensible or kind. It was about taking risks.

'I'm going to Dunadd,' he told Trystan. 'I'm going to find Brangianne.' He would tell her the truth and risk watching her love wither and die. 'And hope she forgives me for marrying another woman.' Because hope, like life, took courage too.

Trystan regarded him steadily, giving no hint of whether he welcomed this decision or not. And perhaps it was a bit of both, for although, eventually, he smiled, it wasn't a smile of pleasure.

'So, you can still surprise me. And you've just lost me a bet. I thought you'd go back to Lothian, but Aelfric swore you'd go to Dunadd.'

Trystan whistled for Rhydian, who trotted over, his hooves kicking up the ash, and Trystan reached up to pull himself into the saddle, but Corwynal caught at his arm.

'Wait – you bet on me?'

Trystan shrugged. 'There hasn't been much else to do. But it was Aelfric's idea – take it up with him.'

He nodded behind him and Corwynal turned around to see horsemen approaching the pyre. Aelfric, Kaerherdin and Ferdiad were riding towards them, their gear strapped to their saddles, the little white dog trailing along behind them.

'So, it's Dunadd is it?' Aelfric eyed him narrowly, then tossed him his own gear, as Janthe trotted over to Corwynal's whistle. 'Thought you might.' He kneed his big roan forward to join him. Corwynal looked at him without comprehension and saw the big Angle flush. 'What? Think you're the first man to abandon your wife for another woman? Not sure if Oonagh will be there, but I'm going to Dunadd anyway. Got a fancy to see it.'

Corwynal felt a loosening of something that had grown tight. Aelfric, who'd wanted to kill him once, was still his friend, and he'd have company on the road at least. But it turned out he and Aelfric weren't the only ones heading south.

'I too have business in Dunadd,' Kaerherdin said stiffly. 'I want reparation from Feargus of Dalriada.'

'And you'll have it, Kaer.' Trystan smiled grimly and pulled himself into Rhydian's saddle. 'Between us, we've a gift for him.'

It was then that Corwynal noticed what was hanging from Kaerherdin's saddle-horn.

'Not the head!' Then he understood one further thing, that Trystan was going to Dunadd too, that he'd always intended to do so. He was torn between relief, fury and concern, and concern won, for this gift would hardly endear Trystan to Feargus.

He rounded on Ferdiad. 'Your idea, I suppose?'

'Trystan's, actually. He's quite capable of making his own decisions. As, it appears are you.' The Fili looked rather put out – had he bet on Corwynal's decision too? – but it wasn't long before his glinting malicious smile reappeared. 'But I'm sure there will be compensations. I must say I'm looking forward to seeing The Morholt's killer walk into Feargus' hall armed only with a head! Well then, since it seems we're all going to Dunadd – presumably together – perhaps we should be on our way? You may all have lost track of time, but I haven't. Lughnasadh's not far off.'

Lughnasadh, The Night of Gifts. And this year, in Dunadd, one of those gifts would be the head of a Dragon.

PART V

DUNADD IN DALRIADA

LUGHNASADH 487 AD

20

A ROYAL WEDDING

'Are you actually praying?'

She was, as it happened. *Let him be alive. Let me see him again. Let him come and find me. Or set me free so I can find him.*

It had been over a month since Brangianne had been forced to leave Loch Abha, and ever since then she'd been imprisoned in St Martin's. It was a comfortable prison, but a prison nevertheless, and she didn't welcome being locked up with her thoughts.

She still refused to believe Corwynal was dead. Kaerherdin had said the Britons had all been killed, but his mastery of the Gael tongue was poor, so maybe he'd mis-spoken. Nevertheless, as the summer solstice came and went and Lughnasadh approached, and Corwynal still didn't come to find her, hope that he ever would began to wither and die. Despite his damaged arm, he'd gone after Trystan moments after promising not to, so must have had a good reason. What had Ferdiad said to him while she'd been comforting Yseult? That she was Feargus' sister? No, it had to be something more serious, and she'd dearly like to have asked Ferdiad, preferably with her hands about his scheming throat. But he'd disappeared too, as had Oonagh, the only two people, apart from her and Yseult, who could give the lie to Eoghan's ridiculous claim. Had Eoghan arranged their disappearance? Might he, were she not Feargus' sister, arrange her own?

So many questions, but as long as she remained imprisoned in St Martin's there was no way to get answers. If Ciaran had been here this wouldn't have happened, but the Abbot was away on some diplomatic mission and wasn't expected back before Lughnasadh. All she could do was to pray to a God who didn't appear to be listening and hope the miracle she'd stopped believing in would happen and Corwynal would come to find her as he'd promised.

So when the chapel door opened and she was aware, behind her closed eyelids, of a wash of light flooding the little stone and thatch building, and heard footsteps, not sandaled but booted, walking steadily towards her, her pulse began to beat raggedly with the first stirrings of hope, then faster still when whoever it was knelt beside her. But when he spoke in that familiar voice, and she was enveloped in a scent she knew just as well – apple-wood smoke and a hint of cedar from his clothes – her heart slowed to a sickening thud of disappointment.

'I *am* praying,' she told her brother and gaoler. 'So go away.'

'I'm not going away,' Feargus replied. 'I'm here to talk to you.'

'How nice of you to recall my existence!' she said acidly, keeping her hands pressed together and her eyes resolutely closed. 'But I've no interest in whatever you have to say, unless it's an apology for not believing your own flesh and blood.'

'If I believe you, I'm forced to disbelieve Yseult,' he replied reasonably, a tone she'd learned to distrust.

'Yseult's lying, and you know it.' She opened her eyes to glare at him.

'I didn't come here to talk about Yseult.' He rose to loom over her, quite unmoved by her fury. 'At least, not directly. It's your marriage I want to discuss.'

'My . . . my marriage?' Her heart rocked in her chest and she scrambled to her feet. Had Corwynal come at last? Had he gone straight to Feargus? That would be just like him! 'Is he here?' She turned to her brother, grasped his tunic in both fists and shook him as if she might, for once, shake the truth out of him. 'Tell me he's here!'

'Eoghan?' He prized her hands away. 'I don't believe so, but your marriage to him is the reason I'm here.'

Hope, cruelly stirred into life, was rudely crushed. 'Eoghan's the last person I'd ever marry!'

'Good,' he replied, to her surprise. 'Then you don't consider yourself betrothed to him? For his part, I gather he no longer wishes to marry you, on account of your behaviour in Carnadail.'

'My *behaviour!*' Outrage sent her voice soaring.

'Quite,' Feargus said dryly. 'Eoghan took it upon himself to . . . make enquiries.'

'You sanctioned that?!'

'No. I didn't.'

She glanced sharply at him, but his face betrayed no hint of his thoughts.

'What are you up to, Feargus?'

There are three devious men in Dalriada. So went a recent triad doing the rounds in Dunadd; it had even penetrated the sanctity of St Martin's. *The first is Eoghan, son of serfs, the second Feargus son of Kings, and the third, and greatest of them, is Ferdiad, son of no man.* It was a fitting triad for all concerned, especially Feargus, for she'd been asking him what he was up to for as long as she could remember. She'd never received a satisfactory answer, however, and didn't do so now, for before he could reply – if indeed he'd intended to reply – the door of the chapel swung open and Yseult came in.

She was wearing white, the colour of innocence. Her eyes were large in her unnaturally pale face, and there were shadows beneath them and hollows below her cheekbones, but these served only to enhance the impression of Yseult as a suffering saint. *If she's suffering, it's her own fault*, Brangianne thought crossly. The two of them had barely spoken to one another since they'd both been incarcerated in the Monastery, Brangianne out of anger at the way Yseult had behaved, and Yseult – she assumed – out of shame. Sand Brangianne hoped Feargus was about to give Yseult the dressing-down she so richly deserved. But he didn't.

'Ah, Yseult, there you are,' he said with a suspiciously benevolent smile. 'I've come to take you back to Dunadd. It's time for you to prepare for your marriage.'

The colour came and went in her face, and she reached out to touch the altar with fingers that trembled a little.

'As you wish,' she replied, with more control of her voice than her body.

'Marriage? To whom?' Brangianne asked Feargus, since Yseult didn't, or couldn't.

'To the man who defeated the Creonn and the Dragon-riders.'

'But . . .' Yseult's eyes flew to her father's. 'You mean he's not dead?' She meant Trystan, Brangianne realised, but Feargus didn't.

'Why should Eoghan be dead?'

Yseult closed her eyes briefly but took the news calmly, as if she'd been expecting it, and it was Brangianne who objected.

'You can't mean it, Feargus! Not Eoghan! Whatever you promised him, you can't honour it, especially when what he claims isn't true. And surely you know how long he's lusted after her?'

'I'm aware Eoghan's admired Yseult for some time and—'

'I didn't say admired. I said lusted after, and he did so even when he was supposed to be betrothed to me.'

Feargus ignored her. 'Yseult needs the hand of someone older and wiser than herself.'

'It's your hand she needs, in the form of a thrashing.'

'She's too old to be thrashed. She's no longer a child.'

'If she behaves like a child—'

'Stop it! Stop it!' Yseult burst out, then, as silence fell, dropped her face into her hands. She wasn't weeping, however, and after a moment she let her hands fall and turned to her father.

'I will marry Eoghan. It's ... fitting.' Her voice was low but unwavering.

'Yseult, please ...' Brangianne stepped forward and touched her hand. Yseult's skin was like ice. 'It's *not* fitting. Tell the truth, and I'm sure your father—'

'My father knows the truth.'

Yseult lifted her head and met Feargus' eyes, green meeting green, and Brangianne looked from one to the other, wondering what it was she didn't understand. But Feargus just nodded.

'Come, then. We'll ride back to Dunadd together. Go and pack. No, Brangianne—' She'd moved to follow Yseult, assuming she was returning to Dunadd too. 'I've something to say to you first.'

'You can't do this.' Brangianne glared at her brother as the door of the chapel closed behind Yseult, the draught setting the candles on the altar dancing, and blowing some of them out. The smell of hot wax and snuffed wick drifted down the nave.

'Yes, I can.' He glared back at her, but once he'd lowered himself onto one of the benches his voice softened. 'I wish you'd trust my judgement as you used to.'

'Your *judgement?!* You're rewarding someone who ought to be punished. Eoghan's a *liar*.'

'Of course he is,' he agreed, and frowned at her when she stared at him. 'Do you think I'm a fool? Eoghan didn't defeat The Dragon. There's only one Dalriad who's ever defeated a Dragon, and that's me. I know everything that happened and why. Do you think I'd be who I am if I didn't? All I'm trying to do is remain as I am – as King – and this marriage is the key to my safety and that of our Family. Listen, Brangianne, you play Fidchell. Badly, I have to say, but you understand the rules and strategy. You know that, to win, some of your moves have to be feints.'

Yet it wasn't Fidchell, with its board and pieces and rules, that came to her mind. It was another image entirely; a juggler in the hall, throwing balls into the air, two, three, four, sometimes five, the balls circling above him to come back, miraculously, to the juggler's hands. Sometimes, however, an ambitious juggler would try to throw too many, and they'd all come tumbling down, to the jeers of his audience. Was Feargus the juggler? Were she and Yseult, even Eoghan, nothing more than balls spinning for the entertainment of the crowd?

'So, this marriage is a feint?'

'Possibly.'

'Possibly? You mean you don't know?'

'I told you I was in trouble a year ago, that we, as a Family, were in trouble. Do you never listen?'

'Yes, but I thought . . .' Her voice trailed away. She'd thought it was over.

'Nothing's changed,' he said. 'I was forced to give Eoghan command of the army because I needed his men. I admit I underestimated the resolve of the Creonn, and overestimated Eoghan's courage—'

'Hah!'

'—which he will pay for – but when it suits me, not you.'

'Then you don't have to give him Yseult. And what if the man who actually defeated The Dragon comes to claim her?'

'Why should he? According to my daughter, they hated one another. Anyway, he's dead, if we can believe that Briton. As for Eoghan, no I don't have to give him Yseult, but I need to promise her to him. I have to keep him on my side. Everything I've done, offering him you, allowing him to lead half my army, now promising marriage with Yseult, is to keep him on my side. Rather than Loarn's.'

'Loarn? But he's your foster brother! He wouldn't . . .' Once again, her voice trailed off. Loarn had always been ambitious. 'Is Loarn planning on deposing you?'

'Almost certainly. And so Eoghan is playing both sides. It's what I'd do in his position.' He smiled grimly. *There are three devious men in Dalriada . . .* 'As long as I promise him Yseult, as long as I pretend to believe he's a hero—' His lip curled. '—it gives me time to ally myself with someone strong enough to defeat Loarn when I have to.'

'Who?'

'I don't know.'

He's lying, she thought. He had something in mind, some desperate gamble, one more ball flung into the air. But if he carried it off, there would still be a price, and that price would be Yseult.

'What do you want from me? I assume this conversation isn't just a desire to demonstrate how devious you can be? Oh, yes, I heard that triad. Second place, Feargus?' She smiled sweetly at his expression. Yes, that would have rankled! 'I've been stuck here for over a month, so why tell me all this now?'

'You were hardly rational a month ago.'

'Rational? I was furious!'

'I didn't need the distraction of your fury, but I was sure, after a period of reflection—'

'You need me,' she cut in. 'It suited your purposes for everyone to believe I was in disgrace, but now you need me.'

He eyed her narrowly, a ball spinning in the air, not quite in his grasp. 'Very well. Yes, I need you. Eoghan has bought off anyone who might disprove his claim, but not everyone believes it, and they begin to mutter. When the time comes, they can mutter all they like, but that time isn't now. The last thing I need at this particular moment is a public statement from my own sister that Eoghan is a liar. So I want your support for this marriage and your acquiescence to whatever happens. I want your silence and your smiles.'

She pressed her lips together and let the silence draw out. Eventually, however, she nodded. 'Very well, Feargus, since you tell me it will protect our Family, I'll do as you ask.'

The tension eased visibly out of him, and he smiled with the satisfaction a juggler might feel when one of his wayward balls slaps back into his hand.

'But there will be a price,' she went on, and was pleased to see his smile falter. 'My freedom.'

'From St Martin's? Of course.'

'That isn't what I mean, and you know it. I want freedom to do as I wish, to take the veil if I choose, or practice openly as a healer. To marry if I wish to marry.'

Feargus' smile vanished entirely.

'You speak of Corwynal of Lothian, I assume?'

'Why not? He's as well born as you or I.'

'And he's—' He stopped. 'He's probably dead.'

'I don't believe it. I won't!'

He eyed her speculatively, weighing up the possibilities, wondering if the price she demanded was worth it.

'When Yseult's married according to my wishes, I will consider it,' he said, but she knew him too well.

'No, Feargus, I want your word now, not your refusal later. If Corwynal of Lothian wishes to marry me, I don't want you doing anything to prevent me from accepting.'

'Very well,' he said eventually. 'If he asks for your hand in marriage, and you agree to take him, you have my word I'll not stand in your way.'

'It's a bargain then.' But she had the unsettling feeling it had been a little too easy. Had she bought her own freedom at the expense of Yseult's? Yet freedom for Yseult had never been a possibility, and everyone knew it. 'I'll keep my silence, Feargus, and I'll smile. Even at Eoghan.'

'Summoned?!'

The young man was one of Feargus' household warriors. Brangianne had treated him for the spotting fever when he was a child, which felt like yesterday but, judging from the way he towered over her, must have been several years before. There were only a few pock-marks on his face, she noticed, but her professional satisfaction was banished by his use of that particular word. Summoned indeed!

'Surely I can't have heard correctly,' she said sweetly, and the boy – he was still a boy really – shuffled his feet in embarrassment.

'I'm to inform you, my Lady—' He was staring at a point over her shoulder as he recited his message. '—that Princess Yseult, daughter of Feargus, King of Dalriada, Lord of Dunadd, Prince of Ceann Tire, Protector of the Isles, and—'

'Yes, yes, I know all that!'

'—that Princess Yseult is to marry Eoghan, Steward of Dalriada—' Here the boy allowed himself a curl of the lip and skipped over Eoghan's many self-appointed titles. He was in love with Yseult, of course. Most of the war-band were. 'She's to marry him at the Lughnasadh feast, and you're summoned, that is, requested, to attend her immediately.'

Brangianne had been back in Dunadd for no more than a few days when Feargus announced his daughter's betrothal. So, was Yseult finally asking for help? Yet getting her out of the situation she'd got herself into would require a miracle, and miracles, in Brangianne's experience, were thin on the ground.

Nevertheless, escorted by the boy, she went to join Yseult on the Royal Terrace, expecting to find her in tears. If she was, Brangianne thought she might forgive her, but only if the right words were said. *Sorry*, for example. The word *summoned* however, should have warned her.

Yseult's lips, grazing Brangianne's cheek in the kiss of welcome, were icy, her expression warming only when she turned to the boy. 'Thank you, that will be all.'

Brangianne waited until the boy, blushing and bowing, had left before turning to Yseult and crossing her arms. 'Well, Yseult? I believe you summoned me. An unfortunate choice of words.'

'Not at all. I told him to use that word. I wanted you angry.'

And she was. Angry with Feargus, with Yseult, with Eoghan, with the world, with God. Brangianne needed no further invitation, and it all came pouring out of her: accusations and demands, threats and wounding remarks, resentment, bitterness and, finally, grief. Yseult bore it in silence, a rock on which the storm roared, a creature who was no longer a girl. Now she was a woman who knew what she'd done and was ready to bear the consequences, including Brangianne's anger, a woman who'd grown up. That growing up, however, hadn't been a happy transformation. It had been dark in St Martin's chapel, but on Dunadd's Royal Terrace, in a break in the clouds that were trailing showers out on The Moss, the light was bright and unrelenting. Brangianne's torrent of fury slowed to a trickle of exasperation as she saw the damage that transformation had done. It was as if Yseult had been burned in a fire, leaving nothing behind but a beautiful husk. Her skin was pale, almost luminous, and drawn too tightly over finely made bones. Her eyes were ringed with shadows, her lips thin and half-parted as if she was struggling to breathe. She smiled, or tried to, but it was little more than a series of movements of her lips, a smile that had nothing to do with pleasure, and it swept aside the last of Brangianne's anger.

'Oh, Yseult, what a mess all this is!' She reached out to her, but Yseult slapped her hands away and stepped back against the terrace wall.

'Don't touch me, and don't you dare cry! I'm beyond the reach of tears.'

'But not hope, surely?'

'Hope?' Yseult laughed, a harsh hurtful sound. 'For what? The miracle my father believes in?' She shook her head. 'No. I'll marry Eoghan for three reasons. The first is that he's a danger to our Family, the second that the alternative might be much worse—'

'So your father told you about Eoghan and Loarn?'

'He didn't need to tell me. I'm aware of how things stand. Eoghan has always wanted power – and me. So has Loarn. I think, on balance, I'd prefer Eoghan. If I can bind him to our Family, he'd have no reason to destroy it.'

Brangianne was uncomfortably aware that if she hadn't fled to Carnadail Yseult wouldn't now be paying for her cowardice. 'I should have married him.' But Yseult shook her head.

'No, it was always me he wanted. And there's a third reason. Marrying Eoghan is the punishment I deserve – because I caused the death of Trystan of Lothian.'

'But you didn't. Anyway, we don't know he's dead.' But Yseult had heard Kaerherdin's words too. *They're all dead . . .*

'He's dead,' Yseult said without emotion. 'And it *is* my fault. I was too proud, too determined to prove my worth. I joined the army because of him. I led the cavalry into a trap because of him. I went back to the clearing because of him, and I said what I said because of him too. And now he's dead, hating me. As if it matters that he hated me. Except it seems it does.' Yseult's composure was visibly cracking, her hands clenching and unclenching, her body wracked with shudders as she paced back and forth across the terrace. 'He's turned me into someone I don't recognise any more, someone without honour. He killed my uncle, Brangianne. He lied to me about who he was. He tricked me and laughed at me and told me I should be thrashed like a child. I *ought* to hate him.'

She stopped in front of Brangianne and grasped her by the shoulders, her fingers biting into Brangianne's flesh. 'Tell me I hate him! Tell me what a fool I am. Remind me how close I came to killing us all, how proud I am, how selfish. Tell me everything he told me and make me believe them, because if I don't I can't do this. I have to believe I did all these things out of pride and honour and hate and not because . . . not because . . .'

Not because you love him. The earth shifted beneath Brangianne as a new thread, silver and strong, tore its way through the fabric of the world, altering the weave forever, as love always does.

'You hate him,' she said because that was what Yseult needed to hear, then gathered her into her arms when she collapsed as if all her bones had turned to ash. She was sobbing wildly now, all composure gone. 'You hate him, Yseult, and he hates you, but, whether he's dead or not, you'll never see him again. You've been a fool, yes, and you're being punished, more than you deserve perhaps, but you'll survive it. I promise you, you'll survive.'

They were just words, words that didn't mean anything. One didn't survive love any more than one survived hate or life or death. It had taken Brangianne a lifetime to understand that, and now Yseult had begun her own harrowing journey towards the same truth. But she wouldn't make the journey without pride. She was Princess of Dalriada, daughter to a King, so eventually she stopped crying and pushed herself away, wiped her face with the back of her hands, and armoured herself with determination, building it breath by breath, allowing it to stiffen her bones, her sinews, her resolve.

'You're right. I'll survive. We'll all survive.' She took Brangianne's hand. 'I'm sorry. I've wanted to say that for so long. Are we friends again?'

'Not friends.' Brangianne smoothed away Yseult's frown. 'We're Family, and that's stronger.'

And for Family, love couldn't be allowed to matter, not even if it meant marriage to a man they both despised. Yseult took a deep breath, and another, until her armour was complete, her smile protecting her face, her feelings. 'Family,' she agreed. 'Come then, let's go to the hall and show everyone what Family means. I'll smile at Eoghan and let him think whatever he chooses. I'll smile and imagine myself a widow, because this marriage won't last long. He'll be dead within the year, by my father's hand or my own, but he'll never know what I'm thinking. I'm Feargus the Fox's daughter, after all, and I'm good at pretending.'

Quite how good, Brangianne discovered later that day in the hall when Yseult sat beside Eoghan and smiled at whatever he was saying. The smile didn't reach her eyes, but few would know it. She clapped her hands with delight when Eoghan, smirking, presented her with some token, and watched her pretend to be an empty-headed girl, flattered by the attention of an older, wiser, but not unattractive suitor. Eoghan's pebble eyes gleamed, and his skin sweated greasily in the heat of the hall as his fingers reached out to touch Yseult on the hand or the arm before drawing away at the last moment. Brangianne could feel his gaze sliding over Yseult's skin as if it was her own, could feel his desire, barely held in check, and his triumph in the prize of this girl who, if he'd known it, looked forward to becoming his widow. Only once did her pretence falter.

The meal was over, the trenchers removed, the dogs whipped away from the bones, the doors and windows shuttered against the night. Then the bards took the floor. Eoghan, who'd no ear for music, was smiling in satisfaction, glancing at Yseult as he did so, for this was yet another gift to her, a bard, recently added to his household, a youth clearly chosen for his looks – plain and rather solid – than his voice, which was thin, or his skills at the harp, which were mediocre. Nevertheless, he'd been schooled in the songs Eoghan thought would please Yseult, and when the bard began to sing it was a song she herself had transcribed, a song Brangianne had first heard sung in Carnadail, one of Trystan's, translated into the Gael tongue in the throes of Yseult's imagined hatred for him. Now it was given back to her, adorned and false, self-important and slightly off–key. She bore it for a verse, her face set, her smile rigid, then jumped to her feet, made some excuse, and ran from the hall. Distantly, Brangianne heard the sound of retching, and half-rose to follow her, but her wrist was caught in an iron grip.

'No,' Feargus said softly. 'Leave her.'

He held her fast, his smile as false as Yseult's for the benefit of any who might be watching, and Eoghan's bard carried on to the end of the song. He looked put out that his principal audience had left and was applauded without enthusiasm. Feargus loosed his grip on Brangianne's wrist and tossed the man a silver ring.

'Dreadful, wasn't it?' he murmured, nodding and smiling at the bard. 'But not enough for you to forget your promise – to hold your tongue and smile. Even at Eoghan. So smile, Brangianne. Smile.'

'There's to be a royal wedding, at Lughnasadh,' Ferdiad announced, having returned from a sortie to a farmstead that lay off the road leading to Dunadd from the south end of the loch.

Aelfric wasn't interested in any wedding, royal or otherwise. What he wanted, right then, was something to eat and somewhere to shelter, preferably with a fire, since his toes had been squelching inside his boots for so long he was afraid they might have dissolved. It was still raining, a heavy drumming downpour that this cursed country specialised in, weather that had plagued their journey all the way along that endless fucking loch and had turned the journey of a few days into a week or more.

'Why this way?' Aelfric had wanted to know as he'd struggled along the high ground on the eastern side of the endlessly long loch, dragging his horse through tangled pinewoods riven with streams and mudslides, with clouds above, mist below, and the incessant rain running down his neck and into his boots. The other side of the loch had looked like easier ground, and occasionally, when the clouds broke, Aelfric had made out island dwellings and fishing boats rowing on the loch. There would have been shelter there, hot food, drink, and somewhere to dry their clothes . . .

'This way's safer,' Ferdiad told him. They were in Dalriada proper now, and it was the Fili who was guiding them, much to Aelfric's relief for, to begin with, the Forest People had led the way. It had been days, however, since Aelfric had seen or smelt them, though he had the distinct impression they were still being watched, even once they descended from the ridge towards the more settled south with its settlements of round houses and farms.

'It's not the little hunters you should be worrying about,' Ferdiad had said 'It's my countrymen.'

Which was a bit much, considering they'd almost died for Ferdiad's countrymen. But Aelfric supposed it made sense, so now they were hiding in a copse of alders a bowshot from the road to Dunadd, a road that was rather too busy for the comfort of five men trying to be invisible. Which meant Ferdiad going to that farmstead had been a risk, especially since he'd come back with nothing but news of a wedding.

'Why is that so amusing?' Corwynal asked sharply, for the Fili was smiling as if at some private joke.

What is it with those two? Aelfric wondered irritably, for the tension between them, bad enough to begin with, had got steadily worse the further south they'd gone. Sure, Ferdiad was a devious Dalriad snake, Corwynal a stubborn stiff-necked Caledonian, but there had to be more to it than that, something to do with Trystan, who was sitting next to Aelfric in the inadequate shelter of a tree, shivering and trying not to cough. The boy had escaped the wight that had sent him mad, and had recovered his sanity, thanks be to Woden, but he still wasn't strong, and the wet and difficult journey along the loch had taxed him badly. Nevertheless, it had been Corwynal who'd been pushing the pace, and Ferdiad who'd insisted they stop to rest for Trystan's sake. And what was wrong with Kaerherdin? He too was even more silent than usual, but it was Corwynal he seemed to resent rather than Trystan. Actually, if anyone ought to have a grievance against the Caledonian, it was Aelfric himself, since, by going to Dunadd, Corwynal was breaking his promise to Ealhith, Aelfric's own sister.

'It's amusing because of who's getting married and why,' Ferdiad said. 'Feargus' daughter, the Princess Yseult, is to marry Eoghan, Steward of Dalriada.'

'Poor girl,' Trystan said with scant sympathy. 'But maybe they deserve one another.'

'I doubt Yseult has much choice in the matter. She's the prize for the man who defeated The Dragon.'

Ferdiad smiled broadly as he said this, then gave a shout of laughter at their various expressions. 'Quite!' he agreed once he'd mastered his amusement. 'But this means it's important to stay off the road. Eoghan may not be looking for you four, because he thinks you're all dead, but he may keep a watch for me since I witnessed his great victory or, rather, didn't witness it. So we'd better cross the river here and head west. There's another way to Dunadd, one not much used these days.'

'Why not?' Corwynal demanded.

'You'll see . . .' Ferdiad replied, still smiling, the sort of answer guaranteed to spark Corwynal's rather fragile temper.

'If this is some sort of trick—'

'Leave it,' Trystan cut in. 'Ferdiad's got us this far. We should trust him and go where he suggests.'

Corwynal looked at Trystan long and hard, but Trystan coolly returned his look, and the Caledonian backed down. 'Fine,' he said, pulling himself into Janthe's saddle. Moments later, screened by a particularly vicious downpour, they left the shelter of the copse, dropped to the river, crossed by a swollen ford, and headed into the broken wooded country beyond. Once over the river, the weather improved at last; the rain eased, and the sun came out, but it was then that the stones began.

'What is this place?' Trystan asked as they followed a faint track that led south between low hills. Along the way stood strange upright stones, their faces carved with odd pock-marked whorls and spirals. Some were arranged in circles, leaning drunkenly, like dancers after a night's revel. Others stood alone, pointing at the sky, and as they rode south, in silence now, Aelfric saw a line of posts on the edge of a field, carved with what looked like faces, dark eyed and ancient, and, here and there, mounds covered with lush grass on which no beast grazed.

The Ghost Woods were old, but this valley seemed older, though the gods of these stones didn't feel threatening. It was as if they'd lost interest, as if the men riding through these avenues, these groves, this valley, merited no more attention than ants beneath the gaze of giants. Nevertheless, it was an unnerving place, and Aelfric wasn't surprised this strange valley was uninhabited.

'Where does it lead?' Trystan asked.

'Originally? I don't know,' Ferdiad replied. 'These days it leads to the Monastery of St Martins that lies a few miles to the north of Dunadd.'

A monastery? Aelfric brightened. He didn't trust the god on the cross or his priests, but there were certain aspects of monasteries he approved of; they welcomed strangers, gave them food and shelter, and didn't ask questions.

'—a monastery we're going to avoid,' Ferdiad went on.

'Why?' Trystan wanted to know. The sun was setting by then, a flame of red in an angry black sky that threatened more rain to come, and none of them relished the idea of sheltering in one of these ancient oak groves.

'We just are.' Ferdiad kicked his horse forward. Then stopped.

None of them had seen the man standing beneath the trees, if man he was. He was as tall as the stones they'd passed, as rooted to the earth. He stood at the edge of a grove of oaks that lay in their path, dressed from head to foot in some dull grey material that took on the colour of the shadows, but when he stepped forward he turned out to be an old man who bore no weapon other than a tall wooden staff.

'Greetings.' The man's voice was low and, like Ferdiad's, faintly amused. 'Welcome to Dalriada.'

'What are you doing here?' The Fili's own voice was harsh and stripped of humour.

'Waiting for you.' The man allowed his gaze to travel from one to the next, and when his eyes fell on Aelfric, he wondered if the man was as harmless as he'd first appeared, for those eyes were dark and deep, like those of the carvings in the valley, and saw more than they ought to. 'All of you,' he added with a smile.

'Who are you?' Corwynal asked. 'How do you know who we are? Or that we'd come this way?'

He threw a glance at Ferdiad, bright with suspicion, and

Aelfric knew he was thinking the Fili must have betrayed them. But Aelfric didn't think he had, for Ferdiad looked far from happy to have met this particular man.

'I have my sources,' the old man said placidly. 'I know where you've been and what you've been doing. I know when you left and how you travelled. And I knew Ferdiad was leading you, so I knew you'd come this way and avoid St Martin's if you could.' He lowered his voice and spoke to Ferdiad alone. 'You've been avoiding St Martin's – and me – all your life.'

Ferdiad, for once, was lost for words, and the man smiled at that before turning to the rest of them. 'I'm Ciaran, Abbot of the Monastery of St Martin's. I'm hoping to persuade you to break your journey.'

'No,' Trystan said. 'We need to press on to Dunadd.'

'I can't prevent you from travelling there, nor have any wish to do so. But you won't get in without my help.'

'Why do we need your help?'

'Because, Trystan of Lothian, Galloway and Selgovia, they name you Morholt's Bane here in Dalriada, though it's Dragon's Bane they should be calling you now.'

Aelfric glanced at Corwynal, saw his eyes light up, his hand reaching for his sword as he turned on Ferdiad, certain now he'd betrayed them. Even Trystan looked at Ferdiad reproachfully.

'Did you say something at that farmstead?'

'Trys, I assure you—'

'No-one knows you're coming,' the Abbot cut in. 'But they will if you don't accept my help. Word will be sent to Dunadd on my order.' He turned and gestured. Further along the track was another priest, mounted and ready to ride.

'Perhaps you won't send that order,' Kaerherdin said. He'd drawn his bow and his arrow was aimed at the old man. His Scots had improved, Aelfric noticed, laying a hand on the haft of his axe.

'Perhaps I won't,' the Abbot agreed, then his voice hardened and took on the edge of a blade. 'But it's not you who'll stop me, Kaerherdin, son of Hoel of Selgovia. Or you, Aelfric, son of Herewulf, of Gyrwum. Drop your weapons!'

Aelfric's hand shot away from his axe as if he'd been scalded, and beside him Kaerherdin lowered his bow and, with a curse, flung it from him. *Not so harmless then*, Aelfric thought, as the Abbot raked them all with his dark implacable gaze. But eventually he smiled and his voice softened.

'Do me the honour of being my guests for the night,' he went on. 'I have a private residence not far from here. It's already occupied by another guest, but I believe I can find sufficient beds for you all, as well as dry clothes. And food of course.' He smiled at Aelfric, a benign old man once more. 'Sufficient, I believe, even for an Angle.'

The Abbot's private residence of Dun Treoin lay a little way to the southwest, a large round house surrounded by a cluster of smaller dwellings, standing on the shores of a rocky bay in which two ships were riding uneasily at anchor. To the east, across a broad expanse of low-lying salt marsh, Corwynal could make out a whale-backed crag ringed with walls and wreathed in smoke, the stronghold, he assumed, of Dunadd. To the south, on the other arm of the bay and in the shelter of an island, was a forest of masts, which must be the famous pirate fleet of Dalriada. So why were the two ships anchored so precariously in the bay? As he watched, a squall darkened the water, and the ships swung perilously close to the rocks, almost colliding with one another. One bore a plain black flag, the other a pennant whose symbol Corwynal couldn't make out since it had been shredded by the wind.

That particular mystery was soon solved, however, for when they entered the roundhouse and saw who the Abbot's visitor was, Corwynal knew what flag that ship was flying. The visitor was a small portly cleric whose head would have been tonsured if he'd possessed any hair at all. But the man was completely bald, his scalp polished to a pink shine, his cheeks gleaming like a ripe apple, his plump well-manicured hands clasped over an ample stomach as if to protect the jewelled cope he wore over his habit of fine blue-dyed wool. There was an expression of benevolence on his face that Corwynal knew to be false because he'd met this man before. He was Garwyn, Bishop of Caer Lual and, since Marc's recent transformation, Bishop of Galloway also.

Bishop Garwyn peered at them in mild alarm, which was hardly surprising since they looked like a band of outlaws. They were travel-stained and filthy, their faces obscured by several days' growth of beard, but when the little man peered at Trystan, his face cleared.

'Prince Trystan! Forgive me. I didn't recognise you at first. I'm very pleased to see you, however. We feared for you in Galloway, you know. Your uncle will be delighted to hear you're alive and well! And your arrival is timely, given that my own was delayed by the weather.'

Timely? Corwynal wanted to ask. Indeed, he wanted to know what the Bishop of Galloway was doing in Dalriada in the first place, but when he opened his mouth to ask the Abbot caught his eye and shook his head.

'Come.' The Abbot held out his arms to them all. 'You're cold and hungry. We'll talk once you've eaten.' He clapped his hands, and several servants came in to build up the fire and light the braziers that stood about the roundhouse and the oil lamps that hung from the roof timbers. They laid out food and drink on a table set with benches and Aelfric set too with a will and looked set to demolish the lot. There was enough for everyone, however, and both food and warmth were welcome, so it wasn't until Corwynal was sitting toying with a piece of bannock and allowing his cup to be re-filled with ale that he acknowledged his growing sense of disquiet.

Who was the old man? *What* was he? Those eyes . . . He shivered at the memory of the old man's gaze as it had swept over him. He'd felt exposed and open and . . . known in ways no man should know another. And why this generosity to a group of travellers whose motives were questionable at best? The man wanted something from them, and nothing was for nothing. He'd been waiting for them, which meant they were expected and, despite Ferdiad's denials, it must have been him who'd given them away. Yet if Ferdiad felt triumphant, he was keeping it well hidden. Indeed, he seemed more unsettled than Corwynal himself.

'Timely,' the Abbot said, as if in reply to Corwynal's unspoken question. 'Bishop Garwyn used that word with good reason, for sometimes God answers our prayers. You've arrived just in time, Prince Trystan – to rescue Princess Yseult from an unwelcome marriage.'

Everyone stared at the Abbot.

'That's not why I'm here,' Trystan said. 'And how could I do that, even if I wanted to?'

'How? I would have thought that was obvious. You have the head, don't you? May I see it?'

Trystan nodded to Kaerherdin who extracted the grisly object from the leather bag in which he'd kept it since the earth-house. It smelled less strongly but was still an unpleasant sight. Bishop Garwyn paled, his hands going to his mouth, but the Abbot took the head by the braid and peered curiously into the dried-up face. 'Poor man,' he said eventually. It wasn't clear to whom he was referring, Azarion or his brother. 'I'll pray for him.' He handed the head back to Kaerherdin and turned to Trystan. 'You realise what you can do with this?'

'I can claim justice for my dead,' Trystan replied with quiet authority. 'That's all I'm here for. I've no wish to embroil myself in Dalriada's politics.'

'You can't avoid it I'm afraid. Claiming justice for your dead will mean discrediting Eoghan, Steward of Dalriada, a trusted servant of the King, a man who won't take that well.'

'He's a liar,' Trystan said bluntly. 'He deserves to be discredited.'

'Quite,' the Abbot agreed with a smile. 'As Dalriada's Steward, he's made himself wealthy at Dalriada's expense but, as a result, has a great deal of support from those who owe their positions to him, or are afraid of him. In one way or another he has a hold on all the principal families of the land. In particular, he has the support of Loarn and Oenghus, Feargus' foster brothers, who rule the North and West, and could, with Eoghan's help, overthrow Feargus and rule Dalriada themselves. The only reason they haven't done so is that Eoghan has been persuaded to support Feargus in return for the hand of his daughter.'

'None of that explains why I should care about the difficulties of your King or his daughter. I owe Feargus of Dalriada nothing. Quite the reverse, in fact. He owes me an apology, a public apology.'

'Kings are not in the habit of apologising. Particularly in public.'

'To own a fault is the mark of a truly Christian King,' Bishop Garwyn intoned sententiously. 'King Marc understands that.'

'*Marc* understands it?' Corwynal exclaimed, never having known Marc apologise for anything, publicly or otherwise.

'Feargus understands it too,' the Abbot said. 'But you'll have to give him something in return,' he added, nodding to Trystan. 'If you're to walk into Dunadd's great hall and call Eoghan a liar, there will be consequences. Only Eoghan stands between Loarn and Oenghus and the ruin of Feargus' family, which means

Feargus won't allow you to discredit his Steward until he has an ally strong enough to back him against his foster brothers.'

'An ally?' Trystan asked, looking first puzzled then angry. 'You can't mean me! Not after he allowed half my men to be slaughtered!'

But Corwynal knew what the Abbot meant, as did Ferdiad, who leant forward and would have spoken if Trystan hadn't worked it out for himself.

'Galloway' he concluded. 'You mean Galloway.'

'There has been considerable correspondence between Galloway and Dalriada,' the Abbot explained. 'It began, I believe, when King Marc wrote to Feargus to thank him for restoring you to him.'

Corwynal would very much like to have read that letter, and to have witnessed Feargus' reaction on reading it, given that he'd sent a shipload of men to stop him and Trystan from leaving Dalriada at all.

'Other matters have been discussed since then, however, including the question of the tribute,' the Abbot went on. 'As you'll know, an accommodation was reached and, in return, the question of trading rights was raised, together with that of shipping and fishing, what to do about the Arainn pirates, that sort of thing. The ship in the bay, the one that accompanied Bishop Garwyn's ship, contains a number of, let's say travellers, from Galloway, bound for an island Feargus has agreed to gift them in perpetuity. There will no doubt be other such arrangements of mutual benefit, as you might expect between the rulers of two maritime nations. All this has encouraged Feargus to consider where his interests might lie, and to whom he might look for aid in certain . . . internal matters.

'But nothing is for nothing.' He glanced at Corwynal, his dark eyes gleaming. 'In return for such aid, an alliance has been proposed, and Bishop Garwyn has come to negotiate the terms on behalf of King Marc. Sadly, his arrival was delayed by the storms that have swept Dalriada in the past few weeks, and Feargus was forced to announce the marriage of his daughter to Eoghan, the prize for his part in the war against the Creonn and the Dragon-riders. Except he played no part, did he?' He turned to Trystan now. '*You* defeated the Dragon. So all you need to do to get your public apology from Feargus is walk into Dunadd's great hall with the head. And claim Princess Yseult for yourself.'

THE NIGHT OF GIFTS

L ughnasadh is the Night of Gifts, the night that marks the turning of summer to autumn. When Brangianne had been a girl, the Druid priests had sacrificed to the Old Gods to ensure a good harvest. Now the Priests of Chrystos gave thanks to the One God and prayed for the harvest yet to come. But little else had changed over the years. Lughnasadh remained a fire-festival, and during the three days of celebration people came to Dunadd from far and wide for the market held on the summer-dry water-meadows. During Lughnasadh, Dunadd was transformed into a tented city full of noise and colour, of strange foreign smells and stranger foreign tongues, of basket-makers and knife-grinders, jugglers and travelling bards, thieves and cutpurses, men for hire and women for sale. Farmers and fishermen came to sell their wares, clogging the roads with wagons piled high with cheeses and smoked meats, bolts of cloth and coils of rope, leatherwork and metalwork. The anchorage at Crionan was crammed with trading ships bearing more exotic wares: wine and oil, gold and silver jewellery, brightly dyed fabrics, manuscripts and medicines. Brangianne was hoping to replenish her supply of poppy and had been concerned about the unseasonable weather, which had brought rain to the north and gales further south. Eventually, however, the winds eased, and the trading ships arrived, sailing in from Dun Averty and Dun Sobhairce, from Strathclyde, Rheged and far-off Gwynedd.

At nightfall on the Night of Gifts, bonfires burned on the fields by the river and high on Dunadd's Royal Terrace. Later there would be feasting in the hall, the giving and receiving of gifts, and few would go to bed sober. Those who did, or had robust constitutions, would rise at dawn to watch the first of the new grain being ground and baked into the Lughnasadh bannocks, which were cooked in the ashes of the fires and eaten dusty and hot, smeared with honey. The breaking of the Lughnasadh bannocks symbolised the sacrifice of Chrystos, or so the priests said, but in Brangianne's youth it had signified the death of Lugh, the God of Summer. In still older, darker, times the King would have sacrificed himself to ensure a good harvest, but those days were long gone. The King was no longer required to give up his life for his people. Only his daughter.

Yet Yseult appeared a willing enough sacrifice and, as Feargus' clients and guests gathered in Dunadd's hall for the Lughnasadh feast, she moved about easily, smiling and laughing as she greeted each new arrival with the guest cup. Only those who knew her well would notice the rigidity of her smile and hear a brittle hysterical edge to her laughter.

'Loarn's arrived . . .' Feargus murmured to Brangianne. 'Try to be polite,' he added before moving to greet his foster-brothers. Loarn, the self-styled Lord of the Isles, was a big man, coarse-fleshed and, by all accounts, coarse in his habits. His brother, Oenghus, a paler, softer version of Loarn himself, followed in his wake, and both paused in the doorway of the hall, Loarn searching for allies and opponents. Brangianne intercepted a look between him and Eoghan, but there was no hint of rebellion in Loarn's face as, having greeted Feargus, he approached Brangianne herself.

'Well, sister . . .' She hated him calling her that, and he knew it. 'You look well.' He regarded her with critical, if curious, approval. Obeying Feargus for once, she'd dressed for the occasion in a rich black dress, heavily embroidered with gold thread, over a fine white underskirt. There were gold brooches on her shoulders, and a cross hung from a heavy gold chain. Normally she left her hair free, but that night she'd covered it with a fine linen veil held in place by a narrow gold filet. Looking in her mirror earlier that evening, she'd seen a stranger, and perhaps Loarn saw the same stranger, for all that they'd known one another since childhood.

'They say you're for the church,' he observed nodding at her attire.

'So I believe,' Brangianne replied with an ambiguity to match that of her dress, which might have been that of an Abbess.

'I expect you've being waiting until the girl was off your hands.' He turned his attention to Yseult, as did so many others, and small wonder. She was particularly lovely that night, dressed as she was in a simple gown of pale green wool that brought out the colour of her eyes. Unlike most unmarried girls, she'd chosen to wear her hair up, and had coiled it into a fine gold net and pinned it up like a crown. The weight of it set off the long line of her neck and shoulders, as did the jewelled collar she was wearing. It was a present from Eoghan, a gaudy thing set with river pearls and faceted crystals that, to Brangianne, had the look of a slave collar. Nevertheless, Yseult looked like a queen out of the old tales, remote and untouchable, and there were few men in the room who wouldn't have imagined that, with Yseult by their sides, they would feel like a king.

'Should have married the girl myself . . .' Loarn mused, half to himself. Brangianne, revolted, opened her mouth to protest but stopped herself. *Be polite.*

'That would have been unthinkable,' she said sweetly, her teeth grinding with the effort of not slapping his fleshy face. 'Given the closeness of your relationship. She's your niece, after all.'

'Foster kin,' Loarn grumbled. 'Not blood kin.'

'As close in the law, my dear brother, as no doubt you know.'

Loarn threw her a look of loathing and stalked off to speak to Eoghan, but Dalriada's Steward didn't appear to be interested in whatever Loarn had to say and was clearly impatient for the feast to begin, for after the feast would come the marriage. His colour was high, and his laugher had the frenetic quality of a man who has a years-long goal in his grasp and can't quite believe it. His mood of feverish gaiety was shared by most of the people in the hall; it was as if they were waiting for something to happen, something beginning with the feast but ending with something other than a marriage, as if, like Brangianne, everyone was praying for a miracle, and Eoghan was the only one not to know it. But Brangianne had little confidence in miracles, so she moved to stand beside the one person who could stop all this.

'You said this was a feint,' she reminded her brother. He was no longer smiling. Perhaps the juggler had too many balls in the air and little expectation of catching them all.

'I said it might be. And there's still time.'

Time for what? She didn't ask, though, and the time he was relying on shrank as the flow of new arrivals slowed from a flood to a trickle. Ciaran had still not arrived, which was strange, for she'd heard he'd returned to Dalriada, if not yet to St Martin's. But, even for the Abbot of St Martin's, Feargus could delay no longer, and he took his place on the tall oak chair that stood on the raised platform at the back of the hall. The crowd drifted towards the benches and tables where servants had laid out platters of roasted meats and cheeses, baskets of bread and bannocks, jugs of heather and honey ale, and imported wine. One of the guardsmen moved to close the main door, but Feargus gestured irritably for it to be left open.

He still has hope. Brangianne went to take her own place, for outside, beyond the hall door, night had fallen on the fortress, and surely no-one would come now? It was then, past time, past hope, past prayer, that the miracle happened.

A tall, white-robed figure appeared in the doorway, a small party of monks in his train. By his side was another tall man, clad in a dark wool habit belted with gold, its hood drawn over his head to obscure his features.

'Ciaran, at last!' Brangianne heard the relief in Feargus' voice. 'Be welcome, you and your guest, who is my guest also – Bishop Garwyn of Caerlual.'

Who?

The question murmured around the hall. No-one, including Brangianne, had heard of Bishop Garwyn or knew where Caerlual was. Yet there was something oddly familiar about the man's gait as he strode forward at Ciaran's side to salute Feargus.

'Not Bishop Garwyn, I'm afraid.' Ciaran's voice was low yet carried throughout the hall. 'But a man you may welcome to Dunadd with equal honour, a man who's come to make a claim.'

'But not a gift.' The man's voice sounded harsh after Ciaran's soft persuasive tones and cut through the murmur like a blade. 'I claim no more than what is mine by right.'

He pushed back his hood, and an appalled silence settled on the hall until it was broken by a woman screaming. Another moaned, and a ripple of consternation ran around the packed crowd. Then, as if a nest of wood-ants had been poked with a stick, people jumped up, grabbed children and spouses, and made for the doors.

Amazingly, miraculously, terrifyingly, The Dragon had come to Dunadd.

'Be welcome to Dunadd.'

To Brangianne's surprise, it wasn't Feargus who'd spoken, for he was still staring at Azarion, ashen faced, a juggler who'd failed to catch all those circling balls that had turned out to be made not of coloured leather but of fragile roman glass and were shattering all around him. It was Yseult who'd come forward, her clear voice reaching to every corner of the hall. At the sound of it, so pure and firm and unafraid, some of the fleeing men and women turned back, curiosity warring with terror, to watch her walk towards The Dragon, the guest cup in her outstretched hands, a smile on her lips, and, for the first time in weeks, a gleam of life in her eyes.

Azarion took the cup from Yseult's hands, swallowed a mouthful, and gave it back to her. A faint susurration of relief ran around the hall as this enemy thereby accepted Dunadd's hospitality, but Brangianne didn't share their relief. *Is he claiming her? This embittered old man?* Even Eoghan was preferable, but Eoghan, as white as bleached wool, was edging into the crowd. Feargus, however, had regained a little colour. Perhaps he'd seen a way of turning this fresh disaster into an opportunity.

'Make your claim then,' he said.

Azarion smiled at Yseult, then turned aside and strode into the crowd to grasp Eoghan by the throat as he sought to make his escape.

'I just want what's due to me,' he hissed, dragging Eoghan back into the centre of the hall.

'Take her then. Take her!' Eoghan squealed.

Azarion snarled in disgust and threw him to the ground. 'She's not yours to give.' Then he turned on Feargus. 'I understand you offered the hand of your daughter to the man who defeated The Dragon.'

'So they say.' Even now, Feargus the Fox was trying to wriggle out of it.

'Then you're less than a father.' The Dragon spoke with deliberate contempt. 'But I'm not here to claim Princess Yseult. I want only what belongs to me – the head of my brother, the man you knew as The Dragon, the man who led the Creonn and the Dragon-riders. He was defeated, as once you, Feargus of Dalriada, defeated my father. But The Dragon doesn't die, and I'm The Dragon now, though in truth I always was. I saw my brother's body hanging from your walls, and I see my brother's armour.' He glanced behind Feargus, at the Champions' swords hanging there, and at The Dragon's golden armour which had been pinned beside them. 'I already have the helmet.' He took a bag from beneath his cloak and pulled out the gold-washed helmet that was shaped like a beast. 'What I don't see is the head.' He swept his gaze around the hall before allowing it to settle on Eoghan. 'What I don't see is the man who defeated my brother.'

All around Brangianne, people began to murmur, speculatively now. This was what they'd been waiting for. This confirmed all their doubts. *I never believed it . . .*

'*I* defeated him,' Eoghan declared defiantly, ignoring the whispers.

He's going to bluff it out! Eoghan must be relying on Yseult's silence, for if Eoghan was exposed as a liar then so was she. If she went back on her story now, it would be put down to the natural apprehension of a girl confronted with the realities of marriage. As for Brangianne, her antipathy to Eoghan had been a little too public. Only Ferdiad might be believed, but the Fili was still missing. So Feargus, for the moment, chose to say nothing

'I brought his body and armour back to Dunadd,' Eoghan went on. 'You may take them if you wish, but there was no head.'

'No head?' Azarion raised an eyebrow in mock surprise. 'Didn't you strike it from his body? After you defeated him?'

'Yes . . . no . . . that is . . . One of your Riders must have taken it.'

Silence fell as everyone concluded that this was a lie, and in that silence a bell could be heard ringing. Perhaps it was to announce some late arrivals, but to Brangianne it sounded more like a warning, though of what she couldn't have said.

'The head doesn't matter.' Eoghan declared, unnerved by the silence and that distant tolling bell. 'The important thing is that I defeated him. Didn't I, Yseult?'

'You didn't, you lying pathetic worm, you miserable excuse for a man! *You* defeat The Dragon? Are you mad? Are you *all* mad?'

It wasn't Yseult who'd spoken. Nor was it Brangianne, who would dearly liked to have said these things herself. One of Ciaran's monks stepped forward and threw back the hood of their habit, revealing a mass of distinctive dark red hair.

Eoghan's eyes bulged when he recognised Oonagh, but he recovered quickly. 'The word of a servant carries no weight in the law.'

'The word of a King does, however.' Ciaran moved to stand between Eoghan and The Dragon, laid his hands on Azarion's shoulders, kissed him on both cheeks, then stepped back to bow formally, before turning to Feargus.

'My Lord King, may I present Father Adarn of St Torran's who was The Dragon and is once more – Azarion, Commander of the Dragon-riders and King of the Forest People.'

Feargus stared at them both, momentarily lost for words, but it wasn't long before he was Feargus the Fox once more. 'Leader of the Dragon-riders you may be, but I thought *I* was King of the Forest People.'

'The Children of the forest have always chosen their own King, and they have chosen me.'

The two men regarded one another steadily, but, in the end, it was Azarion who gave way. 'In their tongue, King is the same word as Father, and I think of them as my children. But that is a matter for further discussion between us. For the moment, I'm just here for justice.' He turned on Eoghan, his hawk's eyes glittering. 'You claim to have defeated The Dragon. Would you challenge his successor?'

He swept his cloak aside to reveal the rusty sword he'd worn before, now stained with dried blood, and threw it at Eoghan's feet as he backed away.

'Go on,' Azarion said. 'Pick it up. Strike off my head as you struck off the head of my brother.' Eoghan made no move towards the sword, and Azarion threw back his head and laughed. 'Except you didn't. It was *I* who struck off his head. That blood is his, and I've sworn never to clean it off, or to bloody this blade ever again, though in your case I might make an exception, you – how did my daughter put it? – you lying, pathetic little worm. *You* didn't defeat the Dragon!'

'Then who did?' Eoghan demanded. 'Let *him* show everyone the head! Let *him* come forward!'

Brangianne glanced at Feargus, but his attention, like that of the crowd, was on the warning bell, the sound of which had drawn closer. Outside, in the courtyard, voices rose in anger and alarm, but there was no clash of arms. Someone was coming, someone who couldn't or wouldn't be withstood. Then six figures appeared in the doorway. One was a cleric of some kind, a short fat man wearing a jewelled cope and head-dress and carrying the hooked staff of a bishop. He stood apart from the others, all of whom were clad in hooded grey cloaks and tunics daubed with black crosses. Everyone near the doors surged back in fear, for those crosses meant these men were lepers.

'What's the meaning of this?!' Feargus jumped to his feet to plant his fists on the bench in front of him, his furious gaze on the cleric. 'Bishop Garwyn, you I expected, but not these . . . these creatures!'

'They're men like you and I, and we had an agreement,' the man said in Gaelic so strongly accented it was difficult to make out, but Feargus understood.

'I expressly forbade you from bringing them to Dunadd! You should have taken them straight to the island I gave you.'

'A gift for which they're grateful,' the bishop replied, ignoring Feargus' anger. 'These men bring you a gift in return, on this, the Night of Gifts.' He turned and gestured to one of the grey-clad men who moved into the hall until he was standing before Feargus. Everyone else backed away, and Brangianne and Yseult were swept towards the wall by the crowd.

The man raised his hooded head, and Feargus turned pale. Brangianne wasn't surprised, for she'd had some dealings with this most terrible of diseases and knew the man's face would be a ruin of skin, his features distorted by scar tissue, his limbs twisted and deformed. He would be a monster.

'I bring a gift for a King,' the man said, his voice surprisingly clear, and those remaining in the hall craned forward to see what his gift might be. 'But not for you, Feargus of Dalriada,' the leper continued. 'You deserve no gift from my hand.' He turned his back on Feargus and went over to Azarion, dropped to his knees in front of him, and held up a large leather bag. 'My Lord King, I have brought you your brother's head.' He swept back his hood to reveal his features, his young, unblemished features, features Brangianne had thought she'd never see again.

It was Trystan.

I knew this was a bad idea, Corwynal thought when the shouting began. There was relief, certainly, but it was mixed with anger, and Corwynal threw back his hood and reached for his sword as the crowd surged forward once more. If it came to a fight, they didn't stand a chance, but he felt safer with a blade in his hand.

He'd argued against this plan; even Trystan hadn't liked it.

'I have a legitimate claim. Why do I need to go in disguise, and why as a leper?' Trystan's lips had twisted with disgust for, despite the old Abbot's assurance that the habits had never been worn, the thought of appearing as one of those doomed outcasts made everyone's skin crawl.

'Because no-one is going to challenge a leper . . .'

And so it had proved. Now they were in Dunadd's great hall, and, whatever Trystan intended, Corwynal was there for one reason only, to find Brangianne, for the Abbot had assured him she'd be here. But he couldn't see her and, in any case, there was Feargus to deal with first. The King of Dalriada was glaring at them, his eyes hostile as he met Corwynal's, before passing on to Trystan, kneeling at the feet of a rival king.

The Dragon took the bag from Trystan and pulled out the head, to gasps of horror from those close enough to see it clearly. It was shrunken but bore such an unsettling resemblance to Azarion himself no-one doubted it was the head of his brother.

'I thank you for this gift,' Azarion said softly.

'I thank you for my life.' Trystan rose to his feet and smiled at the older man, but his smile faded as he turned to Feargus. 'How is it that I owe my life to the man I came to fight and not the man I came to fight for?' His clear voice carried through the hall. 'We came, my men and I, to repay a debt, but we didn't come to fight your battles unaided. So where was your army, Feargus of Dalriada? Where were your men when mine were dying in the Ghost Woods?'

His face was tight with anger as he stepped towards Feargus, sweeping back his cloak and dragging his sword from its scabbard as he did so. A cry of dismay ran around the hall, but Trystan just slammed his sword down on the high table in front of Feargus. 'I will tell you where they were!' Skulking by the loch, led by cowards. Only your cavalry showed any sense of honour, and had they not been led by an incompetent—'

'Enough!' Feargus cut through Trystan's tirade. 'The leader of the cavalry has been punished, and as for the man who led the army...'

Corwynal followed Feargus' gaze to someone trying to push his way towards a side door. Some of Feargus' warband moved to cut off his escape, forcing the man to face Feargus, and Corwynal recognised him as the one who'd appeared in the clearing, weighed down with armour. So, this portly, ostentatiously dressed man was the Steward of Dalriada, the one who'd been betrothed to Brangianne, but presumably was no longer, given that he was claiming Feargus' daughter as his prize. Corwynal thought he looked more like a cleric than a warrior, and, judging from the whispers that were running about the hall, everyone agreed with him.

'I'm confused, Eoghan,' Feargus began softly and patiently, not looking like a man given to either confusion or patience. 'You told me you'd defeated the Creonn and I accepted your word. You told me you'd defeated The Dragon, and as proof you brought back his body and his armour, but not the head. Now it has been brought by one who also claims to have defeated The Dragon. Can you explain this ... discrepancy to me, Eoghan?'

'Why should I have to explain anything, my Lord?' The man's tone was defiant. 'Haven't I been loyal to your interests? Haven't I supported you in so many ways? Why should you believe the word of this ... this boy, rather than the words of your trusted servant and your own Family?' His expression grew sly. 'Will you allow a stranger and an enemy to call your daughter a liar? Will you allow him to threaten your Family's honour?'

Silence fell at that. Corwynal didn't understand what was going on, but he knew a threat had been made, something to do with the daughter. The Steward was scanning the crowd in search of the girl, but the only person who stepped forward was Ciaran, Abbot of St Martin's, who nodded to the King of

Dalriada. Corwynal saw the tension go out of Feargus' body as if that nod confirmed some news he'd been hoping for. His fists uncurled, and his gaze, shifting to the Steward, was no longer enquiring but cold and stern.

'I believe, Eoghan, that you can safely leave the honour of Dalriada and its Royal Family to its King,' Feargus said softly but with an edge to his voice. 'And no man may call my daughter a liar. Everything Yseult has claimed has been with my full knowledge and approval.'

Which meant the Steward had been tricked into the lie by someone less principled and a great deal more cunning. Corwynal almost felt sorry for the man.

'You force me to consider your position,' Feargus went on. 'You're correct; you've been a faithful servant to Dalriada for many years, but perhaps I've overburdened you. I may have forgotten that a sense of honour and justice is bred in bone and blood. I may have overestimated the ability of a man so recently elevated from the ranks of artisans to grasp the concepts those of the aristocracy take for granted.'

There was an intake of breath from around the hall and not a few sniggers.

'—but because the fault is partly mine, I will be lenient,' Feargus continued.

Eoghan, had slipped to his knees as if his legs had given way, but now he looked up hopefully.

'I won't have you executed,' Feargus said with a thin smile. 'Instead, you'll be stripped of your possessions and banished from Dalriada.' He nodded to a couple of his warband. 'Take him to whatever border he wishes to cross.'

Eoghan let out a strangled cry and surged to his feet, looking around wildly, but no-one would meet his eyes. Then he hurled himself at Feargus, seized the sword Trystan had slammed down on the table, and struck out at the King. Corwynal leapt forward, blade in hand, and blocked Eoghan's blow, then grasped him by the shoulder and flung him towards Feargus' men, who seized him and dragged him from the hall.

'I think that makes us even,' he said quietly to Feargus, before laying his own sword next to Trystan's, but Feargus scowled back at him, his eyes cold and hard.

'I think not.'

Corwynal shrugged. The man's opinion of him didn't matter. Nevertheless, he gestured to Kaerherdin and Aelfric to lay their weapons next to his and Trystan's. Aelfric did so, if reluctantly, but Kaerherdin kept his hand on his sword after he'd laid it down.

'Trystan and I have a claim to make,' he said, leaning towards the King.

'Make it then,' Feargus said, looking to Trystan. But Trystan's attention had wandered, and he was scanning the crowd in the hall as if searching for someone. Only when Kaerherdin nudged him did he recall why he was there.

'We've come to claim compensation for the men who died on your behalf.'

Feargus' brows snapped together as if this wasn't what he'd been expecting but hesitated only for a moment before nodding.

'Agreed. They'll be honoured as if they'd been part of our own warband. Is that all?'

'No. I want a public apology.'

The crowd held its breath, for it was a brave man who asked a King to apologise for anything, especially in his own hall, but Feargus just narrowed his eyes.

'If everything you say is true, you'll be due one,' he said carefully, speaking to Trystan but looking to the last of the 'lepers'. Ferdiad had accompanied them to the hall but had remained in the shadows. Now he shrugged off the leper's garb and stepped forward.

'It's the truth. These men came at my request to aid Dalriada.'

'Your request? The last time you spoke in my name, without my permission, you brought us The Morholt's Bane.'

'And, on this occasion, brought The Dragon's Bane.'

The Dragon's Bane . . . The name ran around the room like a tongue of fire.

'Yet The Dragon still lives,' Feargus pointed out, inclining his head to Azarion.

'A Dragon you needn't fear,' Azarion said. 'If you keep to your borders, we will keep to ours. All I ask is that my Children be left in peace in the place they've made their own – the abandoned Ghost Woods of the North. Is that so much to ask, my Lord King? Don't we both want peace? Isn't this boy's gift to you, on this Night of Gifts, the gift of peace?'

Feargus leant back in his chair, a hand stroking his beard. Corwynal had the distinct impression he was smiling behind the hand, that this most devious of men had let himself be driven to give Trystan an apology, not because he had to but because he wanted what would come from it.

'Very well. You have your apology, Trystan of Lothian and Galloway. And I give you the freedom of Dunadd for you and your—' His eyes drifted to Corwynal and chilled. '—your companions.' Then he turned back to Trystan and raised an eyebrow. 'Is there anything else you would ask of me?'

This was the moment Corwynal had been dreading, though for no good reason, for the old Abbot had been convincing. A treaty had been negotiated between Dalriada and Galloway, but it wouldn't be popular. The saviour of Dalriada, The Dragon's Bane, however, could make it so. The Abbot, backed up by Bishop Garwyn, had pointed out that, for Galloway's sake, it was an opportunity that should be seized. Corwynal agreed with them, and Trystan, seeing the sense of it, had allowed himself to be persuaded. So why did he have such a bad feeling about it?

Yet now the moment had arrived Trystan said nothing. He wasn't even listening to Feargus. He was staring at a girl at the back of the crowd, a girl with a pale face beneath what Corwynal at first took to be a head-dress, but which was actually a mass of auburn hair netted in gold and piled on her head like a crown. Corwynal didn't recognise her to begin with, since the last time he'd seen that hair it had been tumbling over the shoulders of a blood and dirt-smeared girl dressed in boy's clothing. But It was definitely Ethlin.

'Anything at all . . . ?' Feargus asked, beginning to frown, and Trystan, with an effort, dragged his attention back to the King and the reason he was there.

'It seems to me, my Lord, that King Azarion is correct. The best way to honour my men would be to make a peace in which their families and kinsmen can live without the shadow of yet another war. Galloway and Dalriada have long been at odds, and much ill has come from that. So let it be over. Let Galloway and Dalriada unite in peace and prosperity.'

There was some muttering at that, but Feargus gestured the crowd to silence and leant forward once more. 'Let me understand you, Trystan of Galloway. Do you, as the man who defeated The Dragon, claim the hand of my daughter?'

'Yes, but—'

Trystan's attempt to clarify his answer was drowned in a roar from around the hall, some shouting in protest, some in approval. What the daughter herself thought of this proposal remained a mystery, however, for no Princess stepped forward. Yet she must be in the hall, for Feargus lifted his head, scanned the crowd and snapped his fingers.

'Yseult! What are you waiting for? Bring the guest cup!'

Corwynal followed Feargus' frowning gaze, and it was then that he noticed a woman standing next to Ethlin, a woman he'd taken for a nun on account of her dress, a rich black gown that set off a large gold cross hanging around her neck, and a fine linen veil covering her hair. Then he looked more closely, and everything about him faded away: the hall, the crowd, the two kings, his disquieting forebodings. It was Brangianne, the other half of his soul.

She had her hand on Ethlin's arm and was speaking urgently to her, but the girl ignored her, braced her shoulders and pushed her way through the crowd. Corwynal glanced around, wondering where the Princess was, but no-one else came forward in answer to Feargus' curt summons, and Ethlin continued on to the high table, took the guest cup from Feargus and walked over to Trystan.

'Ethlin?' he asked in some confusion, glancing over her shoulder as he searched for some other woman.

'Ethlin?' Feargus asked. 'That was her mother's name. This is my daughter, Yseult.'

Trystan stared at her, his confusion gradually replaced by a cold, unyielding expression.

'Ethlin,' he repeated, an accusation now.

'I was Ethlin in Carnadail,' she agreed. 'And you were Drust. Here in Dunadd we have other names.'

Corwynal's eyes flew to Brangianne's and met hers. Her face was as milk-pale as the girl's, and he saw guilt there and something like apprehension. And finally – *finally* – he understood. If Ethlin was Yseult, daughter to Feargus, then Brangianne was his sister.

The understanding drove a sword through the heart of all his plans. He'd come to Dunadd to find the Lady of Carnadail, a healer, but, other than that, a woman of little importance. He'd intended telling her he'd married someone else, and hoped, when she knew his reasons, that she might forgive him. He wanted to ask her to share his life, to become his wife in all but name. They'd have to go away, to somewhere no-one knew them, Rheged or Gwynedd maybe, but surely, if she loved him, a healer might be prepared to do that? But would the sister of a King?

I'm going to kill you! Murder rippled through his veins like wine as he turned on the Fili, the man who'd hoarded the secret of Brangianne's identity for his own purposes, who'd planned all this from the beginning, who'd led him step by step to this final irrevocable understanding, this long-planned revenge.

Ferdiad was watching him, his eyes glittering, his body as tense as an over-strung harp. Corwynal took a step towards him, intending to tear the man to pieces with his own hands, but Feargus' voice dragged him back to sanity. *Not here. Not yet.*

'Yseult!' Feargus called out. The girl was still standing in front of Trystan holding out the guest cup, but he made no move to take it. 'You've lost one husband today, but here, it seems, is another. Will you take him?'

'But I—' Trystan tried once more.

'If he claims me, I will take him,' Yseult said clearly, but her voice had an edge to it. 'Do you claim me?'

Ferdiad's revenge was still echoing around the hall like a plucked chord, but now another note rang out to join it, for Ferdiad wasn't the only one who wanted revenge. Ethlin was a great deal more than a spoiled girl with a taste for music and a longing for adventure, a girl Ferdiad had brought to Carnadail to break Trystan's heart. She was Yseult, niece to The Morholt, whom Trystan had killed. She wouldn't forgive him for that, or his excoriating dismissal of her in the Ghost Woods. *Claim me*, she was saying, *and I will make your life a misery. I will destroy you!*

But Trystan hadn't come to Dunadd to claim her in the way

she thought. She might hate him, but he had no reason to care about that. Nevertheless, Corwynal's foreboding grew stronger as Trystan failed to reply.

Then, like a flash of lightning, something flared in his memory – the moment when Trystan, blinded by the sun, had staggered in a doorway in Carnadail. Except it hadn't been the sun. Why hadn't he seen it? Why hadn't he understood, when it had been exactly the same for him in Galloway all those years before? Just as sudden, just as shattering. Hadn't he, like Trystan, thrown up every shield he'd possessed? Hadn't he pretended a dislike he didn't feel to protect himself from pity? Hadn't he kept his feelings so well hidden his face had turned to a stony mask of derision? Now, too late, he understood why Trystan had come to Dunadd. He wasn't here to claim anything from Feargus. He was here to apologise to the girl he'd been so rude to. Instead, he'd found someone who hated him more than he could have imagined, and he could neither move nor reply to the challenge he wanted with all his heart to accept.

'Don't!'

The word rang through the silent waiting hall. Corwynal tore his gaze from Trystan's frozen blood-drained face and turned to Ferdiad, for it was he who'd called out, his voice raw with desperation, the same ghastly pallor as Trystan in his face, as if he too remembered that moment in Carnadail, as if, like Corwynal, he'd only now understood what it meant. Yet wasn't this what he'd wanted? Wasn't this the culmination of his vengeance, two hearts broken in return for his own? But the triumph of a few heartbeats before had been stripped from his face. He'd believed he'd failed to break Trystan's heart but no longer cared. Indeed, he'd been glad of it. Now, however, whatever his present hopes and plans, they were as broken as Corwynal's own, as he watched Trystan play out the game he could no longer control.

'I claim you,' Trystan said eventually, his eyes on the girl, his voice steady with an effort that left his whole body shaking so hard he couldn't reach out to take the guest cup. All he could do was continue to say the words he'd begun to speak earlier, the words Feargus, knowingly or unknowingly, had interrupted.

'I claim you on behalf of my uncle, King Marc of Galloway.'

22

THE CHOICE

I *claim you . . .*
Brangianne's world crystallised into perfection. It was as
if Corwynal had spoken the words rather than Trystan.
She'd seen him searching for her earlier, but, crushed against the
wall by the crowd, she'd been out of sight and unable to move.
Then Yseult pushed her way forward and he saw her at last. His
eyes blazed from slate to the deepest of blues, but when his gaze
flickered to Yseult, he looked puzzled. Trystan was also staring at
Yseult as she moved towards him, a wash of colour in his face, his
eyes glittering. There was something young and vulnerable about
him that Brangianne understood as if she'd always known it. *He*
loves her! Everything he'd said to Yseult, everything he'd done,
had been nothing more than armour against love. Now that
armour had shattered, leaving him helpless – and confused.

He doesn't know, she realised with a rising sense of horror.
He still thinks she's Ethlin. Brangianne's eyes flew to Corwynal's,
but, to her dismay, they'd turned to granite. He hadn't known
either, but now he did.

It was then that the cracks appeared, and her perfect crystal
began to splinter. Neither she nor Corwynal moved, but distance
formed between them, and she pushed against the crowd,

desperate to reach him, to claim him for herself. But the lie, deception, misunderstanding – whatever it was – was destroying everything. She felt as if she was standing on the surface of a frozen river cracking in the spring spate. The plates of ice beneath her feet were tilting, and she was falling into freezing water, too cold to move, too cold to think. All she could do was watch Trystan understand who the girl holding out the guest cup had to be. All she could do was listen to him speak the words that would change everything.

I claim you on behalf of my uncle, King Marc of Galloway.

Galloway. King Marc of Galloway. His uncle.

No-one moved. No-one spoke. Yseult's hands separated, as if acknowledging defeat, and the guest cup fell, the wine spilling down the front of her dress like a leak of blood from the heart. Metal rang on stone, and there was a crack. At Yseult's feet, the two halves of the cup rocked themselves to silence, and the smell of spilled wine, harsh and metallic, seeped through the hall. Still, no-one moved, and no-one spoke. Yseult tore the pins from her hair to let it tumble over her shoulders, then stripped the jewelled collar from her neck and flung it to the ground. *Look! I'm not Yseult. I'm Ethlin!* Trystan flinched as if a blow had been struck but made no reply, because what could he say? Ethlin was as much an illusion as Drust had been. Here, in Dunadd's great hall, the pretence breathed its last, and Yseult folded in on herself like a flame that has consumed itself and gutters into darkness. Then, in the stunned and immobile silence, she turned and, without haste, walked out of the hall, her head held high, the crowd parting before her as if she was an arrow cleaving flesh.

Corwynal was standing in the middle of the hall staring, not at Brangianne, but at Trystan, his face drained of everything but anguish. *I'll explain,* she thought. *I'll make him understand that who I am doesn't matter.* But not now, not here in this all too public place. She pushed her way out of the hall and followed

Yseult, but, once out of sight of everyone, the girl broke into a run, heading not for her room but the warren of buildings that surrounded the hall, and Brangianne lost her. In truth, she didn't know what she could have said, for right then all she had were questions. Had Feargus known? Had he planned this? Or, opportunist that he was, had he used Trystan's unexpected arrival to discredit Eoghan then manoeuvred him into claiming Yseult for the Galloway King? But others must also have been involved. Ciaran? Yes, Ciaran would have backed this alliance, and that Galloway Bishop wasn't here by chance.

Brangianne was so absorbed by her thoughts she hadn't realised her feet had taken her to the Royal Terrace. It was dark now except for a couple of guttering torches, one by the entrance and the other by the King-making stone. She walked over to the wall, propped her chin on her hand, gazed over the lower levels of the stronghold, and wondered how this appalling situation could be remedied. Maybe if she explained to Feargus that Yseult loved Drust, and he her, he'd be content with an alliance to Galloway's heir rather than its King. Then Yseult needn't go to Galloway until that King died. Trystan would stay in Dalriada, and surely Corwynal would stay also, especially since Feargus had agreed to her marrying him.

Full of her plans, she lost track of time. An owl hooted from the woods below the walls and woke her from her trance. She ought to get back to the hall, but when she turned to go a dark-haired man was standing in the entrance to the terrace, the man who'd come to Dunadd to find her. It was going to be all right. She would make it all right.

The two halves of the guest cup rolled back and forth on the floor, the wine seeping into the cracks between the flagstones. The cup was the only thing moving in the hall; it was as if everyone had taken a breath and held it. Images flickered and blurred in Corwynal's vision; in one moment he was standing in Dunadd's hall staring at Trystan, and in the next he was in the practice ring at Mark's Mote, a nineteen-year-old boy staring at a woman with Trystan's features.

Eventually, however, the two halves of the cup rolled to a stop and Trystan bent to pick them up then pressed them together as if by doing so he might remake a broken world. There was still a little liquid in one half, and he tilted it to his lips and swallowed the wine, a gesture that eased the tension in the hall. Then he met Corwynal's eyes.

'Help me!' he whispered. 'I need you to help me!'

He doesn't need you. Ferdiad had been wrong; he should never have believed it. Now, with Trystan's plea, everything that had gone wrong between them was right again, and Corwynal was able to move once more.

He stepped over to Trystan and gripped him by the arm. 'I didn't know, didn't understand.'

'You weren't supposed to know.' Trystan's smile was broken. 'No-one was. Especially Her.'

Her. That was how Trystan thought of the girl. *She.* Trystan stared at the guest cup for a moment, then opened his hands, splitting the cup apart like a heart, allowing the dregs of wine to spill into the rushes.

'Do you remember?' he asked, his eyes lost. 'The day I married Essylt? You told me I've have to stand by and watch the woman I loved marry someone else. Was this what you meant? Did you see *this?*'

Corwynal shook his head. He hadn't seen the future that day, only the past, only his own mistakes, the doom he'd bequeathed to his son. But Trystan wasn't going to suffer as he had, not if he could help it.

'You don't have to watch. We'll leave tomorrow, go back to the Fort, anywhere that isn't here or Galloway.'

'After everything I said to you?'

'You didn't mean any of it.'

'I meant some of it. I didn't want you to give everything up for me. I still don't.'

'If you mean Brangianne, I have to give her up, Trys, but not for you. For her. She's Feargus' *sister!*'

'You're a King's son.'

'—and I have a wife.'

'If that matters to her, she's not the woman I think she is.' Trystan gripped his arm. 'Talk to her. Explain. Then we'll leave, all three of us. You don't have to choose between us.'

Was Trystan right? Might Brangianne care about him enough to leave behind everything of her life in Dalriada? Did he dare defy a God? Did he dare hope he might keep both of them?

'Go and find her,' Trystan urged him, but it was too late, for a hand landed heavily on Corwynal's shoulder. The smile on Feargus' lips belied the expression in his eyes.

'So, you're the man who made a whore of my sister?' He was still smiling as if making some mild pleasantry and, one hand gripping Corwynal's collar bone, his other arm flung around Trystan's shoulders, he steered his apparently valued guests towards the high table.

'Unless I mistake the matter?' he went on. 'Have you come to Dunadd to request her hand in marriage? But wait – you can't, can you?' He smiled thinly at Corwynal's failure to reply then turned away and raised his voice. 'My Lords, Ladies, honourable Fathers of the Church! You came to celebrate a wedding that will not now take place. Instead, we have a betrothal to celebrate. Please, take your places . . .' He let Corwynal and Trystan go, having led them to two seats close to his own, and snapped his fingers at the servants who rushed to bring out fresh platters of meat. 'We celebrate the betrothal of my daughter and the newly forged peace with Galloway, with all the opportunities this peace will present us with . . .'

His warband muttered and scowled, for there was little profit in peace for warriors, but Feargus' client landholders were mollified by that magic word 'opportunities' and moved towards the tables, curious to see what Feargus the Fox would do now, and what they might get out of it for themselves.

'We'll begin as soon as my daughter has changed her gown.' Feargus gave the rueful smile of a father indulging a girl with little thought of anything but her clothes, and whose precipitate departure had been on account of a stained dress and not, absolutely not, because of the marriage so very publicly made for her. He continued to smile while snapping his fingers at a servant. 'Find her!' he snarled.

'I'm here, Father.' The voice, low and musical, came from behind them. The girl had approached silently and near-invisibly, for she had indeed changed her dress. Now she wore one of unrelieved black, high at the neck and long in the arms, and there was no colour about her at all, for her skin was white, her lips pale, her eyes downcast and her hair, bound in a tight coil around her head, was covered by a linen veil. Even so, she was still impossibly lovely, and, glancing at Trystan, Corwynal saw him quiver with the effort of not looking at her.

'Couldn't you have worn something more appropriate to the occasion?' Feargus muttered as she took her place between him and Trystan.

'I thought this was appropriate. It marks Dalriada's dishonour.' She raised her eyes to her father's. The same green eyes, Corwynal noticed. 'Smile, Father,' she added. 'Everyone is watching.' And, having left Feargus speechless, she turned to Trystan, an empty smile stitched to her lips. 'How is the wound in your hand?' she asked with withering civility.

'It's healed well,' he replied, matching her tone. 'Thank you for asking. Will you take wine?' She nodded and allowed Trystan to pour her a cup of wine but left it untouched. Nor did she eat anything on the plate set before her. Trystan, after a pretence of eating, pushed his own plate away as if the smell of the meat made him feel sick, took a deep breath, and turned to address her.

'My Lady, I have an apology to make, for certain things I said to you. They were . . . unforgivable.'

She smiled her humourless smile once more. 'Then you'll understand if I can't forgive them. I don't doubt you meant them, and that knowing who my father was wouldn't have altered your recommendation that I – how did you put it? – should be given a good thrashing.' She turned to Feargus. 'Did I mention that?' she asked sweetly, then laughed at his expression. 'Oh come, Father! Didn't you threaten me with that very thing? You should be pleased to find someone so in harmony with your own opinions. You imprisoned me in St Martin's as a punishment, but what you've done today is even more of a punishment. I think I would rather have been thrashed.'

'You're to marry a King,' he said sharply. 'Be grateful.'

'I've little experience of Kings. The only one I know is willing to sell his daughter for the sake of an advantageous trading agreement.'

Feargus gripped the bowl of the silver goblet so tightly it began to distort. 'You forget yourself, Yseult!' he hissed.

'I do not! It's you who've forgotten what Family means!'

'Family!' he muttered in disgust. 'Where is my Family when I need them? Where, for example, is that aunt of yours?'

Corwynal, achingly aware of the empty place beside him, would have given anything to leave, to find Brangianne, to say all the things he'd come to Dunadd to say. But he couldn't leave the hall just yet. Feargus was in control of the situation for the moment, but that could easily change. The warband were still muttering; they wouldn't have forgotten the defeat at the Loch of the Beacon and the part he and Trystan had played in it. Some fool might challenge them and, if it came to a fight, they'd be overcome, especially since Aelfric was on the far side of the hall, talking to Oonagh, and Kaerherdin had vanished. Right then, Trystan needed him. His control was fragile, his replies to one of Feargus' landholders, sitting on his other side, very much at random. He could still say or do something stupid. So Corwynal was forced to sit through a feast he had no stomach for, with Feargus' accusation ringing in his ears.

You've made a whore of my sister. That was how the world would see it. It was certainly how Feargus viewed the matter.

'My sister's to take her vows as soon as Yseult's married,' Feargus said, leaning across the empty seat between them. Corwynal had been raising a cup of wine to his lips; now he set it down once more.

'Is that her wish?'

'It will be when she learns of your . . . marital situation.'

'Hasn't she learned of it from you?'

Feargus smiled thinly and unpleasantly. 'I thought it might be best if she was informed by the . . . perpetrator. You married your slave, I believe . . .'

The blood rose in Corwynal's face, and a cold hard stone formed below his heart. So, this was Feargus' revenge for what he saw as Corwynal's betrayal at the Loch of the Beacon. But why punish Brangianne too?

'Your sister has no desire to live behind walls.'

Feargus shrugged. 'Perhaps not, but it will only become necessary if she's so far gone in honour as to choose you over her duty to her Family. Do you understand me?'

The stone below Corwynal's heart pressed on his stomach until he was nauseous.

'It's for her to make that choice, not you.'

Feargus shook his head. 'In the matter of my Family's honour, I make the decisions. I will not permit my sister to turn Dalriada into a laughing stock, so let me warn you; if she chooses to leave with you, I'll hunt you down, both of you, and my reach is long. I'll drag her back, if necessary, and she'll never see beyond the walls of St Martin's until she's repented of her folly. I've done it once, and I can do it again. If, on the other hand, she's not offered a choice, she'll have her freedom. Which means you're wrong. It's not her choice that's at issue here. It's yours.'

Corwynal's dreams had been small ones, ill-formed and clutching at life. Now, finally, they died. Carnadail was closed to him now, as was the whole of Dalriada, joining all the other places from which, in one way or another, he'd exiled himself – Lothian, Selgovia, Manau, and now Galloway. So where did that leave? Strathclyde? Rheged? The Kingdoms of Eriu? Nowhere was beyond Feargus' reach. Only the North held any hope. Might Azarion give them shelter? No, The Dragon's negotiations with Dalriada were at too delicate a stage for him to risk Feargus' wrath. Caledonia then? The cold stone in his stomach lurched. No, he wouldn't be safe anywhere in Caledonia and couldn't protect anyone else. All that left was a life on the run, which was no life for any woman, even if she was willing to share it with him. And that was by no means certain.

'Do you understand me?' Feargus repeated.

Corwynal nodded.

'Go then.' Feargus leant back in his seat with a small smile of triumph, then gestured a servant over and exchanged a few words with him. 'She's on the Terrace.' He nodded at a door at the back of the hall. 'You'll find her there.'

Corwynal glanced at Trystan. His colour was better now, his pose less rigid. He'd survive this appalling feast and in the morning they'd leave Dalriada. Corwynal pushed his chair back and stood up, taking a deep breath and squaring his shoulders as Trystan had done. Only two things were left for him to do before they could leave. To make a woman cry – he'd always been good at that – and kill Ferdiad.

Brangianne's heart was hammering as Corwynal walked towards her, even though she told herself she loved him, and he her, and nothing else was important. But when he reached her his expression was grim. This was no lover come to claim her but a man who'd lied, or at least concealed the truth, and who, like all men, had come to accuse her of the same crime.

'You should have told me you were Feargus' sister.'

There it was. No apology for breaking a promise, for allowing her to think him dead, for appearing unannounced in leper's garb. She'd hoped to step into his arms and weep with relief for herself and sorrow for Yseult. She wanted to hold and be held, to feel her heart fuse with his so that they became one heart, one person, ready to face the world together. This bald accusation was unexpected.

'And if I had?'

'If I'd known, there could have been nothing between us.' His voice, so distant, so controlled, pierced her. Nevertheless, she touched his shoulder and slid her hand to his neck, felt the warmth of his skin beneath her palm, the pulse of his blood against her fingers, its beat as fast as her own. She heard his quick intake of breath at her touch, and the familiar ache blossomed in the pit of her stomach, so when she spoke her voice was husky with it.

'That's why I didn't tell you. Oh, at first it was because I was afraid of you, then I didn't want to admit I'd lied, but later, after we ... afterwards, I wanted what we had to last. I wanted *you*, not caring who you were. I thought you were a man of no consequence, a man who might be afraid to aspire to the sister of a King. But you're not of no consequence. Your blood is as good as mine. They tell me you're a King's son—'

'A King's bastard.'

'You think that matters to me?'

'It matters to the world, my heart.' He placed his hand over hers, pressed it against him for a moment, then stepped away so that her hand fell away, her palm filling with cold night air. 'It matters to your brother.'

'But it doesn't! Feargus may not like you very much, but he cares about me. He told me that if you asked for my hand in marriage he wouldn't stand in my way. He *promised* me.'

Corwynal laughed, a soft bitter sound. 'Well do they call him Feargus the Fox! His promise to you is empty, Brangianne. He knows I could never come here to ask for your hand in marriage because I can't, any more than Trystan could have asked Yseult to be his wife. He has one already, Queen Essylt of Selgovia. And I—' He paused and took a breath. 'I too have a wife. And a child. He's called Caradawc. He must be two years old by now.'

Blow after blow, right to the heart, a knife twisting again and again as he rammed home each appalling fact. A wife. A child who was two years old now, which meant—

'In Carnadail – all that time – you had a wife?!'

'No!' He reached for her hands and gripped them painfully when she tried to snatch them away. 'Not then. Listen to me, Brangianne. I didn't know about the child. Everything in Carnadail was true, as true as it is now. But I believed you hated me and knew you had reason. I thought I'd lost you, that I'd never be happy again, that I didn't *deserve* happiness. That's not why I ... The child was a surprise and not a welcome one, but I thought I could do some good for him at least. So I acknowledged him as my own and married his mother, who used to be my slave. I didn't love either of them – I didn't *know* either of them – but I thought I could give them both a life. And yet, when I heard Dalriada was in danger, all I could think about was you.'

She swallowed hard. Married to a slave he didn't love, as she might, against her will, have married Eoghan. But even if she'd sworn a marriage oath to her God, she would have broken it to be with the man she loved. So why couldn't that man break an oath of his own for her?

'We can still be together,' she insisted. 'We can go somewhere no-one knows us and pretend to be married. Only you and I would know . . .'

His face twisted with something that looked like disgust.

'No,' he said flatly, dropping her hands. She turned away to hide the flush of shame – that she, a King's daughter, a King's sister, should offer herself like that – and be rejected.

'Then why did you come to Dunadd?' she demanded. 'Why did you say you'd find me?'

'I wanted to tell you the truth – I owed you that much. I hoped . . .' He made a helpless gesture. 'I don't know what I hoped for. I thought there was a choice I could make, but now I know there isn't a choice. There never was.'

'There is, but you choose your wife rather than me.' Her voice broke. 'Are you going back to her?'

She'd never felt hatred like the hatred she felt for this unknown unnamed woman.

'I don't know,' he said. 'But I have to leave Dalriada. I need to get Trystan as far away from your niece as it's possible to go.'

'Then it's him you choose,' she said bitterly, knowing that while she might have fought a woman he didn't love, she couldn't fight Trystan.

'He needs me. He's my son.'

'And if I'd borne you a son?'

'But you didn't.'

It was the cruellest thing he could have said.

'I wish you'd never come to Carnadail,' she said, reaching for anger, hugging it to herself and cuffing tears from her face. She couldn't afford to be weak, not yet. 'You left thinking I hated you, though I didn't, not then. But I do now. I hate you, Corwynal of Lothian, and I'll never forgive you for being what you are, a liar and a cheat and a *coward!* I don't want to see you ever again, or hear your name spoken.'

She turned her back on him so he wouldn't see her tears, and was painfully conscious of him standing behind her. But, despite knowing she'd gone too far, that she didn't mean any of it, she didn't look back. Her eyes were blurred, and she was aware only of light and shade, the moon vanishing, dark sweeping across the terrace, the smell of roses and thyme, a curlew calling from the fields, a lonely empty sound, and she whirled around in something close to panic. *Don't go! Don't leave me!*

But it was too late. He'd already gone.

He didn't go far, just to the back of the hall, out of sight of the Terrace, where he leant against the wall and slid down to rest on his heels, coiling himself around a pulsing agony sourced somewhere below his diaphragm.

It wasn't the first time he'd sat in the dark, listening to a woman weep. It seemed to be his role in life to make women cry, so it was only fair that he listen.

It's Trystan you choose. In truth, he'd chosen Trystan eighteen years before. He'd given up his future for him and sacrificed his heart for Trystan's life, but he didn't regret his bargain with the God. Trystan was his son, and there was nothing he wouldn't give up for him, including his own life. He should have understood that limitation and not allowed himself to long for something more, or involve anyone else in those longings. He would never do so again, never give any woman cause to weep. Never.

It was late by then, and the noise from the hall faded away as Feargus' guests left, others having fallen asleep, drunk or sober. The bards and jugglers had gone, the dogs had been whipped out, and it was quiet except for the woman weeping, hopelessly now. He got to his feet and went back to the entrance to the Terrace. The moon, high in the sky and nearing the full, had disappeared behind a bank of cloud and the place was in darkness but for a guttering torch illuminating a plane of bedrock. Brangianne was nothing more than a vague outline against the night sky as she stood, still with her back to him, looking out across the lower part of the stronghold.

He went back to the hall, picked his way between the benches and the sleepers, and found a servant to show him where he and the others were to lodge, a small roundhouse, one of a cluster near the southern rampart. Trystan was lying on a pallet, his hands behind his head, staring into the roof beams, and barely gave Corwynal a glance as he came in. Kaerherdin, sitting with his back against the wall, was smoothing down a bow, and Aelfric was sharpening a knife with a whetstone. Good: they were all there, so he need only say this once.

'We're leaving tomorrow. We'll head north, then west at the head of Loch Abha, then make for the Loch of the Beacon. It's a day's journey from there to the high road. It should only take us a few days to reach Iuddeu. Then we can make for the fort.'

No-one said anything. Trystan abandoned his examination of the space below the beams where the smoke from the fire had gathered and turned on his side to watch Corwynal as he sat down to unlace his boots.

'I'm not going back,' Aelfric said. A flush of colour washed his face and he wouldn't meet Corwynal's eyes.

'I see,' Corwynal said stiffly, trying not to envy him. Aelfric had chosen to stay with Oonagh, despite, like Corwynal, having a wife and a family.

'I'm not going back either.' Kaerherdin lifted his chin in challenge, but Corwynal didn't care. All that mattered was getting Trystan away.

'I guess it's just you and me then, Trys,' he said, making a pathetic attempt at humour, but Trystan didn't find it amusing.

'I'm not going back,' he said. 'Feargus asked me to escort his ... his daughter to Galloway. And I agreed. God help me, I agreed.'

'No! I won't! I can't!'

Yseult's voice, coming from Feargus' chamber, was high-pitched and hysterical, easily penetrating the thick oak planks of the door. Two guards, ostensibly on guard, had their ears pressed against the door and jumped when Brangianne approached. But they recovered quickly, snapped to attention and angled their spears to bar the way. 'The King doesn't want to be disturbed, my Lady.'

'I don't care what the cursed King wants!' Their mouths fell open in shock, and their spears sagged, and she was able to push past them and storm into her brother's chamber.

Feargus was looking both furious and beset as Yseult paced back and forth, weeping hysterically, her eyes wild, her hair disordered, her whole body shaking with emotion. For once he was relieved to see his sister.

'Thank God! Can you talk some sense into this girl?'

He wasn't prepared for Brangianne to step forward, pivot on

her toes and, with the full weight of her arm behind it, land a satisfyingly powerful blow to his jaw.

'Have you gone mad?!' He caught her wrist as she moved to follow up that blow with another, twisted her arm and flung her at Yseult, which had the happy result of putting a stop to the girl's hysterics, but not to Feargus' anger. 'How dare you strike your King! I should call for the guards—'

'I didn't strike my King! I struck my brother. I struck Yseult's father. As for the guards, they've got their ears glued to the door, so go right ahead and call them.'

Feargus strode to the door, jerked it open and growled some instruction, liberally seasoned with curses, that sent the guards scuttling back to the hall.

'Perhaps you'd be so good as to tell me what this is all about,' he said in clipped tones, his eyes dangerous, as he shut the door behind him and leant back against it, his arms crossed.

'You know perfectly well what it's about you ... you *bastard!* You knew all along, didn't you? You made me a promise, knowing it was meaningless. You *used* me!'

But far from looking ashamed, Feargus just raised an eyebrow in surprise. 'What else are you for?' He glanced at Yseult. 'What are you both for? Your duty is to our Family and—'

'If you say that one more time, I swear—'

'Have done woman!' He marched over to his chair and flung himself down. 'I acted in the interests of the Family, which means I acted in your interests. Surely you didn't think you'd be happy as the concubine of a half-breed Caledonian?'

'Concubine?' Yseult looked from her father to Brangianne. 'But wouldn't you have—?'

'—married him? Yes, if he didn't already have a wife. And a son.' She turned on Feargus once more, bitterness curdling into anger. 'And you *knew*, Feargus!'

'Of course I knew! I wouldn't be who I am if I hadn't known!

But you can't blame me for keeping my silence, not when it wasn't *my* secret to tell.' He noticed, for the first time, her swollen and reddened eyes. 'He told you then.'

'Yes, and he didn't ask me to be his concubine!' *I asked him, but he turned me down.*

'Good. Then this madness is over,' Feargus concluded without pity. 'Now you can concentrate on your role as my daughter's aunt and talk her out of this defiance.' He glared at Yseult, who met his look with a glare of her own. 'She's refusing to go to Galloway.'

'I didn't say that!' Yseult protested. 'It's *him!* I don't want to see him ever again! I won't! I hate him. He killed my uncle! I swore *revenge!*'

'And you've had it.' Feargus leant back in his chair and crossed his legs at the ankles.

Both women stared at him. 'How?' Brangianne asked.

'Isn't it obvious? Trystan of Lothian is heir to Galloway. But when Yseult bears Marc a son, he'll be robbed of that inheritance.'

Yseult paled at that before flushing with anger once more. 'That's not what I want! It isn't enough! He'll still have Lothian, won't he?'

'And Selgovia,' Brangianne added sourly. 'He'll have that too, won't he Feargus? Something else you must have known about and didn't think to mention. He's already King Consort of Selgovia.'

'King . . . Consort?' Yseult sat down abruptly on a chest that stood by the wall.

'He's married too.' Brangianne went over to her and put an arm about her shaking shoulders.

'So?' Feargus asked testily. 'Why should she care if she hates him as much as she keeps telling me? Though she'd do well to hide her feelings when she's in Galloway.'

She wouldn't have to, Brangianne thought, remembering what Corwynal had said. *I'll get him as far away from that niece of yours as it's possible to go.* And if Trystan wasn't in Galloway, Corwynal wouldn't be there either. Suddenly, with a swooping sensation in her stomach that robbed her legs of strength, Brangianne knew what she had to do and where she had to go.

'I'll remind her.' She groped for a chair and sat down heavily. 'Because I'm going to Galloway too.'

'But you hate Galloway!' Yseult objected. Feargus' eyes narrowed in suspicion, but she met his look evenly.

'I have to put my hatred behind me, because my duty is to my Family. Isn't it Feargus?'

'Well . . .'

'Isn't it?' she insisted. 'My duty means I have to go to Galloway with Yseult to see her married, as Dalriada's representative. But don't worry – I'll be as regal as you'd wish me to be. I'll carry messages from St Martin's to Rosnat and, since the Britons know nothing of healing, I'll ask this King Marc if I can establish an infirmary to care for the sick . . .' She was talking for the sake of talking in the hope that her own voice would drown out the scream of panic struggling to fight its way free. *He'll be there,* she thought. *The man who led the raiders who killed Aedh. I'll have to confront him. I'll have to take the revenge I promised all those years ago.* Yet if she was going to do that, it would be best to do so from a position of strength, as the respected aunt of a queen. 'I'm going to turn myself into what you've always wanted me to be, a holy woman and a saint. But it won't be here in Dalriada. It will be in Galloway.'

'Is this some sort of trick?' Feargus' eyes were still narrowed. 'Is this about the Caledonian after all?'

'No. It's over between us,' she said. That at least was true. It was why she had to go to Galloway, the last place in the world she wanted to go, because it was the one place in which she'd never see him again, the one place she'd be safe from heartbreak. 'You promised me my freedom,' she reminded Feargus. 'And for once in your life you're going to keep your promise. You said I could go where I wanted, do what I wished. This is what I want, and it's in your interests too, because it's in the interests of our Family. It has nothing, absolutely nothing, to do with Corwynal of Lothian. Why should it?'

Yseult slid her hand into hers and gripped it hard. 'Because my father has arranged for Trystan of Lothian to escort me to Galloway.'

And where Trystan went, Corwynal would be at his side. It wasn't over then, not yet, not by a long, long way.

 **23**

A KNIFE IN THE NIGHT

*H*e was back in Galloway, nineteen years old, and in love as only a nineteen-year-old can be, but trying to hide it. Especially from Her. He was better at hiding his emotions than most nineteen-year-olds, so not even Marc realised it.

'She's to be wed.' Marc looked up from the cup of wine into which he'd been staring. Corwynal had found him in one of the Mote's less savoury taverns beside the wharves. He slung himself over the bench at the other side of the table and reached for the jug to pour himself a cup but stopped at Marc's words.

'When?' It was as if a spear had been driven into his belly. Gwenllian was seventeen, past the age most girls were betrothed, but royal women generally married late. First her father had equivocated, then Marc, but since the war with the Scots had ended Lot had been whispering in Marc's ear.

'Beltein,' Marc said with a scowl. Most marriages were made at Beltein or Lughnasadh 'Don't want to let her go . . .' he mumbled into his cup.

Corwynal poured himself some of the wine. The smell of it made him feel sick, but he took a long swallow and let the fumes dull the pain in his stomach. 'Then don't. You're King. She's your sister. You can marry her to anyone you want.'

But not to him. Even in his wildest fantasies, Corwynal knew Gwenllian could never be his.

'Lot's breathing down my neck . . .'

It would be the eldest son, Corwynal assumed. Only fourteen, but already in his father's warband. Sandy-haired like Lot, with the same stolid looks, he'd seemed a nice enough boy – until today. Being only fourteen, however, the betrothal might be a long one . . . It began to seem less of a disaster.

'Lot's insisting I give her to Rifallyn,' Marc went on with a sigh.

There it was again, the spear stabbing and stabbing. 'My father?! But he's ancient! It's obscene! You can't agree to it!'

'I already have.' *Marc poured the rest of the wine into his cup. It slopped over the edge and spilled down his arm as he swallowed half the contents.* 'Gwenllian made me. Wants to marry a King. That's all that matters to her.'

'Let me talk to her,' *Corwynal begged. He'd warn her about his father, tell her how cold he was, how dark.*

'You?!' *Marc spluttered.* 'She'd never listen to you!' *He leant across the table and dropped his voice.* 'She can't understand why you haven't fallen for her like every other red-blooded man in the Mote. I might have thought you were one for the horse-boys, but . . .' *He punched Corwynal lightly on the shoulder and winked.* 'We both know you're not, eh?'

The blood rose in Corwynal's face. This very tavern had seen some of their wilder debauches, Marc the leader, but Corwynal not far behind. Drink, gambling, fighting. And faceless nameless women who weren't Her. The memories sickened him, but he managed a shamefaced grin for Marc, who laughed reminiscently before turning serious once more.

'She has to marry someone, and it has to be a King. Rifallyn is the only possibility.'

It was true. Except for Marc, his father was the only King in the Lands between the Walls who didn't already have a wife.

'I'd wed her myself if I could,' Marc said.

'That would be incest,' Corwynal pointed out stiffly. He didn't consider it a joking matter.

Marc flushed darkly. 'I know that! Anyway, it's all arranged. She's to marry the old man at Beltein. That's a month off, so there's plenty of time to get there. She'll be taking half our household, I don't doubt, servants and furniture and dresses and the like. I'll have to send a troop with her. Can't spare my best men, not with Strathclyde agitating up north, but I can rake together enough spearmen to fend off bandits. I'll need a good man to lead them, of course, and, given you're the only one of my captains not falling at her feet like a fool, you're the only one I'd trust. You'll do it, won't you? Escort my sister to Lothian?'

And, wanting her, wanting to be with her, he'd agreed. The gods help him, he'd agreed. And now, because of Ferdiad, the whole sorry story was happening all over again.

'Are you *insane?!*'

Aelfric flinched at Corwynal's choice of word and wasn't surprised to see Trystan pale.

'Am I?'

It was the very question Aelfric had been asking himself. The boy had evidently fallen for the girl, though he'd managed to hide it until now. Not that Aelfric blamed him – she was a pretty little thing – but, given the fact that she was now betrothed to that Galloway drunk, it was a bit of a disaster politically. So maybe Trystan's madness hadn't really gone away.

'No,' Corwynal said, after a moment's hesitation. 'Not in that way. But going to Galloway is the worst thing you could do.'

'I know. But I can't help it, and it's too late now. I've agreed.'

'You'll not talk the boy out of it,' Aelfric cut in. 'I've tried.'

'I have to see it through, this . . . this marriage,' Trystan said.

Aelfric agreed with Corwynal. Going to Galloway to watch the girl you'd fallen for marrying your own uncle was a very bad idea. If it had been Oonagh now . . . Not that he was in love with the woman, not in that soppy way the Britons sang about, but he was fond of her, and if she married someone else, he wasn't sure what he'd do.

'After that, we can leave,' Trystan went on, the first sensible thing he'd said all night. 'You'll come with me?' he asked, turning to the Caledonian, a plea in his voice that took years off him. 'To Galloway?'

'Of course,' Corwynal said without hesitation.

But it wasn't that simple. Nothing involving women was ever simple.

'What about Brangianne?' Trystan asked. 'She won't want to go there. She hates Galloway.'

The Caledonian winced as if a blow had been struck, and maybe it had. 'She hates me too.'

Trystan shuddered as if he felt the same blow. 'So, you told her. What did she say?'

On the other side of the roundhouse, Kaerherdin had stopped smoothing his bow and was listening intently.

'That she never wants to see me again or hear my name spoken.'

Aelfric wasn't surprised. Telling a woman you were already married was fraught with danger, as Aelfric knew to his cost. Yet he'd managed to talk Oonagh around, so why couldn't Corwynal do the same with Brangianne? Because the man was a fool with women, that's why. And now he was going to Galloway to get away from her, despite the one aspect of their journey the Caledonian clearly hadn't thought through.

'You realise we're going by ship?' he said, forgetting he hadn't mentioned his own plans.

'We?'

'Oonagh's going with the Princess.' Aelfric shifted uncomfortably. 'Thought I'd . . . tag along.'

The Caledonian gave him a hard look but didn't say anything and turned to Kaerherdin.

'And you?'

The Selgovian shrugged. 'If I'm to go back to Selgovia I can travel as easily from Galloway as the Strathclyde coast.'

That was bollocks, but Aelfric didn't say so. He was just relieved Kaerherdin wasn't making a fuss about Trystan having fallen for a girl who wasn't his wife, Kaer's sister. Maybe the Caledonian was too, since he didn't say anything, and just relaced his boots and reached for his sword-belt. 'Did anyone see where Ferdiad went?'

'Down to the lower town,' Aelfric told him. 'Why?'

'Don't!' Trystan protested when Corwynal made for the door. 'It's not Ferdiad's fault.'

'Of course it is! He planned all this from the beginning. This is his revenge on us both for The Morholt.'

'Don't kill him. You can't rob Feargus of Dalriada's Fili.'

'I don't care about Feargus!' Corwynal snarled and jerked the door open.

'Don't be an idiot, Corwynal!' Trystan sat up and swung his legs to the floor. 'What are you going to do? Challenge him to single combat? He won't accept.'

Corwynal just slammed the door in Trystan's face.

'Don't be an idiot yourself,' Aelfric said when Trystan reached for his own boots. 'That Fili has had this coming for a long time. If I were you, I'd keep well out of it.'

'You're not me,' Trystan said and followed Corwynal out into the night.

Finding one man in a stronghold he didn't know wasn't as easy as Corwynal had expected, and he searched about the fort, the settlement, and the tented village, with the growing conviction that the Fili was just one step ahead of him, slipping behind each building he approached, or into an alleyway, that he was laughing at him from the shadows, his laughter echoing Arddu's amusement.

'Are you satisfied?' he demanded of his God. 'Is this what you wanted? Am I struggling enough for you?' But he was met only by silence.

Eventually, however, he picked up Ferdiad's trail in a drinking place near the river that swept around the base of Dunadd's rock, a place that, judging by the rotting wooden stilts that supported it, must be flooded in the winter. Even at Lughnasadh, in summer, the place stank of mould and damp. It was an unsavoury hole where a man could drink without questions being asked, and it took a deal of silver to open the bartender's mouth on the question of the whereabouts of Dalriada's Fili.

'Went with the boy not long back. Not willing like, but the boy persuaded him.'

'Boy?'

'Good looking lad,' the man said with a leer. 'He likes them good-looking, does our Lord Ferdiad. Golden-haired, he was. Fancied the lad myself, but he's likely above my touch.' His leer widened, revealing blackened stumps of rotting teeth. 'You'll be after the boy yourself I expect.'

'Where did they go?' Corwynal demanded, controlling his desire to smash his fist into that rotting mouth.

The man shrugged and scratched himself. 'Where else is there to go from here but up?'

So his search continued, but Ferdiad was out in the open now and no longer alone. It would be Trystan who was with him, Trystan who must have searched for Ferdiad to warn him Corwynal was coming for him. The trail led him back to the fortress on its rock, which offered a limited number of places they could have gone, and it was in the warren of roundhouses that clustered below the main hall that he finally heard Trystan's voice and caught sight of two men standing at the junction of a couple of alleyways that ran between the sleeping quarters of the royal residence and the kitchen.

'We should go back to the hall,' Trystan was saying.

'Not yet,' Ferdiad replied. 'There's something I want to show you.' His voice was clear enough but had the single-minded tenacity of the not-entirely sober.

'The hall is the one place you'll be safe from Corwynal.'

'You think I'm afraid of him?'

'I think you ought to be. He blames you for everything.'

'Do you?'

Trystan brushed the question aside. 'Come on.' He put a hand on Ferdiad's arm to steer him in the direction of the hall. 'Whatever you want to show me can keep until the morning.'

'You're leaving tomorrow.' Ferdiad pulled his arm away. 'You're going to Galloway.'

'How do you know? You left the hall before Feargus asked me.'

'Because I know him, and I know you, Trys. Listen to me; you don't have to do this.'

'It's too late now.'

'It's not too late. There are other things you could do, other places you could go. With me.'

There was a long silence at that, and Trystan looked away from Ferdiad, into the shadows where Corwynal was standing. He thought he'd been seen, but Trystan didn't react to his presence, and turned back to the Fili. 'Must we have this particular conversation?'

'You owe it to me to listen.'

'Very well,' Trystan said with a sigh, then leant back against the wall of one of the buildings and crossed his arms. 'Take your chances.'

Ferdiad laughed. 'Taking chances has always been my speciality! But not here. Come, it's this way.'

They moved into one of the alleyways, and Corwynal followed. But instead of leading Trystan to the side entrance of the hall, where Ferdiad presumably had quarters, they went to the Royal Terrace where Corwynal had left Brangianne weeping.

Why here? What did Ferdiad want to show Trystan? What was it he needed to say? Curiosity warred with his desire for violence, and curiosity won.

The torch by the entrance had burned out, so he was able to slip onto the terrace without being seen. Only one torch remained, the one by the strange rock in the centre of the terrace, and that was where Ferdiad stopped.

'Do you see that hollow in the rock?'

'Like a footprint? What of it?'

'That's where the Kings of Dalriada claim the Kingship. They place a naked foot on the stone and claim the land. You could claim it, Trys, with my help.'

There was a short stunned silence before Trystan burst out laughing. 'Don't be ridiculous! I'm hardly someone Feargus would choose to succeed him!'

'It's not his choice, though he'll try to make it so. In the old days, Kingship was won, not given, won here in Dunadd by the strongest of the warriors, by Dalriada's Champion. The sword hangs in the hall, waiting to be claimed. Already they call you Dragon's Bane, so the sword could be yours. Oh, not straight away. You'd need to build up your reputation, go to all the places you can't begin to imagine – Laigin in the Old Country, the Court of the Ui Niall, the mountains of Gwynedd, and further, to

Dumnonia, or Armonica across the narrow sea. We could go anywhere you want, anywhere there's fighting and you could make a name for yourself. With my help, you could be everything you always wanted to be, someone to be remembered. They'll sing songs about you, Trys, and the best of them will be mine. We could leave tomorrow. Forget Yseult. She's a spoiled, mean-spirited little girl with a pretty face. I know I tried to make you fall for her, but I was a fool. I didn't know you then, and I was glad when I failed.'

'You didn't fail,' Trystan said bleakly.

'Listen, Trys, whatever you feel now, it will pass. You're worthy of so much more than Yseult. Don't go to Galloway. Come with me instead. Let me help you forget her.'

There was a long silence, and Corwynal's heart contracted. Ferdiad was offering Trystan everything he'd once wanted. *Come adventuring with me,* Trystan had asked him in Lothian, and he'd refused. Now all he had to offer Trystan was a return to the fort on the margins of Arthyr's war, to fight Caledonians who vanished into the mists. Trystan would be forgotten there on the edge of the world, when he craved to be at its heart. Now Ferdiad had offered him the whole world.

'You'd make me into a second Morholt?' Trystan's reply was so quiet Corwynal barely caught the words.

'Why not? You could be as good. You could be better. There's more to you than there ever was to him. Trys, you—'

'I thought you loved him. I thought that was what all this was about. I killed him, in a fair challenge, and almost died myself. For any other man, that would have been the end of it. But not for you, because you loved him.'

'I did. But now, Trys, I—'

'Don't touch me.' Trystan's voice was firm rather than angry, and Ferdiad withdrew the hand he'd reached out to him.

'I'm sorry. I'm a fool and spoke too soon. I just wanted you to know that, whatever you feel for Yseult now, you'll forget her, and when you do, there are others who . . . care for you.'

'Corwynal cares for me.'

'Not as I do, Trys.'

'No,' Trystan agreed. 'Not as you do.'

'You see it then!' Ferdiad said eagerly. 'How he's used you, how he keeps you chained to the earth when you were born to fly free. So forget him now, and be the man you were meant to be. I can help you—'

'No.' Trystan's flat negative was followed by a heavy silence.

'I see.' Ferdiad drew back, his voice losing its animation. 'You're not free because he's poisoned you against me. What has he said? It will be a lie. Everything he's ever told you will have been a lie, because everything about him is a lie. Shall I tell you his secrets?'

He moved closer to Trystan, gripped his arm, and pulled him around to face him, but Trystan jerked away. 'If Corwynal has secrets, he'll tell me himself.'

'No, he won't. Listen to me, Trys—'

'Have done, Ferdiad! I know I killed your lover, but you've had your revenge for that, and I forgive you. But Corwynal did nothing to you, so why break his heart? Not just by lying about Brangianne, but by trying to turn me against him at the earth-house. You almost succeeded, but I should never have listened to you. I thought I didn't need him, that it would be better for him if he didn't need me. I was wrong, and you're wrong too. Corwynal hasn't poisoned me against you. He doesn't like you or trust you, and he calls you a snake, but he's not the first man to do so. It's you who've poisoned yourself against me. *You.* You'll never be anything to me now, not friend and certainly not lover. But you're not my enemy, because I've reason to be grateful to you. That's why I came to warn you, but if your life doesn't matter to you, you can hardly expect it to matter to me!'

He turned and walked away, leaving Ferdiad standing by the stone.

'Wait, Trys. Please. I'm sorry! I shouldn't have—'

'It's too late.'

'But I love you!' Ferdiad's voice was raw with the terror a man feels when he loves.

'I know,' Trystan said quietly, turning back. 'I've known since the earth-house. I've . . . tried to be kind.'

'I don't want your *kindness!*'

'It's all I have,' Trystan said with finality, then, when Ferdiad moved towards him. 'Don't follow me.'

'This isn't the end! Trystan—!'

But he was already walking towards the entrance to the terrace.

'It is for me,' he said over his shoulder, then softly, turning to the shadows by the gateway where Corwynal was standing, frozen with shock. 'Try not to kill him, Corwynal.'

Ferdiad was crouched over the stone as a man will crouch when kicked in the stomach, his head bowed, his hands flat on the surface close to that odd foot-shaped depression, and Corwynal thought he was either weeping or praying. Despite Trystan's plea, he wanted to strike the man's head from his body, but he wanted answers more, so he just touched the edge of his sword to the side of Ferdiad's neck.

'You poisonous worm!'

Ferdiad stiffened, and there was a long careful silence during which he no doubt reviewed everything Corwynal must have overheard. He looked up, and his face, not weeping after all, was a cold hard mask, half-lit by torchlight, half by the blue light of a racing moon, his eyes dull and lifeless.

'I heard everything.' Corwynal had the satisfaction of seeing Ferdiad flinch, but the Fili recovered quickly and, ignoring the blade, rose to his feet and smiled his thin serpent smile.

'Then you know I'm caught in my own trap, which you must find amusing.'

'Amusing?! We're all of us caught in your trap! Two innocent women as well as Trystan and me.'

'Innocent? I think not.'

'You're despicable!'

'Then despise me,' Ferdiad retorted. 'As long as you don't pity me.'

'As Trystan does?'

Ferdiad grimaced, and Corwynal knew he'd wounded the man. Nevertheless, this wasn't going as he'd planned. He'd come to strike the smile from the Fili's laughing face, to drive his knuckles into his pale skin, to beat the man to his knees, and then, when he'd driven him into the dirt, to swing his sword and bring it crashing down on his unprotected neck, then hack through his body to cleave his treacherous heart in two. Part of him still wanted all that, but now, in the shifting light of the moon, he could tell Ferdiad was already beaten, for his smile had faltered as all humour inside him died. The Fili was already on his knees, and Corwynal's anger curdled inside him until it was an impotent knot of unresolved violence.

But the other man still had a little pride. 'As Trystan does,' he agreed, then glanced at Corwynal's blade. 'Are you just going to wave that around? You want to kill me, I imagine. Such a *straightforward* desire. I almost envy you. So why don't you get on with it?' He spread his arms to show that he bore no weapon. 'What's stopping you? Don't you have the stomach to cut down an unarmed man?'

'I'm giving you the chance to fight me, man to man, if you're any sort of man at all.'

Ferdiad's eyes flashed. 'Generous! A trained and armed warrior against an unarmed— What did you call me? Oh yes, a poisonous worm. Not a man at all. So you won't be surprised if I don't accept your offer.' And he smiled and something like humour returned to his face. 'We seem to have reached an impasse. So, what now?'

Corwynal still needed violence. He wanted to break the man's self-possession, and the only way to truly hurt Ferdiad was with words, so words would have to be his weapon.

'Now you tell me the truth,' he said, lowering his sword.

'Me?' Ferdiad seemed genuinely surprised. 'Tell the *truth*? To *you?*'

'I want your confession—'

'Confession to what?'

'That this was never to do with Trystan killing The Morholt. I thought it was for revenge, because that was what any man would have wanted, but you're not a man, are you? It was all to serve your desire for Trystan. You arranged for Trystan to lose his head over that girl, knowing who she was and how much she hated him. You expected him to fall into your arms when he realised it.'

Ferdiad had grown very still, his face a mask once more. Corwynal could see a muscle jumping in his jaw, but his voice was carefully controlled. 'If that was my intention, I failed miserably. And where were you in all this? If it was never about revenge, what were you to me?'

'Someone who'd protect Trystan from you. Someone who stood in your way.'

'Then why did I conspire to break your heart too? Or were you also a target for my unnatural desires?' Ferdiad's lip curled at Corwynal's expression. 'Do you imagine I even find you attractive?' Ferdiad's hands were clenched into fists now, his body trembling with the anger spilling from him.

'Of course not!'

'So what I did to you was nothing more than malice? An opportunist who saw an opportunity to meddle? Don't be a fool, or assume I'm one! Nothing I've done – *nothing!* – has been without reason, without justification. I hate you, Corwynal of Lothian. I've hated you for a very long time, and I fully intended to break your heart because once—' He stopped, breathing harshly. 'But my reasons are of no interest, are they? You think you know why. You really think I'm that simple. Well, I'm not, but you are, and not realising it was my mistake. I assumed you were a man, that you had a heart to be broken, but you don't. Not by a woman, because there's no place in your heart for anyone but that boy of yours. You choose him again and again, and I begin to wonder why.'

'He's my brother.'

'No,' Ferdiad said flatly. 'That's a lie, like so much else. I know about you, Corwynal of Lothian, Talorc of Atholl. Not everything, not yet, but I will, because Trystan was never my target. You were. You still are. This hasn't ended.'

He smiled, triumphant now, a man no longer on his knees. Ignoring the sword, which, to his own surprise, was still in Corwynal's hand, Ferdiad turned and walked away, and Corwynal knew he'd lost the battle of words. But he hadn't lost the war.

'Then end it now!' he yelled. 'If I'm your target, fight me now! Because you'll have to kill me before I'll let you turn Trystan into a second Morholt. He was right, wasn't he? That's what you want – a Cuchullain to your Ferdiad—'

Ferdiad stopped in mid-stride and whirled around. 'How dare you!' He strode back to Corwynal, his eyes blazing, his fragile control broken, and launched himself at him, snarling like a lynx, his fingers reaching for his throat, his eyes wild. The force of his leap threw them both off balance, and they crashed to the ground. Corwynal's sword flew from his grasp, but it didn't matter, because this was the fight he wanted. The knot of impotent violence unravelled as he gripped Ferdiad's wrists and tore his hands from his throat, then braced his legs and heaved upwards to fling him off, striking the Fili hard across the face. Ferdiad scrambled back out of reach and dragged a hand across his mouth to leave a trail of blood on his cheek.

'You can't kill me, you fool! Not a Fili of the gods.'

'The gods don't frighten me.'

'Then you're doubly a fool.'

Fool or not, Corwynal wanted this fight, needed to feel Ferdiad's blood spilling between his fingers. He wanted to slash that handsome mocking face to ribbons, to cut out that singer's tongue, to drive his fists over and over into that smooth graceful body. He wanted to tear the man's heart out with his own fingers. Yet Ferdiad wasn't going to make any of that easy for, as Corwynal's knuckles split against Ferdiad's cheekbone, and he felt the other man's flesh pulp, a fist thudded into the small of his back and a knee was driven into his groin. Murder flared in Ferdiad's green eyes as he clawed at Corwynal's face, splintered nails raking across his eyes, a booted foot kicking his shins.

The music coursed through him, metallic and sweet, and he heard drums beating inside his skull. This time, however, it was met by a counterpoint from somewhere outside him, as if each note of music, each beat of rhythm, was answered by another. The music swelled and soared until it deafened him, and he understood that Ferdiad's hatred was stronger than his own.

He groaned as his ribs and face absorbed blow after blow, and his teeth rattled in his jaw. He sank them into Ferdiad's palm when the Fili's fingers groped for his eyes and tasted Ferdiad's blood mingling with his own. He could no longer see out of one eye, his fist was throbbing, and his damaged shoulder ached. Ferdiad had his strong harper's fingers around his throat, his thumbs digging deep into his neck where the blood runs. A dark, deeper than that of the torch-lit night, was pulsing in from the edges of his vision. All Corwynal could see was the wild white gleam of Ferdiad's triumphant feral grin and the green glint of his eyes. He tried to tear the Fili's hands away, but his grip just tightened. He sought for some sort of leverage to try to throw the man off, but he was crushed against the rock, and its smooth surface provided no purchase. Distantly, he could hear Arddu laughing, and the music inside him faltered as the counterpoint grew stronger.

I could die here, he thought, though he still didn't understand the reason. He struggled afresh, trying to break free, groping for something that would give him an advantage. He felt the cold touch of a jewel set in the hilt of a blade thrust into a small leather scabbard fixed to the back of Ferdiad's belt, a little thing, some effete decoration such as the Fili liked to wear. It would be blunt, he thought as he pulled it free and caught a glimpse of un-cared for metal, but it was still a blade. Distantly, he heard a peal of warning, as of a far-off bell, then, closer, the sound of a breath taken and held.

It wasn't his. Or Ferdiad's. It was a God's.

Corwynal brought the blade down, but Ferdiad must have caught the glint of moonlight on metal, for his crushing grip on Corwynal's throat was gone, and he raised one hand to shield himself from the plunging little knife. But a hand was no shield, and the blade, sharper than he'd expected, sliced through skin, past tendon and grated along bone.

Ferdiad screamed a high inhuman scream of pain and terror, and threw himself back, rolling himself off Corwynal and onto his knees where he remained crouched, curled over his wounded hand, his eyes wide with fear as he looked first at his hand, then at Corwynal and, finally, at the little knife Corwynal was still holding. It was The Dragon's knife, red with Ferdiad's blood, the poisoned knife, the one that robbed a man of everything that mattered.

Corwynal had won. He'd come to kill the man, and he'd succeeded, because he knew with absolute certainty what Ferdiad would do now. The Fili glanced at the knife, which had fallen from Corwynal's suddenly nerveless fingers, and gathered himself to make a leap for it. He'd do what Trystan had wanted to do. Corwynal had stopped Trystan from taking his own life, but he wouldn't stop Ferdiad. Letting the Fili kill himself would be a kindness. Or he could do it himself. It was why he'd come here, after all. Corwynal reached for his sword and kicked the knife out of Ferdiad's reach.

The Fili gave a low moan of despair and, with a visible effort, smiled without mirth. 'I expect you want me to beg. And I'm not sure . . . if I can . . . stop myself. So, please . . .' He glanced at the sword in Corwynal's hand. 'Please . . . ?'

He couldn't do it. In spite of everything. In spite of *everything!* He threw down his sword, ripped off his belt and wrapped it around Ferdiad's lower arm then pulled it tight until the wound stopped bleeding and the Fili's fingers turned white.

'Put your hand on the stone,' he said. Only then did Ferdiad understand Corwynal's intention.

'No!' He struggled, but Corwynal forced his hand flat on the stone and held him down with the weight of his own body as he reached for his sword, pivoted the edge on the rock and brought it down hard. The blade, a vivid arc of grey metal, sliced through flesh and tendon and between bone, to grate against stone. And it was done. Ferdiad's right hand, his fine-fingered singer's hand, was severed at the wrist, and, despite the belt, blood was spilling over the rock, filling the strange foot-shaped depression.

Ferdiad gasped, his breathing a short, ragged pant as he hunched himself over his wounded limb. 'It was a keepsake, that's all,' Ferdiad whispered, his whole body shaking as he stared at his own hand lying on the stone, the fingers curled as if in the act of plucking a harp. 'A *keepsake!*' he snarled, raising his other fist to the sky. 'Are you satisfied, Arddu?' he screamed. 'Is this what you wanted?'

Arddu? The name of the God hung between them in the cold moonlit and torchlit night, and Corwynal remembered something Ferdiad had said. *I'm as much Arddu's creature as you.* Had their fight been nothing more than amusement for the God?

'Never mind Arddu,' he said – as if that was ever possible – then shrugged himself out of his jerkin and tore off his shirt to rip it into bindings for the stump of Ferdiad's arm. 'Brangianne can do this better—'

'Not her. Get me to Ciaran. And . . . and bring that cursed knife.'

He half-supported, half-carried the Fili through the settlement to a roundhouse close to the gate where, to his relief, the Abbot came swiftly to the pounding on the door.

'Oh, my poor boy!' He took the weight of Ferdiad's body and helped him to a pallet by the wall where the Fili collapsed, his wounded arm cradled against his chest. He was still clutching his severed hand.

'Show him the knife,' Ferdiad gasped.

The Abbot took it from Corwynal, sniffed and recoiled.

'How long?' he demanded of the Fili.

'Twenty heartbeats, more or less. Was it soon enough? *Was it?!*'

'I don't know, Ferdiad.' Ciaran frowned. 'Only time will tell.'

Ferdiad's fragile control deserted him, and his face crumpled as he began to weep. Ciaran crouched beside him and put an arm around his shoulders, but the Fili shrugged him off and turned his ravaged face to Corwynal.

'So, this was your revenge for a broken heart?' he snarled. 'Such a little thing, a broken heart. Yet you've taken everything from me that made life bearable. *Everything!*'

'I didn't mean . . . I didn't want *this!* Gods, man, what in The Five Hells did you keep that blade for?'

'To remind me of my own folly. To remind me of the moment I understood I'd trapped myself in my own web. Vengeance is a two-bladed sword, Talorc of Atholl, so don't make the mistake of thinking it's over between us. Breaking your heart is a small matter compared to what I'll do to you now. Because this is *war!* One day, dead or alive, I'll take everything from you, and everyone you hold dear. One day I will *destroy* you!'

'Will he die?'

Ferdiad was unconscious by then, for, with Corwynal holding him down, the Abbot had forced a tincture of poppy past the Fili's clenched teeth. Even then, Ferdiad struggled to stay conscious, the fear of what he might be when he woke so undisguised and painful Corwynal was sick with relief when the Fili's eyes finally fluttered closed and the Abbot was able to start treating his injury.

'Not if I can help it,' he said, laying a knife in the glowing coals of the brazier. 'Though he'll fight me every step of the way.'

'Why is he so afraid of you?'

The Abbot picked up the now red-hot knife and laid it on the stump to cauterise the wound, filling the room with the stench of burning flesh. Ferdiad moaned but didn't regain consciousness.

'Pass me that roll of linen.' The Abbot gestured to the table, then began binding Ferdiad's arm, and didn't reply until he'd finished. 'I'm an old man, Corwynal of Lothian. In the course of my life, I've seen much and learned a great deal, and have come to know things men believe to be secret. They think, therefore, I can see into their souls.' He lifted his dark penetrating eyes to Corwynal's, who shivered. 'I can't, of course,' the Abbot went on with a faint smile. 'But Ferdiad doesn't want to take the risk, because he's a man with a great many secrets.'

'Who is he? What does he have to do with me?'

'Both good questions.' The Abbot tied off the bandage with a neat knot. 'Ferdiad, if that's his real name, has a hundred stories for who he is. Who can say which of them is true? Now he's afraid I'll find out, so afraid that only the threat of madness has persuaded him to seek my help. Perhaps he's right to be afraid, because he's a talented man and I won't hesitate to use him once I know the secrets of his heart. As to what he has to do with you, that I don't know, but if I were to speculate, I would say it has to do with your own secrets, Talorc of Atholl.'

'You know nothing about me,' Corwynal insisted, with the unsettling conviction that this was very far from the truth, and wasn't surprised when the Abbot just smiled.

'Not everything, certainly, but not nothing. Do you think your secrets belong to you alone? Given who you are? I and others are trying to build something to last beyond the storms that gather on our horizon, and we'll use everyone and anyone in pursuit of that goal. You have your place in that, as does Ferdiad. This alliance between Dalriada and Galloway is just the beginning.'

'So we were nothing more than tools, Trystan and I,' Corwynal concluded bitterly, but without surprise. 'You had Ferdiad bring us to Dalriada so you could use us. You knew Brangianne was Feargus' sister, that Ethlin was his daughter, but said nothing.' Then something else occurred to him. 'And so did Blaize.' Corwynal would have a few sharp words to say to his uncle the next time he saw him. 'You kept silent for the sake of your precious alliance. You let me think—'

'That you'd be happy? Men like you aren't fated to be happy.'

'I don't believe in fate.'

'For someone who doesn't believe in fate, you spend rather a lot of time fighting against it,' the Abbot said dryly. 'Listen to me,

Corwynal; this isn't a game, and you're a great deal more than a piece on the board. Much as I'd like to control the affairs of men, they insist on doing the unexpected. Ferdiad, for example, acted unpredictably in persuading you and Trystan to come to Dalriada. But that's not to say he was wrong or that the outcome wasn't to be desired. Peace, after all, is a rare commodity in this world of ours. So ask yourself, Corwynal of Lothian, if you wouldn't have done the same things and kept the same secrets, if it had been Lothian's future at stake. Because what, truly, has been lost? A boy's heart? A man's heart? A woman's heart? Would you really set those in balance against the lives of countless men and women?

'No, you wouldn't, so don't blame me for making the most of the opportunities that presented themselves. Blame me, if you must, for sending Brangianne to Carnadail. If I hadn't done so, your life would have been quite different. And hers. Blame me for not knowing Trystan had lost his heart to a girl called Ethlin. Blame me for the human failures of an old man for whom the passions of the body are just a dim and distant memory. Blame me because you need to blame someone.' The Abbot spread his arms wide. 'So here I am. Blame me. But don't imagine I don't understand you. I know you're angry and I know why. It's because you're afraid you'll never see Brangianne again, and that Trystan will repeat your mistakes. You know you have to try and stop him, but you're afraid you'll fail.'

This was too accurate, too effortless a stripping away of all his concealments, that Corwynal's anger curled up on itself.

'Will I fail?' he whispered, sinking down onto the stool.

'Are you asking me for prophecy?'

He shook his head. He'd learned how deceitful prophecy could be. Nevertheless, there was one thing he had to know.

'Will I see her again?'

'You'll see her tomorrow, though that's not what you're asking me. You mean in the years to come.'

Corwynal nodded, and the old man sighed, then tilted his head to one side, his eyes changing as Blaize's sometimes changed, growing more distant, as if he was seeing not through the wall of the guest hut and the stone of Dunadd's rock and out into the night, but through the veils of time itself.

'I see you meeting in woodland. A thrush is singing. She has a child in her arms, and she gives it to you. You're both weeping, but whether for joy or sorrow I can't tell.'

'Is the child mine?'

The Abbot's gaze sharpened and returned to the here and now, and his expression grew regretful. 'No,' he said quietly.

He should never have asked. 'Curse you, old man.' Corwynal got up and made for the door.

'Wait. Let me do something about your face before you go.' The Abbot moved towards him, but Corwynal backed off.

'Don't touch me.' He was afraid that if the old man touched him, he might weep and the last of his anger would evaporate. He needed his anger as a man needs strong drink, and he wrestled desperately with the door bar with his swollen hand.

'I'm not your enemy,' the Abbot assured him. 'And nor, in his heart, is Ferdiad. He could have killed you, or worse, but chose not to. None of us are your enemy, not even those in Atholl whom you fear so much.'

The bar finally lifted, the bones in Corwynal's hand grating against one another as it did so, and he was out, into the night and the dark, if not entirely into silence, for the old man's voice followed him. 'Ask yourself, Corwynal of Lothian, who your enemy really is.'

He didn't go back to the guest hut. He didn't want to face Trystan and have to explain what he'd done to Ferdiad. He didn't want anyone to see his face, because someone might take it into their head to send for Brangianne and, much as he wanted to see her again, he didn't want her to see him like this. One eye was half closed, blood crusting his lid shut. His scalp was bleeding sluggishly, and his hand and cheekbone were swollen. His whole body was aching, especially his shoulder, and his ribs were bruised, his shin bleeding, his hip throbbing from falling against that rock.

The guard at the gate looked at him oddly as he passed through to the lower town but didn't challenge him. His role was to stop suspicious characters getting into Dunadd, not out. Getting back into the fortress might be a difficulty, but Corwynal would worry about that later. Right then, all he wanted was to find somewhere dark and quiet in which to rail against the fate he didn't believe in, to blame himself for his own folly, and imagine how different his life would have been if this hadn't happened or that.

The night was still and quiet, the setting moon obscured by a bank of clouds, but the river reflected the torches that burned by Dunadd's gates and on the battlements, and there was enough light to reveal a wild-fowler's track leading into the Moss and heading for a thicket of willow that grew by a bend in the river. Once he'd reached it, Corwynal sank onto a pale tussock of grass and dropped his face into his hands.

It was over, the adventure that had begun on the Rock of Carraig Ealasaid the previous year, when he'd set off across the sea in search of healing for Trystan and found a healing of his own. What would have happened if he hadn't faced the sunset and chosen to risk everything? Knowing what he knew now, a year and a few months later, would he have turned away?

Dunadd was far behind him now, its torchlight pinpricks of amber, the rock itself looming black against the more distant hills, almost invisible. Out on the Moss, he was surrounded by birds; a pair of curlews wailed down the night, and a dark-plumaged bird fluttered into the branches of the willow above him. A voice whispered from the rushes, the voice he'd come to find.

You could have killed him.

'The old man?'

Ferdiad.

'Did you mean me to? Why? He's your creature.'

As are you. Do not forget it. I will neither be ignored or summoned. Or threatened.

The dark bird hopped closer.

'Is that my crime? Is that why you sent Ferdiad to take everyone I care about?'

He failed. He allowed himself to be . . . distracted. You could have killed him, but you chose not to.

'Because he's not my enemy, is he? You are.'

The bird cawed loudly, like a God laughing.

Your enemy? You poor fool! I'm not your enemy! I'm your doom. *Do you think to fight your doom? Do you think to fight a God? I made you. I can unmake you just as easily. Look at yourself – broken, unloved, without country, without people, without honour. Everything you have, you have at my whim. You are nothing without me.*

'Everything you've given me was for a price, a price I've paid. You asked for a heart. You have it now.'

Next time it will be your soul.

'Never!' Corwynal picked up a stone and flung it at the bird. It flapped its wings, hopped to a higher branch and peered down at him.

'I won't be used by you or anyone! I won't be lied to!'

Except by yourself . . .

The bird spread its wings and lifted into the air, flapping to clear the trees, then swooped towards him, a shadow beneath the moon, a threat in the night, its wicked beak grazing Corwynal's cheek and leaving behind a cold fetid air that blew out of an uncertain future.

Who is your enemy, Corwynal? Who?

Then the bird was gone, the voice with it, and he was alone beneath a vast black sky and an indifferent moon, his body aching, his heart sore, his stomach sick with fear. *Who is my enemy?*

Was it Ferdiad? The Abbot? The God? Was it all of them? Was it everyone who wanted to take from him anything he wasn't prepared to give – his life, his obedience, his soul?

No, it was himself, the man who'd wanted more than he deserved, who, like Ferdiad, had allowed himself to be distracted by love, to long, to dream, to hope. He'd made a choice eighteen years before, and nothing, not love or vengeance, not promises or threats, should have made him forget it. He'd given up everything for Trystan, and a man should give with his whole heart, not part of it. He understood that now. It had been a long journey to reach that understanding and a hard fight, but, like Ferdiad, he would survive, mutilated and beaten perhaps, aching and bleeding in body and soul. But not defeated.

To the east, behind the hills, light was growing, washing away the night, and all around him the birds of the Moss, reed-warbler and curlew, blackcap and thrush, began to fill the world with song.

EPILOGUE

En route to Galloway

Lughnasadh 487

SHE MUST NEVER KNOW

T he wind died before the dawn, and Corwynal, waking exhausted and confused after barely an hour of sleep, wished he'd died with it.

He was lying on something that tilted and lurched beneath him, his head pillowed on a pile of rough sacking that stank of mouldy grain, bilge water and vomit. The woollen cloak in which he'd wrapped himself was sodden and offered little protection against the morning chill, and some ancient creature had crawled under his tongue and died. As if all this wasn't bad enough, a demented stonemason was driving a nail deep into his brain.

'How are you feeling?' The voice was concerned and sympathetic, and Corwynal opened his eyes to find out who'd asked this remarkably stupid question. But all he could see was a confused tracery of wooden spars and ropes that spiralled dizzily against a dull, ashen sky, creaking and groaning as they did so.

He was on a ship, he remembered, his gorge rising at the thought, a ship going to Galloway. They were escorting Princess Yseult to Galloway so she could marry Marc. Accompanying her, to his astonishment and horror and a bitter, fruitless relief, was Brangianne. *The Princess Brangianne*, he reminded himself, thinking back to the moment when she'd marched onto the ship with Yseult and he'd had to face her, one eye half-shut and still crusted with blood, his lip split, the left side of his face swollen and purpling, his hands scraped. Her mouth had fallen open at the sight of him – or his face – and she'd started forward but stopped herself and turned away. They hadn't exchanged a single word since they'd left Dalriada two days before, for which he'd been profoundly grateful, since he'd been seasick the whole way.

So how *was* he feeling? Sick to the stomach and the heart, aching, old, tired, humiliated. Afraid.

'Fine,' he croaked, before lurching to one side, retching feebly. But after two days on the ship, there was nothing in his stomach, and all that came up was a trickle of sour bile.

'Here. Drink some water.' A water-skin was thrust into his hands. The water was stale and brackish, but it served to swill some of the sickness out of his mouth. He spat and swallowed, then closed his eyes and lay back on the stinking pile of sacks, gasping for breath, his heart thudding. He opened the one eye that could still open and peered at his torturer, saw blue eyes, hair the colour of a ripe field of grain, lips curled with mocking amusement. There had been a girl like that once . . . But this wasn't a girl. Nor was it a boy. It was a man, his features shaped by experience.

'God, you're pathetic! It's a flat calm!' Trystan declared, half-exasperated, half-affectionate. He was swaying easily to the lurching motion of the boat, as at home on the deck of a ship as on the back of a horse. 'You'll feel better if you're on your feet,' he added bracingly, holding out a hand.

Corwynal waved it away. He might be sea-sick and conscious of every one of his thirty nine years in the stiffness of his joints and muscles, but he had his pride. With the aid of one of the nameless ropes holding up the mast of this thrice-cursed boat, he got to his feet and stood there, clinging to the rope and peering out over the side.

'Where in The Five Hells are we?'

A grey sky was heaving uneasily above a grey sea, furrowed and ridged by an oily cross-swell. A single gull, bobbing on the surface of the water, eyed him derisively before lifting into the air and beating its way into the wan light. It wasn't long after dawn, and a reluctant light was seeping from behind the low-lying clouds, and Corwynal could make out the vague shapes of land. Behind the ship lay a dark mass that must be the Mull of Ceann Tire. Ahead, between the light and its half-hearted reflection, was the darker line of the low-lying Rhinns of Galloway. Closer, to their left, lay an island with a frill of broken water about its base, the Rock of Carraig Ealasaid, where Trystan had defeated The Morholt and almost died himself, and where Corwynal had made a foolish pledge to a God who'd taken him at his word.

'We're halfway across the Sound,' Trystan said. 'The master thinks the wind will pick up once the sun comes up. Aelfric agrees with him, so I reckon he's right. We should reach the Rhinns about noon and the Mote by nightfall, and then—'

He broke off, a muscle leaping in his jaw, his hands clenching on the rail as he stared out to sea. Corwynal was aware of movement behind them, close to the ship's bow, and glanced around. Then, like Trystan, he looked away. The Royal Women of Dalriada, the women who held their hearts in their hands, were emerging from the shelter near the bow. They were guarded, as ever, by Oonagh, and also by Kaerherdin, who seemed to have made himself Brangianne's personal servant.

'I don't think I can bear it,' Trystan whispered in a voice of quiet desperation and clutched Corwynal's arm with something close to panic. 'I should never have agreed to this. I knew it as soon as I said it. I can't go through with it. You have to help me, tell me what to do, what to think, how to . . . to be.'

Time stopped, then moved backwards, faster and faster, until Corwynal was nineteen years old and in Lothian once more, watching the woman he loved marrying his father. He too had thought he couldn't bear it and had only got through the day with the aid of an inordinate amount of wine. There had been no-one to confide in or seek advice from. He had no friends in Lothian apart from Blaize, but his uncle had been off about his mysterious business somewhere among the Lands between the Walls and hadn't returned for several months, by which time it was too late. Corwynal had done the worst thing he could have done. He'd stayed. Wanting all of Her, he'd tried to satisfy himself with little more than snatched moments, a glance exchanged across a crowded hall, a fleeting touch as they brushed past one another, a whispered assignation and a brief fumbled embrace. He'd hated every sordid moment of it.

But that past wouldn't repeat itself with Trystan, because Corwynal was going to stop it. This was now, not then. Trystan wasn't him, Yseult wasn't Gwenllian, and Marc wasn't his father. There were a hundred differences, and the greatest of them was that Trystan had asked Corwynal for his help, and he wasn't going to let him down.

'You *can* bear it.' He squeezed Trystan's arm reassuringly. 'You must. If you run away, She'll know.'

It was shameless manipulation, but it worked. Trystan's lips thinned with determination, and his shoulders straightened. 'She must never know,' he muttered. 'I'd rather die.'

'Then you'll have to watch her wed, but then we'll leave. The two of us.'

'And go where?' Trystan asked doubtfully. 'Not Lothian or Selgovia. So where does that leave? Strathclyde? Manau? I doubt we'd be welcome in either. Gododdin? No, Lot isn't to be trusted, and Arthyr won't have us back, not after we abandoned him. Where then?'

'We'll go south,' Corwynal said. It was where he'd planned to go with Brangianne. 'To Rheged, maybe. Or Gwynedd, even Kernyw.' Ferdiad had offered Trystan the same thing and been rejected, but Trystan was interested now. 'Do you remember, back in Lothian, before all this began, you asked me to go adventuring with you?'

'You refused.' A smile flickered about Trystan's lips.

'I was a fool then, but it's not too late. Let's see what the world has to offer us. We could go to the old Roman lands in Gaul, then on to Rome itself.'

'We'd have to cross the Narrow Sea for that, and you'd be sick all the way!' But the smile had reached Trystan's eyes.

'I don't care.' *Anything*, he'd promised a God. How much easier it was to make the same promise to a boy who needed his help. 'I'll go anywhere,' he said, returning Trystan's smile.

There was a touch on his face, a cold air on his neck. Aelfric, dozing at the steering oar, woke up and leapt down from the steering platform to kick the ship's master awake. After more shouting and kicking, the crew threw aside their blankets and jumped for the ropes. The sea was changing, the oily grey swell darkening to slate as the promised wind riffled the water. Someone began to beat on a drum, and the crew hauled on the ropes to pull the sail on its heavy wooden boom slowly up the mast. Ropes creaked as the boom swung and the sail caught the wind, bellied and snapped taut and full. The ship slid through the swell, gradually gathering way until its wake streamed behind them. The Mull of Ceann Tire fell away and Carraig Ealasaid slipped by on their larboard side. Ahead, the coast of Galloway eased its way out of the haze until Corwynal could make out beaches and fields, smoke rising from settlements and, behind, the soft swell of the hills.

Everything that was grey vanished as the sun burned away the last of the mists and leapt blazing into a new morning.

AUTHOR'S NOTE

I very much hope you've enjoyed reading *The Swan in Summer*.

If you have, I'd love you to **post a review on Amazon**. It needn't be an essay – a couple of lines would be fantastic. Reviews are particularly helpful for authors like me who're just setting out into the stormy waters of self-publishing. It would be great to know you've got my back!

If you've spotted any typos and would like to let me know about them, please contact me through my website or DM me on Instagram. I do really want to know so I can fix them.

If you'd like to find out about the next book in *The Trystan Trilogy*, *The Serpent in Spring*, see the next page, and/or:

Subscribe to my Newsletter

Not only will you receive exclusive extracts from *The Serpent in Spring*, but free short stories, regular newsletters, and notifications of new blog posts about writing in general and the world of *The Trystan Trilogy* in particular.

Go to **barbaralennox.com/subscribe** or scan the QR code:

THE SERPENT IN SPRING

The story concludes . . .

One day you'll have to stand by and watch the woman who's the other half of your soul marry someone else.

Corwynal's prediction comes true when Trystan is forced to watch the girl he loves, Yseult of Dalriada, marry his uncle, Marc, King of Galloway. But Trystan isn't willing to give her up completely, and Corwynal has to stand by, helpless, as the lovers endanger the fragile peace between Galloway and Dalriada. Only when they risk their own lives is he able to act. He helps them escape to the one place they'll be safe, the one place he doesn't want to go – Atholl in Caledonia.

There he'll not only have to face the judgement of the Druid Council for a crime he committed as a boy, but the long-planned revenge of Ferdiad, Fili of Dalriada, for a crime he doesn't remember committing at all.

Corwynal will have to decide where he belongs and what and whom he loves the most, unaware that his decisions will lead to the final tragedy that is the story of Trystan and Yseult.

Read the opening of *The Serpent in Spring* on my website.

HISTORICAL NOTE

The mediaeval romance of Tristan and Isolde was compiled on the continent in the 12th century and later incorporated into Malory's 15th century Arthurian fantasy, *Le Morte D'Arthur*. But it was based on much earlier tales derived from Irish and possibly Pictish sources. These early tales acquired a Welsh flavour, following the resettlement of Britons from Strathclyde in Gwynedd at the end of the 9th century. Subsequently, the same stories were taken to the other Brythonic lands of Cornwall and Brittany where they absorbed local references, and the story is now thought of as being Cornish/Breton. But the original stories were probably set in Scotland/Ireland.

In *The Trystan Trilogy*, the legend has been reworked to include many of the familiar elements of the story, but not necessarily in the same order, and has been set against the 'historical' background of late 5th century 'Scotland'. Historical is a very loose term in this context. Virtually no texts survive from this period and location, so the settings and characters are an amalgam of the little that is known about earlier and later times. Galloway and Strathclyde, for example, are later names, given to the lands of the Novantae and Dumnonni tribes detailed by Ptolemy in his 1st century map of Britain. The Votadini tribe of the east coast gave their name to the later Kingdom of Gododdin. Lothian, a modern term, comes from a reference to Tristan's traditional home being Loonois, which has been equated with Lothian. Dalriada was a real Irish Kingdom, existing both in Ireland and Scotland. It was supposedly founded by Fergus,

Loarn and Oenghus, but they are probably mythical. The Caledonian, or Pictish, tribes are also mentioned by Ptolemy, and a list of their kingdoms appears in a 9th century text. The name Atholl probably derives from Alflotha, or new Ireland, a name given to it after the area became part of a Scots-controlled territory.

The character names were taken from the various versions of the Tristan and Isolde legend, and from the oldest Arthurian texts, but have been 'adjusted' to give them more of a 'Welsh' look since the people of the Lands between the Walls (a made-up name) would have spoken Brythonic, a precursor of Welsh. Some names, such as Dumnagual and Ciniod, come from genealogies and king-lists of the period. They may even have been real people, though the historicity of genealogies is very dubious.

All Celtic nations would have celebrated the four fire-festivals of Imbolc, Beltein, Lughnasadh and Samhain, but these are the Gaelic names, since I was unable to find reliable 'British' names for them.

The Trystan Trilogy is a work of fiction, and my intention was to give the reader a flavour of the cultures of the period rather than sticking strictly to the known facts – or lack of them. I've researched as widely as I could on these matters but, inevitably, will have misinterpreted or simply missed available evidence, and for that I apologise.

For further information and a bibliography of sources, refer to my website:

(barbaralennox.com/resources/bibliography)

ABOUT THE AUTHOR

I was born, and still live, in Scotland on the shores of a river, between the mountains and the sea. I'm a retired scientist and science administrator but have always been fascinated by the early history of Scotland, and I love fleshing out that history with the stories of fictional, and not-so-fictional, characters.

Find out more about me and my writing on my website:

Barbaralennox.com

Connect with me on the following:

Twitter.com/barbaralennox4
Instagram.com/barbaralennoxwriter
Goodreads.com/author/show/19661962.Barbara_Lennox
Pinterest.co.uk/barbaralennox58
Amazon: viewauthor.at/authorprofile

ALSO BY BARBARA LENNOX

Song of a Red Morning, a short story, which takes place in 6th century Scotland and is set at Dunpeldyr, was published in 2019.

getbook.at/Songofaredmorning

'Thoroughly absorbing and beautifully written.'

The Man who Loved Landscape, a collection of 40 short stories, many of which are set in Scotland, was published in 2020.

getbook.at/Manwholovedlandscape

'Simply the best book of short stories I have read in years.'

The Ghost in the Machine, *poems of love, loss, life and death*, a collection of 69 poems, was published in 2021.

getbook.at/theghostinthemachine

'This is an excellent book, nuanced, accessible, human.'

Related and forthcoming novels:

The Wolf in Winter, first volume of *The Trystan Trilogy*, was published in 2021. getbook.at/Wolfinwinter

The Serpent in Spring, third volume of *The Trystan Trilogy*, will be published in 2023.

ACKNOWLEDGEMENTS

I would never have written anything if I hadn't attended the 'Continuing as a Writer' classes, part of the University of Dundee's Continuing Education Programme. These classes were tutored by Esther Read, whose support and encouragement has been unstinting and invaluable. Esther, I can't thank you enough, not only for your help and advice as I mastered the art of short story writing, but for manfully reading through early drafts of *The Wolf in Winter*.

I'd like to thank my beta-reading team at The History Quill for reading the almost-final manuscript. Their comments were so encouraging and helpful.

I have to give a shout-out to all my Instagram pals from whom I learned such an immense amount about the process of self-publishing, and who were always there for inspiration, support and encouragement. Thanks, guys and gals!

At home, my writing buddies, Harry, Rambo and Oscar, the best cats in the world, were with me all the way, usually asleep.

Almost finally, but not least, I'd like to thank my husband, Will, for putting up with all the scribbling and not asking any awkward questions.

My biggest thank you, however, goes to all my readers, especially my ARC team – you know who you are – without whom this book would be nothing more than a footnote in my own imagination.

Printed in Great Britain
by Amazon